W9-CCG-091

EVEN STEVEN

Also by John Gilstrap

Nathan's Run
At All Costs

EVEN STEVEN

a novel

JOHN GILSTRAP

POCKET BOOKS
New York London Toronto Sydney Singapore

This book is a work of fiction. Names, characters, places and incidents are products of the author's imagination or are used fictitiously. Any resemblance to actual events or locales or persons, living or dead, is entirely coincidental.

POCKET BOOKS, a division of Simon & Schuster, Inc.
1230 Avenue of the Americas, New York, NY 10020

Library of Congress Cataloging-in-Publication Data

Gilstrap, John.
Even Steven / John Gilstrap.
p. cm.
ISBN 0-671-78666-0
1. Missing children—Fiction. 2. Childlessness—Fiction. 3. Kidnapping—Fiction I. Title.

PS3557.I4745 E9 2000
813'.54—dc21 00-033636

First Pocket Books hardcover printing September 2000

10 9 8 7 6 5 4 3 2 1

Designed by Jaime Putorti

Printed in the U.S.A.

QF/

For Dad, with thanks for setting the bar so high.

ACKNOWLEDGMENTS

FIFTEEN YEARS AGO, I married my best friend in the world. A day never dawns that I don't thank God for sending her my way, and the sun never sets without me wondering why she continues to put up with my antics and my dreams and my sixth-grade sense of humor. What I am, I owe to you, Joy. I love you.

In the years that I've been fortunate enough to write for my supper, my son, Chris, has grown from a little boy to a fine young man. The journey proceeds with impossible speed, and with each step he makes me prouder than any father has a right to be. Keep it up, kiddo. And thanks for making my world shine.

My job is one big what-if game. In writing *Even Steven,* I asked myself what I would do if I found myself facing prosecution for murder. Answer: I'd turn to John Bevis, the best defense attorney I know. A thousand thanks, John, for making my imaginary attorney sound as if she knows what she's talking about. For the record, whatever details are wrong are my fault, not John's. He's but one of a long line of teachers to find out that I'm not the most attentive student.

Thanks also to Dorothy Amarandos, for her help on the classical-music front. I wonder sometimes if she knows how many lives she makes more livable just by being who she is.

The book business can be treacherous, where friends can become predators without warning. I recently took my first turn in the shark tank, and I learned that an author is often only as strong as the people who represent him. That being the case, words can't express my gratitude to my agents, Molly Friedrich and Matthew Snyder. Many thanks for the counsel, the critique, and the hand-holding.

Finally, I want to say thanks to all the folks at Pocket Books, my wonderful, shiny new home in the publishing world. In particular, I'd like to thank my editor, Jason Kaufman, for being damned good at what he does.

EVEN
STEVEN

1

BUNDLED TIGHTLY AGAINST the cold, the young couple lay on an outcropping over the Catoctin River, looking up at the cloudless sky, and wondering which of the countless millions of stars was truly the one that delivered wishes.

"You asleep?" Bobby whispered.

"Not yet." Susan's throat still sounded thick.

He pulled his bride of five years even closer and kissed the top of her head. "Happy anniversary."

Susan snuggled in, burying her face in his jacket.

The calendar had lied. After such a brutal winter, he liked to think that April would have brought warmer temperatures. Out here in the mountains, though, where West Virginia reached closest to God, the air still smelled of February. He'd never been so ready for spring.

This wasn't at all how he'd planned it. The spot was perfect, yes; and the night beautiful, but he'd hoped the sadness would have dulled by now. There had to be a way to make the pain go away. There *had* to be. If he were a better husband, he'd know what it was. Susan's thick brown hair—invisible in the darkness—felt warm and soft against his hand as he gently massaged lazy circles on her scalp. She liked it when he did that.

"We'll just try again," he whispered, hoping she didn't hear the tremor in his voice. "And again, if we have to. And again and again and again."

Susan just burrowed her head deeper. Her anguish felt like razor blades in Bobby's gut. He pursed his lips and stared at the sky, desperately trying to hide the little hitch in his breathing. His role required strength. If she sensed that dimples had formed in his armor of optimism, he wasn't sure how either of them would hold up.

They'd come so *close* last time; they'd let themselves believe. As much as he craved children, Bobby wasn't sure he could handle the cycle of hope and disaster anymore. He wasn't sure that anyone could. His tear tracks turned cold quickly in the night air.

It had been a week since the doctor had pronounced Susan's internal plumbing to be healthy and normal, and this was to be their weekend of healing. The tears were all a part of it, he supposed, as was the pain, but he worried about the anger. Sometimes when he was alone—only when he was alone—he raged about the injustice of it all, cursing God and Susan and himself for denying them the one blessing that would make their marriage whole. The anger ate at him sometimes, and on nights like these, as his best friend succumbed to wave after wave of grief, he wanted to hurt something just to exorcise the rage.

Time was the answer. He knew this, both from experience and from the advice of others, but it was the one element in the world that he could not manufacture.

Time heals all wounds. What a crock.

The river ran fast and loud just below them, swollen by melting snows. Every now and then, a few drops would rain down on them from an errant eddy that had slapped against the vertical face of their rock ledge. The thunderous noise of the water filled the void of the night, bringing to Bobby a momentary glimpse of the peace he'd hoped they'd find out here. What is it about water, he wondered, that settles the soul?

On a different night, he might never have heard the rustling in the bushes that bordered their secluded outcropping. It was a tentative sound, too random to be the wind, but bigger than a coon or a possum. Out in these parts, there was only one reasonable thought when you heard a sound like that.

"Oh, my God, it's a bear," Susan breathed, speaking their common fear. And it stood between them and their campsite.

Bobby was way ahead of her. Rolling quietly to his side, and then onto his feet, he rose slowly.

"What are you doing?"

"I'm gonna scare him off," he said.

"You're gonna *piss* him off. Just be still."

Bobby had never actually encountered a bear in the woods, but the common wisdom agreed that they had no real interest in people. As long as they didn't feel cornered, and their cubs weren't in jeopardy, they'd much rather run away from a noisy human than face him down.

"Go on!" Bobby shouted at the top of his voice, waving his arms. "Get out of here! I see you there in the bushes! Get out! Run away!"

Susan pulled at his pant leg. "Bobby!"

As the rustling stopped, Bobby turned in the cold moonlight and flashed a grin. "See?"

Then it charged. Squealing like a frightened pig, the beast bolted out of the trees, coming straight toward Bobby at first, then breaking off to the right, across the rocks toward the river.

Only it wasn't a bear.

"Oh my God!" Susan yelled. "It's a little boy!"

And he was scared to death. Screaming, he ran in a blind panic toward the edge of the rocks, and the roiling waters below.

"No!" Bobby shouted, and took off after him. "No! Don't! Come back!" But the kid moved like a water bug, darting with amazing speed but no visible effort, turning at the last possible instant away from the water, and back toward the woods, screaming the whole way.

"I didn't mean it!" Bobby called. "Stop! Really! I didn't mean it!" His words only seemed to make the boy move faster.

Finally, an old-growth oak tree ended the footrace. The boy looked over his shoulder long enough to see if Bobby was closing in on him, and he slammed into it; a glancing blow on his shoulder that might have killed him if he'd hit it head-on, but instead sent him ricocheting into a sapling, then onto the hard ground.

Bobby closed the distance in eight strides.

At first the little boy just sat there, stunned, and then the pain kicked in and he started to cry—a wailing sound that went beyond pain, combining fear and anger and frustration. He simply gave himself up to it, rolling over onto his tummy and sobbing into the leaves on the ground.

Bobby just stood there. He had no idea what to do. He stooped down and hesitantly reached out a comforting hand. "Hey, kid, settle down, okay? I didn't mean any harm."

"Here, let me in." Susan shouldered Bobby out of the way and scooped the boy into her arms. He fought at first, but then he looked into Susan's face, and he liked whatever he saw. He seemed to meld with her, clamping down hard with his arms and legs, his face burrowed into her shoulder.

Susan shot a look to Bobby, but he didn't know what to say. The boy looked tiny—maybe three years old—and he was filthy. Dirt caked his hair and his ears; his skin was crusty with it. He wore only a pair of footy pajamas, with little red choo-choo trains stenciled on the flannel. The toes on his left foot protruded through the tattered cloth.

"What do you think?" Bobby whispered.

"I don't know. He's so small. And he's freezing. You should feel him tremble."

Bobby looked around, hoping to see a terrified parent somewhere, but all he saw were woods and sky and water.

"Hey, little guy, what's your name?"

The sound of Bobby's voice made the boy cringe and pull himself even tighter against Susan.

"He's going to break my back," she grunted.

Bobby stripped off his down jacket and wrapped it around the boy's shoulders. "Here you go, tiger. Let's get you warm." To Susan, Bobby added, "Let's get back to camp."

During the walk back, Susan tried to talk to the boy, asking him his name, and how old he was, but all he'd do was cry and hang on.

"This is bad, Bobby," she said softly. "What's he doing out here without clothes in this kind of cold?"

Bobby shrugged. "Maybe he wandered away from his campsite." What else could it be?

"But how did he get so dirty? I mean, look at him. This isn't just a little dirt. This is weeks of dirt. Months, maybe, and even then, he'd have to live in a garden."

She had a point. There's dirt, and then there's *dirt*. This kid looked as if he'd been rolled in mud.

In two minutes, they were back at their campsite, such as it was. Primitive was the name of the game here. Their Explorer was parked a good mile away, at the bottom of the trail. What little they had in the way of creature comforts they'd packed in on their backs. The campfire, built for aesthetics and warmth rather than cooking, had burned down to a pile of shimmering red embers.

"I'll build this back up," Bobby said, peeling off from the others.

Susan went straight to their igloo-like dome tent, and the warmth of the sleeping bags inside. She stooped to her haunches outside the little doorway and tried to pry the boy's hands from around her neck, and his feet from around her waist. He grunted and instantly reattached himself.

"No, no, sweetie, you're okay now. You're safe. We'll make sure you get back home, okay?"

No, it wasn't okay. It wasn't okay at all. He remained glued to her, and the more she tried to pry him away, the more desperate he became to hang on.

"Why don't you sit with him for a while inside, Sue?" Bobby suggested, drawn back to the tent by the noise. "Wrap him up in a sleeping bag and just hold him until he settles down. He must be scared to death."

"Then what?"

Bobby's eyebrows twisted. "I don't know. I guess we hike out with him in the morning and take him to the ranger station. They'll decide what to do with him from there." Bobby stayed in the doorway for a moment, watching the two of them settle into a sleeping bag. "Tell you what," he proposed after they were lying down. "Why don't I make some hot chocolate? If nothing else, maybe it will loosen his tongue a bit."

At the sound of the phrase *hot chocolate* the kid's eyes lit up, but as soon as Bobby shifted his gaze to meet them, the boy quickly looked away and remelded with Sue.

Having put the cooking equipment away hours ago, Bobby had to reassemble it all from scratch. The camp stove was a single-burner job, fueled with white gas, and it took all of about three minutes to put it together, the satisfying blue flame telling him that he'd done it correctly. He poured water from his canteen into an aluminum pot, put it on the burner, and set about the business of resuscitating the campfire. He carefully stacked what remained of the kindling they'd collected in the daylight and knelt low, so that his elbows were on the ground, and his face nearly touched the dirt. From there he blew on the embers, a thin stream of air that made them flare orange before finally blossoming into a satisfying yellow flame.

He added larger pieces of wood, and within minutes, it burned freely, the flames reaching a good foot above the pile of sticks.

This whole thing had him spooked. Why in the world would a toddler be wandering around the woods in his pajamas? If he'd indeed been separated from his parents, where were the teams of rangers and police that should be out here looking for him? Where were the helicopters and the dogs? A sense of foreboding prickled his skin and he found himself obsessed with the notion that someone was watching him.

A loud snap drew his attention up ahead and to the right, toward the darkness that lay beyond the illuminated circle cast by the campfire. What was that? Most likely, just his imagination.

But he heard it again. Whatever it was—*who*ever it was—was approaching cautiously. Bobby closed his hand around a club-sized piece of firewood and stood casually, keeping it hidden as best he could behind his leg as he moved to the edge of the light circle.

"Bobby?" Susan asked from inside the tent. "Is something wrong?"

"Shh. I don't know. Be quiet for a second."

There it was again, only this time a rustle of leaves preceded the snap, and again the movement stopped, as if someone were attempting a stealthy approach and getting frustrated.

"Hello?" Bobby yelled. His words seemed five times louder in the silence of the night. "Who's out there?"

2

SAMUEL CRINGED AT the sound of the breaking stick and froze without waiting for Jacob's hand signal. He knew he'd screwed up again, and he knew that Jacob would have one of *those looks* on his face. He hated those looks. Samuel Stanns wasn't nearly the idiot that his brother thought he was.

Okay, so he'd let the boy get away. That was a big mistake, but to hear Jacob piss and moan about it, you'd think he'd done it on purpose. He never screwed up on purpose, and if he knew how to stop screwing up by accident, then he'd do it, wouldn't he? Of course he would.

Hell, it was dark out here. How are you supposed to avoid stepping on a stick? It was just hunky-dory terrific that Jacob was able to do it, but not everyone was as good at stuff as Jacob was. Samuel tried his best, and as his mama used to tell him, trying was sometimes the best you could hope for. His mama had understood that, and so did Jacob most of the time, even though his daddy . . . Well, what his daddy thought didn't matter much anymore.

Didn't matter at all right now because Jacob was pissed, and when that happened, the whole world had better start paying attention. Ever since they were kids, Jacob'd had a temper, and everybody who knew him knew to stay away from it.

"Are you listening to me or what?"

Jacob's harsh whisper broke whatever spell had locked up Samuel's mind and brought him back to the present. He nodded yes—that he was listening—because he knew it was the right answer, but Jacob still repeated himself.

"You just stay here," he commanded. "Don't go anywhere and don't say anything. I'll take care of this."

Samuel nodded, but then Jacob got mad again anyway.

"Did you hear me?"

"Yes." Samuel was never very good at whispering, so the best he could do was sort of a soft regular voice. "But you said not to say anything, so I thought I wasn't supposed—"

"Shut up, Samuel."

Susan poked her head through the door flap. "What's going on, Bobby?"

He didn't even look as he waved her back inside. To the woods, he said, "Howdy. You scared me. What can I do for you?"

"Well," a new voice said, its gravelly tone sounding twice as loud as her husband's, "I'm hoping you can help me find my son."

At the sound of the voice, the boy bolted upright in his sleeping bag and made a keening sound as he scrambled to Susan for protection. His eyes bore the look of a frightened pup, pleading and helpless as he pulled with hands and feet to drag Susan back into the tent and embrace her. She tried to quiet him down, but it was useless. The boy was utterly terrified.

Outside, Bobby recognized the boy's cries for what they were, and he caught the flash of contempt in their newest visitor's eyes.

"I'm Tom Stipton," Jacob said, extending his hand. "I see you found him. Quite a handful, isn't he?"

"I'll thank you to keep your distance," Bobby said, retreating a step and tightening his grip on the club. At six-two if he was an inch, the stranger looked like someone who'd been in his share of fights, and he moved with the confidence of the one who usually prevailed. Bobby's mind raced with possible bluffs, but with the kid making so much noise, he wasn't sure what he could do. "How did you lose him?"

The visitor seemed amused, as if he knew that his lies were transparent but decided to humor Bobby anyway. "Oh, the wife and me was drivin' down the road when we broke down. I fiddled with the engine for a while, and when I looked up, dear little Samuel was gone."

The words sat wrong with Bobby. "Dear little Samuel" had a troubling ring of sarcasm, and the delivery wasn't right. This guy should have been ecstatic to be reunited with his son. Instead, he seemed angry.

Bobby needed to do something. None of this added up, and he'd be goddamned if he was just—

The gun came from nowhere, materializing in the visitor's hand as it swung up at arm's length to point at Bobby's chest. It moved so fast that he never really saw the weapon, but the motion could only mean one thing. The odd smirk never left the man's face.

Bobby reacted without thinking, ducking to his left even as he swung his club. He connected with the back of the man's hand just as the weapon fired, the explosion deafening him momentarily as he rolled to his side and struggled to find his feet. He waited for the agonizing impact of a bullet, but instead saw the stranger on his hands and knees, brushing through the leaves on the shadow-strewn ground.

The gun! I must have knocked it out of his hands.

Bobby charged, with his club raised high over his head, but the stranger saw him coming and drove a fist deep into Bobby's belly, knocking the air out of his lungs. Gasping for a breath, Bobby never even saw the vicious backhand that buckled his knees.

His consciousness wavered, and he tasted dirt in his mouth. It made a foul, muddy mixture with the blood that leaked from a gash inside his cheek. The whole world spun at a weird, tilted angle, and as he attempted to find the ground and grab on to it, he knew with absolute clarity that if he passed out now, he'd die.

He tried standing once, fell back again, his hand landing in the fire, trigging a yelp of pain. The singed fingers helped him to focus, though, and as his vision cleared, he saw the stranger back in the leaves, trying to find his pistol.

Jesus, the pistol.

The fuzziness in his head evaporated. This man was going to kill him. Him and Susan. And the boy. He had to stop him. But how?

With a rush of clarity, he remembered the pot of water simmering on the small stove. It was his only chance. Scrambling to his feet, he staggered toward the dim blue flame and snatched the boiling pot from the burner, the metal handle burning the folds of his knuckles.

At that instant, the stranger made an odd, growling sound as he triumphantly snatched his gun from the leaves.

Bobby never even slowed down. Charging full tilt, he slung the scalding water in an awkward underhand softball pitch, catching the intruder squarely in the face. Jacob howled and clawed at his scalded eyes, but Bobby kept coming, catching him full in the throat with his shoulder, and sending him sprawling backward into the dirt.

"Samuel!" Jacob yelled. "Goddammit, Samuel, help me!"

Bobby hit the ground hard and instantly scrambled back to his feet. He needed the gun. He needed this man to die. But the weapon was still clutched in the stranger's hand. He kicked out wildly with his boot, targeting Jacob's head but mostly hitting the arms he used to shield himself.

"Samuel!"

Bobby went for the gun. He grabbed the weapon by its barrel and pulled. It fired. Bobby yelled and fell to the ground, certain that he'd been hit, but surprised by how little it hurt. His right forearm felt as if it had been set on fire by the muzzle flash, but as he glanced at the damage, he was shocked to see that he'd come away with the gun.

"Motherfucker!" the killer roared. Still blinded from his burns, Jacob turned onto his belly and thrust his hand out to close with crushing force around Bobby's ankle. "I'll kill you. I swear to God, I'll kill you. Samuel!"

Terrified, Bobby tried to kick himself free from the man's grasp, but there was no getting away. He sighted down the barrel of the big pistol at the top of Jacob's head.

He'll kill you. He'll kill Susan . . .

But his finger wouldn't work on the trigger.

Then the scalded eyes found him. The man looked straight at him. Even through the blisters, the coldness of his eyes chilled the night air.

"I'll fucking kill you!" he yelled, and he lunged forward.

The pistol bucked in Bobby's hand, blinding him with a brilliant white flash, and then it bucked again. He couldn't even see what he was doing anymore, but he had to kill this monster.

• • •

Susan shrieked at the sound of the gunshots, and so did the boy. They desperately hung on to each other inside the tent as she tried to make some sense of it all; to figure out what she should do.

If Bobby was dead, then so was she. And the boy, most likely.

The fight had raged outside for an hour, it seemed, and as she tried to piece together all that had happened, all she heard now was quiet. After so much noise, the quiet was most terrifying of all.

Samuel felt the tears coming, and he fought to stop them. Only pussies cried. He'd heard Jacob say that a thousand times.

He'd said not to move, dammit! And he'd said not to say a word, so when he started calling for help, that was really, really confusing. How could Samuel know that Jacob wouldn't get mad all over again? Besides, Jacob never liked it when Samuel got into the middle of his fights. He said that he could handle himself, and that his little brother only fucked things up when he tried to help.

But from where Samuel stood, it sure looked as if Jacob needed some; the way he just lay there, not moving. It reminded him of the way other people lay frozen on the ground when Jacob was through with them. He couldn't be dead, could he?

No, Jacob was too tough to die. He might get beat up real bad sometimes, but he'd never die. He promised. He'd always be there for Samuel, no matter what. He said that all the time.

But he sure wasn't moving.

Samuel started to cry, in spite of himself. He always cried when he was scared, and right now he was more frightened than he'd ever been. At least since he was a little boy.

But Jacob would be okay. He promised.

Samuel had to suck on his hand—that place between his thumb and his forefinger (because everybody knows that only pussies sucked their thumbs)—to keep his crying quiet enough that no one would hear.

"Come on, Jacob," he whined in as near a whisper as he knew how. "Come on and get up. Please get up, Jacob . . . "

Bobby couldn't take his eyes off the man on the ground. He just watched, numb, as the blood leaked out of him, forming little rivulets in the mulchy forest floor. The trembling started from Bobby's shoulders and raced down his body; uncontrollable spasms that made him sit down heavily, doing his best all the time to hold his aim.

"Oh, my God, Bobby, are you alright?" He looked up to see Susan staring down at him, her face a mask of horror.

"I think I killed him," he said. His voice sounded as if it belonged to someone else.

Susan put the boy down and sat next to her husband, gathering him into her arms. "Oh, my God," she said, then said it again.

It was all more than Bobby could comprehend. Not a half hour ago, he was comforting his wife in the moonlight. What the hell had happened? Jesus, he'd killed a man!

Susan jumped, as if shot with electricity. "No, don't!" she yelled, and Bobby braced for another attack.

"What? What's happening?"

Susan jumped to her feet. "Oh, no, Jesus, no! Don't do that." She darted over to the body, where the filthy little boy straddled the man's back, pounding him as hard as he could with his fists. "Stop it!"

As she wrenched him away, the boy continued to flail and scream, Susan's head and shoulders absorbing the force of the pummeling. She didn't try to say anything to him; she just held on to him, and in time, he settled down some, his panic dissolving to sobs, and then a muffled whimper before he finally fell asleep in her arms.

3

SUSAN HELD THE boy tightly in the crook of her shoulder, patting his back and trying to get him to stay settled. To keep him turned away from the body, though, she had to face it, and what she saw made her stomach churn. He lay so *still.* With his left arm at his side, and his right hand raised, he looked like the toppled statue of someone who'd been waving good-bye. They were the hands of someone used to hard work—big, beefy hands that looked as if they could never be cleaned, not even after an hour of washing. They were mechanic's hands. What she noticed most about him, though, was how flat the body looked; as if he were once a balloon, and now half the air had leaked out of him.

But that wasn't air she saw leaking through his thinning hair, nor was it air that stained his denim jacket black. That was blood. Blood from the bullet holes her husband had punched into his body—the bullets that had likely saved her life. The shadows cast by the flickering light of the campfire turned the corpse's eyes into dark hollows, and as the black smear of a nose shadow danced along his upper lip, she saw that his front teeth were smeared with blood. In just a few minutes—or certainly within a few hours—the blood would crust over and turn brown. She shuddered as she found herself licking her own teeth the way she might before a formal dinner, to guard against lipstick-teeth.

"Who's Samuel?" Bobby asked out of nowhere.

"Huh? What?" It was as if Susan had already forgotten about the fight.

"Samuel. He kept calling for help from Samuel. Who the hell is he?"

"Isn't that what he called the baby? He said they turned around and Samuel had run away."

Bobby nodded pensively. That's right. He *had* said that, hadn't he? So, was he trying to get the boy to come to his aid? This tiny little boy? The one who had pummeled his dead body? Not likely.

"We need to get out of here," Bobby said. "I think he's got friends, and I don't want to meet them."

"It's dark! The trail's too dangerous at night."

"Well, it's safer than staying here." Bobby nodded toward the body on the ground. "Besides, do you want to spend the night with him? The sooner we report this, the better off we're all going to be. It's stupid to stay here."

Susan patted the boy's head and kissed his filthy hair. "But what about the baby? He can't walk all that distance. He's exhausted as it is."

"We'll carry him, then. We'll wrap him up real warm and then we'll carry him, but we've got to get out of here." Bobby looked at the pistol he still clutched in his hand, then stuffed it in the waistband of his jeans. "It's just not safe."

For the first time, Susan saw it all for what it was, and she whipped her head from side to side, scanning the woods for more gunmen. A giant fist squeezed her stomach. "Okay. Okay, I'll get some things to wrap the baby in. We'll come back later for our stuff, right?"

Bobby nodded. "Right. Just leave everything."

As Susan wrapped the boy up in a jacket and a sleeping bag, Bobby couldn't take his eyes off the corpse. Jesus, he'd killed a man; damn near been killed *by* him. Why? What the hell was going on? And why would he want to harm such a small child?

Bobby realized now that he needed to know who this guy was. If there was a Samuel out in the woods somewhere, waiting to come in and help his pal, Bobby didn't want him dragging the body off to cover his tracks. If nothing else, he needed a wallet or a driver's license from his attacker—some name to give to the police.

He moved cautiously, as if the body might suddenly lash out at him. Ridiculous as it was, scenes from all the slasher movies he'd ever seen flashed through his mind, and he didn't think he could deal with a sudden awakening from the dead.

The corpse's wallet bulged plainly from his back pocket. Bobby stood for a long time, gathering the courage he needed to take the next step. His skin puckered at the very thought of touching a dead man.

Straddling the body, he used only his thumb and forefinger to reach in and grab a corner of well-used leather. The man smelled of urine, and up this close, the spilled contents of his bladder radiated a nauseating warmth.

"What are you doing!"

The suddenness of Susan's words made him jump a foot, and he fell backward into the leaves. "Jesus Christ!"

Susan just stood there, at the opening of the tent, the bundled boy in her arms. "Are you robbing him?"

"No, I'm not robbing him!" Bobby was aghast that she would even ask such a question. "I want to get his ID so we'll be able to put a name to all of this."

"Oh, honey, I don't know . . . "

"It'll only take a second." He went back to work, again using only two fingers to pull the wallet clear of the pocket, and opening it. He couldn't see much in the darkness, but the billfold had an odd shape and weighed more than he thought it should. When he turned it over in his hands, he saw why, and for just a fraction of a second his heart stopped beating.

A gleaming silver badge stared up at him. Suddenly light-headed, he reeled and once again sat heavily on the leaf-strewn forest floor.

"What?" Susan said, moving toward him. "What is it?"

"He's a cop." Hearing the words shot an icy chill through his belly. "Oh, my God, Sue, I killed a cop."

Terror bloomed in Bobby's chest. Cop killers went to jail, pure and simple; that much he knew just from watching television. Provided, of course, they lived long enough to make it there.

Susan took a quick three steps forward, then stopped. "But so what?" She tried to sound light and confident, but the brittle edges of panic showed through anyway. "So what if he was a cop? I mean, he's just another man, right? Self-defense is self-defense."

Oh, Christ, but was it *really* self-defense? This cop came into their campsite looking for a child to whom the Martins had zero rights, and when Bobby showed resistance, the cop drew his gun. Whose self was being defended?

No, don't think that way. He was going to shoot. I saw it in his eyes. He was going to shoot.

But he *didn't* shoot, did he? At least not until Bobby lunged at his gun and started to fight with him. What the hell else was he supposed to do? All the cop knew was that some stranger had his kid, and when he moved to get him back, Bobby refused. He was a *cop* for God's sake.

"Bobby? Bobby, what's wrong? It *was* self-defense, wasn't it?"

All at once, it crystallized for him. They had to get out of there. Right now. They had to disappear, make it look as if they'd never even been there. Stuffing the wallet back into the man's pocket, Bobby stood and whirled to face his wife.

"We've got to go. Take everything. And I mean *everything*. I don't want to leave so much as a trace."

"You're scaring me, Bobby," Susan whined. "Tell me what's happening."

He didn't have time for this. Neither of them did. "Think about it, Sue. I killed a *cop*."

"In self-defense." She said the words as if she were speaking to a dense child. Then she saw the look in his face, and her shoulders sagged. "It was."

He didn't know where to begin. Everything had happened so fast. Everything was just flashes and impressions. "I don't know for sure," he said at last, and he saw his wife's eyes widen with terror. "I mean I was sure at the time, but I don't know now. I mean, if I thought he was a cop, maybe I would have done things differently. If he'd identified himself as a cop—"

"But that's just it," Susan said quickly. "He didn't identify himself. I was here. I heard that. And by not identifying himself, you had every right—"

"What about the other cops, Sue? The ones who investigate all of this? They're going to see a dead cop, and they're going to hear about a child we don't know from Adam, and a story about an attack that's making less and less sense even to me. What are they going to think?"

"So, what do we do, then?"

"We get the hell out of here."

"You're at least going to call, right?"

"I don't know. I don't know anything right now. And to top it all off, we've got *him.*" Bobby gestured to the sleeping boy, who'd finally found his thumb. "Not to mention good old Samuel, whoever the hell he is." Bobby stepped over the body and started policing the area. "For all I know, this is the worst thing we could do, but it's the only thing that sounds right, okay?"

No, it wasn't okay, and her face showed it. But she didn't have a better idea.

"Now, put the kid down someplace and let him sleep. I need help here."

He moved at a frantic pace, darting from one corner of the campsite to the next, playing his L.L. Bean miner's light all around, hoping to find any trace of themselves that they might have left behind. He got the food and the trash, and he remembered to pick up the pot he'd slung at the intruder.

While the little boy slept at the base of a tree, Susan shoved their belongings into their backpacks. Bobby's sense of urgency had infected her, and she found that her hands couldn't move fast enough. Every second, she felt that they were on the verge of getting caught. She still wasn't sure what that would mean exactly, but she'd never seen Bobby so distraught.

She made it a point not to look toward the body. Anything left over there was left forever, as far as she was concerned. She just wanted to be off this mountain and on to someplace safe and friendly where she could talk some sense into Bobby's head. They had nothing to hide, dammit. To run was to admit otherwise. She knew this. And she knew that Bobby would know it once he started thinking straight again. For now, all that mattered was getting back to the car.

Samuel hadn't moved in a half hour, and neither had Jacob. It really was true, wasn't it? Jacob was really dead, and these people had killed him. If it hadn't been for those two nosy nellies, everything would be just fine.

But why are they nosy nellies to begin with?

He whirled at the sound of Jacob's voice, only to find himself staring deeper into the woods.

"Jacob?" he asked the night, still in his quietest voice. He looked nervously toward the campsite again, and at the body, which still hadn't moved. "Where are you?"

No answer. Jacob was like that sometimes, asking questions just to get Samuel thinking straight.

He stewed the question over in his mind. Why were they nosy nellies to begin with?

Because of the kid. That damned kid, who refused to do anything he was told to do. That kid who wouldn't do anything but scream and whine and never say a fucking word to anybody. For the life of him, Samuel couldn't figure out why Jacob had wanted the kid in the first place.

You let him get away. You fell asleep.

That time, he knew the voice came from inside his head. The picture that Jacob wanted him to see started to focus in his mind, and once it did, Samuel wished it would disappear.

If the kid hadn't gotten away, then the nosy nellies would never have known a thing. And if they had never known, then Jacob wouldn't have been shot. So, if Samuel hadn't fallen asleep when he should have been watching . . .

Samuel gasped, clapping a hand over his mouth to keep anyone from hearing him.

Oh God, oh God, oh God, it can't be. I killed my own brother.

Finally, they were ready. The backpacks were full, the stuff sacks stuffed, and the woods where their campsite had been looked pristine.

Susan wanted to carry the boy, but with her full pack, she couldn't manage the weight, so Bobby took over. The child stank of urine and filth. He tried to carry the boy with the little one's grimy head on his shoulder, but the straps of his backpack got in the way. In the end, he had no choice but to carry him cradled in his arms.

Bobby led the way, illuminating the path with his goofy-looking headlamp. The boy couldn't weigh much more than thirty pounds, but dead to the world as he was, he felt much heavier. Combined with the fact that Bobby could no longer see where he placed his feet on the narrow, steep, rocky trail, the thirty-minute walk to the Explorer might as well have been an hour and a half.

The woods seemed abnormally silent tonight, the blood pounding in his ears all but drowning out the distant rushing of the river. Where it had once brought a sense of peace, that hissing roar now made him worry that someone might more easily sneak up on them.

"I see the car," Susan said from behind.

Bobby shifted his head, and sure enough, he caught a flash of white through the naked trees. "Thank God." The little boy now felt as if he weighed three hundred pounds. Bobby's arms trembled.

"Okay, little guy," Bobby said as he walked around to the side of the truck, "I've got to put you down for a second." The boy stood as Bobby lowered him to the ground, but he never really woke up.

Just to be sure, Susan steadied the boy as Bobby's trembling hands fished for his keys. With two presses of the little button on the fob, the locks popped up and he pulled open the door.

Susan hoisted the boy onto the backseat, where he instantly curled onto his side and stuffed a thumb in his mouth.

Next came the backpacks, which they shoved through the tailgate. It was time to leave.

"I'll ride in the back with him," Susan announced.

Bobby opened his mouth to object, then closed it again. Why the hell shouldn't she ride in the back? The boy needed to be with *somebody,* after all.

Thirty seconds later, the truck was heading down the treacherous, unpaved switchbacks that would lead to the road home. Ruts and rocks bounced them all over the interior of the truck, and Bobby found himself riding the brakes even after shifting the transmission into low.

"How are you guys doing back there?"

"I'm hanging on, and he's doing great." Susan's voice bounced right along with the suspension.

"Shouldn't be more than a couple minutes till we're out of here."

If anyone had asked him yesterday, Bobby would not have been able to imagine a circumstance in which he would make this drive after dark. Not unless someone was gravely ill.

Or dead, with a bullet in his brain.

Finally, they made it to the bottom, and Bobby let out an audible sigh. They were back on solid pavement, and they'd put plenty of distance between themselves and whoever the cop might have been traveling with. For the time being, the worst was over.

Or so he thought, before he saw flashing blue lights closing in on his rear bumper.

Samuel had taken a trip. That's what he called those times when he left the real world and traveled off to think thoughts that no one else could understand, and when he got back, darkness had returned. The campfire and the flashlights were gone, and the darkness pressed in all around him. Even the moon had dimmed.

The stiffness in his shoulders and his knees told him that he'd been gone a long time, but not as long as he used to go when he was a kid. His pants were still dry.

He didn't like the dark; never had. Bad things happened in the dark, and for as long as he could remember, he'd always kept lights on around him. At least a flashlight, but Jacob wouldn't let him carry one of those tonight.

In the darkness, with all the other people gone, Samuel decided that it was okay for him to cry. No one could see, so no one would call him a pussy now. Certainly not Jacob.

Because he was dead.

Sadness flooded up all the way from his tippy-tippy toes and burst over him, making him wonder if maybe he would drown in it. Samuel put his hands over his ears and pushed as hard as he could, hoping that the horrible feelings could be kept inside, but they all rushed out anyway. He sagged to his knees and sobbed there in the darkness, not even caring about the snot and the drool that leaked out onto his shirt.

Jacob was never coming back. He was dead. And there was nothing Samuel could do about it.

It took another half hour for him to summon the courage to move out of his spot and do what he had to do next. The moon didn't provide a whole lot of light, but it was enough for Samuel to pick his way through the trees without getting hurt. He moved a step at a time, still trying his best not to step on any sticks.

Through the bushes, an iridescent white rectangle drew his attention. He bent down for a closer look and found a piece of paper with writing on it. Samuel liked paper, and he liked writing, so he folded it up and stuffed it in the pocket of his jeans.

You're not out here to pick up trash.

He knew that, and it angered him that he could so easily be distracted. Returning to his original course, he took only six more steps and then he was there. His brother still hadn't moved; he was just a black stain against the night.

Samuel knelt as close as he could and rested his hand on Jacob's shirt, hoping that maybe he would feel it and wake up. "I'm really, really sorry, Jacob," he said. And then, choking back a sob and wiping the snot from his nose, he leaned down and kissed his big brother good-night.

4

WE'VE GOT TROUBLE, Sue," Bobby groaned, trying his best to squeeze the terror out of his voice.

Susan saw the strobing blue shadows and strained to look out the back window. "What do they want?"

"What do you think?"

"How could they know? How could they possibly know?"

Bobby pulled over to the side of the road, nursing a distant hope that the cop behind them might be chasing someone else. Yeah, right. The strobes slipped in behind them.

"What are you going to do?" Susan asked.

"I don't know."

Bobby's mind raced. What were his options? By his calculation, he had exactly none. Maybe this was for the best. They'd done what they'd done, and maybe it was best for them just to fess up to it and face the music.

Out of nowhere, he remembered the pistol he'd casually tossed onto the passenger seat as he climbed into the truck, and he quickly reached over to get it out of sight. Through his side-view mirror, he saw the cop's door open, and his heart did a quick somersault. The very last thing he needed was to greet the cop with a gun in his hand. Hesitating for only an instant, he tucked the weapon under his butt and tried to look innocent.

Ten seconds later, the cop was at the window, and Bobby pressed the button to lower it.

"Good evening." To his own ear Bobby sounded petrified.

The cop shined a flashlight in his eyes. "Howdy." Next, he shined the flashlight in through the rear window. Bobby noted with a tiny flutter of hope that the man's weapon was not drawn. "Y'all okay?"

Hope bloomed even larger. "I think so," Bobby said, forcing a smile. "Any reason I shouldn't be?"

The flashlight came back around, but this time at a less imposing angle, aimed more at his door than his face. "None I can think of. We just don't get many people driving the roads this time of night. You haven't had anything to drink tonight, have you, sir?"

Bobby had to fight off a giddy little laugh as relief washed over him. Could it really be this simple? "No, sir, not a drop. Water and coffee, that's it."

With the light redirected, the top half of the cop's body was a faceless shadow, but Bobby readily saw the man's gold badge on the green shirt. This guy wasn't a cop at all. He was a park ranger. "I see y'all been camping. Is there a reason why you're bugging out so early?"

Bobby startled himself with his answer. "I'm afraid the wife's not cut out for the out-of-doors life. I could stay awake all night explaining sounds, or I could drive us back home. This seemed to make more sense." He marveled at how easily the lie materialized, and how rational it sounded.

The ranger laughed. He'd been there, done that. "I don't suppose you have a camping permit I could look at, do you?"

This time, honesty served Bobby well. "Yeah, I do, but it's on my pack in the back. Do you want me to get it for you?"

The ranger thought about it, but after another quick glance in the backseat, he shook his head. "No, that's okay. I'll take your word for it. I'm sorry your trip didn't work out better for you. Have a good night, and drive carefully for me, will you?"

"You bet." Bobby smiled. "Thanks." As his window climbed its track, he shook his head and allowed that giggle to escape. "Would you believe that?"

Susan saw none of the humor. "Just get us home, okay, Bobby? Just get us home."

• • •

Once the adrenaline high subsided, leaving only the monotony of a long drive in a quiet car, reality began to sink its hooks.

Jesus, he'd killed a man.

You can't murder another human being and just walk away. Life doesn't work like that. You do something wrong, and you step forward to take ownership of your crime. Throw yourself on the mercy of the court.

But he was a cop.

Why couldn't he have been anyone else in the world but a cop? Bobby didn't buy for a second that the guy was the kid's father, but maybe he was on the feather edge of solving a kidnapping case. Or, maybe, like the Martins, he was minding his own business in the woods when he saw this kid in his filthy, torn pajamas, and like any other public servant, he stepped forward to do the right thing.

But I didn't know that, Judge, Bobby imagined himself saying in a future courtroom. *He scared me so badly that I rushed him, and then when he pulled his gun, what choice did I have but to wrestle it away and shoot him?*

His stomach tumbled at the very thought of it. They'd never believe him; not in a million years.

But they didn't see his eyes. They didn't hear the boy's reaction to the sound of his voice. Even with all of his doubts and all of his questions, Bobby couldn't escape the notion that the cop wasn't there to help anyone. He was there to hurt people; specifically, the little boy. And if he did that, then he'd have to do something about Bobby and Susan, too, wouldn't he? Of course he would.

It was self-defense, dammit. Bobby had nothing to hide. Why the hell was he acting like he did?

If he'd been anybody but a cop . . .

Yeah, if only.

If he stepped forward, people were going to want to know why his first instinct had been to run. He could explain it as panic, he supposed. How was he to know that the stranger didn't have an accomplice out there in the woods with him? Somebody named Samuel?

Well, tell me, Mr. Martin, if there were an accomplice, wouldn't he have, well, helped a little? Maybe stepped in sometime between the start of the fight and your killing his friend?

These people wouldn't understand that thoughts get all jammed up in your head when you're fighting for your life. Not everything was *going* to make sense in the calm afterglow of hindsight. Things that seemed perfectly logical were going to sound ludicrous. Surely they would all understand that. They'd *have* to understand it, because it was the truth.

Innocent people don't run, Mr. Martin.

And that's the truth, too. Ask anyone, and they'll tell you the same thing. The truth is a powerful weapon, they say. It will set you free.

So long as the evidence bears out your story.

And so long as your victim is not a cop.

Holy God Almighty, what was he going to do?

Bobby had been tracking neither the mileage nor the time, but his gut told him that he was still a good hour, hour and a half, away from home, and the gas gauge had dipped below the one-quarter mark. The lighted Amoco sign consequently caught his attention more readily than it might otherwise have. He slowed the Explorer smoothly, slapped the turn signal, and slid behind the row of pumps closest to the road.

Sensing the change in direction, Susan mumbled something he couldn't understand and then set her head back down on the headrest. An instant later, her jaw dropped, and she was back asleep.

"Must be nice," he grumbled as he carefully and quietly opened his door. The way he felt now, he doubted that he'd ever get a restful night of sleep again. He walked with one foot on the curb as he slid between the truck and the pump, reaching for his wallet as he went. He had his credit card in his hand, ready to insert it into the gas pump when the sensibly paranoid lobe of his brain reached out and gave him a good slap.

If ever in his life there'd been a bad time to use a credit card—with all of its traceability—this was it. It'd have to be cash. He checked his reserves, found two twenties, and went ahead and set the pump. He lifted the nozzle, flipped the lever, just as he was supposed to, and nothing happened.

It shouldn't be this complicated, he thought, and then the speaker popped in the roof of the pump island, startling the bejesus out of him. "You've got to pay first," said a groggy adolescent voice. Bobby peered through the windows of the Explorer to see a zit-faced kid behind the glass, waving at him.

Leaving the pump handle dangling out of the tank, Bobby stepped over the hose and made his way toward the squatty glass building that advertized itself as a Mini-Mart. An electronic bell pinged as he opened the door, and the kid behind the counter wrestled himself to his feet.

"How much do you want? Whoa, are you okay? What happened to your face?"

Clearly the visual effects of his fight were worse than the physical ones. "I was just born ugly, I guess." No way was he going to explain anything to this kid. "Let's shoot for twenty bucks' worth. You'll give me change, right, if it doesn't take it all?"

"Course," the kid said. "Wouldn't stay in business very long if we stole people's money."

A Kit Kat bar on the first rack inside the door caught Bobby's attention, and as he reached for one of the orange packets, a picture of a smiling baby on a box distracted him. They sold Pampers here, too. Well, he could sure use some of them. And some of those wipe things, too, to clean babies' butts.

He brought his booty to the checkout counter and nearly fell over when the kid said, "With gas, that'll be forty-four dollars and thirty-seven cents."

"Holy cow," Bobby gasped.

The kid smiled. "We ain't the cheapest, but we're the only place open for thirty miles."

You had to give him credit for honesty. "Tell you what, then," Bobby said. "Put me down for fifteen dollars in gas, and then the rest here."

Susan still had not moved by the time he wandered back to the truck, though she stirred as he opened the back door.

"What's going on?" she asked.

"I just stopped to get some gas and essentials."

Susan saw the diapers and smiled. "That was sweet." She shifted around in the seat, drew one leg under her, and closed her eyes again.

The Explorer drank every bit of the fifteen dollars' worth, with thirst to spare. Bobby returned the nozzle to its slot in the pump and was on his way back to the driver's seat when he saw the pay phone at the far edge of the parking lot.

This was his chance, he told himself; his chance to do the right thing. But what would he say?

Hi, there, my name's Robert Martin, and I just killed a police officer. . . .

No, that wouldn't do at all, would it? Truth be told, he didn't have to say anything to anybody. He could just go on his merry way, and maybe nothing would ever come of any of this. Maybe no one would happen by the body in the woods for months—until long after the remains had been carted off by animals, or at least until the body had deteriorated far enough that it was no longer recognizable. How long would that take? he wondered. In this weather, as cold and dry as it had been, probably a long time.

He found himself approaching the phone booth even before he knew what he was doing. *Just let it go,* his brain screamed. *Just drive on and take your chances.*

But a man was dead, goddammit. When somebody did get around to finding the corpse—and one way or another, he knew they would—they'd call it a homicide, and the hunt for the killer would never end. *Never.* The statute of limitations on murder ran without end in every state in the Union. He knew that much from a lifetime of cop shows. Over time, he'd crumble under the weight of it all. He knew he would.

Bobby's mind conjured up the image of a retirement party one day. He'd be surrounded by colleagues and family when the police came, knocking down the doors and hauling him off to prison. How would he feel then, starting a life prison term at a time when he'd probably be getting released if he'd only fessed up earlier?

And none of this even touched on the issue of the boy. What the hell were they going to do with him? Bobby supposed there were still orphanages somewhere, but they couldn't just drop him off on the front step of some building.

He placed his hand on the phone and paused. This was it. The point of no return. What the hell was he going to say?

Nothing. You say nothing. You just go back to your car and let fate take care of this.

And when they finally caught up to him, how would he explain forgetting about the guy he killed five, ten, thirty years ago?

"Okay, Bobby, you can do this," he said aloud. After another pause for a deep sigh, he settled himself down and made his phone call.

5

APRIL SIMPSON OFFERED up a little prayer of thanks that she'd been able to drive all the way home without falling asleep. She feared sometimes that this pace might kill her. Eight hours at McDonald's followed by another four cleaning offices downtown was only half of the available hours in a day, but as the baby in her belly continued to bloom, she needed more sleep than she could find.

Some nights, she lay awake in her bed crying, wondering how she was ever going to get by with two children to care for. She remembered those endless nights when infant Justin refused to sleep, crying and crying and crying until she finally had to leave the apartment for fear of doing something to hurt him. Now her son was nearly three, but still terribly two, and she was going to have to find a way to deal with *another* infant. She wasn't sure she could do it.

Not that she had a lot of choice anymore. She'd decided to keep the belly squirmer, and that's all there was to it. To hell with what William thought.

William was a pig. He'd been a pig for as long as she'd known him, and if it hadn't been for the night of drunken passion that had created Justin, she'd never in a million years have married him. William wasn't the father, but he was a man, and at the time, that's what she thought she needed most.

April pulled into her space at The Pines and scanned every compass point for signs of trouble before turning off the ignition and climbing out of her tiny Geo. Her little Chevy served as her symbol of freedom—her statement to the world that she wasn't completely useless. It also was the only asset that she owned outright and in her own name. One day, it might just be her ticket out of here.

Making sure she'd gathered all her stuff, she didn't bother to lock the doors as she walked away. Better that a thief get into the car and find nothing to steal than break out the windows and leave her with a big mess in the morning. If they wanted to steal the car itself, more power to them. She could use the insurance check.

As she crossed the dark playground on her way to her building, she kept her hand in her coat pocket, wrapped around the tiny .25 that she'd bought six years ago but never fired. William liked to say that she could empty a whole clip into someone and only piss him off, but if that bought the time she needed to avoid a rapist or a weapon bigger than hers, then that was just fine. Killing wasn't her bag. Surviving was.

She kept her eye on the cluster of kids over by the sliding board, watching without turning her head, as they did the same to her. What could they possibly be doing outside at four in the morning? Where were their parents? And why would they want to be outside on such a cold night? In the summer, it almost made sense, as a means to escape the stifling heat of the apartments, but not tonight. Here in Pittsburgh, spring felt too much like winter.

Twenty, thirty yards away, the kids posed no immediate danger, but as one of them took a step closer, her hand tightened on the pistol's grip. When it turned out that he was merely moving around to sit on the end of the sliding board, she relaxed. She tried to tell herself that her paranoia was silly, but it was the kind of silliness that kept you alive in The Pines.

She'd once counted the steps, from her parking space to her front door, and the number 182 remained burned into her brain forever. One hundred eighty-two steps, exposed to the whims of whoever might decide to take advantage of her. Yet, no one ever had. She wondered sometimes why that was. Maybe it was because she stayed clean and sober and never hassled those who could not make the same claim. Maybe she was seen as a kind of Switzerland among the warring drug factions. She liked to think of it that way.

Soon, though, Justin would grow from a toddler to a little boy, and along about the time he started school, the druggies would come after him. Not to use—that came in junior high—but to carry money from one spot to another. The gangs liked to use little ones because police didn't hassle them as badly. Even when they were caught, the kids were usually home with their parents by the next morning.

That's if they were just carrying money. More and more, the dealers were using little ones to shuttle guns, and that scared the daylights out of her. Guns brought death, it was that simple. Just like in the pocket of her jacket right now. How close would she have let that kid on the sliding board approach before drawing down and threatening him? And once drawing, how much closer still before she pulled the trigger?

Sometimes, the world seemed bleak as hell.

Finally, she arrived at her apartment door, relieved to find it locked. Usually, that meant that William was reasonably sober, and there'd be no fight. There'd be sex instead. William liked getting laid in the mornings, after a good night's sleep for him, and an endless workday for her. Her friends called his demands a power play—lofty psychological analyses from the Oprah school of medicine—and they were probably right, but what the hell? Five minutes of grunting and sweating beat the hell out of the whining and yelling that were the only alternative. Jesus, it wasn't even a contest.

April had to turn all three dead bolts, and as the door swung open, she nearly screamed. William was waiting for her on the other side, sitting in the La-Z-Boy opposite the door. In the blue light of the television he looked like somebody's ghost.

"My God, William," she exclaimed. "You scared me to death."

He didn't seem startled at all. "Sorry," he grunted. "I've been waiting up for you."

"What's wrong?" Call it woman's intuition or a premonition or whatever, but she knew that something terrible had happened. She felt it in the pit of her stomach.

He didn't say anything. He just pivoted his head, and then she saw the bruises. Mottled shades of black and red marred the whole left side of his face, swelling his eye shut, and drooping his lower lip.

"Jesus, William, what—" She took a half-step closer, then froze. "Justin," she breathed.

Dropping her purse to the floor, scattering keys and change everywhere, she bolted down the short hallway toward the baby's room. She slapped at the light switch, missing it twice before the single, dangling sixty-watt bulb jumped to life and bathed everything in a dim yellow light.

Justin didn't sleep on a bed per se, but rather on a mattress on the floor, and that mattress looked for all the world to be empty. "Justin?" she said, first at a whisper, and then as her panic grew, she shouted it. "Justin! Where are you!" Frantic, she fell to her hands and knees and tore at the covers, trying to convince herself that her son was under that mess somewhere. He'd just rolled off, that was all. He just was lost somewhere among the covers.

But he wasn't lost. He was gone.

"William!" she screamed. "William, where's Justin?" She bolted back into the living room, panic boiling hot in her belly.

William hadn't moved. He still stared at the blue light, studiously avoiding eye contact.

"Goddamn you, William, talk to me. Where is Justin?" She reached out to strike him, but quickly retracted her hand. She'd never seen him like this before. She worried what emotions might accompany the stare.

As his eyes finally came around—only one of them would open all the way—she noticed the tears, and her legs buckled. Sagging to the floor, she covered her mouth with her hands and gasped, "Oh, God, is he dead? Please tell me he's not dead."

William shook his head, just a barely perceptible movement, but she understood it for what it was. "He's not dead. At least, I don't think he is."

"Tell me!"

William winced against her scream, looked as if he might cry. He waved his hands in an odd, circular motion, as if to draw the words out of his body, but nothing came.

April changed tacks. She put her hand on his forearm and gently squeezed it. "Tell me," she said again, much softer this time. "Just tell me what happened. Don't worry about the right words, just tell me what happened to Justin."

He took a deep breath and finally made that subtle nodding movement again. "They took him."

The words cut like razors. "*Who* took him? What are you talking about? Who would take Justin?"

"Two men. Cops. They beat me up really bad."

"Why! Goddammit, William, stop with the mystery and tell me what happened."

"I don't know!" William blurted. "They pulled me over while I was driving Justin over to Wilson's and—"

"You were taking a two-year-old to a bar?"

For just an instant, the grief disappeared from William's face, replaced with a flash of anger, which just as quickly went away. "I don't know why I was doing that. I know it's wrong, but I was being a piece of shit, okay? I did it. Or I tried to do it."

April realized that she really had no interest in Wilson's or the fact that her boy would be taken there. "Okay," she coaxed. "You were on your way to Wilson's and what happened?"

"They pulled me over. These two cops in an unmarked car. I was over there off of Tyson Boulevard, you know, in that stretch where everything's boarded up after five?"

It was a good half mile out of the way, but April didn't bother to ask why he was over there. Tyson's dead-ended about a block from Wilson's, and by going that way, he avoided any breathalyzer traps that the cops might have laid. "I know where it is. What happened?"

"Well, they flashed their lights at me and pulled me over, and then when they came to the window, the big one just dragged me out of the car and started beating on me. I swear to God they broke my jaw." His *S*'s slurred into a sloppy, juicy sound, making *swear* sound like *shwear.* "When I got up, they had Justin, and they were taking him back to their car. I tried to stop them, but they just kept going. Honest to God, April, I swear I don't know why. They just came out of nowhere."

April's brain raced to piece together the puzzle. "The police don't do this sort of thing, William."

"Well, these did."

"Then we need to call some more. Jesus, you haven't done that yet?"

He shook his head. "No, I thought—"

"William! We've got to call the police."

"No. I don't think that's a good idea."

There was that look again. This time it wasn't anger, but fear. As if he'd been caught at something. Suddenly, she knew he was sandbagging. He knew more than he was telling her.

"What?" she demanded. "What's the rest of it?"

The hurt face returned. "I don't know what you're talking about."

"You're lying," she yelled. Suddenly, the .25 appeared in her hand, and his pretend fear became very, very real. "Tell me what happened to Justin!"

"Jesus, April, put that away!" He tried to cover himself up with his arms and hands. "Look at me. They beat the shit out of me."

"Then it had to be for a reason. I want to know the reason."

"I don't know—"

She raised the gun even higher and moved in closer, to a range where even she couldn't miss.

"Okay, okay," he said, cowering in the La-Z-Boy. "I think they were working for Logan. Logan's guys took Justin."

Suddenly, the room seemed short of oxygen. April had to breathe hard to keep from passing out. "Why? Why of all the children in the world would Patrick Logan want my little boy?"

"I—I d-don't know."

"Don't lie to me!" Honest to God, she was ready to shoot him. Her finger tightened on the trigger.

"Jesus, April! God, okay, okay, I'll tell you, you crazy bitch. God. I owe him some money."

It just got worse and worse. "You owe Patrick Logan money? You borrowed money from that drug-peddling son of a bitch? Are you *crazy?*"

"I didn't borrow money from nobody," William said, somehow inflating a little as he spoke the words, as if there were more respectable business dealings with a man who killed people for sport. "I rolled a guy last week who turned out to be one of Logan's mules. He wants the money back, and he took Justin as insurance that I'll get it for him."

"How much?"

"About a thousand dollars."

April brought her hands to her head and squeezed, gun and all. "A thousand dollars! A thousand dollars? What, did you think that someone walking down the street just happened to have a thousand dollars in his pocket? You had to know it was Logan's money. Or Ortega's or somebody who runs drugs."

William shrugged again. One more time, and April swore that she'd shoot the son of a bitch just for the thrill. "I guess I wasn't thinking."

"You weren't thinking. That's what you have to say? You weren't thinking?" Jesus, a thousand dollars was more money than April had ever seen in one place in her entire life. A thousand bucks could *buy* a life, for God's sake. "Give it back. Give it back, and we'll get Justin back. Is that what he said? He'll give him back if we pay up?"

"It's not that simple. I don't have it anymore."

"How can you not have it? You spent a thousand dollars in a *week?*"

Another goddamn shrug. "Well, there's interest, too."

This was too much. April couldn't believe what she was hearing. "I don't give a shit about interest! How can you spend that much money in a single week?"

"It just went. I don't know, I bought a couple of rounds at Wilson's, and I guess my luck wasn't so good at cards there one night."

"Jesus Christ," she growled. "My God, William, you lost my son over booze and cards? Are you out of your mind?"

Something in her tone transformed William's demeanor. Like flipping a switch, he became angry. "Hey, it's not like I'm proud of it, okay? It's not like I offered him up for sale. They *took* him, April. And they kicked the shit out of me in the process. Thanks for noticing, by the way."

What? *What?* Surely he didn't think she gave a shit about his bruises. If they'd have killed him on the spot, that would have been just fine with her. Saved her the trouble of doing it herself. This was not happening. Not as hard as she worked to keep things together. Who did Logan and those assholes think they were, stealing her child? What would possess them to think that they could get away with such a thing?

Without a word, April turned on her heel and headed for the kitchen.

"Where are you going?" William said quickly, pulling himself out of his chair and hurrying after her.

"I'm calling the police."

"No, you can't."

"The hell I can't. I don't give a shit if you go to jail."

William grabbed her roughly by the arm and spun her around to face him. "That's not it. They told me that if I called the cops, they'd kill Justin. Said they'd never even tell us where they hid the body."

Again, April's knees sagged and she leaned against the wall for support. Until that instant, the reality of it all had not hit her. Her son—her beautiful two-year-old little boy—had been *kidnapped!* By people who wouldn't hesitate to kill him or anyone else to get their way. Logan was an animal. Everyone knew that. And now that animal had her child. "So, what are we supposed to do?"

"He gave me a week to come up with the money. His men promised me that they'd keep him alive that long. But not a day longer. But they said that if Logan so much as heard a rumor about cops, he'd kill Justin."

"So I'm supposed to trust Logan? Is that what you're telling me? I should just let some goon hold on to my child for a week because this murderer *told* me to?"

"We don't have a choice!"

"The hell we don't!" April yelled. "I'll call the whole goddamned army down on him and they'll throw him away forever!"

"And Justin will die!" Those words brought total silence to the room. "He'll fucking die, April. Is that what you want?"

April shook her head. She didn't want it to be true. "Then Logan will fry in the electric chair."

"No, April, he'll walk away a free man. Don't you get it? There were no witnesses out there. Nobody saw anything. Who's going to believe my story when the only witnesses work for Logan? We don't have a choice here."

The wave of hopelessness started in a place deep down inside April's body, and it spread with amazing speed, until her hands quaked uselessly and the gun clattered to the parquet floor tiles. Images of her adorable little boy bound and gagged and shoved into a closet somewhere flooded her mind and took her breath away. "Then what are we going to do?"

"We'll have to get the money back. I'll have to get it from somewhere and pay him back. I have a week."

"We *don't* have a week! We don't have an hour! I will not allow my little boy to be handled by that man and his people for a single second."

William scoffed, "Well, we're gonna have to be a *little* patient, anyway. It's not like I can go outside and shit a pile of hundred-dollar bills."

The smugness of his tone, the lightness with which he spoke the words, made something snap inside April, and she smacked him across his face, hard enough to make his head snap to the side. "How dare you—"

Then, just as quickly, he fired back, a stunning blow to her cheek. Stars flashed behind her eyes and she fell sideways onto the floor.

"Don't you ever lay a hand on me, bitch," he snarled. "Don't you ever talk to me that way again. I'll get the fucking money, all right? And I'll get your fucking kid back, but don't you ever, *ever,* hit me again." He disappeared into the bedroom.

April couldn't bear it anymore. Lying there on the floor, she buried her face in the crook of her elbow, and as a door slam shook the apartment, she started to cry.

6

SUSAN'S NAP DIDN'T last long after the Explorer started moving again. Her mind reeled with all the countless things that needed to be done. The diapers were a good first step. She had cleaned his bottom and replaced the tattered pajamas with a clean T-shirt from Bobby's backpack. He was still caked with dirt, but she felt as if she could at least hold him now, without cringing against the stench and the crusty feel of hopelessly soiled clothing.

Through all her fat-fingered fumbling in changing him, he never really woke up, though he never seemed fully at rest, either—no doubt pursued in his dreams by the same people who'd done this to him.

Well, he was safe now. Susan would make sure that nothing bad could happen to him anymore. He lay with his head in her lap as they traveled in silence down the highway toward home. Toward their house, really. It wasn't a home yet; would never be until they added the sound of a child's laugh and the sight of fingerprints on the wall; until she could sit down with all her friends and participate in the conversations about what the little darlings were learning, and what mistakes they were making. As it was now, the Martins' rambling brick colonial—their dream home, set in the woods of Clinton, Virginia—stood merely as a shrine to what might have been; to what nearly was.

Susan had known grief in her time, from the death of her mother just a few years ago, to every one of the three miscarriages that had plagued the early years of their marriage. She thought she could be strong, that she could handle grief as it came her way. But then when Steven died, she learned that what she'd thought was grief was really just meaningless discomfort, disjointed training-pain that made you feel depressed for a few days, but then faded away.

To lose Steven, though—to lose him the way they had—was a sharp, enduring, Technicolor kind of pain that just never dimmed. With each passing moment, in fact, the grief only deepened and widened, to the point where sometimes she wondered if she could possibly haul herself through another day.

They'd taken all the usual precautions, refusing to tell anyone about the pregnancy for the first four and a half months—until, in fact, her belly was so obvious that people had begun to troll for hints. "Have you been gaining a little weight?" was the standard from family members, but less intimate contacts would use the more subdued approach: "Do you have any news for us?"

In the past, the miscarriages had all occurred during the first trimester, right in step with all of the predictions from the doctors and the baby books. The first time it had happened, Bobby and Susan had both cried, and they had both felt a sense of loss, but they'd been able to rationalize it away.

It's God's way of making sure our baby is perfect.

The second time around was many times more traumatic, the baby hanging on until the end of the eleventh week before the bleeding started, and the cramping and the anguish. She'd seen the hurt in Bobby's eyes that time, and the look continued to haunt her to this very day. It was as if someone had betrayed him, as if some invisible force were conspiring to hurt his family. With the third pregnancy, Bobby had refused to get his hopes up. He'd steeled himself against the bad news that he knew was inevitable, and which ultimately proved itself to be true. He held her hand through it all, and he said all the right words as their third attempt at parenthood leaked from her body onto the ambulance sheets, but his eyes never so much as moistened. He knew this was going to happen, so it had just been a matter of time.

Then along came Steven. The first trimester was a breeze, without so much as a bout of morning sickness, and as they passed that magical third month, they celebrated with a bottle of sparkling cider. Everything felt so *right.* They dared to dream again; to think the thoughts of expectant parents, rather than expectant mourners. Eventually, even Bobby's skepticism turned to optimism. They bought furniture, they attended showers, they even established a savings account for the college fund. Listening to the experts, you couldn't start saving too early these days.

Because of Susan's history, that pregnancy was monitored more closely than a moon shot. She visited her OB/gyn every week for a while there, and she endured every test known to God or babies. Over the months, they'd assembled an entire album of sonogram photos, none of which were legible to her, but that didn't really matter. They were finally, *finally* going to be parents. All systems go. Everything A-OK.

The only real crisis they faced during those wonderful weeks was whether to learn the baby's sex. Deep down inside, everybody loves the mystery, but on a more practical level, why not know when the answer is already out there? Fact was, neither Bobby nor Susan were wild about the color yellow, and if you wanted to maximize your take from baby showers, it never hurt to know for sure.

It was a boy. Bobby's dream come true. The first of what he'd teased would be five sons, all of whom would choose lucrative careers in professional sports, earning millions of dollars per year, allowing him to retire from the information-systems sales business early. All that, and never a wedding to pay for.

Nothing else mattered back then. The entire world revolved around the hyperactive baby as he boogied without pause, ultimately finding a rib with his foot, and thrumming it in rhythm to a tune only he could hear. Bobby made it a point to be in the bathroom for Susan's nightly baths, just to watch Steven wriggle in response to the hot water.

They were the happiest and healthiest days of Susan's life. People used to stop her in stores just to say how radiant she looked in her maternity clothes, and she would blush and beam. It was all true, and she knew it. Those were days to be remembered, and she saved everything for the scrapbook that she expected to build. She kept the receipts for the furniture; she cataloged all the gifts. She even saved the parking receipts from her trips to the hospital.

March 13 was the targeted big day, and as Christmas became New Year's, and then Washington's birthday rolled around, they were home free. Even if she went into labor at that point, Steven would merely be another preemie, just like millions of others who entered the world earlier than scheduled but went on to be perfectly normal.

With Lamaze classes completed and bags packed near the front door, all they had to do was wait. Bobby figured that Steven would look just like him—the carrier of all the dominant genes—with his thick brown hair and matching brown eyes. Truthfully, Susan hoped he was right. She'd always thought her own complexion to be too light—especially for a boy. But as long as he came through the tunnel screaming and wiggling, the rest meant nothing.

March 1 was a cold, cold night—only the third they'd spent in their new house, their baby-house—and Bobby decided to inaugurate his half of the two-seater bathtub they'd had installed. The sparkling cider was chilled, the lights dimmed, the heater cranked to deep-fry, and all was right with the world as he helped her into the tub, then dropped his robe and slid in across from her. The CD player eased out the John Tesh album that Bobby thought she liked so much, but which she couldn't in fact stand. She just didn't have the heart to burst his bubble. Secretly, she figured that Bobby wanted Steven to perform his dance routine to a real rhythm.

But Steven didn't dance. He didn't twirl, he didn't roll over, he didn't move. Susan nudged him playfully, but her belly remained perfectly still, the only movement being the vibration of her racing heart.

"He's probably just tired," Bobby said, but the look she saw in his eyes was the most horrific expression of fear she'd ever seen, and although he instantly tried to cover it, she knew what he was thinking.

"He's fine," she said, stroking her tummy lovingly. "You're right, he's just tired. He's been jumping and twirling all day. He's got to rest sometimes, too, you know."

Sure. Sure, that was it. Had to be. They'd come too far for anything to go wrong now. Bobby tried to make small talk, discussing troublesome clients and recalcitrant employees, but that look in his eyes never dimmed, and she never heard a word he said.

Everything would be just fine.

Something was terribly, terribly wrong.

"We're just borrowing trouble," Bobby said, finally addressing the issue head-on. "We worry so much about things that they become premonitions. I'm sure that's all that's happening here. Steven is fine. Tomorrow morning, he'll be doing the coffee shuffle just as he always does. Just wait and see."

And so they waited. She remembered now how hard she had tried to think positive thoughts, to keep the endorphins or the seratonins or whatever the hell they were high enough so as not to let her baby know that anything was wrong. Everything would be just fine. In bed that night, they both lay awake, each pretending for the benefit of the other that there was nothing to worry about, and each of them battling the panic that grew exponentially with each tick of the clock.

Please, God, she'd prayed. *Please let him be all right. Let me have just this one thing, and I promise I'll make amends for everything else I've ever done. Please.*

Bobby skipped work the next day to accompany Susan to the doctor. Not that he expected anything to be wrong, you understand, but simply to be there to help her through the waiting-room nervousness. Once they found out how foolish they'd been to worry, it would be off to the deli for a nice sandwich and maybe a flute of that sparkling cider they'd never touched.

By the time the nurse finally called her name, Susan calculated that it had been twelve hours since she'd last felt Steven move. She practically ran into the examination room, and Bobby helped her undress while they discussed everything—nothing, really—surrounded by photographs of happy little babies with their slick, wet chins and sparkling, bright eyes. It took every bit of an interminable ten minutes for Dr. Samson to arrive.

Ever Mr. Cheerful, the doctor greeted them both with a comforting smile. "So you're worried that the dancing stopped, are you?" He eased Susan into the familiar sonogram recline.

"This happens all the time, right, Doc?" Bobby said lightly. "Nothing in the world to worry about, right?"

Susan watched Dr. Samson carefully as he made his studiously noncommittal face. "Let's just see what we see," he said, and in that moment Susan knew that her baby had died. As the flimsy gown came up over her protruding belly, and the doctor reached for the microphone, Susan closed her eyes. Suddenly, she didn't want to know.

She heard Bobby move in close, and she heard a muffled scraping sound through the speakers as the microphone looked for the perfect angle from which to observe her son, but as the doctor finally settled the instrument into place, she clamped her eyes even tighter, silently mortgaging her soul to any power in the universe that could produce for her the familiar *whoosh, whoosh* of Steven's heartbeat.

"What do you see?" Bobby asked, his voice cracking from the blossoming fear.

Dr. Samson repositioned the microphone and filled the room with still more silence.

"He's okay, right?"

Susan opened her eyes to see her steady rock of a husband quivering at the end of the table, his mouth forcing a smile, while every other part of his face twisted into a mask of grief. She reached out for his hand, but he recoiled, overwhelmed by his realization of the truth.

The doctor put the little microphone back on the stand and turned off the machine. For a long time, he didn't say anything, instead staring at his hands and collecting his thoughts. When he looked up, his words were unnecessary. His face said it all.

"I'm afraid the news is as bad as it gets." Bobby turned ashen, and he helped himself to a corner of Susan's exam table. "The baby seems to have died." Dr. Samson appeared to be pushing himself through the words, making them come out of a throat that wanted to say anything else in the world.

"What happened?" Bobby gasped. "How could that be?"

The doctor pursed his lips and furrowed deep wrinkles into his forehead as he wrestled with the answer. "There are a thousand things that might have gone wrong. It could be a congenital defect we missed, or it could be a virus, or it could be just about anything. I'm afraid we won't know until after he's born."

"No," Bobby groaned. "This can't be happening. You have to be wrong." A crimson flush worked its way through the pallor of his cheeks. "How do you know that you're not wrong?"

Dr. Samson blushed as he opened his mouth to answer, but then closed it when he thought better of it. "This is terrible news for both of you, I know. I wish—"

"What did you do?" Bobby asked, moving in close to the doctor. "What did you do wrong?"

Susan gasped and reached out for her husband. "Bobby, please . . ."

"What did you do?" His tone dripped accusation, and his posture said that he wanted to exchange blows with the man.

Dr. Samson didn't even flinch. "It's not like that, Mr. Martin. There's nothing anyone did or didn't do. Casting blame accomplishes nothing."

To Susan, Bobby said, "Did he give you any drugs, honey? Any new medications?"

"Not a thing. Not a thing."

Bobby looked unsatisfied. These things didn't just happen. His son didn't just *die.* For Christ's sake, *somebody* had to be held accountable here. Susan had never seen him like this, and the image of her trembling husband frightened her. Ever the source of calmness in their lives, she wasn't ready for him to lose control.

But then, just as suddenly as the anger had flared, he seemed to find the handle for it, and he wrestled himself back under control. His jaw locked, his eyes hardened, and he grasped Susan's hand hard enough to crush it.

For her part, Susan remembered entering a space in her mind where she'd never been before, an emotional closet of sorts, where she could shelter her sanity from the rush of pain that welled up inside. She remembered feeling as if she were floating as she listened to the doctor explain why she needed to carry Steven's remains in her tummy for another couple of weeks, while her own body adjusted to the changes in chemistry that were on their way. She didn't understand the logic of it then, and she still didn't, even today. All she knew was that her son—once such a source of pleasure and anticipation—now rolled around dead inside her, his real and imaginary movements a disgusting, sickening parody of those smiling babies on the doctor's wall.

As she lay in bed those nights, she would dream of young Steven, afloat in his amniotic cocoon, eyes open, tongue lolling off to the side, like some prop from a horror movie. She'd wake up drenched with sweat and once didn't quite make it to the bathroom before she vomited up what little dinner she'd been able to force down.

They'd wanted her to wait for two weeks, but after nine days, Bobby called the doctor in a panic. "She's not going to make it," he'd said to the answering service at four o'clock one morning. "This thing is killing her from the inside. Please, you have to do something."

The very next morning, they took Steven from her. They gave her the shot to induce labor at about ten-thirty, and by two o'clock, he was on his way out. Susan insisted that she remain awake throughout the ordeal, and Bobby sat in a chair by her side, coaxing her along, just as they had learned in class. She breathed and she rested and she sucked on her ice chips, and as the intensity of the contractions peaked, she imagined things the way they were supposed to be, with family and friends waiting out in the lobby, and the room decorated with flowers and balloons. In her wide-awake dream, everyone smiled, and they cheered when Steven emerged and surprised them all with a boisterous wail.

Instead, her son passed from her womb into a silent room, where the lights had been dimmed out of respect for the dead. In those last moments of her labor, Susan watched Bobby. She saw his face cloud and his eyes redden, even as his mouth remained firmly set. He would not break down, he'd told her. He would be strong, and they would somehow put their lives back together when all of this was done.

But as Steven emerged, and the last of their unreasonable grasps at hope evaporated, so did her husband's resolve. He opened his mouth as if to cry out, but instead took a deep breath and covered his silent scream with his hand. Tears tracked down his cheeks, but he quickly wiped them away, and as he looked down at Susan to see if he'd been caught, she was quick to look away.

"I have him here, Susan," the doctor said. "Would you like to see him?"

The horrific images she'd conjured in her mind loomed huge, and she wanted desperately to say no. Who in the world wants to look at a dead child? Who would even dream of saying yes to such a request?

But that's exactly what she said.

Again, she watched Bobby for a sense of just how bad it would be, but as his features relaxed, so did she, though it still took her a long moment to turn her gaze toward her son.

He was the image of his father, with those thin lips and his wavy, dark hair. He wasn't green and purple and bloated as he'd always been in her dreams, but instead looked like any other baby. Just so still. And silent. He even felt warm to her touch.

The atmosphere in the operating room thickened as the Martins said hello, and then good-bye, to their infant son. It was as if no one knew for sure what to do, waiting for some sign from the parents.

"How could this happen?" Bobby whispered. "He's so beautiful."

Dr. Samson cleared his throat to draw their attention and immediately looked apologetic. "Listen, Susan, and Bobby. I don't know if this hurts or helps, but I know what went wrong."

The couple said nothing, but spoke a thousand words in a shared glance.

The doctor cleared his throat again. "He, uh, well, it seems he tied a knot in his umbilical cord." Somehow, the explanation seemed intrusive at that moment, and Dr. Samson looked to the nurses in the room for affirmation that he was doing the right thing by sharing this. "I just wanted you to know that you did nothing wrong. Perhaps it will help to remember that he died playing."

Died playing. Susan loved that phrase, and she loved the image that it conjured. The son she knew so well, despite having never seen him, was a troublemaker, and secretly, that was the type of son she'd always wanted. A little boy who would test his boundaries and her patience every single day. A *real* boy. *All* boy.

Whose voice she'd never hear. Who'd never throw a temper

tantrum, never score a soccer goal, and never cry in her arms over a lost love. The sadness came with the force of a collapsing wall, crushing her soul, and leaving her gasping for breath. How could Steven be dead when he was here in her arms? How could they tell her that this fine, handsome, beautiful little boy would never kiss her goodnight?

The unfairness of it all was unspeakable, and that's when the sobbing started. She had the sense that the air in the room had turned horribly stale, and as she fought for her breath, she was dimly aware of someone taking Steven away from her, even as she fought to hang on to him. Maybe if she offered to suckle him, he would quit this horrible, naughty game he was playing, and she heard a distant groaning sound from Bobby as she exposed her breast to her son and she tried to get him to eat.

"Oh, please, God, Susan, don't do that. Not that. Please."

That's it, Stevie, that's it. Just a little before your nap.

But no one would listen. She screamed at them, shrieked at them, yet no one would listen. They took him from her then hurried him off into another room as a nurse moved quickly to inject something into her IV line that made the pain dim and then finally go away.

It came back, though. Every morning, afternoon, and evening, the pain lived on, its edges just as sharp and jagged as they'd been six weeks ago. Susan prayed for the day that it would dim, if only just a little bit, or if only for a few minutes. She knew from her shrink and from her own reading that six weeks was nothing on the grief timetable, little more than an eye-blink, but she didn't know how much more of it she could take. Sometimes it seemed that the very next minute would edge her into lunacy.

Those were the times when Bobby miraculously appeared for her, his strength restored, his optimism unblemished. God, how she loved him.

She found herself watching the back of his head as he piloted the truck through the night, studying the strong set of his chin, his unshakable concentration on the road. When he shifted his position in his seat, he moved slowly and deliberately, no doubt assuming that she was asleep and not wanting to disturb her.

Watching him this way brought a glimmer of warmth. All of this really would pass, she told herself, and if she emerged whole on the other side, it would be because Bobby had never let go of her hand. She used these thoughts to edge the other horrors out of her mind as she leaned back against the headrest and closed her eyes.

An hour later, as the Explorer swung the turn into the long, wooded driveway, Susan was sound asleep, the fingers of her right hand tangled in the boy's filthy mop of hair. In her dream, Steven was with her again, his head on her lap and listening intently as they read together from *Winnie the Pooh.*

7

RUSSELL COATES CINCHED the seat belt even tighter and willed himself not to look out the window. He focused instead on the altimeter, where the needle rested just above five hundred feet, and he did the math. The mountains themselves had to be at least three or four hundred feet, and then you add tall trees on top of that, and by his calculations, they were already dead. Maybe the window wasn't so bad after all.

"Are you okay, Agent Coates?" the pilot asked over the intercom.

He did his best to smile. "Peachy."

"I've been doing this for years, sir. Since Vietnam, in fact, so you can relax."

All that meant was he was as old as Russell and all the more likely to have a heart attack and pitch this rattletrap eggbeater into the trees; there to be found and eaten by the descendants of the *Deliverance* gang.

"There's the crime scene down there." The pilot pointed through the windows at their feet. In another few weeks, once the leaves had bloomed, the cluster of cops on the ground would have been invisible. "Now, we can lower you on a winch, or—"

"You're out of your mind."

"The alternative is a long walk, sir."

"Always my preference over a long fall. Just land this thing and let me out, okay?" Russell wasn't sure what part of his statement was so funny, but the pilot thought it was hysterical.

Russell's headset crackled. "State police chopper, this is the FBI ground unit below you. Is Agent Coates on board with you?"

Russell recognized the voice of Tim Burrows, his ASAC out of the Charleston field office, and he beat the pilot to the mike button. "I'm here, Tim. We're just looking for a place to park. Hold what you've got and I'll be on scene in a half hour, tops."

As police agencies go, the Charleston, West Virginia, Field Office of the FBI was not exactly Murder Central. They did their share, of course, but most murder investigations fell within the jurisdiction of local police forces, with additional support from state agencies. Because this particular killing had occurred in Catoctin National Forest, however—on federal property—it was a federal issue. Moreover, because it had occurred on Russell Coates's first day back from a Bahamian cruise, it had become the Bureau's version of a welcome-home fruit basket.

A hiker had discovered the body earlier this morning and made an anonymous phone call to the nearest ranger station. They, in turn, had called the local police, who notified the FBI. Somewhere in that daisy chain of telephone calls, someone thought to roust Russell out of bed on what should have been his last day of vacation to catch a state police chopper out to the middle of nowhere. Technically, he could have said no thanks, but such were the words that could get an agent stranded in West Virginia for life. As it was, he didn't know whom he'd pissed off to get himself landed out here, but a day didn't go by that he didn't fantasize about being someplace else.

That Tim Burrows, the wonder boy, had been standing in for him all week didn't help matters a bit. At thirty-something, Burrows looked twenty-something and sported that kind of raw enthusiasm and ambition that made Russell nervous. As assistant supervisory agent in charge of a field office that generated precious few national headlines, Tim would sacrifice his left nut to personally command a murder investigation. If things went well, and the bad guys were apprehended with the appropriate flair, a young agent could fatten his personnel file with the right kinds of letters and commendations. All of these things defined the reasons why Russell had busted his butt to make it out here to East Jesus at zero dark early.

Properly restrained, Tim was a genuine asset to the Bureau; not to be confused with the genuine ass he often made of himself when you didn't sit on him from time to time. Russell didn't fully understand what had happened with the academy graduates of Burrows's era, but somebody had pumped their egos with helium. Never a group known for low self-esteem, the younger agents in the field these days floated somewhere between annoying and insufferable.

Of course, it could just be that Russell was getting old, but he refused to believe that. Outside of the National Football League, forty-three didn't meet anyone's definition of over-the-hill.

As the ground dropped away below them, Russell saw four smoke trails rising from the ground where someone had used road flares to mark out a makeshift landing zone around what appeared to be a narrow fire trail. He took it on faith that the pilot had a good feel for the length of his rotors, but held his breath anyway as the Aerospatiale chopper approached from upwind and then flared gracefully before touching down without so much as a bump.

"On the ground safe and sound, sir," said the pilot.

Russell reached across the center console and shook his hand. "Nice job. Glad it's not mine." He ducked low under the rotor disk as he jogged away from the big machine. Something about a bazillion horsepower guillotine overhead just made you want to be shorter.

Russell headed for a group of rangers gathered around a Park Service vehicle, and as he did, one of the cluster—a midthirties blonde with that hearty woman-of-the-earth look that seemed so common among park rangers—broke off from the pack and walked out to meet him.

"Sarah Rodgers," she said, extending her hand. "I'm the shift supervisor."

Russell grasped her hand, noting from her grip that she was no stranger to physical labor. In fact, she could probably take him in two rounds without breaking a sweat. "Russell Coates, FBI. Special agent in charge."

"You're the 'SAC' I've been hearing so much about. I guess I was expecting something in burlap."

Sack. Burlap. Funny. First time he'd ever heard that one. He smiled. "Actually, it's the Secret Service that pronounces the word. We only spell it. It's *S* period, *A* period, *C* period. What kind of resources we got working up here now?"

As she talked, Sarah tried to lead him back toward her fellow rangers, but he stood still, bringing her back in closer to him. It's the little things that let people know who's really in command, and he'd lived through enough jurisdictional wars to know the importance of coming on strong at the beginning.

"Well, there's a few of your people up at the scene with the body, along with a few of mine, and a few local and state police thrown in for good measure. If you want specific numbers, I'm afraid I don't have them."

Shit. Too many people. "What about hikers? Is the area closed off to them?"

The question amused her. "This is a national park, Agent Coates. People come and go, and they don't always use the trails. I assume your agents are controlling the scene up on the mountain, but if you're asking if we've shut the gates, the answer is no. And if you're about to ask me to do that, the answer again is no."

Why did he have the feeling that they'd gotten off on the wrong foot? He smiled as best he could. "Look, Ms. Rodgers, I don't mean to offend, okay? I'm just a little disappointed that the whole world might have traipsed through this crime scene before I've even had a chance to see it."

"Ditto about the offense," Sarah countered. "Please understand that my people are trained in all aspects of running a national park, but homicide investigations are a bit out of our league. If we've done something to screw up your case, then I assure you it was done accidentally, and with the best of intentions."

Fair enough, Russell thought. "So, where am I?"

Sarah retrieved a weather-beaten, plastic-laminated map from the back pocket of her green trousers and unfolded it. It had been a long time since Russell had had to translate contour lines into meaningful data, but as she traced the map with her finger, it came back to him pretty quickly.

"Here's the spot where we found the body," she said, pointing to a place on the map next to a meandering blue mark that could only be a river. "That's about a mile up that trail"—she pointed to a worn patch of foliage to his left—"which is right here on the map. We call it Powhite Trail. Currently, you're standing right here, on Fire Road Seven. Technically, people aren't supposed to drive up here, but many do, just to get a head start on the Powhite."

"You don't ticket them?"

Sarah shrugged. "Not so long as they stay off to the side and don't block fire equipment access. Frankly, we don't get but maybe five or six parties a month that come up this way. It's not an easy hike."

Russell pictured what she had told him and arched his eyebrows high, suddenly struck with an inspiration. "When people drive in, do they come from the top of the mountain or the bottom?"

She thought about that for a second. "Both, I guess, but the vast majority probably come from below."

Russell nodded as he let an idea percolate. "Okay, Ms. Rodgers—"

"Call me Sarah, please."

"Okay, Sarah." He recognized this as the opportunity for him to return the favor of informality, but he kind of liked his title. "I need to head up there and see what's happening, but while I'm gone, I'd like you to make sure that none of the vehicles I see here are moved. Not an inch. And I want you to make sure that no other vehicles are permitted to come within a hundred yards of this place."

"For how long?"

"Until I tell you otherwise."

"What am I supposed to tell the police and the media when they come flooding in here?"

Russell laughed. "Tell the media whatever you'd like and send them away. If the cops are halfway professional, they'll understand."

Sarah looked at him as if he were crazy.

"Look, if our bad guy parked along the side of the road, his tires likely left an impression. That means we have to make castings of every tire print around here, and I need you to keep your vehicles in place so I can rule out their prints from all the others."

If any of this impressed her, she didn't show it. "How long is that likely to take?"

He shrugged. Frankly, such things didn't matter to him. "I don't know. Probably the better part of the day, by the time we get the technicians organized and mobilized. Welcome to police work, Ms. Rodgers. Now, can you spare someone to escort me up to the crime scene?"

Tim Burrows stood with his back to the perimeter barricade tape, arms folded, admiring his work. Two hours ago, this patch of woods had looked just like the thousands of acres that surrounded it, distinguishable only by the presence of a dead human being among the matted leaves and black mulch. Now it teemed with people, fifteen experts, all of whom knew their jobs better than anyone else on earth, and all of whom reported directly to him. After such an expert beginning, it wasn't fair that Russell Coates would be allowed to just step in and steal all the glory.

Simply put, Coates was too old, too cranky, and too burned-out to be doing this stuff anymore. He'd already disgraced himself once, for God's sake. After that snafu in Atlanta, Tim couldn't figure out whose dick Coates must have sucked to keep his job at all, let alone to get himself assigned as a supervisory agent in charge of a field office. But that was the Bureau for you, sometimes brutal and sometimes gentle, but always in defiance of logic.

For Tim's part, the real crisis swirled around what effect working as second fiddle to a confirmed fuckup might have on his own career. This was all that Tim had ever wanted to do—what had driven him to perform in college so he could get into law school. All of it had been training for the Bureau, and now that he was here, he hated like hell to think it could all go away at the hands of a boss who clearly disliked him. Funny how that works. You get assigned to work for a man who doesn't know his ass from a hole in the ground, and then it's the incompetent one who gets to write the performance evaluation.

Tim couldn't stand it. He couldn't stand Coates's folksy ways and his casual dress, and he couldn't stand the way Coates always put him down in front of subordinates. Discipline required a solid chain of command, and the strength of that chain was tested every single day by every other agent who was trying to make something of himself. With his snide little comments, and his refusal to let Tim do his job without interference, Russell Coates tried to poke a hole a day into the rising balloon of Tim's career, and there wasn't a thing in the world that he could do about it.

Somehow, there had to be a way to make the people who counted understand how helpless he was, bathed in Coates's shadow. One way or another, he needed to create an opportuntiy to shine brighter than that shadow; so brightly that the shadow would disappear, and the powers that be would see him as the future of the Bureau—the FBI as it was supposed to be.

In the meantime, he had to put up the good front; to give the appearance of support for the boss he couldn't stand, even as he created new ways to aim shots below the waterline. With luck, if everything worked out the way it should, everyone would see that Coates just was not up to the task anymore. If only by comparison, then, Tim's light would burn its brightest.

But these things took time. Frankly, he'd hoped that Coates would decide to sleep through this investigation and give him a shot at solving it himself. He'd even considered not notifying him, even though Coates was back in the country, but to do that would have been to invite a fusillade of criticism on himself. The Bureau understood and even supported the fact that everyone's advance came at the expense of someone else, but the rules of engagement punished any combatant whose agenda was too obvious.

That was okay. He'd been out here in hell for eight months so far, leaving only sixteen more before he could move on. He just wanted to make damned sure that his next move was up and over. He'd had enough of this lateral-transfer shit. He wanted the glory and he wanted the power, and he didn't much care if everyone knew it. The ones who claimed lesser ambitions were either useless burnouts like Coates, or they were just plain lying. In any case, it wasn't Tim's style to hide his feelings.

He checked his watch and shifted his feet. Typical of Coates, the half-hour arrival he'd promised was already running ten minutes late, and Tim had yet to see any sign of an approach. It couldn't possibly be much longer, even if the old fart was using a walker to climb the hill. Tim liked that image—a man so hopelessly out of shape and over-the-hill that he needed assistance climbing the trail. Tim smiled at the thought of it, then turned back to the business at hand. He had an investigation to run up here, and no matter how much of the glory Coates ultimately stole, this one was going to go down in the books as strictly by-the-numbers.

And if it got thrown out of court one day because Coates had yet again screwed up the chain of evidence, then Tim would have over a dozen witnesses to testify to the fine job he'd done up until the time when incompetence arrived on the scene.

One glance told Russell that Tim Burrows had a good handle on things. Judging by the hundreds of feet of barricade tape that had been stretched among the trees, he saw that the crime scene was a big one, roughly defined as the entire mountain. A sheriff's deputy challenged him as he approached, but stepped aside when Russell flashed his credentials.

Tim looked more like a jungle grunt than an FBI agent, dressed in camouflaged BDUs with his H&K nine-millimeter strapped low on his thigh in a Velcro and nylon holster. Russell wondered if there'd ever been a time when he himself could have looked that good in a uniform. As it was, Russell sucked in his gut so it wouldn't bulge over the waistband of his jeans.

"Hey, Tim," Russell opened as he approached his ASAC. "Bring me up to speed."

Burrows imitated a warm smile and led with his hand. "Hey, Russell. How's the golf game?"

"Didn't even bring the clubs. Decided to rip the lips off fish instead." After years of stress at the end of a golf club, Russell had finally determined that it wasn't his game. He'd take a smooth lake or a roaring surf anytime. Just him and the fish.

Tim handed Russell two heavy rubber bands for his shoes—all investigators wore them to differentiate their footprints from the others—and led the way toward a blue paper sheet that they'd anchored against the breeze with a half dozen stout rocks. Russell figured correctly that the star of this investigation lay underneath. As they approached, a potbellied deputy kicked the rocks off one long side of the sheet and let the wind flop it over to reveal the corpse.

"I figure time of death at twelve to eighteen hours," Tim said. "He's rigored up tight, and you can see the lividity for yourself."

Indeed Russell could. The dead man lay on his stomach, and all the low spots of his body had turned purplish black from the stagnant blood pooled in his tissues.

As he followed Tim in close to the body, Russell did his best to conceal his revulsion at the odor. Local homicide investigators had the luxury of getting used to this sort of thing. As infrequently as Russell did it, every murder was a new adventure in stamina.

"The guy's a cop. Thomas Stipton from Pittsburgh, Pennsylvania. We found his badge and ID in his back pocket."

Russell's right eyebrow scaled his forehead. He nodded toward the empty holster on the corpse's hip. "Where's his weapon?"

Tim shook his head. "Haven't found it yet. Doubt that we will."

"Shot with his own gun, you think?"

"Hard to say till ballistics gets done with the bullets. Here, take a look at the entry wounds." As Tim spoke, he pointed out the different holes with the point of his pen. "We've got one here in the shoulder, sort of between his shoulder blade and his collarbone, one here at the suprasternal notch, and another here on the top of his head."

Tim dug using phrases like *suprasternal notch.* Russell would probably have called it the top of the breastbone, or maybe the base of the throat.

"High, downward angles," Russell observed. "You figure the killer was hiding in a tree?"

Tim shook his head. "I thought that at first, yes. But look down there in the woods. You see that orange evidence marker? That's a stray bullet lodged in a tree trunk."

Russell could see the scar itself, gouged in the base of a tree about twenty feet away. "So, what are you telling me? The guy was crawling?"

"Well, that's the million-dollar question, isn't it? I figure maybe it was a foiled rape attempt. Judging from the powder burns, this guy was shot like point-blank."

Coates stood again and scanned the area around him. "But his pants are up and his pecker's tucked in, right?"

"Sure looks that way. Maybe he was still trying to subdue her when he got shot."

Russell's head bobbed as he considered that. "Okay, so why didn't she call the police when she got down off the mountain? And why steal his gun?"

"Scared, maybe? I don't know, rape victims freak out all the time. You know that."

"Maybe." Russell strolled in a small circle around the body, trying to imagine a scene as it might have unfolded. Suicide was out, if only because of the angles of entry. What does that leave? Murder, certainly, but how? And why out here?

"There's something else—"

Russell silenced Tim with a raised finger. He saw something. Not sure what it was, exactly, but it was *something.* Call it insight, call it intuition; but whatever it was, he'd learned to trust it. Something about the arrangement of the leaves. There it was, right over there: a cleared spot among the mess of rocks and leaves. If he used his imagination a little, he could almost see a faint circular imprint in the ground.

He walked over to the spot, and still not saying a word, he stooped and then knelt, feeling along the ground for a telltale sign of—

"Here it is," he announced. "The stake hole from their tent." Removing his pen from his pocket, he gently probed the hole. Sure enough, it extended down at an angle; and from the angle, he could guess where the other stakes had been. "There was a campsite built here last night. I want plaster casts made of these stake holes, Tim. And I want casts made of every footprint and of every tire track down there on the fire road."

"That'll take forever." It wasn't a complaint; merely an observation.

"You've got more pressing business, do you?"

Tim smiled.

"You were going to show me something else," Russell prompted.

"Oh, yeah. Damnedest thing. Parker over there found these." Tim led his boss out farther into the woods. "Look."

Russell followed Tim's arm down to two more footprints. "Am I looking at something that is more than it appears?"

Tim started to wipe away the leaves for a clearer picture of the print.

"Don't touch those," Russell snapped. "Nothing gets moved until

Crime Scene is done with everything. Make your point with your hands in your pockets."

Tim blushed. "Parker noticed that these prints are deeper than the others, and that they're unusually close together. The boot treads seem to match, so it would seem that both feet belong to the same person."

Russell laughed, then grew instantly apologetic once he saw the expression in ever-serious Tim's face. "Relax, Timbo. I suddenly got this image of a guy walking around with someone else's foot." Still no laughter. "Go ahead." *And lighten up, asshole.*

"Well, Parker thinks the depth can only mean one of two things. Either the guy is really heavy, or he stood here for a very long time."

"Or both."

"Right. Or both. Still, don't you think that's odd? Somebody standing out here watching somebody else get killed?"

Russell shrugged. "I don't know. If I had stumbled by a murder in progress, I might be inclined to stand real still and be quiet. Better than being drawn into the fight."

"So that puts at least three people on the scene of this thing now. And of those three, one of them is dead, another did the killing, and a third stood by and watched."

"How do you know he didn't stand here before or after the murder?"

Tim started to answer, but then stopped. "Well, I guess I don't know that for sure, but what would be the point? I mean, who's going to stand out here in the middle of the woods like that? Long enough to make an imprint this deep? And as far as hanging around after the murder is concerned, that doesn't make sense either. Christ, this guy has a dead body on his hands. He's going to get the hell out, isn't he?"

Russell nodded and walked back toward the campsite. "It's also interesting that they took plenty of time to clean up before they left."

"Your point being?"

"Look around. If it weren't for the body on the ground, you'd never know anyone was here. I mean, they even scattered the ashes from their campfire. Seems kind of odd to me that someone who's just been attacked would have the presence of mind to cover their tracks so well."

Tim thought it over. "Okay, so why not conceal the body?"

Damn good question. "How would you do that? I mean, as a practical matter, you could bury him, but that would mean a big fucking hole. Not exactly something you can dig with the spoon from your mess kit. I figure they saw the futility of it and decided to use the time to their advantage and just concentrate on doing away with all vestiges of themselves."

And how naive a decision it was, he didn't say. Even the smartest criminals leave something behind. Beyond the footprints and tire tracks, there might be cigarette butts, toothpicks, hair or blood samples. All he had to do was piece those things together, use a little imagination and logic, and with a little luck, he'd have himself a murderer in no time.

8

BOBBY MARTIN SHOT upright in bed, instantly awake, and instantly aware of all the horrors the new day brought. Jesus Christ, he'd killed a cop!

Had he really called in and reported it? Had he really been that stupid? So much of what was happening jumbled in his head like somebody else's terrible dream that he felt momentarily lost between fantasy and reality. But *none* of it was fantasy, was it? Every detail, every mistake, every *second* was bona fide, certified, USDA-choice reality.

Whipping off the covers, he swung his feet to the floor, surprised to see that he was still wearing his pants and socks from yesterday. He'd been so exhausted when he lay down on the bed—just for a few minutes, he'd promised Susan—that he'd neglected to undress.

He didn't bother to call out to see where she was. He knew. She'd be right where she was the last time he saw her: in the baby's room, watching the little boy sleep. The hallway still smelled of fresh paint and new carpet, and as he crossed the bridge that separated the grand foyer from the expansive great room, he walked gently, hoping not to wake anyone.

He still didn't quite understand how he'd allowed himself to be talked into buying this barn of a place. What good were five bedrooms when you only had furniture for two? Even at that, everything was so undersized from their previous town house that most of it would have to be replaced anyway. But it was the house that Susan wanted, and thanks to last year's bonus he'd been able to put enough money down that the monthly payments didn't hurt too much. It was their dream house, purchased in the frenzy of dreams about Steven.

What wonderful times they were, back when everything seemed so ordained. He loved every minute of the excursions to baby stores and fabric shops, choosing paint and the bunny-rabbit border print for the nursery. Finally, after so long, they were going to be a family. A *real* family, with kids and messy diapers and toys underfoot.

And at long last, well-meaning busybodies would stop asking the baby question, and he and Susan could stop pretending that the questions didn't hurt. He recognized that they'd brought a lot of the insensitivity on themselves, refusing as they had to share with anyone else the devastation of the miscarriages, but who wanted to be burdened with such news from their friends? Talk about a conversation killer. Instead, they'd spent four years just shrugging and offering their standard line about taking their time.

Once they'd passed the critical first trimester, though—with a couple of extra weeks thrown in just to be sure—they'd gone public about Steven, and everyone they knew offered nothing but good wishes. They were inundated with baby showers, providing them with enough clothing and paraphernalia to keep the kid going for the first three years.

In the weeks since the baby had died, however, they'd heard precious little from anyone outside the family. People didn't know what to say, and truth be told, Bobby didn't know how to reach out to anyone. He couldn't get past his anger that everyone else he knew—*everyone*—could pop out babies at will, all of them perfectly healthy, while he and Susan could only produce corpses.

The Martins were good people, dammit. They were well educated, they had good jobs, they made a lot of money, and they had this untapped reservoir of love for which God had twisted the valve shut. It wasn't fair. Hell, half of the people he knew couldn't afford the kids they had, yet it seemed that someone new was popping up pregnant every day.

Most people couldn't even make it to Steven's funeral, citing dozens of schedule conflicts, and when he thought about it rationally, he couldn't say that he blamed them. Nothing made people squirm quite as quickly or as thoroughly as the thought of a dead child, and they would go to extraordinary lengths to rationalize it away. If one more person tried to comfort him with the adage that miscarriages happen all the time, he was going to throttle them. At full term, it's not a miscarriage; it's a dead son. Why couldn't people recognize that?

In the hallway outside the nursery, Bobby paused to look at the little shrine he'd built to Steven's memory. At the hospital, a nurse had thoughtfully clipped a lock of his son's hair and presented it quietly to Bobby, tucked away in a sealed envelope, along with a picture of the baby.

"I know it's painful now," she'd said, "but in years to come, I thought you'd like to have this."

It was the kindest, most sensitive thing that anyone had ever done for Bobby, and not a day had passed in the last few weeks that he hadn't thought of her, and how she had sat with him in the hallway, holding him as he struggled to find the strength Susan would need. He'd recognize the nurse's face anywhere, but for the life of him, he couldn't remember her name.

Now, the dark wisps of corn silk lay permanently encased in a Lexan frame, on the wall above the impossibly tiny booties that they'd had bronzed, even though they'd never been worn.

As for the picture, he threw that away. He wanted to remember his son for his gymnastics in his mother's tummy, for his boogying in utero. If ever he felt compelled to remind himself of what Steven had looked like, he always had the sonograms. He couldn't make head nor tail out of them, but at least they triggered happy memories.

He found Susan in the nursery, where she hadn't moved since last night. She still sat in the Mother Goose rocker, stroking the sleeping boy's filthy hair through the crib rail. She looked up at Bobby and smiled. "He's beautiful, isn't he?"

He was, indeed. Even through the dirt that caked his face and his ears, the boy would have been the darling of Madison Avenue. His dark brown hair and olive complexion gave him a Latino look, but with the long, slender features of a Scandinavian. Sleeping on his tummy as he was, with his head canted toward them, he looked like the very picture of contentment.

Bobby smiled back. "Has he awakened at all?"

"Hasn't moved. He was exhausted."

Bobby got the feeling that Susan would stay there for days on end, or even weeks until the boy opened his eyes again. Seeing her this peaceful made him feel warm in a place that had been cold for too long. But he also felt fear.

"Honey, we have to talk."

"Later." She didn't bother to look at him this time.

"No, I really think we ought to do it now. There's a lot—"

"Who would do this to a child?" she interrupted. "Who would take such a beautiful baby and neglect him so?"

Bobby moved around and knelt next to his wife. "That's what we need to talk about, Suz. What are we going to do with him?"

She looked at him as if he'd lost his mind. "What do you mean?"

Bobby's jaw dropped. "What do I *mean?* What do you think I mean? We have to turn him over to the authorities."

Susan shook her head. "I don't think so. He's been traumatized enough. He needs someone to love him."

"Exactly. And that someone must be scared to death looking for him."

"Whoever did this doesn't deserve to have him back."

The finality in her voice shot a chill the length of Bobby's spine. "Honey, he's not a stray puppy. You can't just keep somebody else's child."

Susan shrugged, as if this were merely an annoying detail. "Who's to say he doesn't belong to us now?"

Oh, this wasn't right at all. He got up and moved around to the other side of her chair, so she had to look past him to see the little boy. "Who's to say? The world is to say. Jesus, honey, we don't even know what his name is."

"Then we'll name him."

"Susan!" The boy jumped at the sound of the raised voice, but he didn't wake up.

"Bobby, hush. You'll wake him."

He closed his eyes tightly and shook his head, as if to rattle a loose chip in his circuitry. "Do you hear what you're saying?"

She said nothing. She just continued to stroke the boy and to watch him sleep. But her jaw set, and so did her lips, the way they did when she was lost in thought.

"Susan?"

When she finally brought her eyes around, they showed anger. "Don't ask me to explain it, because I can't. But I know this. I know it's true. I prayed to God for a child, and even as I was praying, there he was, standing there, wanting only me. He wanted nothing to do with you or anyone else. He wanted me. God sent him to me. I don't know why, or how, but I know as surely as I know anything that this baby belongs to me now, and there's nothing you can do or say that will change my mind."

Bobby couldn't believe what he was hearing. "How about if I say 'kidnapping,' Suz? If I say that, might I change your mind?"

"You say kidnapping, I say murder," she shot back. "You can't prove one without admitting to the other."

The words hit like a fist. "Oh, my God, Susan, are you threatening me?"

For a long moment, she just glared, as if weighing her words, and then her eyes cleared. She shook her head and she ran her free hand through her hair. "I'm sorry. Of course I'm not threatening you. Think of the box we're in, though. We need to think everything through before we do anything."

The sudden shift in mood made him uneasy. "That's what I wanted to talk to you about."

"I know. And I guess I just don't want to deal with it right now. Let me just sit here for a while longer, okay? Let me just be here when he wakes up. After that, we can talk."

Bobby didn't know what to say. Surely she didn't believe that there was some circumstance where they could just keep this child and pretend that he was their own. Even if she talked herself into it, how could they possibly explain such a thing to friends and relatives? And how could they live with themselves if they even tried?

Seeing the dream painted there on her face, though, he couldn't bring himself to shatter it. He couldn't bring himself to say the things that he needed to say. Not now; not with her looking the way she did. Not with the baby lying right there where he could hear everything.

"Okay," he said finally. "We'll wait. But just for a little while. You realize that, right?"

She smiled and tilted her head up for a kiss. He obliged her.

"Later today," he said.

"After I've had a chance to rest a little."

And then she turned back to the boy. At that moment, Bobby didn't even exist to her. He was invisible, a nonfactor. As he exited the nursery, he heard her start to sing a lullaby.

Bobby thought about showering, but decided to unpack the Explorer first. As he passed through the kitchen, he glanced at the digital clock on the stove and was shocked to see that it was only 7:14. It had to be later than that. He thought for sure that he'd slept for more than three hours.

To feel so wide-awake on so little sleep typically meant only one thing: that in a couple of hours he was going to hit the wall big-time. Hoping to delay the inevitable, then, he put on a pot of coffee, doubling his usual recipe. It'd look like ink and taste like crap, but by God he wouldn't be taking a nap anytime soon. Like until next week.

While Mr. Coffee gurgled and steamed, he headed out to the garage, thumping the button for the overhead door as he descended the short flight of steps. Thank God for three-car garages. It was the one feature on which Bobby would not compromise as they were drawing up their dream-home specifications. He and Susan were both acknowledged pack rats, and he'd be damned if he was going to have to walk sideways through accumulated junk just to get to his truck.

Instead, he had to step carefully through a minefield of junk that was scattered all over the floor of the center bay. One day, he was going to clean this place out. Really.

The morning chill still had a bite to it, and he found himself wishing that he'd stopped to put on a jacket. No matter, really; he had one in his backpack. After lifting the tailgate, he reached inside and pulled his navy blue Kelty pack closer to him, so he could dig into the big main pocket. The tubular aluminum frame had been old technology when he bought it secondhand back in college, and nowadays, he considered it a source of pride that the ancient pack gave evidence of his status as an old hand at the outdoors. Space-age composite frames might be lighter, but at $400 a pop, he'd take a little extra exercise any day of the week.

He took care easing back the flap, hoping to avoid an avalanche of socks and underwear, but as it turned out, none of that mattered. His palm landed on something sharp, and it recoiled from the delicate silver wire that stood up from the angle of the frame that would have been closest to his left shoulder. There were two strands there, braided together with a half dozen twists.

He felt something tumble deep inside his chest as he realized that the paper camping permit that the wire had once fixed in place was no longer there.

9

BY TEN O'CLOCK, Russell Coates was about ready to move on. The crime-scene technicians had arrived in a swarm around six, and he'd learned a long time ago that the smart man stays out of their way. By the time they finished, half the mountain would be bagged, tagged, and cataloged, as the first step in the hunt to find that one critical piece of evidence that would pull the whole case together.

In the meantime, Sarah Rodgers had already approached him twice about speeding things along and releasing her vehicles and personnel. The first time, she did her best to conceal her annoyance, but apparently didn't feel so compelled during round two. Russell thought it was kind of cute how her ears turned crimson when she shouted, but the little specks of spittle that accompanied a few of the hard consonants were definitely a turnoff.

Now, here she was again, striding up the hill toward the yellow corral of barricade tape, carrying a sheaf of papers in one hand and a portable radio in the other. Russell couldn't fathom anyone better suited by disposition to her job. Bears and cougars no doubt ran for cover when they saw her coming with her mad-face on.

"I think she digs you," Tim said softly from behind.

Russell groaned, "I'm a magnet for chicks who can bench-press me." Pasting on his best official smile, he walked carefully through the maze of evidence techs to meet her at the tape. "Sarah, we're working as fast as we can, I promise you."

Her head came up at the sound of his voice and she looked confused. "What? Oh, that. They finished with my folks a good hour ago. They've all gone back to work. Thanks."

So much for round three. And for being on top of his own investigation. "What can I do for you, then?"

She handed him an enormous stack of manila-colored cards. "These are the park registrations for the past week. I was supposed to give these to you, right?"

Russell took them and smiled. "Yes, thank you."

Then Sarah took them back and spun them around so that they could both see. "You asked for them all, so that's what I brought, but that's probably five, six hundred registrations." She shuffled through the cards until she found the smaller stack she was looking for. "But look here. We've only had about three dozen parties in here to camp over that time, and of those, it looks like only fifteen or twenty of them entered at a spot that would likely bring them this way."

Russell didn't know what to say. "Why, thank you, Sarah. That was very . . . helpful."

She laughed, and for the first time, he saw that under all that Ranger Rick crap was a beautiful smile. Russell was a sucker for beautiful smiles. "You don't have to seem so surprised."

He laughed uncomfortably and shrugged. "That was a little transparent, wasn't it? I just figured that after our first discussions, you might be, well . . . "

"Pissed?"

"Pissed works."

"Well, I was. But once your people got off their asses and let my people get back to work, I got better." She made a real effort to smile, taking the sting out of her words.

Russell looked more closely at the registration cards, each of them obviously the carbon backing from another sheet. Names, addresses, phone and license-plate numbers, the whole nine yards.

"Now, I must warn you that not everyone registers," Sarah advised, triggering an eyebrow. "There's also a five-dollar fee that goes along with it, so it's not unheard of to find the occasional hiker who tries to dodge the system. When we find them, we kick them out of the park and hit them with a seventy-five-dollar fine, but not everyone is afraid to take that risk."

Russell nodded. "Especially the ones who are here to commit murder. Gives us a place to start, though."

"Ms. Rodgers?" Another ranger approached from up the hill, with two backpackers in tow: a man and a woman, both in their twenties, who looked disgustingly healthy and about three days overdue for a bath.

Sarah turned and offered a broad smile. "George! How are you?" She greeted him as if they were at a high school reunion. Then, turning to Russell: "Agent Coates, this is our brightest new star, George Majewski. George, meet Agent Coates with the FBI."

Russell shook the man's hand and nodded, but the young ranger looked about to burst with news.

"These people have some information that might be useful."

Russell slid under the barricade tape and approached the young couple. "I'm the agent in charge of the murder investigation." He addressed the comment to the hikers but knew he was answering George's unasked question as well. In his peripheral vision, he noted that Tim was moving in closer to listen.

"Gary Combs," the man said, offering his hand. "This is my wife, Mandy."

Russell shook her hand as well. "Pleased to meet you. What have you got?" This was about as close to charming as Agent Coates could manage.

Gary nodded toward the blue sheet in the distance. "Is that him?"

Russell's eyes narrowed. "How did you know it was a him?"

Instantly, the young hiker looked terrified. "I—I didn't. I mean, I did, but—"

"I told him about the murder," George offered. "I'm sorry, was I not supposed to?"

He was *supposed* to stay the hell out of the investigation and chase squirrels, but Russell kept to the high ground. "No, that's okay. You did fine."

"We don't need lawyers, do we?" Mandy had a little girl's voice and a set of boobs that weren't nearly as natural as the granola she no doubt grazed on for breakfast.

"Not unless you're going to confess to a crime." Russell meant that to be lighthearted, but no one seemed to take it that way. What was it about West Virginia that seemed to erase people's sense of humor? "No, you don't need a lawyer. I just need you to tell me what you know."

The couple exchanged nervous looks, silently bidding the other to tell the story. Finally, they started together, then clammed up again.

"You start, Gary," Russell prompted.

"Okay, well, I don't know if this really means anything or anything, but last night around midnight we heard some yelling out here, as if somebody was trying to hurt someone."

"Well, we can't say for sure that anyone was being hurt," Mandy corrected.

"No, no, well, of course not, because we couldn't see anything. But don't you think that's what it sounded like?"

"I know that's what we said at the time, but now that I think back on it—"

"You heard yelling," Russell interrupted. He felt his blood pressure rising. "We'll just keep it at that. Yelling, but you can't say for sure what it meant."

"Yes, exactly," Gary said.

"Right," Mandy agreed. "I mean, we thought it was angry, but, you know, out here at night, it's hard—" Something she saw in Coates's glare caused the words to harden in her throat.

He turned back to Gary. "Yelling."

"Right. It sounded like a little kid."

Tim came under the tape now and stood shoulder to shoulder with his boss. "Now, that's interesting," Russell said. "Could you make out what they were saying?"

"No, not really. In fact, I'm not sure they were really saying anything. That's one of the reasons I think that a kid was involved. You know how they just sort of yell, but don't really say anything?"

Gary had just described both of Russell's ex-wives. "How close were you to these screaming people?"

Gary and Mandy silently conferred again with their eyes. "Oh, I don't know," she said. "Hard to say in the woods, but I'd guess they were probably a hundred, maybe a hundred fifty yards from our campsite."

"And how far was your campsite from here?" Tim asked. Sometimes, Russell wondered if Tim thought his vocal cords might atrophy if he didn't exercise them enough.

Gary turned to George. "Well, we were more or less where you first saw us, so how far is that?"

"Half a mile, maybe? Straight up this path."

Russell paused for a moment, giving his brain a chance to make something of this information. How could an argument with a child cause a shooting all the way down here?

"When did you hike in?" Sarah asked. Now everybody wanted in on Russell's interview.

"Last night," Mandy said.

"From the top of the mountain or down below?"

"Down below."

"So did you pass the people who were camped here?"

Another silent conference. Gary said, "I remember seeing a camp here, but I don't remember seeing the people. I'm willing to bet, though, that at least one of them was a woman."

Please don't make me ask, Russell thought in the silence that followed.

"They had a cute little flower wreath hanging on the front of their tent," Mandy volunteered. "We commented on that as we passed by."

Russell looked down at the cards in his hand and started shuffling through them. "Ranger Rodgers, I don't suppose you remember how many of the campers on our short list checked in as a couple, do you?"

She answered without hesitation, "Six."

"Really?" Russell couldn't keep the surprise out of his voice. "You know this?"

Sarah smiled. "Photographic memory. Four-point-oh business grad from Harvard."

Why did this surprise him so much? He stuffed the cards into his jacket pocket. "Six. Well, that really will narrow down our initial search, won't it?" Then to George and the young couple: "Let's hike back up to where you were when you heard this yelling."

• • •

April Simpson checked her watch one more time, then walked to the tall windows to see if the used-car manager was anywhere in sight. It had been fifteen minutes since he'd taken her Geo on a test drive, and in that time, he should have been able to make a decision. April prided herself on the condition of that car, and she expected a top-dollar offer.

She dumped the cold coffee into the trash can, then checked the imprint on the bottom of the cup before tossing it in, too. The jack of spades fit in with the rest of her instant poker hand to give her a pair of nothing. Zip. No one could ever say that her luck was not consistent.

Scanning the horizon, past the sea of parked cars and the spiderweb of banners and little whirly-gigs overhead, she saw no sign of the fat manager in the ill-fitting suit. Across the lot, a pair of old folks drooled over a champagne-colored Caprice, while a hotshot sales guy drooled over them. April had happened to see the price tag on that boat of a car on her way in, and it angered her that people would even consider spending $40,000 on a vehicle—nearly twice what she made in a whole year, working two jobs. Before taxes. Jesus, life was unfair.

What did you have to make to afford a car like that? A hundred grand a year? As for grandma and grandpop out there, they were probably already retired and living off their investments, so that made them worth what? A million bucks? A half million, anyway. All the money in the world.

And April was trying to scrape together enough pennies to buy back her son.

The shame of it all gripped her insides with an iron claw, lacerating that part of her where faith resided. The world shouldn't have such extremes; there shouldn't be an opportunity for rich old people to be planning for their carefree retirement at the same moment when she didn't even know if her little boy was still alive.

The old couple looked pleased as they lifted their heads out of the Caprice's trunk, and as the lady pointed to the sticker, her expression seemed to say, "Not bad at all."

April hated them both.

How could everything—*everything*—have gone so wrong in her life? What had happened to the days when she and her dad used to dream about her acting career? God knows she had the looks for it, with her lush auburn hair and long Scandinavian features, and she'd been the star of every show her high school produced.

The plan had always been clear: her father would continue to work double shifts for as long as it took for her to graduate from the North Carolina School for the Arts, and then, when she finally made it on Broadway, she'd build a special wing for him in her home in the Hamptons. Her dad needed to escape the mills, and after all the sacrifices he'd endured to make their life together decent and respectable—just the two of them—she owed him something better. She could see the desperate hope in his eyes whenever they dreamed aloud, and the mere fact that he had never said she was being ridiculous made the dream seem that much more feasible.

Never in all its thousands of iterations, however, did the dream ever include a tumor. She'd just completed her second full week of college in Winston-Salem when she got the call to fly home. Her father had collapsed in the front yard after mowing the grass, and the prognosis was as bleak as it could get. Cancer had been entwining his brain stem for years, the doctors told her. Even if he'd noticed the symptoms, there was likely nothing they could have done. As it was, they gave him two months to live.

He only took three days.

Just like that, she was an orphan at the age of eighteen. With one deft swing of his scythe, Father Time had left her an adult, in all senses of the word, and with adulthood came all the realities: her father was broke. Worse than broke, actually, with debts far exceeding his ability ever to dig himself out.

Unless his only daughter and only child had struck it big in Hollywood.

Those double shifts could have kept revenue flowing long enough and fast enough to cover his finances for a few years, she supposed, but when she really looked at the books he'd kept, the whole thing was embarrassing.

She could have walked away; *should* have, probably, but to allow everything her dad had worked for to be sold at auction seemed terribly unkind—sacrilegious, almost. He'd never once turned his back on her in life. How could she abandon him in death?

The logic of it all made sense at the time, even as her dad's business friends tried to talk her out of it, but she'd inherited not only his penchant for dreams, but also his bullheadedness. April let all the unsecured debt just go away, and by reducing credit card debt alone, she was able to knock a hefty five figures off the depth of the hole he'd dug. That left her with the house, the car, and miscellaneous household gadgets bought on time, most of which she got to keep gratis, if only because she dared the collections weenies at Sears and Monkey Wards to come and take their stuff away from a grieving orphan.

Each victory came after a vicious fight, but at least the victories were hers. "Come on by," she'd said enough times that the words became almost reflexive. "I'm sure the news coverage will be great publicity for you."

But the fight for the washing machine and the refrigerator were just the warm-up bouts, and she knew it. The *real* war would be fought over the mortgage on the house, on which only ten years remained unpaid. The bank manager, a pompous prick named Morgan, told her in no uncertain terms that her father had already missed three payments on the note and was technically already in default when he died. Morgan was just as sorry as all get-out that things weren't going well for her, but, well, business was business.

Morgan gave her two choices: she could walk away from the property, in which case the bank would foreclose and subsequently enjoy a 300 percent return on their original investment, or she could refinance the mortgage and try to make a go of it herself.

"What would the payments be?" she remembered asking.

The question prompted a flurry of activity as his long lady-fingers flew across the keys of his calculator. When he looked up, he was so damned proud of himself that she'd wanted to puke. "Looks like your P and I would be about eight-fifty a month. With taxes and insurance, maybe just north of a thousand."

"A thousand?" April had breathed. *"Dollars?* Every *month?"*

Morgan laughed at her reaction, and that moment lived on to this day—well, until earlier this morning—as the instant when she had come closest to killing another human being. "I'm afraid so, miss," he'd chuckled. "Is that more than you can afford at present?"

She could still feel the heat building in her face and neck as she sat there in the polished lobby of the Milford Bank and Trust Company. She knew deep in her gut that she should have just walked out, but even in retrospect, that wasn't possible. Not remotely so. "You arrogant shit," she'd said, louder than was proper in those surroundings, but then, that was sort of the point. She wanted the entire world to know how this asshole was treating her.

"Miss Fitzgerald, really," Morgan blustered. "I don't think—"

April never dropped a beat. "Yeah, it's more than I can afford. I'm eighteen years old, you prick. How am I supposed to afford a thousand dollars a month?"

As she'd hoped, every eye in the bank had turned toward her.

"My mother *died* four years ago, Mr. Morgan. My father *died* last week! They left me with nothing but this house."

"If you could just keep your voice down—"

"I'm not keeping anything down, Mr. Morgan! That's *my* house, and you're throwing me out of it! Is that the way you treat your customers?"

Throughout the bank, people eased their way toward the doors, even as the security guard approached. April turned on the blue-clad rent-a-cop and leveled her forefinger at him. "You touch me, asshole, and I'll sue you all the way into the next decade. I haven't done anything against the law here, and I'm going to have my say."

Morgan stood. "You're disrupting business, Miss Fitzgerald. If you don't stop, then I'm going to have to call the police."

"Call 'em," April dared. "Shit, at least I'll have a place to sleep. Your way, I won't even have that."

Morgan nodded to an assistant, who picked up the phone and dialed.

"I don't believe this is the way you make your living, Mr. Morgan. You should be ashamed of yourself."

"I'm not the one making a fool of myself, Miss Fitzgerald."

Oh, God, how she hated that man. If she'd had her little .25 with her that day, he'd have been dead for sure. But she didn't, and in the end, she left without changing anyone's mind. On her way out, she tossed off the challenge, "You know where I live, Morgan; at least for the time being. Feel free to send the cops on over."

It took sixty days for those cops to arrive, and when they did, it wasn't to arrest her. It was merely to throw her out onto the street. There were a lot of them, too, apparently alerted by her good buddy Mr. Morgan that she was a hothead. The efficiency of it all was stunning. They arrived at eight in the morning, and they descended like locusts, moving everything out of the house, and finally sealing the door with a huge padlock. The whole thing took less than an hour.

It wasn't till they were leaving that April thought to ask for a suggestion where to stay, but none of them seemed to have the time to answer. They just kept their heads down and did what they had to do.

Thus began the never-ending thrill ride down the shitter, spiraling ever faster toward the ultimate darkness that was her future. She marveled that the memories were still so clear after nine years; how the pain they brought hadn't dulled a bit. She missed her father unspeakably, and she missed the comforts of her life growing up, but more than anything, she missed the hope that had once dominated her childhood. Sometimes, when she had a few quiet moments to rub together, she'd close her eyes and try to remember what that felt like.

She knew now, with the benefit of hindsight, that youth dies when you stop believing that you can affect the hand you're dealt at birth. The reality is, sometimes you just draw shitty cards, and no matter how much you plan, and no matter how hard you work to be good and to go to church and to think the right thoughts, there's nothing in the world you can do to get a reshuffle.

The sudden appearance of her Geo just outside the glass snapped April back to the present. She watched as the used-car manager pried his girth from behind her steering wheel, ignoring the anger in her gut that he'd readjusted everything to take his spin around the neighborhood.

An obnoxious little bell slapped against the glass door as Mr. Simenson waddled back inside the sales office. Despite the forty-degree weather, he'd managed to work up a sweat, and April found herself hanging back a bit to avoid whatever odor he might exude.

"I don't suppose you have maintenance records, do you, ma'am?" he asked, wedging himself into his squeaky metal chair.

April shook her head. "What kind of records are you looking for?"

Mr. Simenson made a big deal of opening a file folder and leafing through the pages as he talked. "Well, I'll look at whatever you've got, but I'm specifically looking for any brake adjustments, oil changes, tune-ups, that sort of thing."

"I've kept pretty much current on all of those things."

"But can you *prove* it?"

The anger flared a little hotter. What would you bet that the old folks looking at the Caprice didn't have to *prove* anything? What would you bet that their sales guy actually looked at them while he spoke?

April took a long time answering. "Well, when you put it that way, I guess I can't."

Simenson's head bobbed as his fat fingers worked his calculator, and he jotted some numbers on a pad. She tried to read them, but he shifted just enough to block her view. When he reached for his blue book—which was actually red—April leaned forward in her chair, daring a whiff of cheap, fruity cologne.

"I took a look in the library before I came here. The blue-book value on the car is about fifty-three hundred."

Simenson laughed. "Well, I guarantee you I'm not gonna offer that kind of money. I've got to turn a profit, you know."

April's eyes narrowed. "How much then?" *You sanctimonious fat slob.*

He didn't answer at first, choosing instead to write himself another secret note. Finally he looked up and smiled from the nose down. "I can give you seventeen fifty."

April's jaw dropped. "Seventeen fifty! What is that, the down payment?"

Simenson grunted out a little courtesy chuckle, then chased it with a shrug. "Like I said, I've got to turn a profit."

"But I've taken terrific care of that car! It's in great shape!"

"Mileage is a little high, and the paint is beginning to fade a bit. You can't get top dollar with it in that condition."

"But, Jesus, seventeen fifty? You've got to be able to do better than that."

Simenson raised his hands as if surrendering. "Maybe I could on a different day, ma'am, and I'm certainly not the only game in town. If I were you, I'd maybe try selling it myself. That way you can get *retail* price. It's your call."

April glared. Something in Simenson's face put her on edge, as if he knew something that she didn't. Or, perhaps he knew *everything*. Was that even possible?

Then, she got it. He sensed her desperation, and in his business, that was all he needed. Desperation meant weakness, and weakness meant an easy kill.

"Unless you're in a hurry for the money," he added, and for the first time, the grin became genuine.

10

SUSAN AWOKE WITH a start, frozen with fear and not sure why. She'd heard a thump (was it a door slam?), and whatever it was, it had been loud enough to rock the whole house.

"Bobby?" she whispered. She wanted to yell, but only a whisper escaped her throat. "Bobby! What's happening?" Still, her vocal cords would not engage. She tried to stand, but when she found herself rooted in the Mother Goose rocker, as if tied in place by invisible ropes, she knew that it was all a dream. She'd have laughed at her silliness if she didn't hear footsteps climbing the stairs; someone heavy enough to make the risers pop under the strain of his weight.

Okay, this is enough, she thought. *It's time to wake up.*

But her mind wouldn't let her. It *was* a dream, wasn't it? She looked around. The boy still rested in his crib, and all the decorations on the wall were exactly as they were supposed to be, but somehow night had returned, the moonlight casting the kind of twisted, fingerlike shadows that only occur in the movies. It *had* to be a dream. The double-reverse dream where you convince yourself that you're really awake even as you sleep.

The footsteps never stopped. They climbed with an inhuman rhythm, so precise and so slow that they were meant to frighten. Whoever was approaching the second floor—whoever had glued her to her rocker—wanted to scare the living shit out of her, and he was doing a terrific job.

Susan tried screaming again, just for the hell of it, but now, even the whisper was gone. *Oh, Bobby, oh, God, Bobby, please help me . . .*

The footsteps stopped abruptly just outside the door to the nursery, and Susan found she suddenly had a superhuman ability to zoom in on the doorknob. As she pulled in very, very close, the knob began to turn.

If it were a movie, the door would have groaned as it opened, but the Martins' house was still too new to have squeaking doors. Here, everything was pristine, in perfect working order, except for the places in the master bathroom where the molding was pulling away, or in the shower where the grout had never fully sealed the gaps. No, the door didn't squeak. But it would have if this were a dream, wouldn't it? Did that mean that this was real?

Oh, God, Bobby, why aren't you here for me?

For an interminable moment after the door swung open, all she could see were the visitor's feet. He wore work boots that were covered with mud and blood, the rolled cuffs of blue jeans all but covering the tattered laces.

"Who are you?" she managed to say, but the visitor remained mute.

He took a step closer, holding something in his hands, arms outstretched, as if making a religious offering. Susan tried to see what it was, but her vision remained cloudy, the offering just out of focus, even as she saw the stoutness of the visitor's fingers, and the dirt matted under his fingernails. She concentrated hard, and as the zoom lens in her eyes started to move in closer, she found herself distracted by something that fell onto the offering. It splashed when it hit, making her jump.

What is it?

The man moved closer, and as he did, she thought she recognized the flannel shirt and denim jacket he wore. The jacket had holes in it, and they oozed blood, turning the blue denim black against the darkness of the nursery.

A chill seemed to set her back aflame and she tried to scream. But screams weren't allowed.

That's when she noticed the blood crusted on the man's teeth. And the hole punched in the top of his head.

But I didn't do it, she pleaded. *Bobby did it. Bobby is the one you want.*

But the dead man shook his head. He wasn't here for revenge. He was here to make a trade. His gift for something she had. He thrust the offering closer to her, then motioned with his marble eyes for her to take it from him.

She knew what it was. Instinctively, she knew, and she wanted nothing to do with it. She pulled against the invisible forces that kept her mounted to her rocker, and she tried to scream, and she tried to call to Bobby for help, but nothing worked.

Unable to stop the inevitable, Susan finally dropped her gaze to the dead man's hands, and there lay Steven, so tiny in the corpse's giant palms, the umbilical cord still coiling out of his tummy and tied in a knot. The agony of going through this another time was more than she could bear. Her poor, poor baby lying lifeless in the visitor's hands.

And then the baby's feet kicked, and she saw him breathe. He was alive! Oh, sweet Jesus, Steven was alive! But why? Why had this demon brought him back? What was it he wanted?

The little boy from the woods stirred in his crib.

But of course. He wanted to trade. A baby for a boy! She could just hand over the stranger and then have her beloved Steven back. But what would happen then? What would happen to the little boy? She knew, of course, but did she care? Wasn't the trade worth it?

Honest to God, her heart actually hurt, it was pounding so hard. What was she to do? How could anyone ask her to make a decision like this?

And then Steven moved again. He stretched, as if awakening, then yawned. Creases formed in his little forehead as he contemplated waking up, and then finally, his eyes opened. They were big and brown, just like his father's, and as he looked at her, she saw the love in them, and the recognition. He wanted to be with her. He wanted to be alive again.

The little baby opened his mouth, as if to speak to her, and as he did, a huge gob of blood from the dead man's head landed squarely on Steven's nose, obliterating his features.

Noooo!

This time the scream came easily. It rose like a siren from the darkness of the room, abrading her throat and bringing tears to her eyes. It rose and rose in volume and pitch, peaking in a tone that she'd never heard before.

The images of the man and the baby disappeared in the fog of noise, and with them, the darkness went away, too. It had been a dream, after all.

But the screaming. It just kept going, rattling her nerves and hurting her ears. But it wasn't she who made all the noise. It was someone else.

The boy!

Instantly, she was wide-awake, and she launched herself out of her chair, eyes wide open, scanning the room for whoever or whatever was harming the boy.

God only knew how long he'd been like that, shrieking his head off, the bars of the crib clenched tightly in his hands as he rocked his body violently back and forth in an effort to get away. His dark eyes were huge, just like before, but in the daylight the fear that burned behind them looked somehow even more desperate.

Susan was on him in seconds, scooping him up and hugging him tightly to her. He was beyond hysteria, beyond anger, in a place where she'd never seen anyone, let alone a child so young. He fought her at first, struggling to free himself from her grasp, but then he seemed to recognize her, and he finally agreed to hug her back. His face felt hot against the base of her neck, and while the fear seemed to have drained from him, he still fought for control of his breathing, each inhalation coming in halting, choking sobs.

"Shh, shh, shh," she cooed, stroking his filthy, matted mane which seemed easily two inches too long for a boy so small. "You're fine. Everything's just fine."

But nothing was fine, and she found herself wincing against the lie. Things were as bad and as terrifying as they'd ever been. Whatever unspeakable traumas this boy had endured, they both knew that they wouldn't go away merely with a hug and a place to stay. Someone had hurt this child deeply and scared him beyond any level of fear that

Susan could comprehend. Even if the person responsible for that violence lay dead in the woods, the emotional trauma would live on inside this little boy forever.

Susan made a silent pledge right then and there never to lie to this helpless child again.

"I don't know what happened to you, sweetie, but I promise you that no one will ever hurt you again so long as I am here. At least you're safe, okay? I can promise you that much. You'll be safe." She rocked him as she whispered the words in his ear, over and over again. She thought as she cooed nice words that perhaps it didn't really matter what she said exactly, so long as the tone was right. This boy needed loving more than he needed assurances he didn't understand, and as she carried him back to the rocker, he seemed to relax, and his breathing returned to normal. He still clung tightly, but she could feel his little muscles relaxing.

Within five minutes, he let go completely and was looking curiously around the room. The knot of anxiety had left his face, too, leaving behind a look of peace; neither happy nor sad, but at least the terror was gone.

And God, did he stink! Susan wasn't sure that a mere bath would do what needed to be done for this little boy. A steam cleaning, perhaps. Between the combined smell of sweat and grime and a dirty diaper, the odor was enough to take her breath away.

"What do you say we clean you up?" she asked lightly, and her words ignited a violent protest.

"No!" he yelled, and he arched his back, sliding out of her grasp and landing on his feet.

The reaction startled her, even as she was pleased to hear a voice out of the little guy. "But you stink, little buddy. We need to give you a bath."

He stomped his foot once and shook his head. "No."

"I won't hurt you."

"No, no, no, no, no!" And he took off for the door. Fast little bugger, too. He was at the door with the knob turned before Susan could even rise out of the chair.

"Wait!" she shouted, but her voice only propelled him faster. What could be wrong? What had she said to frighten him so? By the time she got to the door, he was already halfway down the stairs, turned backward and sliding down the risers on his tummy. He was free, and he wasn't about to be caught again.

"I'm sorry!" Susan yelled. "Come on back." *Oh, my God, what have I done?*

Then she caught the look on his face. That wasn't fear she saw; it was a smile, and at that second she realized that this was part of some long-standing routine. He wasn't afraid of the bath; he was playing the chase-me game.

Well, two could play at that.

"Come back here, you stinker!" She laughed and hurried down the sweeping steps hoping to catch up. No way. He had cleared the foyer and was loose in the house. Susan rounded the corner into the barren living room in time to see a shadow dart across the floor of Bobby's library. She heard the sound of casters against the hardwood floor and looked up in time to see the desk chair swivel just a little bit. He was hiding under the desk.

Susan stepped through the doorway into the library, but made a point of turning her back and peering into the kitchen.

"Where, oh, where, might that little boy be?" she asked the room. "I wonder if maybe he's in here?" With dramatic, exaggerated movements, she made a show of peering behind the bookshelf and the curtains and the door. She even checked under the rug; everywhere but under the desk. "Well, that's a shame. I was really hoping that maybe that cute little boy and I could get a clean diaper and a clean face and maybe eat a couple of cookies. What a terrible, terrible shame."

She stood still for a long moment, peering through the library's French doors into the living room, and beyond it into the front yard. Behind her, the chair moved again, and she heard a shuffling as the boy rose to his feet.

"I guess I'll just have to have those cookies all by myself."

When she heard the giggle, she spun around and clasped her face with both hands. The boy was peering around the side of the desk, just his huge bright eyes grinning past the corner. "There you are!" she exclaimed, and the boy jumped the rest of the way out in a classic "ta-da" pose. "You little stinker, you really had me guessing!"

He giggled again and brought both fists to his mouth—a gesture of pure glee.

"Would you like a cookie?"

The hands stayed in front of his mouth as he nodded.

"Are you going to let me give you a bath?"

Another nod.

"Okay, then, come with me."

Susan faced the kitchen and held out her hand. The little stranger showed no hesitation at all as he hopped over to her and grabbed on to a finger. As they touched, Susan felt a rush of warmth, as if someone had turned on a light inside her body, and her eyes filled with tears. She was getting through to him. This little boy, who was so frightened and alone just a few hours ago, was trusting her now.

She did a funny little Charlie Chaplin walk as she led him through the side door of the library down the short hallway into the kitchen, and the sight of her made him giggle again. She realized then that she was becoming addicted to that sound.

She took him to the pantry—a big walk-in affair lined with shelves that bore far more pasta and soup cans than they did sweets, but somewhere in here she knew they had a box of vanilla wafers—a full box if Bobby was true to his word about dropping a few pounds. "I know they're here somewhere," she told the boy as she rummaged through the shelves, rocking the items on the front of the shelves out of the way of the items hiding in the rear.

Finally she found them, tucked all the way back behind the frosted flakes that Bobby refused to outgrow. Brownie points for her husband: the box remained unopened.

"You like these cookies?" The look she got in return told her that brand names didn't matter. This kid just wanted a cookie. The expectant anxiety in his face made her laugh. "Okay, then, let's just pry this box open."

The three wafers she offered to the boy disappeared in seconds, prompting her to offer three more before declaring, "That's it for now. Nobody needs more than six cookies." She heard these words from her own mouth and smiled at just how motherly she sounded.

As she placed the box on the cooking island, she noticed for the first time a note, written in Bobby's nearly illegible hand:

Dear Suz,

I couldn't sleep and I couldn't sit still, so I decided to go out and grab a few supplies. Be back around noon.

Luv ya,
B

So, that was where he'd gone. She'd figured he'd run off somewhere to get his head together—that's how he always dealt with stress—and she was glad to hear that he was putting the time to good use.

"Okay, Mr. Stinky-Pants," Susan announced to the boy, "it's time for you to get cleaned up."

She halfway expected another romp through the house, but was pleased to see that the little guy understood when a deal was a deal. He led the way back up the stairs, using both hands to steady himself on the stairs as he scampered up to the second floor and on into the nursery.

Doesn't he ever just walk?

She figured he had maybe a five-second lead on her, and by the time she caught up, he was already back in the nursery, staring eye to eye at a stuffed tiger someone from Bobby's office had bought for Steven as a shower gift. It was a plush toy—probably more expensive than Susan wanted to know—and it looked like a cross between the tiger on Bobby's cereal boxes and Tigger from *Winnie the Pooh.* Most importantly, this little boy with the filthy body and stinky diaper had obviously fallen in love.

"Do you like that tiger?" The boy's head whipped around to display a huge smile. Susan laughed. "You can give him a hug, if you'd like."

The boy responded instantly, gathering the tiger in a two-arm choke hold. If he wasn't careful, that grin would rip his face.

"Aw, that's a nice tiger, isn't it, sweetie?"

The boy nodded.

"Would you like to keep him?"

If possible, the nod became even more enthusiastic.

"Okay, then, Tiger is officially yours."

The purity of the joy brought tears to her eyes all over again.

"Okay, now it's time to get you clean."

This time Susan led the parade as they marched into the bathroom off the nursery. "Diaper first," she said, and the boy knew exactly what to do. Never loosening his hold on Tiger, he lay on his back on the little rug in front of the vanity and presented himself for a diaper change. Susan ran the water hot in the sink while she removed the messy diaper and threw it away, then cranked it down to warm before soaking a washcloth and wringing it nearly dry.

The boy made her look better at it all than she truly was. He knew when to raise his bottom and when to lower it, and Susan found herself following his lead.

The bathwater came next, and she checked and rechecked the water temperature a dozen times before settling on tepid.

"Okay, sweetie, can you climb in the tub?"

The boy hesitated a moment, clearly in a quandary over what to do with Tiger. Finally, he gently laid the toy on the floor, then braced himself with his hands on the edge of the tub and swung his legs one at a time over the side.

"Not too hot, is it?"

No answer.

"Too cold?"

No answer.

What was wrong? she wondered. Why had he stopped speaking?

As she soaped up a new washcloth and gently scrubbed him clean, she hummed softly and made sure that she met each of his glances with a smile. *Hush, little baby, don't say a word, Mama's gonna buy you a mockingbird . . .*

She took care to use soft, gentle strokes on him, avoiding a brilliant purple bruise over his left shoulder—no doubt the remnants of his collision with the tree—and worried about finding another painful spot by accident. "Did you get a boo-boo? Oh, that looks sore. Do you have any others?" Truthfully, she didn't expect a reply anymore, but the steady stream of words seemed to keep him calm, while preventing her mind from wandering to the problems that lay ahead.

So, what did she know about this boy? He looked healthy enough, besides that one bruise, and to her admittedly untrained eye, he looked well enough fed. Certainly, he didn't look like any of the starving children they paraded across the television screen during late-night appeals for money. For what it was worth, she noted that he was uncircumcised, which in her mind translated to a poorer upbringing, and when she washed him down there, he didn't recoil from it, leading her to believe that he'd at least avoided the most hideous forms of abuse.

In a wild, disjointed thought, she wondered if bathing a child without a parent's permission constituted a crime during these times of hypersensitivity to children's issues. In an instant, her pulse rate doubled. The list of laws they'd broken in the past few hours spun wildly through her head, making her dizzy, and closing an invisible hand around her heart.

Oh, my God, she thought, *I'm going to jail.*

She felt a kind of paralysis looming over her brain, like a dark shadow that threatened to block out any other thoughts. But what had they done wrong? All they had done was rescue a child.

And kill a man.

Well, what else were they supposed to do? She couldn't just leave this baby out there all by himself. He might have frozen to death. As it was, he was lucky some animal hadn't already mauled him to death. And she certainly couldn't let that terrible man with the bloody teeth have him.

These were stupid, self-destructive thoughts, and she knew it. She pushed them away, turning instead to the needs of the little boy whom God had sent in answer to her prayers.

"Lean your head back for me, honey," she said, and the boy did just that while she poured a stream of water over his long hair, then rubbed in some shampoo. He closed his eyes, and when it came time to rinse, he leaned way back again.

When they were done, she lifted him from the tub and wrapped both the boy and Tiger in a thick green towel and gathered them onto her lap while she gently combed the tangles out of his hair. Her breath caught in her throat as she realized that she'd never seen so beautiful a child. With the grime scraped away, those eyes got bigger still, and that look of growing contentment turned her heart to Jell-O.

"Are you ready to talk to me, sweetie?" she asked as she carefully carved a part into his dark brown mane. "You want to tell me your name?"

It was as if he couldn't even hear her.

"Well, silly, you've got to have a name. Everybody has a name." She tickled him and he giggled again, but he still refused to say a word.

"Okay, then, I'll just give you a name, how's that? A special name. We'll call you Steven. Steven Martin. My son. And you can call me Mommy."

11

APRIL'S PURSE FELT hot against her shoulder, as if everyone on the bus and on the street could see the wad of cash inside. In her mind, the money glowed, a great neon beacon to everyone in this miserable neighborhood who wouldn't hesitate an instant to kill her for seventeen dollars, let alone seventeen hundred.

She should have haggled more. She should have left the dealership in a fit of moral outrage, and tomorrow, after she had her son back, and everything was safe again, she would undoubtedly kick herself for being such a wimp, but for the time being, it was worth a $1,000 a minute just to keep Justin from enduring any more fear or pain or misery than he had to. And now that she had the money for his release, she prayed that she would be allowed to keep it from the street thugs long enough to give it to the street thug of her choice.

The bus driver looked oddly at April as she made her way to the door, as if to ask if she knew what neighborhood she was stepping into. It was a kind gesture, she thought, and she acknowledged it with a little nod before climbing down the three short steps into hell. Fear tugged at her heart as the bus pulled away from the curb, cutting her off from her only route of escape, but she calmed herself with the observation that the streets seemed uncharacteristically clear. An outsider might have been confused by the stillness of the place, but April had spent enough time on this very spot to know that the neighborhood's primary business flourished only at night.

How was it, she wondered, that everyone in the world knew where Patrick Logan lived, and what he did for a living, but the police could never figure it out? How was it that the mayor and the city council and all those other fat cats who made speeches every four years about the necessity of strong neighborhoods and safety for the children never seemed to make it down here in time to see what really went on? As long as the drugs and the AIDS and the used condoms stayed with the locals, no one seemed to give much of a shit; and on the occasions when a more noble resident of the city was found among the bodies in the Dumpster, the media-driven crackdown that followed never lasted more than a week—two, on that one occasion when the corpse turned out to be an assistant to the mayor.

April started down the street, then paused to make sure she had her bearings straight. As if it were possible, she would have sworn that the neighborhood looked even worse than when she'd last left it, nearly four years ago. Gang tags marred every surface, from the once-grand stone walls of the brownstones to the roll-down metal grates that locked the homeless out of the abandoned buildings that might have provided some shelter from winter's bitter cold. Nothing was spared destruction in this war zone. Broken glass littered the streets, trash cans overflowed, and the heavy, sweet stench of trash permeated everything.

Just being here brought a flood of memories that April thought had been permanently exorcised from her brain. Thanks to the drugs that ran her life in those days, the memories were more visceral than visual, bringing back feelings of continuous fear and unrelenting cold. She'd made a living back then, such as it was, dancing in any number of the sleazy strip joints that lined the block, but she'd never once succumbed to Patrick Logan's daily entreaties to join his band of whores.

It was the one source of pride that she could take with her from those awful times, though looking back on it all now, it seemed like precious little.

A half block ahead, on the opposite side of the street, three punks in designer jeans and bulky winter coats talked and played grab-ass at the base of the steps leading to a brownstone that was conspicuously devoid of graffiti, and whose windows above the street level were free of the ubiquitous iron bars. This was Patrick Logan's house, and those coats on his bodyguards concealed more firepower than a SEAL team. As April approached, the grab-ass stopped, and the three of them closed ranks. They seemed genuinely surprised when she stopped and addressed them.

"I need to speak to Logan," April said, getting right down to business. Beneath her jacket, her heart hammered at a thousand beats a minute, but to have any chance at success, she knew better than to show it.

The two thugs on the outside turned to the taller thug in the middle. "Yeah?" said the middle one, growing even taller. "Well, I don't think Mr. Logan is taking visitors this morning." The formality of his tone made the other two giggle.

"Just tell him I'm out here, will you? My name's April Simpson and I have money for him."

Thug Left perked up at this and took a half step closer. "Oh, yeah? And how much money do you have?"

This was April's cue to shrink away, but she refused. "Every penny that I owe him."

The middle thug pulled his partner back in line and held out his hand. "You can give it to me. I'll make sure he gets it."

This time it was April's turn to laugh. It sounded as forced as it felt, but she was making a point here. "I don't think so."

"You don't trust me?"

April recognized a tough moment when she saw one. This guy doing all the talking was obviously the one in charge, and neither he nor she could afford to have him lose face in front of his friends. "What's your name?" she said.

The middle thug answered, "Ricky," then looked surprised that he'd said anything.

"Look, Ricky, I don't want to make a big deal out of this, okay? And I'm sure your boss wouldn't be thrilled with me discussing his business out here on the street. Just do me the favor of telling him that April Simpson is here to give him the money he wants, and that I want to discuss the return of something to me." A frigid icicle of guilt stabbed her insides as she heard herself refer to Justin as an inanimate object.

Ricky considered this for a long moment, then finally nodded and made his way to the top of the concrete steps, where he disappeared behind the massive door, which she now saw was actually made of steel. Two minutes later, the door reopened, and Ricky beckoned for her to join him.

As she got to the top, with only ten feet to go till she was inside, Ricky blocked her path, lowering his voice as he said, "I'll be right there with you the whole time. Move funny and I'll fucking kill you, do you understand?"

The absolute coldness of his tone took her breath away. Suddenly unable to find words, she simply nodded, and Ricky let her pass, stepping in quickly behind her. Logan stood waiting for them in the foyer, wearing slippers and a bathrobe and sipping a glass of orange juice. Nearly as wide as he was tall—but not fat—Logan combined all the worst elements of his Irish bloodline. His red hair might have looked violet in a different light, and his big, round face joined his shoulders directly, seemingly without the intervention of a neck. A bulbous red nose completed the package, even redder than his ruddy complexion, and streaked with the road-map capillaries that showcased his affection for whiskey.

Logan's eyes narrowed as April stepped into the foyer, then widened again as he placed her face. "April!" he exclaimed as if meeting up with an old friend. "My God, I never thought I'd see you again."

April found herself embarrassed by the recognition and said nothing.

Logan suddenly remembered his manners and stepped off to the side to usher her deeper into the house.

She didn't move. Just being inside the door felt way too close to the spider's lair. Instead, she reached into her pocket and withdrew the manila envelope stuffed with cash. She counted out ten hundreds and thrust them toward her host. "Here's your money."

Logan looked genuinely confused. "You're here to buy something?"

"I'm here to pay my husband's debt."

Logan shot a look to Ricky and got a shrug in return. "Who is your husband?"

April's blood pressure shot up eighty points as her face flushed hot. *My God, he doesn't even know.* "He's the man your goons stole my son from."

Suddenly, a trace of recognition. "I'm not sure I know what you're talking about," Logan said warily.

"Kidnap that many toddlers, do you, that you can't keep them all straight?" She scared herself with her words, but stood strong nonetheless. She had a mission here, and she wasn't leaving without completing it.

Logan's eyes hardened. "Be very careful, April. Perhaps you've forgotten who you're speaking to."

"I haven't forgotten anything, you pig. I want my son back. Where is he?"

Logan chuckled and shot a glance to Ricky. "Let's say just for the sake of argument that I had your child. Do you think that I would take him without due cause?"

"There is no due cause," April spat. "Your business dealings with my husband have nothing to do with my son."

The Irishman's head cocked to the side. "Nor with you, yet here you are. Is your husband so afraid of me that he sends the missus to do his work?"

"I want him back." April was not about to let herself get side-tracked.

Logan held her eyes for a long moment, then gestured for the money. Their fingers touched as she passed the stack of bills, and she stifled the urge to wipe her hand.

The big Irishman counted the bills then frowned. "There's only a thousand dollars here." he said.

"That's what he owed you."

Logan laughed again. "My God, April, just what kind of man did you marry? The amount he stole from me was more like eighteen hundred. With reasonable interest, that comes to more like twenty-two hundred. Plus another thousand for expenses."

April felt the blood drain from her head and she reached out for a wall to balance herself. Neither man made a move to help. "Expenses," she gasped. "What kind of expense is there to take a little boy from his mother?"

"Surely you don't think I would take care of such a messy business myself," Logan scoffed. "I hired some special talent for that."

Special talent? Special talent! Jesus, he spoke of this atrocity as if it were some legitimate business. Couldn't he see? Justin was all she had in the world. He was her son!

Suddenly, all the fight evaporated. "Please," she begged. "I only want my little boy. My little Justin."

Logan handed the bills to Ricky, who stuffed them in his jacket pocket. Then, the big Irishman moved closer to April and put his hand gently on her shoulder. "You can have him as soon as you come up with the extra twenty-two hundred. Twenty-seven by this time tomorrow."

The feel of his paw made April shudder, and she used her forearm to knock his hand away. "Don't touch me," she growled.

Logan recoiled, then smirked. "Suit yourself, April."

"How can you do this?"

"How can I do what? How can I do *what?* Your husband robs me of my money, and you ask *me* how I can do this? I let the stupid motherfucker live, didn't I? All I want is my money, sweetheart. And you see? I already got a down payment, so this method works good for me." To his buddy, Logan added, "Ricky, grab her purse."

April didn't bother to fight as giant thug stripped the bag from her shoulder.

Logan accepted it from Ricky and opened it up. "What about the rest of what's in here? Is that for me, too? What do we got here?" Logan counted the bills quickly, riffling them like playing cards. "Another seven hundred and fifty bucks. See, April? Only two grand more and you're home free."

April couldn't take it anymore. Her fear and her grief welled up from a place deep inside her soul, and poured forth in a choking sob. "But I can't get that money," she gasped. "I already sold my car to get what you have. I've got nothing left."

"Look at me, April," Logan said quietly.

Her eyes came up to meet his. Where anger had burned just moments ago, her face showed only sadness.

"You've got to find it." Logan stroked the underside of her chin with his forefinger. "Rob a bank if you have to, I don't care. But you've got to find the money, because I'll only keep him alive for a week. Do you understand that? A week. Seven days from last night."

Logan smiled, and she looked away.

"Did your worthless fuck stick mention what happens if you go to the police, April?"

She cast her eyes down, but he rocked her chin back up.

"I need an answer."

April nodded. Even if she tried to say something, she knew that her voice wouldn't work.

"You'll never even see the body, April. You'll never, ever know for sure. And that will kill you, too."

12

DON'T TOUCH ANYTHING," Russell told Ranger George for the 874th time. Why was this such a difficult concept?

"I'm just looking," the ranger replied as he crouched down even farther.

Russell shot a look to Sarah, who interpreted it for what it was and said, "George, I need you to head down the trail and make sure that everybody finds their way, okay?"

George obeyed and left, looking like a kid who hadn't made the height cut on a roller coaster.

Russell smiled at Sarah. "Thanks. You were much more diplomatic than I would have been."

"He means well."

"They always do. That's why I always feel so bad for shooting them when they get in my way." Russell laughed to make sure she knew he was kidding.

"Ma'am, you don't belong here either," Tim declared, striking a dynamic pose with his fists on his hips.

Russell shot his assistant a glare that should have knocked him over, but the other man held his ground. "Tell you what, Tim. Why don't you head down there, too, and act as my liaison with Ranger George?"

That one got him. Tim looked as if he'd been slapped. "You know I'm right, Russell. She doesn't belong here."

"As I'm sure your notes will so indicate. Now, if you don't mind doing as I asked . . . "

"Send her." Tim nodded to Sarah. His voice took on a squeaky, adolescent quality that Russell found amusing.

"I'm sending you." He could have made up some excuse or tried to justify his decision, but he didn't feel like it. And while there was no denying that Sarah's presence at the crime scene bent the investigative protocols a bit, no protocol is more basic than the one which says that the assistant agent in charge has to do what the agent in charge tells him.

Tim created a new shade of red around his ears before he stalked off down the trail, leaving the two of them alone.

Sarah looked uneasy as hell. "Look, Agent Coates, I didn't mean to—"

"Don't worry about it. You've done nothing wrong. You're here because I invited you."

She looked confused. "You don't like him too much, do you?"

"Can't stand the son of a bitch. He's brash and rude and he won't keep his mouth closed long enough to learn something."

"Not everyone can be a shy, retiring type like you, huh?" She smiled again, and the effect was blinding. "You're not as tight as most feds I've known."

"I've loosened up a lot since I started wearing boxers."

This time she laughed for real, and Russell couldn't help but feel a little proud of himself for finally breaching the wall.

"You like being unpredictable, don't you?"

Russell shrugged. "I don't know what I like anymore. I've been doing this shit for too long. Pricks like Agent Burrows there are the future of the Bureau."

"He seems dedicated enough."

"Oh, dedication is his long suit." Russell laughed. "Just don't forget to check out exactly what it is he's dedicated to."

"And that would be . . . ?"

"Himself. His own career. The number one social goal of the millennium. Advance your career at all costs."

Sarah cocked her head curiously. "I hear bitterness."

"You hear reality. Pragmatism." Russell felt no urge to elaborate.

Instead, he turned away from Sarah, and from the trail behind her, and directed his attention to their newest discovery.

He'd released the Combs couple as soon as they'd pointed out their campsite from the night before. They clearly didn't know anything, and if he found himself with questions later, he had their address and phone number.

Starting from that spot, the four of them—Russell, Sarah, Tim, and George—had spread out through the woods, looking for something that might possibly explain the sounds the couple had reported. For the longest time, they found only more woods. Then, about thirty minutes into the search, they'd struck the mother lode.

Russell walked to the edge of a roughly rectangular pit; maybe four feet by eight feet, and six or seven feet deep. Dirt had been stacked up high on both ends of the hole, and inside, it looked as if someone had done a makeshift job shoring it up with two-by-six lumber. Until the crime-scene technicians arrived, there wasn't much for him to do but stand and gawk.

Sarah joined him. "Is it a grave?"

"Maybe," Russell replied, but he didn't think so. If you want to bury a body, you just dig a hole and fill it in. The shoring materials spoke to a plan far more chilling.

Sarah leaned forward, her hands forming a tripod with her knees as she tried to get a closer look at the bottom of the pit, where a couple dozen little jars lay strewn about. "Is that baby food?"

Russell nodded. "That's what they look like to me."

"They were burying *baby food* jars? What are they, squirrels?"

It was Russell's turn to laugh. "No, I'm afraid our victim was being buried alive."

Sarah gasped, reflexively standing straight again, as if to put space between herself and the horrible thought of what had nearly happened here.

"The baby food is a new twist though," Russell went on. "Good idea, actually. Portable, reasonably nutritious, and requires no can opener. With that much food, a person could keep himself alive probably for a week or two."

"But who would do such a thing? And why?"

Russell smiled. "Well, those are the big questions. When we answer those, we'll have ourselves a killer."

He inexplicably thought of Tim as he explained these things and found his conscience stinging him. There was no excuse for treating a fellow agent the way he had, and one day, when the roles were reversed, he knew he could count on vicious revenge. He should have sent Sarah packing as soon as he realized that they had a new crime scene, but truth be told, he enjoyed her company. He also welcomed the opportunity to show off a little. Later, when Tim inevitably made a stink about it all, Russell would simply point out that she was the official representative of the National Park Service, and that he had thought she might have important insight. Senior rank brought senior benefit of doubt.

Oh, yeah, the payback would be hell.

"Be very careful where you step and what you touch," Russell warned, but judging from Sarah's nervous stance, and the depth to which her hands were stuffed into her pockets, his warning was probably unnecessary.

Russell gently strolled around the perimeter of the pit, hoping to awaken that spot in his brain or in his gut where he made his connection with the crime scene. Over there by the edge opposite where he stood, he thought he recognized boot-tread imprints similar to the ones on the body. The forensics people would make that final determination, of course, but he already knew, just as he knew that the key to this case lay with the link that tied the two crime scenes together.

So, what did he have here? A hole in the ground, a stack of baby food jars, and a collection of footprints. Anything else? Nothing jumped out at him, but that was all right. Something else was bound to show up, but even if it didn't, maybe they already had enough. If the baby food bore serial numbers, for example, they might be able to trace it to a specific store and a specific time. From there, they could talk to the clerks and maybe get a description of the person who'd bought it. Twenty-plus jars is a big purchase. Russell figured chances were good that it might have stood out.

Maybe the forensics lab would learn that the boots that had made these particular impressions were unique to a particular part of the country, or that the person who wore them had an unusual foot deformity.

Russell never ceased to be amazed by the amount of data that could be gleaned by the forensics techs from seemingly mundane little details.

As fascinating as all the Mr. Wizard stuff was, though, it was people like Russell—the analytical thinkers—who really won the day. He considered himself to be more of a macro investigator than a micro one. All of that physical evidence and those trace analyses meant nothing without motive and a clear picture of what likely transpired. Without those logical linkages, all the proverbial smoking guns in the world meant nothing. Nobody in the Bureau was better than Russell at the tedious task of placing those smoking guns in the hands of the bad guys who had pulled the triggers.

Crime scenes, like accident scenes, were really inanimate witnesses to incidents that occurred in exactly one way, and once you learned to listen to what these scenes were telling you, the most complicated, elusive investigations became obvious. More times than not, once all the evidence was collected and sifted, and the puzzle finally solved, he wondered after the fact how it could have taken him so long. He called those cases forehead smackers, and he sensed that this was one of them.

He liked his initial notion that someone was being prepared for a live interment. The more he thought about it, the more it seemed to fit the physical evidence. Early in his career, live burials were rare, but in recent years that seemed to be the outcome of virtually every kidnapping. Russell blamed the trend on a couple of high-profile feature films. Leave it to Hollywood.

Fact was, if Russell were himself a kidnapper, he'd bury them, too. In the old days, when kidnappers stashed their victims in warehouses or in a basement somewhere, finding the kidnapper almost always meant finding the victim as well. The bad guy had no leverage. An off-site burial, on the other hand, raised the stakes for everyone. If the kidnapper got an inkling that the good guys were getting too close, all he had to do was keep his mouth shut, and even if he got caught, without a victim to point to, he stood a damn good chance of staying free. Besides, SWAT snipers hesitate to blow the head off the only person who knows the whereabouts of the victim.

The end result, then, was a trend toward families who simply paid the ransom, without reporting the crime to the police. In Latin

America, kidnapping had become a boutique industry, with kidnappers raking in cash by the pound. Of course, there in the Third World the kidnappers had to be true to their word if they were going to stay in business, and more times than not, the victim was reunited with his family as soon as the ransom was paid. Here in the States, unfortunately, the record wasn't as encouraging. In Russell's experience, most American victims were dead long before the first ransom note was written, and the rest were killed within hours of ransom delivery. And why not? With virtually identical penalties for kidnapping and murder, why not go for broke and make sure there are no witnesses?

Russell pulled on his lower lip as he sifted it all through his mind. He'd have to check the boards when he got back to the office, but as far as he knew, there were no outstanding abduction cases out here. What was the deal with that? he wondered. Surely *somebody* should have noticed that a cop was missing.

"Am I interrupting if I talk?" Sarah asked.

Russell had moved to the far end of the excavated rectangle. "I'll tell you if I need you to be quiet."

She smiled. "Can you tell me what you're doing? What you're looking at so intensely?"

He shrugged one shoulder. "I don't know exactly. I'm just looking to see what I see. You ever buy an Oriental rug?"

The question surprised her. "Can't say as I have."

"Well, neither have I, but my first wife was into Oriental rugs. Seriously into them. In fact, the rugs became an issue during our divorce. I made her fight like hell to get them just so she'd feel like she'd won a battle." He chuckled, but when he saw that he'd confused his audience, he went on, "Anyway, one of the things I learned about Oriental rugs is, each one has a dark side and a light side. If you look at it from one end, it looks one way, but then when you view it from the opposite end, it's like a whole new rug. Even the colors are different."

Sarah still didn't get it.

"Crime scenes are the same way," he explained. "You look at them from only one angle, and you see only a part of the story. You have to walk around and look at everything from all sides. When you do, you sometimes get a whole different feel for what you see."

He turned the third corner around the grave and paused. A big grin bloomed on his face. "Like right over there." He pointed toward a small stand of bushes. Something lay in the tangle of branches, but from where he stood, he couldn't quite tell what it was. Sarah followed as he moved closer.

It looked like a discarded solid-core door, bigger than most, and someone had cut a round hole through the middle of it, maybe three inches in diameter.

"What is it?"

Russell didn't answer. Instead, he craned his neck to see past the door into the woods. "Aha," he said triumphantly, and he waded through the undergrowth over to a five-foot coil of what could have been dryer vent hose. He didn't touch, but he knew right away what he'd found. "This is their ventilation system. Once you get your victim down into the hole, you cover it with that door to keep the dirt from crushing the guy, and this tube runs from the hole in the door up to the surface here so your captive can breathe."

"How horrifying," Sarah gasped.

"It beats the hell out of a noseful of dirt." He said that in such a cavalier way, but the very thought of the panic and the claustrophobia made Russell's stomach hurt.

"So, are you thinking that the kidnappers captured the police officer and tried to bury him? And that he somehow got away?"

Russell pulled his lip some more. Is that what he thought? The evidence supported that theory, but something bothered him. First of all, what would the motive be? It sure as hell wasn't because he had a rich family (cops never had rich families), and if it was about revenge, why go through all the hassle of keeping him alive?

One thing was sure: this had been well planned, and Russell was willing to bet that it wasn't the perpetrators' first effort. That was good. If they'd done this before, there'd be a pattern for the computer to find. On the other hand, if they were professionals, how did they let their man get away? Why wasn't he hog-tied and under tight guard the whole time? Given their line of work, it was a pretty stupid mistake.

Finally, why hadn't word of a missing cop reached his desk? This one really bugged him. Granted, he'd been away for a while, but surely

Tim would have made that connection right away. Any crime that specifically targeted a cop as its victim swept through the law enforcement rumor mill with breathtaking speed. It became the stuff of chatter in every coffee room where badges were present. Yet, this one had gone unreported. Interesting.

Troubling.

Just as crime scenes spoke to you if you were willing to listen, they also told lies to investigators who ignored facts that contradicted their pet theories. The problem of no missing cop reports rang a huge warning bell for Russell. If only he knew what it meant.

He wandered back to the excavation. Why the hell didn't they just shoot their guy on the spot when he started to run? It didn't make any sense that they let him get away.

Maybe they never got him this far, he thought.

Nope, not possible. The footprints clearly showed that the victim had walked around up here. Whether it was minutes before he died or hours, Russell couldn't tell, but clearly he'd been up here.

"You look really confused," Sarah observed.

He nodded. "I'm just trying to figure out the series of events. Say you're being kidnapped."

"Let's not."

"Just for the sake of argument. Help me talk this through. You're brought up here and maybe you see what they're going to do to you, so you panic. That makes sense, right? I mean, you're not going to say, 'Oh, okay, let me just climb into my own grave,' right? You're going to fight like hell."

"Right."

"So, where are the signs of the fight?"

She made a halfhearted pantomime of looking around, but this obviously was not her department.

"Well, there aren't any," Russell answered for her. "At least none I can see. So, instead of fighting, maybe you just run off. Why don't the bad guys shoot you down where you stand?"

"Maybe they missed."

"Maybe. We'll certainly look for any signs that a gun was fired, but that would have been the first thing my buddies Gary and Mandy would have mentioned. Anyway, shot at or not shot at, you go plunging through the woods, with kidnappers right on your tail. How do you end up getting killed a half mile downhill?"

Sarah thought that one through. "I suppose the people who pitched the tent were waiting for him."

Russell nodded. The pieces were beginning to fit together. "Okay, so you stumble onto these people who are somehow in on the plot, and they pop you." A buzzer rang in his head. "No, wait. That won't work. Remember the burns on the guy's face? They fought first."

She looked horrified. "Burns?"

"I forgot you didn't see the body. Yeah, he had burns on his face. They looked like scalds, actually."

Sarah shuddered. "That's terrible."

"Very. But why? How?"

Sarah didn't seem to have a problem with that at all. "I don't know, you're cooking eggs, maybe, and this guy comes crashing through the woods, and he startles you, and you react with the first thing you can get your hands on."

"Okay, then that would mean they *weren't* part of the plot, right? I mean, who boils water in the middle of a kidnapping?"

"So, they weren't involved."

"Until they shot him." Russell rubbed his eye with the heel of his hand, and the answer flashed in his mind. He didn't quite know what it was yet, but he knew he had it, just enough information to put the pieces together. It was like having some little guy in his brain playing peek-a-boo, opening the answer door just enough to give a quick wave and then disappearing again.

"Agent Coates?"

He held up his hand, calling for silence. Their victim—this Thomas Stipton of Pittsburgh, Pennsylvania—came to the campsite on purpose. Was he looking for help? If so, why did the campers shoot him? If the campers were part of the plot, why did he come all the way up here, and once he was killed, why didn't the campers bury the body?

No one was acting logically here, and that meant he was chasing a dead end. All of it lay out in front of him. He just wasn't bright enough to see what it meant.

Then he had it. The thought materialized just like that, whole and fully formed. When he looked up again at Sarah, everything suddenly made sense.

"We've been coming at this from the wrong direction," he declared. "We've been assuming that the dead cop was the good guy, and the killer was bad. But suppose that the grave was meant for our campers."

Sarah's eyes grew big as she fit it all together for herself.

Russell continued, "So, our victim goes through all of his final preparations for this thing he's going to do, and then he sneaks up on our friends down the hill, only all hell breaks loose. They struggle, they douse him with boiling water, and when it's all done, our cop is dead."

"But what about the screaming?"

"Huh? What screaming?" Then, he remembered. The screaming that had brought them up here to begin with. "Oh. Well, shit. I don't suppose that the noise would travel all this way at night?"

Sarah shook her head and made a sympathetic face. "No, I'm afraid not."

"Damn." Okay, so one major detail still didn't fit, but that didn't necessarily trash the entire theory. Maybe the bad guys were having an argument among themselves. There could be a thousand explanations. But suddenly, Russell found himself mentally married to the notion that the victim was the bad guy; more accurately, that he was *a* bad guy. For all Russell knew, there were no good guys at all. Maybe this was some gang-related druggie shit where the only disappointment was that someone walked away from the fight at all.

If he liked the idea that Officer Stipton was the bad guy, he *loved* the notion that the mystery campers were the nominal good guys. Russell's mind re-created a crime scene down the hill: A young couple was minding their own business when this guy with a gun came out of the night, threatening to kidnap one or both of them. One of the campers was able to distract the good officer long enough to douse him with the water, and from there, it's all about the ensuing fight. They're on the ground, rolling in the dirt. The good guy gets his hands on Stipton's gun and he fires.

By God, that explained the angles of the wounds, too, didn't it?

Yessir, this was the answer. The campers killed in self-defense. And then they ran. Why on earth would they do that? What did they have to hide? Well, when he closed that little loop, he'd have the whole mystery solved, wouldn't he?

Russell liked being this close. He liked being able to see the mystery solve itself. All he had to do was stay out of the way of the crime-scene techs, talk to the campers on Sarah's list, and he was willing to bet that he'd have this one ready to file by noon tomorrow.

Noise on the trail told him that his team was on its way.

13

SAMUEL SAT ATOP the big old tractor in the barn, his hand poised over the ignition switch, staring out through the sagging double doors at the house across the hundred yards of turfy, unkempt grass. He had chores to do and he intended to get to them right away, but inside his head he couldn't quite figure out what had gone wrong. Nothing felt right without Jacob around to tell him what to do, and the more he thought about things, the more he realized just how much was left undone.

Sometimes when he thought about things too hard—things he had to do and things he had to remember—the thoughts grew so large in his mind that they seemed to suffocate themselves, and then he'd get so confused that he couldn't do anything. He hated it when Jacob bossed him around, but at least the bossing kept things in the right order in his head. Now, it was all a big clot.

Because Jacob was dead.

Leaving him there in the woods like that was the hardest thing Samuel had ever done. Everybody knows that dead people left outside get eaten by animals. They get torn apart and split up among the herd or the pack or whatever they are, with the strongest getting the biggest pieces, and the weaker ones settling for what is left. When Samuel closed his eyes, he could see the wild animals from those television shows fighting over his brother's arms and legs, and the images made him want to start crying all over again.

And what about *those* parts? he wondered. What about the *private* parts? Would they get torn off and eaten, too? And his toes and his eyeballs?

Oh, please, please make the pictures stop.

He felt terrible for leaving him there. Just terrible. And he'd feel terrible every single day for the rest of his life, but what else could he have done? If there was one thing that Jacob had made clearer than anything else, it was that you never, *ever* touch a body after it's dead. Not without wearing gloves, and Samuel didn't have any of those with him. His brother had told him a million zillion times: "Whenever you touch the bodies, you leave a little of yourself behind, and that's how you end up in the electric chair."

Samuel didn't understand how it worked, exactly, but he knew that the electric chair burned you all up, and he sure as hell didn't want little bits of himself falling off because he had touched someone, even if it was his only brother. He couldn't imagine how badly either one of those things would hurt, and he had no intention of finding out. Besides, it wasn't important that Samuel understood. Jacob had worried about that stuff a lot—a *whole* lot—and if it was real enough to worry him, then it was real enough to worry Samuel.

So, who was going to do the worrying now? More importantly, who was going to tell him when it was time to worry? Samuel just wasn't good at that stuff. Hell, he'd almost forgotten to undo the burglar alarm before he walked in the front door! The alarm, for God's sake! Think of what might have happened then. Forgetting the alarm was right near the top of the list of worst things you could possibly do.

Stop worrying, you pussy. Jacob's voice seemed to come out of nowhere, making Samuel jump in his tractor saddle.

"Huh? Jacob? Is that you?"

But now the voice wouldn't answer.

"Come on, Jacob, if you're playing one of your jokes on me, I don't think it's very funny. Now come on out!"

You drove the truck home safely, didn't you?

Now whose voice was that? Like out in the woods, it was getting harder and harder to tell.

Maybe you're a pussy, but at least you drove the truck home. Anybody smart enough to do that is smart enough to do house stuff.

"But that was luck, Jacob. That was just pure, dumb luck. I didn't know what I was doing."

But you did *it. That's what counts. You'll be fine.*

"I left you out in the woods to be eaten." Even as he spoke aloud, Samuel felt stupid. He knew that Jacob wasn't there—he'd seen the body, for God's sake—so why was he talking to him? Samuel's head started to hurt.

What choice did you have? I told you not to touch me. I told you not to touch anybody, didn't I?

Samuel felt his lip start to quiver, and he knew what was coming next.

Stop that crying shit, you pussy. Be a man. You have to be the man, now that I'm gone.

"You're gone because I killed you."

Those nosy nellies killed me, Samuel. That man at the campfire.

"But I watched."

You did what I told you.

"So I did good?"

You did good, Samuel. You did real good. Now, don't you have some chores to do?

As always, Jacob was right on all counts. Samuel did have chores to do. And he did drive the truck back safely, and all by himself. Without so much as a scratch. Not everyone could do that, you know. No, no, not just everyone. Not for the whole fifty-five minutes without a scratch. You have to be a little special to drive the truck all the way home by yourself.

He'd been sitting there in the barn for a long time with his hand just hovering over the ignition switch, and when he finally moved his arm, his shoulders felt stiff. He kicked out the clutch, opened the choke, and turned the key. For a few seconds, it seemed that maybe the battery hadn't survived the winter, but finally, the starter turned and the big engine coughed to life. It was like this every year for the first cutting of the season. Certainly, it had been this way for the twenty-odd years that Samuel had been doing it. The big old engine ran rough as gravel for the first minute or two, belching thick, blue exhaust out of the tall stack that rose like a tree from the cowling, filling the whole barn with the smell of poorly burned gasoline.

Every year when Samuel would start up the motor, Jacob would be out there to make a big show of coughing and gagging at the smell, swearing that he was going to put a bullet into the beast one day. Actually, Samuel sort of liked the smell, and he knew that Jacob was only kidding about the bullet. He'd never shoot an old friend like his tractor. Not even Jacob would shoot an old friend.

Checking once over his shoulder to make sure the mower deck was still attached (and who would have taken it off in the past fifteen minutes?), Samuel gently eased the throttle forward, engaged the transmission, and lifted his foot off the clutch. The big John Deere moved forward smooth as melted butter. Samuel forced himself to concentrate on the view straight ahead. This was the hardest part, getting the big machine through the opening of the barn. With only about three feet to spare on either side, you had to be careful not to pull the big wooden doors clean off their tracks. He'd done that once, a long time ago, and lordy, lordy, that wasn't something he ever wanted to do again. He'd learned years ago that if you look to one side or another when you're trying to squeeze through a tight spot with the tractor, you're bound to hit exactly where you're looking. The only way to go straight was to look straight.

As he broke out into the cool sunshine, he brought the machine to a halt again. What pattern should he cut today? And where should he start? Way off to his left, up on the top of the hill, the little graveyard beckoned him to come and cut up there first. While the rest of the lawn had gone only about six months without a mow—and truthfully didn't need that much of a trimming, this being early April and all—that little patch up there hadn't been cut in the better part of nine months, and the grass had reached the top of the rotting white pickets. The tombstones themselves would probably be completely invisible by now.

For sure, that was where he should start. He should just climb off the tractor and drag the push mower all the way up the hill and through the narrow gate and just start cutting there first. Give his mama and daddy a chance to see the world around them again.

But he didn't want to. He never much liked going in there, not for as long as the graves had been dug. It was okay when it was just mama, he supposed. He sort of liked talking to her about the things that happened during the day. But once they'd planted his daddy—well, once

Samuel had planted his daddy (Jacob would have nothing to do with it. "Let the son of a bitch get picked apart by birds" is what he'd said)—it just wasn't a happy place to go.

Besides, he wasn't ready yet to tell them about what had happened to Jacob. His brother was always Daddy's favorite, and when he heard that Samuel had got him killed, Daddy was going to be some kind of pissed off.

The graveyard could wait.

Instead, Samuel decided to concentrate on the bigger yard—the twenty acres that spread all around everything. Even with a mower this size, it'd take the better part of six or seven hours to do it right, and Samuel needed to do something that would kill the time.

There was a time—Samuel could even remember it—when their twenty acres was more like a hundred, and they used to keep animals. Once their folks passed away, though, Jacob said that farming work was for suckers, and he let everything but the fields closest to the house and the barn just go to hell. Once, those other fields grew corn and soybeans and all other kinds of farm goods. Now, to look at them, you'd think that nobody even owned them.

Somewhere out there in all that mess was the old chicken coop, with its low roof, wire cages, and little wood-frame doors. It's just a pile of charred sticks and greasy feathers now, of course, but sometimes he swore that he could still smell the stink of that place; usually at night, after he'd had his eyes closed for a while. He still laughed when he remembered the sight of Mama chasing those birds through the yard as they made the mad dash to save themselves from the dinner pot. She always made it look a lot harder than it really was because she knew how much it made him laugh to watch.

Samuel felt a kind of affection for chickens, though for the life of him, he could never say why. Maybe it was like his daddy used to say: that they were the only creatures on God's earth that were stupider than him. Jacob, on the other hand, always hated the squawking, stinking animals and enjoyed being the one to wring their necks and dress them for dinner. Samuel could never bring himself to watch that part. He didn't mind eating them, but he didn't like to watch them die.

He used to name them, even after his mama told him to stop doing it. She thought it was terrible to name a creature you were planning to eat, but Samuel saw it more as an issue of dignity. It wasn't as if he made friends with them or anything—they weren't dogs, for crying out loud. It simply seemed nicer to call something Gracie or Agamemnon than to just say, "Here, chick, chick, chick, chick . . ."

Hey! Wack-job! You're wasting time again!

"Yeah, yeah, yeah. I'm getting to it." He engaged the PTO, and the whole vehicle shook as the blades came up to speed.

Sometimes, Samuel knew things that Jacob didn't, and this was one of them. He wasn't wasting time. He was planning his cut. Mowing was *Samuel's* job, and he was good at it; maybe the best there ever was. He liked to make perfectly straight diagonal lines across the open spaces and to finish them off with a flourish of perfectly symmetrical arcs at the corners where he made his turns. Sitting up high like this, dragging the bush hog behind him, the hours would fly by in mere seconds. Six, seven hours at a time—more, if he decided to do a diamond pattern, instead of the simple straight lines—and no one ever yelled at him or called him names or even tried to get him to stop doing the one thing to start another. Those hours on the tractor were his and his alone, and things just didn't get much more perfect than that.

It took years of practice to learn how to finish cutting at just the right spot where he could pull the tractor into the barn without backtracking and messing up the perfect pattern. It was silly, he knew, because the pattern was ruined as soon as anybody walked across the lawn, but doing it right still mattered. Sometimes, he even caught Jacob watching him—with that smile on his face.

It'd be another few weeks before the springtime grass took on that deep green color—almost blue—and Samuel couldn't wait. Next to Christmas and Thanksgiving, the moist, fresh smell of newly cut springtime grass was Samuel's favorite aroma in the world.

So who was going to cook the big holiday meals this year?

Samuel felt the panic swell inside his chest, and he quickly took a deep breath, holding it tight, to push the fear back down where it belonged.

Samuel got scared a lot. A whole lot, in fact. Sometimes, he could make the fear go away by holding his breath, or sometimes by saying a prayer. But last night, while Jacob was fighting the nosy nellie and screaming for Samuel to help, neither of those things worked. He'd never felt such fear. It was as if somebody had thrown a big old lock onto his bones so that none of his joints could move. He'd told himself—and he'd told God and he'd told his brother—that he didn't move because Jacob had told him not to, but that was a lie. He was just plain too scared.

That's when he went on his trip.

He always went on trips when things got too big for him to understand, and with all that was happening out there in the woods, between that little boy struggling in the gunnysack, and then all the screaming, and finally with the kid running away, too many things had happened too quickly for him to keep up. Plus, Jacob was *so* mad; madder than Samuel had ever seen him. Mad enough that Samuel was a little afraid of him, too.

Why did he have to be afraid like this? Why couldn't he be brave all the time like Jacob is—was. Oh, God.

Samuel was a goddamn pussy, just as they'd always said. And now Jacob was dead. Oh, great God Almighty, what the hell was he going to do now? Out here in the big field with the aroma of grass filling his nostrils, he tried to find peace—he tried to *invent* peace—but the pain just wouldn't go away. He wondered if it ever would, and as the thought passed through him, it left a white-hot wake, searing his guts, and causing him to double over in the tractor's saddle.

Hey, you pussy. It's done. It's over. Water under the bridge; the horse is out of the barn. Last night was last night; today is today. Start thinking, *Samuel.*

But how was he supposed to do that when he felt so terribly, terribly frightened? It was as if his heart and his brain and his stomach were completely full, and nothing else could possibly get in.

I told you to stand there, and you did what I told you. I was the dummy this time, Samuel, not you. You were just doing what I told you to do.

"But if I hadn't fallen asleep, then none of this would have happened. You'd still be here."

It's my fault, Samuel, not yours. Mine. And those nosy nellies.

Oh, those nosy nellies. If they'd just done as Jacob wanted them to do—if they'd just handed the little boy over so they could get on with their game—then there'd have been just a quick snot-pounding, and then everything would have ended just the way it was supposed to. The way it always had before.

About the time that Samuel was tracking the bush hog oh so carefully along the fence line out on the far edge of the property, the sadness started to change. That awful heat in the pit of his stomach started to cool off, and his heart started pounding hard as his face flushed hot. He realized that he was getting *angry*—something that he rarely did, that his daddy would never have tolerated back before the accident. His mind focused on all that he had lost, and on just how quickly it had all gone away. He focused on what those nosy nellies had done. Forever and ever and ever, Samuel would be stuck out here on the farm by himself. Even if he got himself a wife someday, he'd still be stuck out here all by himself. Nobody could ever learn how to cut the grass as perfectly as him, so he was stuck out here forever. Alone. Like Robinson Crusoe, but without the help of Friday.

Just you, buddy boy, forever and ever and ever and ever.

All because of the nosy nellies. He made the turn and headed back toward the house. What would Jacob have done, he wondered, if things had been reversed out there in the woods last night? What would he have done if Samuel had called for help when the nosy nellies were snot-pounding him? You bet your sweet ass Jacob would have jumped right in there to help. And if they'd killed Samuel? (Well, that would never have happened if Jacob had stepped in to help, but what if they had?) Without a doubt, Samuel knew exactly what Jacob would have done. Jacob would never have rested until he'd gotten revenge. An eye for an eye, one of Jacob's favorite expressions. He'd have found out who those nosy nellies were, and he'd have tracked them down for the snot-pounding of their lives.

I wouldn't have just stood there in the woods crying and snotting and drooling, that's for sure.

"Shut up, Jacob."

Funny thing about anger. Once you tap that well deep down inside your gut, and the anger starts to trickle out, there's no controlling it. The trickle turns to a flood, and when you try to turn it off, you might as well try to put a nozzle on a garden hose that's turned on full. The harder you try, the worse it all gets, with anger just splashing everywhere, over everything.

That's how it was with Samuel and the nosy nellies. If he could just find out who they were, then get his hands on them, he'd get even, yes siree.

Teach you a lesson you won't forget, you stupid shit.

This time, the voice in his head took Samuel's breath away. He hadn't heard his daddy's growl in years, and swear to God, hearing it now made his heart stop for a second. What was Daddy doing here? Samuel didn't go up to the graveyard specifically so he didn't have to hear his daddy's voice. He didn't even like to *think* about him, just as he intentionally never thought about the bogeyman or that thing he still thought was waiting for him under his bed sometimes. He'd learned a long time ago not to think about the things that scared him most. If you didn't think bad things, they never came to get you.

"Go away!" Samuel shouted. "You're dead. You just go eat some dirt!" He tried to sound like Jacob when he spoke, but even he could hear the tremor in his voice. Suddenly, he was drowning in a torrent of voices and forgotten memories.

In his mind, he was a little boy again, back in the chicken coop.

No, no, not there. Please not there.

His daddy was about to teach him a lesson.

A lesson that even a stupid shit like you will never forget.

Samuel had already cut his switch, and he'd made it a big one. (Cut it too small and Daddy used the ax handle.) As he undid the suspender clasps, his denim coveralls dropped to the ground, the little hourglass ring landing in a dollop of chicken shit.

"Please don't hurt me," he pleaded.

But it *was* going to hurt. Bad. Lessons you never forget always do.

It was a chilly day, too, the kind that made you shiver if you stood still for too long, but made you sweat if you ran around and played. That made it a spring day, or maybe early fall. The smell of those filthy chickens was overwhelming, and little boy Samuel breathed through his mouth so he wouldn't have to inhale the putrid stench.

"You know what to do, boy. Don't make me tell you again. You know the drill."

The drill. Always the drill, and always out here with the chickens.

Samuel did, indeed, know what to do. His underpants were next. Hand-me-downs from Jacob, they swam on his butt as it was, and it took only a light tug to make them drop in a fabric puddle around his ankles. The chicken coop had a ledge that ran all the way around the front, a kind of windowsill where the chicken wire attached to the filthy, stained pine walls, and that's where Samuel put his hands. The wood held his weight—all sixty, seventy pounds of it—as he "assumed the position." He curled his fingers into the hexagonal holes in the wire.

"Shirttail," his daddy growled, and Samuel reached behind to pull the flannel flap out of the way.

He looked between his feet, down where the toes of his orange work boots pecked out from the mess of blue denim and gray cotton, and watched as a big fat hen explored his underwear with its beak. Samuel kept his eye on that bird in case it decided to look up and take a bite of the little worm he had growing between his legs. A peck of a pecker. The very thought of it terrified him.

The switch whistled as it cut through the air, and it bit the skin of his backside with the sting of a hornet. Samuel didn't hear the sound of the impact, but the hen did, and it scurried for cover.

"One, sir," Samuel said, focusing every dram of energy on the task of keeping the pain out of his voice. No clenched teeth, no yelling. It was all part of the drill.

Off to his right, through the corner of his eye, he saw his daddy's shadow, three times bigger than normal in the late-afternoon sun, as he brought his arm way, way back and over his head. The switch was invisible in the shadow, but it whistled again as the shadow's arm became a blur, and then it bit even harder into the exact same spot.

"Two, sir." Oh, God, oh, God, it hurt. He wanted to cry. He wanted to scream out as loud as he could, but he knew if he did, the switch would become a fist, and it wouldn't be lashing his bottom anymore, but his face, and then he'd have to stay home from school for a week while the swelling went down, and he'd be out here every damn day.

Thwack! Oh, yes, he heard it that time. The whole world heard it that time, and as it landed, a lightbulb popped behind Samuel's eyes, and the lightning bolt of pain reached all the way up into his belly.

"Three, sir," he gasped.

"I can't hear you, boy."

"Three, sir!" Christ on a crutch, that was too loud. Way, way too loud. His instinct was to shut his eyes in anticipation of what had to be coming, but if he did, he was afraid he'd squeeze out some tears by mistake, and everybody knows how tough the drill was on pussies who cried. Oh, please, oh, please don't—

Thwack!

"Four, sir." His daddy was sweating now. He knew better than to look—he didn't want to look—but Samuel could tell from the rancid whiskey odor that mixed with the stink of the chicken shit and whatever sweat or blood was inching its way down Samuel's butt cheeks and on into his crack.

"Five, sir."

"Six, sir."

Six was twice the normal number, but barely halfway to ten, and Samuel didn't know if he could make it. Out in front of him, where his fingers curled tightly around the chicken wire, beads of blood oozed from the folds of skin under his knuckles, and in his mind he could see the galvanized hexagons eating right on through the bone. At his feet, the hen had returned to take another peek. Or was it *peck?*

"I can't hear you!"

"Seven!" Samuel wheezed, but he wasn't at all sure that was the count. In fact, the lightbulbs were popping with every stroke now, and on whatever number that last one was, somebody had lifted the latch that kept his legs straight, and they just folded under him. He'd never fallen like this before—a slow-motion sag that he tried desperately to fight but couldn't. He heard a rushing sound in his ears and was dimly aware that he was about to faint. He found it—interesting, not frightening at all. He kind of liked the idea of being unconscious for a little while.

The hen saw him coming and scampered away again, maybe to go lay another egg. Samuel wondered if maybe it wasn't a relief to have somebody wring your neck and just get it over with.

He tried to get his hands out in front of him, but they didn't want to work. For a long moment, they seemed cemented to the chicken wire, and as he headed for the ground, they pivoted him around just enough that when he landed, it wasn't on his knees as he'd been planning, but on his ravaged bottom, and smack in a pile of chicken shit.

That's when he yelled. He couldn't help it. It was as if every body part suddenly acted on its own, bypassing the filter in his brain that told him when he should act like a man, and when he should keep a stiff upper lip. But this was more than a yell. It just poured from his throat, loud enough to hurt his own ears. He tried to stop it, but his damn throat just wouldn't listen.

And as he'd predicted, the switch became a fist.

14

BOBBY THOUGHT OF the decor in the offices of Donnelly, Wall, and Bevis as lawyer-light. As the largest firm in Prince Edward County, its attorneys enjoyed the status of hugest fish in the mud puddle, and the waiting room boasted the very best that the local discount stores could offer. Vinyl looked enough like leather to pull it off, and the veneered pressboard looked enough like mahogany to make a client feel that the $140-an-hour fee wasn't as exorbitant as it might otherwise seem.

As he passed through the doorway into the wine-colored reception area, the fist that had been clutching his heart all day clenched tighter still. He was going to talk to a *lawyer,* for God's sake. About shooting a man. Whatever delusions he'd nurtured about none of this being as bad as he thought evaporated as he stepped inside. From this moment on, he realized, he maintained only partial ownership of his life. He was going to share a secret that by rights no one else on the planet should know. And once the secret was out, nothing would ever be the same again. While attorney-client privilege protected him from direct harm, it was hard to imagine what the atmosphere would be like the next time they got together for lunch, or when they were waiting to tee off at the next charity golf tournament.

So, Bobby, how's that murder rap thing going?

Just fine, thanks. They still haven't caught me. Think I should use a driver or a three wood?

Jesus Christ, what had he gotten himself into?

Bobby handed his business card to the prune-faced receptionist as she rested her phone on the cradle. "I need to speak with—"

The phone rang and the receptionist raised a finger for silence. "Donnelly, Wall, and Bevis." Then, three seconds later: "Just a moment, I'll check to see if he's in." She punched a button, passed the call to someone else, and then looked up at Bobby. He saw her eyes focus on his bruised eye, but she was way too practiced at her job to say anything.

"I need to see Barbara Dettrick right away."

Something in his manner put her on edge. "Is she expecting you?"

"Just tell her who it is, and tell her it's an emergency."

The phone rang again, and as the woman moved to answer, Bobby reached through the window and covered her hand with his. "It's an *emergency,* ma'am."

The receptionist looked for a fleeting moment as if she was considering filing assault charges, but the expression faded as he withdrew his hand. Looking straight at him, she picked up the receiver on the third ring. "Donnelly, Wall, and Bevis. Hold please."

She punched three buttons this time and after a short pause looked at his business card and said, "I have a Robert Martin here to see Ms. Dettrick. He says it's an emergency . . . I don't know . . . Okay, I'll tell him." When she looked up again, she told Bobby, "She'll be with you in ten minutes."

It turned out to be more like twenty. He helped himself to a squeaky, button-studded, faux-leather chair that could have been fashioned from wrought iron. As tacky as it was, he imagined how palatial this would all seem a year from now, after he'd had a few months of prison time under his belt. By then, a nervous wait in a reception room might be the highlight—the pinnacle—of his day. Hell, for all he knew, this very moment might be as good as it would get for a very, very long time.

God help me.

The lobby door opened, and Barbara Dettrick stepped out to greet her client. "I'm sorry, Bobby, but I was in the middle of a conference call and couldn't get away." She stepped forward and thrust out her hand. An avid golfer and outdoor enthusiast, Barbara looked taller than her rightful five feet ten and never failed to be in good humor. "Nice to see you—My God, what happened?" She reached out to touch his bruise, but he shrank away.

"Can you come with me for a minute?"

She looked confused. "Come *with* you? Where are you going?"

He hooked her in his right arm and guided her toward the front door. "I'll explain in the car. Fact is, I've got things to do, I'm running out of time, and since you're going to send me a bill anyway, what difference does it make where we meet?"

Looking thoroughly confused, Barbara allowed herself to be led out into the parking lot, and from there into the front seat of Bobby's Explorer. "Where are we going?"

Bobby climbed in behind the steering wheel and started the engine. "We're going shopping."

"Shopping? Bobby, what's happening?"

Bobby smiled. "I'm on a really tight leash, okay? Just let me talk, and I think everything will fall into place for you."

Barbara shook her head, waiting for the words to make sense. "My secretary told me that this was an—"

"An emergency; yes, it is. But I'm not supposed to be meeting with you. So, I've got to work fast to complete the shopping I used as the ruse to get me out here. Understand?"

"Not a word."

Bobby took a deep breath and held it. Of course she didn't understand. He didn't understand all of it himself. He started twice to form the words he needed to speak, but both times they refused to come out. Finally, he defaulted to the direct approach.

"I'm in serious trouble, Barbara. I broke the law, but haven't been caught yet. *Yet* being the operative word here."

Barbara's eyebrows came together to form a single line. "What are we talking here? DWI?"

Another deep breath. "Kidnapping, I think."

Barbara's face sort of expanded, her eyebrows launching up, while her jaw dropped. "*Excuse* me? Kidnapping? You're kidding, right?"

He pulled out into traffic and headed for the Kmart Plaza. "And maybe murder."

The silence that followed made him turn his head to check if she was still there.

"Jesus, Bobby."

He nodded. Well said. "You want to hear the details?"

"Holy shit." Clearly, this was her first capital case of the day. Of all the people in the world that Barbara Dettrick could reasonably have expected to see walking through her door, Bobby Martin wasn't even on the list. Mr. Conservative; Mr. Cross-Only-at-the-Corner. This was the same Bobby Martin who had gone on endlessly in college berating bottom-feeding defense lawyers and using her desire to become one as evidence that she had no moral center.

No, she didn't want to hear the details, but clearly she was about to. She surrendered to the inevitable. "Okay, sure. Let me hear it."

"Attorney-client privilege applies, right?"

Barbara nodded. "Don't worry about that. You *are* innocent, aren't you?"

He responded with a look.

"Oh, shit."

"I'm not guilty, either," Bobby said quickly, and he dove into the details of last night's encounter in the woods. He did his best to leave nothing out, and when he got carried away with the emotion of it all, and the facts started to jumble, Barbara slowed him down and asked a few probing questions.

"I don't know where I made the biggest mistake," Bobby concluded, "but now I'm stuck with this little kid in my house, and I don't know what to do with him. If I turn him in to the cops, I'm confessing to the murder. If I keep him—well, hell, we all know I can't do that. So what do I do?"

Barbara Dettrick had been a hair-twister for as long as Bobby had known her—ever since third grade—and now, as they sat in the Kmart parking lot discussing matters of life and death, she worried the strand in front of her left ear into an unruly spike that no longer joined the rest of her coiffeur. They were quiet for a long time as she thought things through. Finally, when she spoke, Bobby thought he noted a hint of dread in her eyes.

"How likely do you think it is that this guy you shot was going to do you harm?"

"Well, looking back on it, I really don't know."

"Don't look back on it, then," she snapped. The sudden appearance of anger startled him. "Tell me about when it was all happening. How fearful were you of him harming you or Susan?"

Bobby had seen enough lawyer shows on television to know that there was only one right answer here, but he wanted to make sure that it was also the truth. At a time like this, the last thing in the world he wanted to do was lie to his lawyer.

"I think I was dead certain at the time. Once he heard the boy making noise, something changed in him."

"So he lunged first?" Barbara prompted.

"Well, you see, that's where—" Her eyes flashed, and Bobby cut the words short. "Yes." Her head nodded almost imperceptibly. "Yes, he definitely lunged first."

"So you had no choice but to defend yourself?"

"Right." Bobby was getting the hang of this now. "Right, after he moved toward me, I moved toward him with the club."

"And what do you think would have happened if you hadn't wrestled the gun from him and killed him?"

Bobby thought again before answering. "He would have killed me. And he would have killed the others, too."

Barbara nodded more enthusiastically. "That's good. That's the basis for a solid case of self-defense. And I assume that Susan witnessed all of this?"

Bobby's shoulders sagged. "Well, that's where—"

"Because it would be enormously helpful to your case if she was a witness. That way, it wouldn't just be your word against the remains of a dead cop."

Bobby held her gaze, trying his best to understand exactly what she wasn't saying to him. "I'll talk to Susan," he said finally. "I'll find out what she saw."

"Good. Let's just hope she saw the same events that you did. What about the gun? Do you still have it?"

"No, I stopped on a bridge on the way home and dumped it into the river. I wiped it clean first, and I'm pretty sure no one saw me. You know, I almost got caught with it that one time and—"

"That's okay, Bobby," Barbara interrupted. "Just give me a second here."

They sat for a long time there in the Explorer, each of them lost in a flood of thoughts. "Do you think that we could carry this on in the store?" Bobby said finally. "I'm supposed to be picking up supplies for the baby, and if I'm not back soon, Susan will worry."

Barbara nodded, but then scowled. Something wasn't right here. "You said that Susan didn't know you were here."

Bobby nodded. "Yeah, that's what I said. She doesn't know that I'm talking to you. I don't want her to know."

"Why?"

Another deep sigh, and suddenly Bobby's emotions were like an open wound, raw and weepy. "She, uh, she's sort of bonded with this baby." His voice was barely a whisper.

"Well, why wouldn't she? I mean under the circumstances—"

"It's not like you're thinking, okay? She thinks that God sent us this baby. To be ours to raise."

"Come again?"

"We've had a few miscarriages over the last couple of years," he explained softly, "and you know about Steven. It was looking like we'd never be able to have kids. That's really why we were out there camping in the first place. We wanted to get things right in our heads, you know? Anyway, when we were down there on the rocks, we said a prayer together. We said a lot of prayers together. Hell, I even wished on a star. We prayed, we cried, and then there he was. Now Susan thinks it's a kind of predestination."

When he looked over to Barbara for an answer, she just looked away, twisting her hair and staring at the glove box.

Bobby didn't want silence right now, so he kept going. "I've got to be honest with you, Barb. In the past—what is it, twelve hours?—I've wondered myself if she isn't right. They say that God works in mysterious ways. Who's to say this isn't one of them?"

Barbara nodded, clearly overwhelmed by it all. "They also say, 'Be careful what you wish for.'" A beat, and then she was all lawyer again. "I assume you're looking for some legal advice here, right?"

"Of course."

"Okay, then, let's deal with the murder first." Bobby recoiled at the word, and she grew still more serious. "I'm sorry, but you know that's what people are going to assume when they find this body. From that point on, they'll do their best to identify who the killer is. Your challenge, then—" Something in Bobby's expression made her stop. "What?"

"I don't think it's a huge stretch for them to figure out who did the killing. When I was unloading the car this morning, I noticed that our camping permit was missing. I think it probably got torn off sometime last night."

Barbara's eyes grew even larger. "What are you telling me?"

Bobby couldn't look at her as he confessed to the ultimate in stupidity. "I think it's probably up there at the murder scene."

"Oh, my God," Barbara breathed. "How did that happen?"

Bobby laughed. "How did it *happen?* Well, I promise I didn't pull it off and leave it there on purpose. I guess it just came off. Maybe during the fight, I don't know. It's only a piece of paper held on with a wire."

"And it's got your name and address on it?"

"You betcha."

"God, Bobby."

"That's why I'm here, Barb! I told you this was an emergency. Any second now, somebody's going to show up at my door with a pair of handcuffs, and I need to know what to do."

Barbara turned suddenly pale, and her eyes looked sad. "I don't know what to tell you. It's too early to panic, though. It'll take time for someone to discover the body, and maybe—"

This time, Bobby paled.

"What?" Her expression said she was waiting for him to drop another bomb.

He cleared his voice and tried not to look stupid. "I, uh, I called the police on our way out of the park this morning. They found the body a long time ago. Maybe before we even got home."

The attorney looked as if she'd been slapped. "Are you crazy?"

"Excuse the hell out of me! I'm happy to say I don't have a whole lot of practice at this stuff, Barb. I knew that running would make us look guilty as hell, and I thought that by reporting it myself, my shit wouldn't be as weak if I ever got caught. I didn't know that I'd left my fucking calling card there."

Barbara looked disgusted. And a maybe a little frightened that anyone who'd achieved some level of success in his life could do something so patently stupid. "God, Bobby, I just don't know what—" She cut herself off again, and her look of horror transformed itself into something more closely resembling bemusement. "Wait a minute . . ." Bobby turned to face her. "How long ago did you call?"

"I think it was around four."

She checked her watch. "Okay, and it's nearly noon now. Here's my question: How come they haven't already come to get you?"

Bobby started to answer, then stopped. Finally he shrugged. "I don't know."

"I mean, how difficult a thing could that be? They've found the body, they've got the name and address of the person who last camped there. How tough could it be to just come by and have you hauled in? Especially with the victim being a cop."

"So, what's your point?"

"My point is, I don't think they've found your permit," she said, a smile finally invading her otherwise bleak features. "Could be it's under a rock they haven't turned over, or it could be that you lost it someplace else, in which case they don't have much on you."

"How do you figure?"

"Think about it. I mean, you'll have to stipulate to being there at the park last night, right? If you filled out a form, then they're going to have the office copy right in front of them. But you're not the only people to be there. If they can't place you directly at the scene of the crime, then they don't have much of a case. Here's hoping that your permit fell off on the trail somewhere."

"But they're still going to come looking, right?"

"Sure they will. Just as they'll be looking at everyone who was there last night. The difference is, without evidence to tie you directly to the scene, they'll come *just* to talk, instead of to execute a warrant."

"And what do I say to them when they start asking questions?"

Barbara noticed with a start what she'd been doing to her hair, and she quickly unwrapped her finger and made a futile effort to smooth the twist. "Let's think this through." Her voice took on a new intensity as she plowed her way through the logic path. "You said this happened in a national park, right? So that means the FBI has jurisdiction." She made a clicking sound with her tongue and shook her head. "That's bad news."

"Terrific."

"Well, unlike dealing with local police departments, it's actually a crime to lie to federal investigators. Or even to mislead them."

Bobby scowled. "You mean it's okay to lie to a county cop or a state trooper?"

"Well, I'm not sure it's 'okay' exactly, but you can't be sent to jail for it. In all other jurisdictions, if you're not under oath, you can say pretty much whatever you want, especially if you're trying to cover your own ass. Prosecutors sometimes try to paint a little white lie as obstruction of justice, but not usually. That's why your local beat cop is always so cranky. He just assumes that everyone he talks to is a liar. But with the FBI, you've got to be more careful."

"So, if he says, 'Did you kill this guy?' what do I say?"

Barbara thought this through for a long moment and finally sighed. "You're putting me in a tough position here, Bobby. I could be disbarred for instructing a client to lie about anything to anyone."

"But hypothetically?"

"Well, hypothetically, if I were in that position, I guess I'd have to weigh the relative advantages and disadvantages of making up a story. On the one hand, I could confess and guarantee myself a trip to prison, or I could try to float a coherent story that would keep me out. If my story was later found to be untrue, then, of course, I'd have to worry about the additional punishment. You know, the punishment that would be tacked on to the end of the death sentence."

Bobby felt as if he'd been punched in the gut. Jesus, the death sentence. Was there no bottom to this pit?

"But that's just a hypothetical," Barbara reiterated. "If, on the other hand, I felt confident that I had indeed acted in self-defense, then I might be inclined to step forward and just tell the whole story. Maybe even before the FBI showed up at my door."

Bobby sucked in a lungful and held it as he rested his head on the back of his seat. He knew in his heart that he should turn himself in;

that he should just fess up to everything, exactly as it had happened. He'd known that all along—ever since he'd placed his anonymous phone call from the tiny mini-mart. And if everything he'd told Barbara had been 100 percent true, maybe the answer here would be simple. The *real* truth was that Susan hadn't seen any of what had transpired, and no matter how much he and his wife practiced a response to investigators' questions, he knew with perfect certainty that one or both of them would cave under the pressure. When that happened, he'd be in a world of misery.

"I'm not sure I can do that," Bobby said finally. "For reasons that you probably don't want to know."

Barbara gave him a little resigned smile. "For reasons that I probably already know without you telling me."

"So when the feds come to my door and start asking questions, at what point do I call you?"

"The instant that they lead you to believe that you're a suspect."

"They wouldn't be there if I weren't."

"Okay, then the minute they lead you to believe that you're more of a suspect than everyone else who traveled through the park that night."

Bobby wasn't sure what he was looking for, exactly, by coming to see Barbara, but he knew that he wasn't finding it. Maybe he wanted a script to follow, a set of planned responses for every conceivable question that might arise.

Or, maybe he was just looking for someone to say that he really had absolutely nothing to worry about. What he had gotten instead was more worry, and the strongest possible hint that he was out there all alone on this one. A headache bloomed somewhere near the center of his brain and grew with amazing speed to occupy every space from ear to ear.

"What about evidence, Barbara? All the stuff that can connect me to the campsite? You know, the tent, the remains of our food, our clothes, that sort of thing. What do I do with all of that stuff?"

Barbara looked at him as if he were crazy. "Bobby, you've got possession of a human being who doesn't belong to you. I don't think that your tent is on your top-ten list of problems."

15

AT FIVE-FOOT-TEN, 165, Carlos Ortega could have been a movie star, sporting perfect white teeth and a flawless olive complexion. He wore his thick mane of jet-black hair short and combed straight back, and he favored a business-casual look. He sat perfectly still, his whole face smiling, as he watched little Christa settle into her chair. Nothing had moved since the last time they'd played together here in the music room, but his daughter was a twelve-year-old perfectionist. The seventh-grader double-checked the strap on her rock stop, making sure the buckle lay exactly on the white line that her father had inscribed across the width of black nylon. That done, she eased the point of her cello's end pin into the cup, settled the scroll just so over her left shoulder, then poised her bow over the strings. She was ready.

"Okay," Carlos said, "I'm going to give you two measures of the bass part, and then you come in."

"I know, Daddy." Christa sighed, and issued her patented eye-roll.

Carlos laughed. He loved it when Christa got so serious about her music. She had a gift, bestowed by Saint Cecilia herself, the patron saint of music, and gifted children needed to appreciate and respect the responsibility that came with their unique talents.

At the piano, Carlos's right hand remained on his lap as the fingers on his left stroked the opening notes of Pachelbel's Canon, a staple at every wedding he'd ever attended. He never tired of the delicious, rich melody of the piece, and as Christa entered exactly on her cue, his eyes welled with pride. Tonight at the concert, the string ensemble would play the piece as a round, with Christa switching in the third verse to the obbligato, playing the solo that was written for a violin, but which was nonetheless granted to her in deference to her talent. Here in this final rehearsal, Carlos played all the other parts on the piano, even hitting the wrong notes that he anticipated from the other children in the ensemble.

"Listen to your part, Christa. Don't let the violas drag down the pitch. Let them adjust to you. Hear the *music,* not the notes. *Feel* the music."

And she did. Music blossomed from her bow and rose to fill the glass-walled music room. She improvised a trill, but her father intervened immediately. "This is a performance, sweetheart. Never experiment in a performance."

Christa smiled, as if to say she'd done that on purpose just to get a rise out of him, and Carlos laughed. "All right, Miss Smart Aleck, you got me. Now, we'll keep going all the way through without breaking, okay?"

Christa responded with a nod, then became one with her music again.

Behind him, over his right shoulder, Carlos sensed movement, and he pivoted his head to see Jesús Peña standing in the doorway, his perpetual scowl only slightly less severe than normal. Now *there* was a man who needed more music in his life. Eye contact was all that Peña had been waiting for, and once it was made, he retreated out of sight. Knowing how much his boss cherished his time alone with Christa, this was as close to an interruption as Peña would dare.

The Canon doesn't end as much as it just dies away. When they were done, and the final notes hung about them in perfect harmony, father and daughter shared a smile.

"That was pretty," Christa said, ever the champion of understatement.

"That was *beautiful,*" her father corrected, and he slid out from behind the piano.

"Aren't we going to practice some more?" Her voice dripped disappointment.

Carlos rumpled her hair. "No, not today. Not with the concert tonight."

"The concert is why I need to practice more."

"The concert is why you need to rest. Sometimes you can overcook before a performance; play too many times and you lose your edge on the piece."

Christa wasn't buying it. She craned her neck to see past her father, but the doorway to the music room was empty. "It's Tío Jesús, isn't it?" The Ortegas rarely spoke Spanish in their home anymore, but *tío*—uncle—had somehow survived as Christa's honorific for Peña, who in fact shared no blood with the Ortegas, but was such a permanent fixture in her life that he might as well have.

"Sweetie, I have work to do."

"But this is *our* time. You said so yourself."

Carlos patted his daughter's face. "It was and it is. But sometimes, things interfere. I know you understand this. Now, please, Christa, I want you to go upstairs and finish your homework. After the concert, your mother and I want to take you out to celebrate, and I don't want our plans scuttled by math, okay?"

Christa tried to pout, but couldn't quite pull it off. She understood all too well how business sometimes got in the way. Gently placing her cello on its side, she stood, gave Papa a hug, and then headed for the door. "You can come in now, Tío Jesús," she called even before she reached the threshold. As she passed through the doorway, she playfully stuck out her tongue at him.

When he appeared, his scowl had become a smile, and his ears had turned red. "I'm terribly sorry, Carlos."

Carlos waved him off and smiled. "I swear to God she's thirty, not twelve."

Peña smiled. He'd about reached his limit for small talk.

"Tell me what's on your mind, Jesús."

"Someone is here to see you. She says she knows you from a long time ago, and she seems very upset. Her name is April Simpson. I told her you were busy, but she seemed very insistent. She begged me, actually."

"I don't know an April Simpson."

"She said she used to be April Fitzgerald."

Carlos cocked his head to the side and allowed his jaw to drop a bit. What on earth could possibly bring that bitch out to see him? "What does she want?"

"She wouldn't tell me. She just said that she had to see you and that it was very important."

"Important." Carlos seemed to be tasting the word.

"Life and death is what she said. I can send her packing if you'd like."

Carlos thought about that. There'd be more than a little satisfaction in turning her away without so much as a nod; but for her to come here, her life must have taken a terrible turn, and something told him that he might just enjoy hearing the details.

"No," he said at length. "Send her in."

Peña waited to see if there was more, then left the music room, closing the door behind him. Carlos moved quickly to position himself on the white leather sofa in the far corner from the door.

Twenty seconds later, the door opened again, and in stepped April Fitzgerald. She looked terrible, her once beautiful blue eyes stained red and darkened by heavy rings underneath. She'd cut her hair since high school, transforming that shiny, long mane into a kind of auburn helmet that Carlos didn't find attractive at all. Looking at her now, in fact, he wasn't sure what he'd ever seen in her.

He said nothing for a long while, allowing the discomfort of the moment to make her squirm; to force her to drink in the opulence of her surroundings. She seemed dwarfed by the ten-foot ceiling and the ornately carved walnut paneling, and in the way of most people who visited him here, she remained deferential, waiting to be told what to do. If it were another lady, Carlos might have considered rising to greet her.

"It's been a long time, April," he said at last.

She nodded and forced a smile. She couldn't hold eye contact, though, casting her gaze down to her hands, where she'd worried a Kleenex to tatters.

"How long, April? Ten, twelve years?"

April didn't answer. He didn't expect her to.

"Please," he said, gesturing to the lush leather chairs across from him. "Have a seat."

She moved hesitantly, as if afraid that he might lash out at her, and gently sat on the very front edge of the left-hand chair. As she came closer, Carlos noticed that she'd dressed up for their meeting, but that the pink frock under her jacket seemed unusually lightweight for days as chilly as these. Her ample breasts swayed and jiggled as she moved, and were it not for the obviously pregnant belly, she might have intrigued him.

"I haven't heard from you," Carlos baited. "No Christmas card, no dinner invitations, no nothing."

April remained silent, pulling at her dress where it bound against her tummy.

"Could it be that you still think that I am a—let's see if I can remember how you put it before—ah, yes, 'a worthless, stinking spick'?"

She wound the Kleenex tighter and tighter in her fist.

Carlos leaned forward and rested his elbows on the desk. "Look at me, April."

She raised her eyes.

"You have to say something. You can't just come in here and take up my time without speaking."

"You tried to rape me." The words came out as a statement of fact. No anger, no accusation, just fact.

Carlos laughed, but when the moment passed, he turned deadly serious. "You open those pretty thighs for everybody else, but when I make a pass, it's rape."

Silence. She hadn't come here to argue.

He leaned back in his chair and folded his hands across his chest. "It must be difficult to be so much better than everyone else." His eyes scanned her appearance. He didn't need to tell her how far she'd fallen from her lofty dreams.

More silence.

"Look, April, I thought you came here wanting something. If you're just here to sit, do it on your own time."

It took a moment for her to say the words again. Just hearing the syllables was like reliving the nightmare. "My son has been kidnapped." There, she said it. The words came out in a rush, but at least she'd said it.

It wasn't what he'd been expecting. He'd assumed that this was about money, but seeing the anguish on her face, he should have known that it was something far worse than that. Something changed behind Carlos's eyes, and he lifted a gaudy brass box of tissues off the coffee table and hovered it in the air while she helped herself. He waited patiently while she struggled with her emotions. When she looked ready, he said, "Go on."

"My husband, William, took some money from a man who works for Patrick Logan. You know him, I assume? Logan?"

Carlos kept his expression completely neutral as his neck flushed hot. "I might have heard the name." Instantly, he knew the rest of the story, without April's having to say another word—not the details, of course, but this was exactly the kind of shit that Logan had tried in the past.

She told the whole story, so far as she knew the details, covering William's bonehead mistakes, the kidnapping itself, and her efforts to repay the debt on her own. "We don't have that kind of money, Carlos. I've done what I can, but I just don't have that kind of cash."

Carlos shook his head when she was finished and made a clicking sound with his tongue. "This is a terrible thing, April, but why do you come to me?"

She looked away again and shrugged. "I guess I thought that maybe you could do something."

Oh, he'd do something, all right. God *damn* that Logan for pulling this kind of shit. Yes, Carlos would do a lot. He'd dance on that fucker's face when he was done here, but that did not concern this woman. "I'm a businessman," he said in his most soothing tone, "not a policeman. I don't know what help I could possibly be."

"You're a drug dealer, Carlos." She spat the words at him, and he surprised himself by recoiling. April saw the reaction, and she leaned forward in her chair. "You're in the business of intimidating people, the business of getting things done. You can talk the same language as Logan."

Carlos recovered quickly. "Oh, I do speak the same language, April, but I conduct my business in a whole different way. Still, what would you expect a man to do when someone steals over a thousand dollars from him? Merely shrug and forget about everything?"

That was it. April reached her breaking point. She slammed her hands down on the coffee table and shouted, "He's not yet three years old, Carlos! Logan's not threatening to kill William—the man who stole from him. He's threatening to kill a little boy!"

The outburst brought Peña to the door, but he retreated from his boss's nod.

Carlos thought a long time before saying anything. His anger built like steam in a kettle as his mind raced through all the shit that Logan had pulled over the years. Every breath that stupid mick took was a gift from Carlos. If he watched a sunset, ate an ice cream cone, or made love to one of his whores, it was because Carlos had decided to let him live for one more day. Why could he not get it through that thick skull that he wasn't just a punk anymore; that he was part of a team now?

There was nothing new or unique about Carlos's business dealings with Logan; it was the same compromise he'd negotiated with every other upstart tough guy who'd decided to try his hand at competing against Carlos. Rather than going to war against them, Carlos wooed them to his side. For a 50 percent stake in everything they brought in, Carlos allowed them to live—live well, in fact, if they were any good at what they did. In return, Carlos and Peña and the people they trusted most helped them to defend their turf from encroachment by outsiders. Everyone profited from the strength of the group as a whole, thus reducing the need for violence and all the police meddling that bullets brought.

The system had worked well and profitably for nearly seven years now; to the point where Carlos sometimes felt as if he were running an insanely profitable pizza franchise or a chain of burger joints. He'd found that by keeping a tight rein on his network of suppliers, he could avoid the kind of violence that raised the ire of police chiefs and city councilmen. People had their vices, and he was the entrepreneur who helped them find happiness.

Logan had no idea how close he'd come to dying. Twice, Carlos had been given reason to believe that Logan was holding out on him, and twice the stupid shit had been within five hours of being whacked before he voluntarily came forward with what he called bookkeeping corrections. People who played so fast and loose with their own lives made Carlos nervous.

Then again, Logan was good, regularly turning fifteen, twenty grand a week in crack, angel dust, and meth, but he was a sick, sadistic fuck who couldn't separate his ego from his business sense. Not every affront required the kind of nuclear overkill that had become the mick's trademark. And this kind of shit—this stuff with April's kid—was *so* over the top that it threatened everything that Carlos had built.

You don't shit in your own nest. How many times had Carlos said this to his franchisees? If you want to make money off of people's vices, you make yourself the most desirable neighbor, the most reliable friend. You don't sell junk to kids; you protect them. You make sure that they get to and from school safely, and you make sure that some other fuck from another neighborhood thinks five, ten, a thousand times before he even considers challenging your turf. Why was it so difficult for Logan to understand these things?

"Look, April," Carlos began, after cleansing his lungs with a giant sigh. "Your hubby made a bad, bad move here. Logan is an animal. What was he thinking?"

"It's not about William. This is about Justin. I have no idea where William's head was. I don't care. I only want my boy back. I'll give you whatever you want. I'll *do* whatever you want." The words made her choke and she reached for another tissue, clasping it over her mouth as she fought her sobs.

Carlos finally understood, and he felt an unfamiliar sense of sadness. "Is that what this outfit is about, April? With the swaying breasts and the light-weight fabric? You're offering to trade yourself for your son?"

She looked straight at the floor. "Please just tell me it's that easy."

"It's not that easy, April. It's not even close to being that easy."

When her eyes came up, they were as hard and as cold as onyx. "I want my son. And you can get him for me. My Justin had nothing to do with any of this. You were once a nice boy, Carlos, and now you're a powerful man, and that's why I came to you. If I was wrong, then I'm sorry. And I'm sorry for your daughter when she finds out what her father is."

That last comment brought darkness. "Did you just threaten me, April?" Threats never worried Carlos. Too many had been made over the years, and people in his line of work knew how to deal with them effectively. But something in the set of April's mouth rang a little bell of fear, deep inside his head.

"I made a promise," April said, her voice growing softer and more intense. "I swear to God, if I don't get my son back, everybody in the world will know what kind of business you're in. I'll name names, I'll—"

"You'll die."

April nodded, her eyes now clear and animated. She saw that she was making her point, and the realization energized her. "Perhaps. I expect you'll try. That's why the first paragraph of my letter begins, 'By the time you read this, I'll likely be dead at the hands of Carlos Ortega and Patrick Logan.'"

Carlos leaned closer. "Letter? What letter?"

This time it was April's turn to be smug. "*The* letter, Carlos. The one that will be in tomorrow's mail if I don't get my way."

"You're bluffing. You have no evidence."

"I have a missing son, and I'll do whatever I have to do to bring him back."

"You stand to make some powerful enemies, April."

"If I have powerful enemies, it won't be because I made them. It will be because they volunteered."

Carlos watched her for a long time, searching for the sign that she was frightened, that this was all part of a game. All he saw was determination. "Why not go to the police now, then, if you're so hell-bent on revenge?"

"I believe Logan when he says he'll kill Justin if he smells police. He would be stupid not to. For right now, though, nothing's happened that can't be undone."

"Why won't he just kill you both?"

"Maybe he will. I'm hoping he won't. But either way, I want my son back, and I was hoping that you might be the one to talk sense into him."

Carlos took in a deep breath, then let it out as a sigh. "You've got balls, April, I'll give you that. You understand, don't you, that no matter what happens, I won't be able to protect your husband?"

April sensed that a deal had been struck. "I wouldn't ask you to."

16

IF RUSSELL COATES were elected king, he'd have found a way to decree that FBI agents could have a stellar career within the Bureau and still remain anonymous to the media. Back in the Hoover days, that's exactly how it was, as Melvin Purvis—John Dillinger's nemesis—had found out the hard way when the newspapers had dared to tout him as a hero during a time when J. Edgar preferred to work the spotlight alone. For Melvin, it got so bad that he ultimately ate his own pistol.

These days, the opposite was true. Media attention steered careers. Face time mattered in a high-profile case, and the more you got, the better off you were—up to the moment you stepped on your own dick, at which point your career took on all the aerodynamic properties of an anvil.

Russell wanted none of it. He saw every reporter as a snake, ready and willing to trash any investigation for the sake of the story, and he was physiologically incapable of concealing his hatred. Not a good trait when you're doing a live television interview.

Thus, Russell apologized to no one for establishing his command post up at the murder scene, rather than down on the fire road where it would be much more comfortable. The decision frosted Tim Burrows's ass, he knew, but that was just icing on the cake. Why else would Tim have dressed in his GI Joe suit if not to preen a little for the cameras?

Russell chose as his own seat a deadfall—oak, it looked like, or maybe ash (hell, he didn't know from trees)—while the others either stood or sat Indian-style, reminding him of campers gathered around the campfire for a ghost story. Burrows was there, directly across from his boss, and so was Henry Parker, the chief criminologist on the scene. Lieutenant Homer LaRue was supposed to be there, too, representing the West Virginia State Police (only in West Virginia, Russell thought, do parents actually name their children *Homer*), but he was still on his way up from the parking lot. At the very end of the line sat Russell's new pal, Sarah Rodgers, unofficially representing the Park Service, and in general helping him to conclude that maybe midlife wasn't such a bad place to be.

"Okay, Henry, why don't you start?" Russell said, jump-starting the meeting. Parker had the best eye for detail that Russell had ever encountered, and he routinely counted on him to get everybody thinking in the right direction.

A big man, with huge shoulders and a thick waist, Henry Parker looked more like a bouncer than one who made his living plucking the magic needle out of ten-story haystacks. He had the kind of voice that made bears and lions change direction in midstride, for fear of entering the wrong end of the food chain.

"Well, it'll be a day or so before we have a coroner's report back, but I'm guessing the firearm used here to be a big one—I'm guessing .44 or .45. We've got big holes in the victim and a big scar in a tree, but no slug recovered yet. It appears that both the victim and the shooter were on the ground when the shots were fired, but because the decedent's clothes are all in place, I tend to discount the rapist theory.

"I think we've already ruled out the rapist scenario," Tim Burrows said, exercising his vocal cords again.

Parker shot him a look. "I'm thrilled to hear that, Agent Burrows. You want me to stop?"

Burrows blushed. "No, please continue. I just thought you'd like to hear what path we were on."

By Russell's calculation, Tim Burrows was learning to ride a two-wheeler when Henry Parker was closing his first case. The older man did not suffer mouthy agents well.

A snappy retort passed Parker's mind—it was right there where everyone could see—but he opted to keep it to himself. "Continuing, then. In examining the casts of footprints, I've got at least a dozen possible unsubs here, not counting the victim."

"He's not a cop!" a new voice boomed from behind. They all turned to see Homer LaRue hurrying in from the path. Paunchy yet athletic, he had the look of a man who left little doubt in the minds of his prisoners that they'd by-God been arrested. "Our dead guy's not a cop. At least, he wasn't the cop his badge says he was. I checked on this Stipton guy, and the Pittsburgh PD reported that *their* Thomas Stipton was on duty this morning, working a double shift. He did, however, report his badge stolen about two months ago." Homer remained standing as he joined the little circle.

The intrusion obviously annoyed Parker, who started to speak again, before Russell cut him off. "This puts an interesting spin on things," Russell said. "Now we have an armed man in the middle of the woods masquerading as a police officer. That right there is a detail I don't want to see in the media, okay?" To Homer: "Lieutenant, who else knows what you just told us?"

"Nobody, I guess. I made that call myself."

"All right, then," Russell warned. "If I hear it in the press, I'll know it came from this group, and I assure you that I will not be a happy camper." He looked a little too directly at Agent Burrows as he added, "I will make it my personal business to plug any leaks with the toe of my shoe. Anyone have any questions on that?"

Russell scanned every face and saw what he wanted to see before turning back to Parker. "Sorry, Henry."

Parker cleared his throat and acknowledged his cue with a quick nod. "I was saying we have footprints from about a dozen unsubs. Now remember that unsubs are just that—unknown subjects. All that means is that twelve or more pairs of shoes walked around the two identified sites up here. For all I know, it was one guy with a shoe fetish. Now, here's what's interesting: of those footprints, only three sets are found both here and at the grave or pit or whatever the hell we're calling that big hole in the ground up there."

"*Grave* sounds good to me," Russell said, and Parker nodded. It sounded good to him, too.

"And of *those* three, one of them appears to belong to a child, maybe two or three years old. I'm guessing from the imprint that he was wearing something on his feet, but nothing very substantial. Maybe a pair of moccasins, or even a pair of socks, but he was definitely in both locations."

"You say he, Henry," Russell interrupted again. "Does that mean—"

"It means I'm not comfortable calling a child it. But I have no reason to suspect boy over girl, or vice versa."

Russell gave a quick nod and gestured for Parker to continue.

For the first time, Henry consulted a set of notes, just to make sure he was getting the details right. "Okay. Now, the second of the three common sets of prints belong to our dead cop—er, our dead *guy.*" Henry wasn't used to correcting himself in public. "The third set belongs to that set in the woods, where somebody apparently stood for a long time. Big guy, too, judging from the depth of the prints. Let's call him unsub one. Two will be our noncop dead guy, and three will be the kid. Y'all with me?"

Everyone nodded, Sarah more enthusiastically than the others, making Russell smile. *Chicks dig cops.*

"Good. Unsubs four and five are a man and woman, or man and adolescent, I guess. How's big and medium? Anyway, prints from four and five are everywhere here at this scene, but nowhere up the hill. Curiously, though, I found prints from four and five *and* the kid down on the fire road, next to some tire tracks that I'm guessing belong to some kind of sports utility vehicle."

Everybody stared, waiting for more. "That's it," Henry said. "At least until I get lab reports back from the trace evidence we've picked up."

"And you'll have me some manufacturers and model numbers on all those footprints and tire treads?" Russell asked.

Henry shrugged with one shoulder. "Well, certainly I can get you a make and model on the tire. Hell, I can have that for you before bedtime tonight. The shoes might be a little harder. Particularly for unsubs four and five. I'll know more after I study the casts, but at first glance, they look like standard Vibram soles. You can narrow that down to a few dozen brands, I suppose, but tighter than that'll be tough. For unsub two, you've already got the whole body, so that shouldn't be too much of a challenge. I have the most hope for one. Those prints out in the woods look kinda unique to me. I'm not sure I've ever seen that lug pattern before. I could be wrong, but I'll know the details tomorrow."

Russell closed down Henry's turn with an abrupt nod. "Okay, Tim, you're next. Tell me what we know about possible suspects."

Tim seemed startled to be called upon. "Well, I'm not sure there's much there that we didn't know hours ago." He recapped the claims of the young hikers Gary and Mandy, who seemed to think that they saw signs of a man and a woman down here, but never really eyeballed anyone. From there, the short list of potentials had been narrowed down to just a half dozen couples. Tim took a good four minutes to prove his initial assertion correct: he had nothing new to add.

"Oh, wait a second," Tim said, just as Russell was about to move on. "Henry, did you say the vehicle with the cluster of unsub prints was a sports utility vehicle?"

Henry half-sneered, "It's refreshing to know that everyone pays such close attention. Yes, that's what I said."

Tim finally grew a backbone and fired a fuck-you look to the criminologist. "Well, I've run all the names on that list, and only one of them owns an SUV." He shuffled through his notes till he found what he was looking for. "That would be a Robert Martin, 7844 Clinton Road, Clinton, Virginia."

Russell's eyebrows danced a little. Sometimes this police work wasn't as difficult as they liked to pretend. "And what's his history?"

Tim shook his head. "He doesn't have one. Not so much as a parking ticket, so far as I can tell. I can call the Richmond or Alexandria field office and have somebody at their doorstep in a couple of minutes."

Russell thought about that, then rejected it. "No, I think I'd like to pay a call on them myself. If I'm gonna be building a case, I'd like to look them in the eye." Too many agents these days liked to run investigations in which everybody else but the SAC did the legwork. If he was going to charge somebody with murder, he wanted it to be based on more than just the physical evidence on the scene. He wanted to get a feel for the people themselves, the way they met his gaze, the way they became indignant or defensive. These kinds of value judgments were a part of every field agent's report on an interview, but because they were so subjective, Russell preferred to be the one who jumped to his own conclusions.

"I'll start down there tonight, I think. Maybe see what I can find out."

Next, Russell turned to Sarah. "Ranger Rodgers, you're up."

"Me?"

The look of utter shock in her face made Russell laugh. That she laughed, too, instead of taking offense, raised her stock even more. "Yes. I need you to get these names and tag numbers to all of the entrance stations and tell your rangers to keep an eye out for them."

"You think they're coming *back?*"

"It's a cliché, I know, but it happens enough that we really should keep an eye out for it."

"Remember now," she added before Russell could move on. "Those entry stations are only manned eight hours a day. The rest of the time, people sign in on their honor."

Her comment ignited a ripple of groans through the assembled law enforcers. "Well, shit," Homer said, seeming to sum it up for the rest.

"What?" Sarah said, suddenly embarrassed and not even knowing why.

"That's a detail you could have mentioned a few hours ago," Tim grumbled.

"But I did—"

"That's enough," Russell barked, silencing everyone. "It's also a question we could have asked a few hours ago, so lighten up."

When Russell turned to Sarah, he seemed annoyed, but at the others rather than her, and for the first time she got the sense that maybe he was giving her special treatment. She felt her ears heat up, and she prayed that no one would notice.

"You said not everyone paid, but we didn't know that the stations weren't manned all the time," Russell explained. "That means that this short list of names we've got isn't necessarily as short as we'd hoped. Truth is, if I were going to come in here to commit a murder, I would probably wait until your people went off duty, and then I probably wouldn't worry too much about the honor system."

"Oh," she said, and cast her eyes downward. Okay, that was something that should have occurred to her all on her own. She knew, after all, what they were thinking about those names, and if she'd just—

"Don't worry about it, Sarah," Russell soothed. "You haven't hurt the investigation. You just made us realize that we're actually going to have to earn our salaries on this one. Really, it's not a big deal."

Russell had a nice smile. She hadn't noticed it before—certainly not in the early minutes of their time together this morning, when all she could see was one giant asshole—but now that she did, she found herself wondering if maybe he was really a nice guy. Could it be that he was actually *trying* to be nice? Not bad looking, either, with his high-and-tight sideburns and barely thinning light brown hair. She admired the way he seemed so determinedly unself-conscious. Everyone in authority had a role to play, she realized, and she liked the way he chose to play his hard professionalism without the bullshit that seemed to always come with the badge.

The meeting ended shortly thereafter, with the only remaining discussion being the rationality of trying to maintain a crime scene out here. In a perfect world, Russell would have loved to hermetically seal the entire area until after the arrests were made and the trials completed, but as a practical matter, that was never possible. The closest they could get on some cases was to keep a residence or an office sealed until they were 100 percent certain that every microscopic bit of evidence had been collected, but out here, where winds blew at random and rain fell whenever it wanted to, trying to preserve the crime scene in a pristine condition would have been a waste of time.

"I'm inclined to shut things down here," Russell said. "Henry? Any objections?"

Henry shook his head. "We might not have enough physical evidence to tell you where to look, but if you bring me a suspect, I got more than enough to either nail him or rule him out." And in the vast scheme of things, that was a hell of a lot more than they often had.

"Besides," Tim said, "once it gets dark, we're not going to be able to certify that the scene wasn't tampered with. Not if our bad guy gets himself a halfway decent lawyer, anyway."

Russell clapped his hands. "That's it, then. Our work here is done. Ranger Rodgers, you can have your park back."

"I appreciate that," she said.

"Thank you, ladies and gentlemen, for a very nice day's work. Henry, the instant you know any helpful details—"

"I'll get them to you, Russell. I haven't let you down yet, have I?"

Russell responded with a clap on the big man's shoulder and turned to Agent Burrows. "Timbo, I want you to make sure that the grave site or whatever the hell we're calling it—"

"Secondary crime scene."

"Right. I want you to make sure that the secondary crime scene is put back together. Fill in the hole with something. I don't want somebody falling in there and suing Uncle Sam, okay?"

Tim nodded.

"Oh, and make sure that everything we've done here is documented and assembled. Triple-check to make sure the chain-of-custody forms are filed exactly according to SOP. If I find a bad guy, I don't want it kicked because of something administrative."

Tim's face darkened. "I thought we were going to talk to that couple on the registration form."

Russell shook his head. "No, *I'm* going to talk to the couple on the registration form. You're staying here to make sure the scut work gets done."

17

APRIL SIMPSON STEPPED off the bus without even knowing where she was. Farther out in the suburbs, to be sure, but which one or which direction, she wasn't sure. She'd chosen this stop because of the shopping mall across the street, and because she felt that she needed to be with strangers for a while. She needed to be with people whose concerns today dealt with topics other than death and missing children. She needed to see that such a world still existed, because the one in which she really lived had begun to strangle her.

She needed to see a glimpse of sanity.

The weatherman had said that today would be warmer than yesterday, but it sure didn't feel that way. As she walked across the street, and then across the expansive parking lot, she drew her coat closer and tried to control the shivers that kept invading her spine.

He'll be okay, she told herself. *Carlos promised. Nobody would be foolish enough to go against him. Not even Logan.*

She'd given herself three hours to concentrate on thinking about nothing; three hours just to wander and pretend that everything was just as it was supposed to be. One of those hours had somehow already evaporated, and she'd need a second one to work her way back to the apartment, leaving her just sixty minutes to dream.

It was nearly three o'clock, and it occurred to her that she'd forgotten to call into work this morning. She was supposed to be running the lunch shift, too. No doubt there'd be hell to pay for that in the morning, but you know what? Right now, she didn't give a shit. The public could damn well make their own Quarter Pounders this afternoon.

He'll be fine, she told herself for the millionth time. *I know he'll be just fine.*

No matter where she looked, or what she forced herself to think about, all she could see was little Justin, cowering in a corner someplace, crying out for her, only to receive silence in return. Or worse yet, a smack or a kick.

The king of all drug dealers had given his word that her son would be returned to her unharmed. It had seemed like a victory at the time, but now that she thought about it, she wondered, where was the value in a promise from a thug? What would happen if Carlos made his pitch and Logan just told him to go to hell? Suppose he decided to kill Justin just for the hell of it—because April had had the balls to go and rat on him to Ortega? What would she do then? What would she be *able* to do?

Inside the mall, the heat had kicked in, making it ten degrees too warm. No one seemed to have told the furnace that it wasn't below freezing anymore. Given the hour of the day, April was surprised by the crowd, amazed by the numbers of shoppers with nothing else to do on a Monday afternoon. The pace seemed different, too. No one had that hard-core shopping stare that she always found so amusing to watch. These people—these ladies, really, because there wasn't a man in sight—seemed to be out for a carefree stroll, each of them with a little boy or a little girl in tow.

Everyone looked so happy. That was the hardest part. They looked so goddamned *happy.* They had their children in backpacks or in strollers or tethered to their sides by a tight handhold. Everyone was so normal. God, what she would do to change places with any one of them; to feel just the slightest trace of happiness somewhere inside her soul. What did these happy shoppers know about pain, anyway? They probably were afloat in money, wandering here through the mall in the middle of the day just looking for an excuse to spend some of it. They had smiling husbands toiling away at real jobs to provide for their families, and they'd never heard of the likes of Carlos Ortega or Patrick Logan. They didn't know what it was like to be abandoned by everyone and everything they had ever cared about.

Wandering the wide avenues of this indoor palace of a mall, past the Macy's and the Neiman Marcus and the Bloomingdale's, April realized she wasn't welcome here. She'd caught the sidewards glances from a few of the shoppers, and at first she hadn't quite known how to interpret them. Then, in a flash of realization, she was able to read their minds just as clearly as if they had been speaking directly to her.

April Simpson represented a part of the world that these ladies with their $100 slacks and $1,000 baubles couldn't possibly understand—a world they wanted to know nothing about. April remembered those days from her own youth, back when things were secure and bills were paid on time and the worst problems she faced on any given day had nothing to do with survival but only with shades of lipstick. Back in those days, success had nothing to do with luck or with social positioning. Success was what happened when you kept your head down and worked hard for long hours.

April watched these pretty, rich ladies and their babies and somehow knew that they'd blame all of this on her. They'd all assume that she'd been a bad mother; that she'd somehow brought this misfortune onto herself. Their assumptions would make them feel better about the thousands of dollars they spent on jewelry every year while giving maybe $100 to charities that helped people like her get a leg up on life.

These people didn't want her here because she represented all the things that made them uncomfortable. None of this would happen to them. They didn't live in neighborhoods where life was so cheap. They didn't hang out with the likes of Carlos Ortega, and they didn't allow people like William into their lives—people who stole money from other people on the street, and tried to take their two-year-old sons on outings to the local bar.

I had no choice! April's mind screamed. But suppose she had known that Justin would be taken from her one day at gunpoint. Would she have been able to find another option then?

You bet your ass.

She knew the risks of her neighborhood; they frightened her every day of her life, but she lived with it anyway. Marrying William had been an act of pure panic. In her haste to find somebody who could take the edge off the fear that came with her pregnancy, she'd chosen him as the simplest solution. But in choosing that safety, she'd knowingly put herself—and her innocent child—in the path of unspeakable dangers.

As she passed in front of a fancy cookie shop—Jesus Christ, $1.50 for one cookie!—she crossed gazes with a little boy in a stroller. He was the same size and coloring and bone structure as Justin, and he smiled as she stared. She smiled, too, but something in her expression sparked a panicked response in the boy's mother, who obviously felt something in the air and whirled to face April.

"Can I help you?" the woman said, sounding anything but helpful. She moved quickly to position herself between her son and this unshowered, frazzled woman in front of her.

April kept the odd, crooked smile, her forehead wrinkling against the pressure of tears behind her eyes. "I was just admiring your son." She'd meant it to sound friendly and easygoing, but the words came out laced with desperation. "He's beautiful."

"Go admire someone else," the woman snapped. Her tone was angry but her eyes showed fear. With that, she quickly wheeled her little boy away. When he turned to wave good-bye, the mother snapped at him to face forward.

That's when she saw that the little boy was Justin. The stranger was taking her baby away!

"Wait!" she yelled, and the woman started to run. "No, wait!" April hurried to catch up, but the woman just moved faster. This wasn't possible. It just wasn't possible. Why would that woman have her little baby? Was she the kidnapper? Surely not.

Off to her right, another woman came out of the BabyGap store, an overstuffed plastic bag in one hand, and then, there he was again, gripping her other hand. The two kidnappers had traded off somehow, and now Justin was with this other woman, who looked much younger than the first, but equally well-dressed. April pulled up short and gasped loudly enough to make the lady with the bag look around.

"Are you all right?" the woman asked.

Suddenly, April couldn't get enough air. *All right?* Was this woman nuts? *She has my baby, for God's sake!* April wanted to scream out; to get the attention of every person in the mall, but all that would come out of her throat was a tiny squeak.

And there was Justin! Again. Not with the bag woman, but with someone else down the hallway. Somehow, they had exchanged him off again. What the hell was happening?

"Oh, Christ," April breathed. "Oh, my dear sweet Jesus Christ." Justin was everywhere! And not just one at a time, either! He was back there at the cookie shop again! And over there in the stupid-looking fake park they'd constructed in the middle of the mall! Everywhere.

The woman with the bag moved forward and took April's elbow. She said something that April couldn't understand, and she knew that such an approach by a kidnapper should frighten her. It should scare the living shit right out of her. But she didn't feel frightened. She didn't feel anything, in fact.

The lady helped her across the shiny tile hallway, over toward an oak-colored park bench. April didn't feel her feet hitting the floor, but rather felt as if she were floating across the mall. Someone told her to put her head down between her knees, and the very thought of it made her want to laugh. She did it, though, and a moment later, the world started to make sense again. Colors returned to normal, and the sounds all around her started to have real form and meaning.

"Are you all right?" someone said.

April looked up, and there was the lady with the BabyGap bag. Next to her stood a frightened little boy who really looked nothing at all like her Justin.

April didn't know what to say. She should never have come here. She should have gone right home after visiting Carlos Ortega—gone home and waited by the phone; waited for some sign that everything would be normal again. She was just one phone call away from the greatest celebration of her life.

And one phone call away from a tragedy she couldn't bear to consider.

"Is something wrong?" the woman asked, confused.

"You have no idea," April responded, but the irony in her voice came out as sarcasm, and the woman took offense, clutching her son by his arm as if he'd done something wrong, and rushing off into the crowd, leaving April on the bench by herself, alone with her fears of going mad.

People all around her stared—the way people stare at a bum on the street who talks to himself. Their faces showed mild amusement, even as they struggled to look concerned. April hated them all. Who were they to judge her? Who were they to think whatever thoughts they entertained about her?

Suddenly, the mall felt too small. April scurried away from the crowd and willed her head to stop spinning. She needed to get home, regroup, and come up with an alternative plan of action. She'd placed the fate of her baby in the hands of killers and drug dealers. Logan had him, and Carlos was getting him back. Jesus, was she crazy? April was Justin's mother, not Carlos Ortega. It was *her* responsibility to get him back. Certainly, it was her responsibility to make sure that Carlos didn't screw things up.

What was it that Logan had told her about the money? Two thousand dollars by tomorrow and he didn't give a shit how she got it. Two thousand or two hundred thousand, it was all the same when you didn't have it.

Rob a bank if you have to.

Those were his very words. Rob a bank if you have to.

Suddenly, the little .25 in her jacket pocket weighed twenty pounds. Could it really be that simple? Could she really just march into a bank and walk out with all the cash she needed? People did it all the time. They got caught, sure, but all she needed was a couple of hours. Just long enough to get the money to Logan and to get Justin back home. After that, they could arrest her or do any other damn thing they pleased. Justin would be safe, and that was really all that mattered.

A couple of hours. She could do this. April tried to envision herself in front of the teller window with a gun in a little old lady's face, demanding all the money from the drawer. The lady would do it, of course, because that was what they were trained to do, and with the money in hand, April could solve all of her problems in one quick stroke.

Maybe she wouldn't even need the gun. She could just push a note under the teller cage, asking for what she wanted, and no one else would ever have to see anything; not until it was too late.

A couple of hours. That was all she needed.

Jesus, what the hell was she thinking? Robbing a *bank?* Was she out of her mind? People went to jail forever for bank robbery. Nobody cared what the justification was. If you threaten somebody's money, then you can absolutely count on a long ride to a jail cell. Do not pass go, do not collect . . . well, it had better be more than two hundred dollars.

April had wandered into Macy's and found herself staring at a rack of shirts. Men's dress shirts, wrapped in plastic, their folds knitted together with a thousand straight pins.

Along the back wall, over the display, April saw the words Credit Department, written in pewter-colored relief over a squared-off archway. The same letters went on to announce Customer Service, Public Phones, and Rest Rooms, but April didn't care about any of those other things. The credit department was where they kept the cash. She knew this from the time she'd gone to Monkey Wards to fight for her refrigerator and they kept her waiting on plastic furniture while the credit executive took care of more important matters. If this place was anything like that one, the credit department looked very much like a bank, complete with teller cages and cash drawers. Plus, so far as she knew, robbing a credit department was a local crime, not a federal one, for whatever that was worth, and it had to be worth something, didn't it?

Two thousand dollars would mean nothing to these people. They had single dresses in here that sold for more than that. Dresses that were worth more in their eyes than the life of her son. What kind of world was this, anyway? What kind of world would ever spin so far out of balance?

The lights were brighter on the other side of the archway, and the surroundings much less opulent. The business conducted in here, she realized, was the business of money, and where money is involved, no one has time for decorations and plush carpeting. Besides, how many reasons were there for customers to come back here? Certainly the rich ones with their perfect credit and their limitless Visa cards never had to deal with people behind cages. No, this area of the store was set aside for the deadbeats.

Only two tellers worked behind the elevated bank of windows, both of them women, and of the two, only one seemed to be receiving customers. The other, younger than the first by at least thirty years, seemed lost in counting money for her drawer. Cash. Thick stacks of it, and it didn't take but a small stack to make two thousand dollars. She knew this because it had only been a couple of hours since she'd carried nearly that much in her purse. The older woman, who looked maybe fifty years old and needed a trip to the hairdresser to take care of a root problem, sat closest to April and seemed to be suffering some kind of indigestion as she lifted her drugstore-issue reading glasses from their perch on her sagging breasts and planted them on her nose so she could squint at whatever it was that the customer had slid over to her. She started shaking her head even before she started reading, setting into motion the loops of the little red chain that tied the glasses to her neck.

"No, you see, dear, this isn't proof of anything. This is the letter that you sent to us. I need to see what we sent back to you."

The customer, who appeared way too young to have three children clinging to her legs, looked as if she might cry. "But I couldn't find my copy," she whined. "Don't you people keep copies of your own letters?"

The lady behind the cage laughed. "Oh, sure. I happen to keep copies of every letter the company writes right here in my pocket."

The words, and the tone with which they were delivered, angered April. She had no idea what had transpired, but she sure as hell recognized the body language. This mother was late on her debts, and the store was making her life miserable. They'd make sure that no other credit card company would trust her, and they'd file reports that would render even her checks useless. If she was more than a few weeks late, they'd start calling her home every night, and they'd talk to her boss and coworkers, ostensibly to locate her, but in reality doing everything they could to ruin her reputation. April had come to understand that debt collection was a form of legalized blackmail, and unless you were lucky enough to be one of the victims who attracted the attention of a television news program, nobody would give a shit.

April tried to look like the very essence of calm as she strolled over to the little writing podium across from the teller cages, but felt as if she were wearing a Watch Me sign around her neck. On the podium, she found cubbies full of forms and catalogs, and even a stack of stubby, poorly sharpened pencils, but no scratch paper. Finally, she found a Customer Comment form with enough space at the bottom for her to write what she needed. The block she chose on the form read, "Please tell us any way that we can make your visit to our store more enjoyable." In big block letters, and with an amazingly steady hand, April wrote:

> *Give me all the money in your cash drawer. Do not panic, and do not set off any alarms. I have a gun.*

Once done, she looked at the note for a long moment, making sure that it said exactly what she wanted it to say, then slid into line behind the woman with the squirming kids. She should be feeling panicky, she thought. Her heart should be racing, and her hands shaking, but she in fact felt a surge of pride that she was doing none of those things. Maybe it was because there was still time to change her mind. Up until the instant when the bitchy clerk read the note, she could just walk right on out of there and no one would be the wiser.

It's for Justin, she told herself. *Anything's legal when your son is in jeopardy.*

"I can help you over here, ma'am."

Startled, April looked up to see the young lady in the other cage flashing a bright, genuine smile at her. She waved her arm at April. "My drawer is ready now. I can take care of you."

April shot a glance at Queen Bitch, who sneered back at her.

Her mind screamed, *Wait! I'm not ready yet. I need to speak with this lady.* But she didn't say that. She didn't say anything, in fact. She just sidestepped out of the line and walked the five paces over to the teenager whose name plate identified her as Debby.

"What can I do to help you?" Debby asked.

Oh, Christ, she was friendly! April didn't want to have to look in the eyes of someone who was friendly. She wanted that sour-faced bitch who was making the young mother cry. How could she go through with this?

"Are you okay, ma'am?" Debby asked, her face wrinkled into a look of genuine concern.

April managed to nod, but that was all. Her voice refused to engage.

Those emotions she'd noticed were gone had all returned now, and suddenly, she didn't know what to do about it.

"Can I help you?" Now Debby talked to her as if she were slow-witted. Perhaps if Debby spoke slowly and enunciated carefully, her customer could understand.

Still speechless, April looked down at the slip of paper in her hand, and then back to Debby. Hesitantly, her hand slid forward across the ledge that separated them.

Their fingertips met, and Debby had to pull hard to slide the note out from under April's hand.

As soon as the note left her touch, April knew that she'd made a mistake. "No, wait," she started to say, but Debby had already unfolded the note and read it in what felt like two seconds. Color drained from the teller's face, and her mouth dropped as she inadvertently took a step backward, away from the counter.

"Oh, my God," Debby breathed, and she brought a hand up to her mouth. Her eyes filled with tears. "Oh, my God!"

The old bitch next door heard her and turned away from the customer with the kids. Instantly, she recognized the look for what it was and moved quickly to open Debby's cash drawer. "Just give it to her," the older teller said urgently. "Just give her what she wants."

But Debby continued to unravel. She couldn't move, her trembling fists clenched on either side of her jaw. "Please don't kill me," she begged. "Please, please don't shoot me."

Now the mother with the kids understood, and her eyes grew huge as she pushed the little ones behind her and started inching backward toward the door. "Oh," she moaned. "Ohhh . . . " Under different circumstances, she would have sounded like a ghost.

The older teller pulled handfuls of bills out of the drawer and shoved them onto the counter, not saying a word, and studiously avoiding eye contact. "Here you go. Take whatever you want. Take it all if you'd like."

April still hadn't moved, frozen in place by the fear of the others. In her jacket pocket, her hand closed more tightly around the little .25, and as it did, she felt a dash of panic herself. Everything was happening so quickly, yet it felt like entire days. The money stacked up on the counter—mostly twenties and smaller bills, it looked like, but she saw a couple of hundreds in there, too.

"Take it," the woman said again, shoving it closer to April. "Just don't hurt us, okay?" Several of the bills fell over the edge and floated lazily toward the floor.

That's when someone screamed. Not a bloodcurdling scream like in a horror movie, but a high-pitched, piercing "Oh my God!" that made everyone whirl to face the door. A young mother with a baby stroller had just entered and, at the first sight of what was happening, yelled and dashed back out toward the men's department. When the mother was out of sight, April heard her shout, "Oh my God, somebody's robbing the store! She's robbing the store!"

Shit!

The panic was very real now, and April realized that she didn't have a chance anymore.

"Take it!" the old teller insisted, and for an instant, April wondered if this woman wasn't *anxious* for her to take the money and get away.

April reached for it, then hesitated. She needed two thousand dollars. Every penny of it. Eight hundred or twelve hundred wouldn't do it, and with the bills forming such a loose, unbound pile on the counter, she'd never be able to grab that much and still get away. If she'd be able to get away at all.

"Take it!"

No. It wouldn't do. It wasn't enough, and taking too little would ruin her life for nothing. She decided to leave it there.

Saying nothing, she turned for the door. The abruptness of the move made the customer with the clinging kids yell and fall to the floor, protecting her children with her arms and her body.

Back in the men's department again, April moved quickly, winding her way through the maze of racks and shelves. She told herself that this was a stealthier—and therefore safer—route than the wide, unobstructed main aisles. Her meandering path made it impossible for her to run, but maybe that was okay. Maybe by not running, she'd be able to slip out of the store before this all grew to be too large to control.

"There!" someone yelled, and April whipped her head over her left shoulder to see a small army of young men and women approaching.

None of them wore uniforms, and none had weapons drawn, so she could only assume that they were store security people.

April broke into a run. She was busted now; no sense in trying to take her time or to blend in with the surroundings. They had her dead to rights, and her only chance for getting away was to make a break.

It had been a long while since April had run full tilt, but in the old days she'd been pretty fast on her feet. Despite the baby in her tummy, the racks of clothes flew by as she zeroed in on the big opening leading to the mall. Salespeople and shoppers alike shrank away as she headed toward them, and in the spot near the men's shirts where the aisle narrowed to virtually nothing, she collided with a wide, round rack of half-priced shirts and lost her balance, stumbling into some stacked cubbyholes and launching a ridiculous mannequin to his death.

Up ahead, she saw a woman about her size break eye contact and walk casually on a collision course while talking into a paper bag. More security. Christ, this place was tighter than Fort Knox.

April wished she had a plan. She realized now how stupid she'd been to even consider robbing a high-end store such as this, what with all of its cameras and security guards, but there wasn't much she could do about any of that now. Getting away—even for a few minutes—was her only priority. Behind her, she could hear the pace of footsteps pick up as the army of security people closed in on her. Up front, still more closed in on the doorway from the sides, even as she saw uniformed guards approaching from out in the mall, and it occurred to her that with every security guard in the Western Hemisphere descending on the front entrance of Macy's, other robbers could have the run of anywhere they wanted.

This was going to be tight. Shooting a quick look over her shoulder, April focused on that one undercover lady with the radio in her shopping bag. Only about twenty feet separated them now, and the guard stood flat-footed, hoping to block her quarry's path. April never even slowed down as she headed directly for the other woman, her shoulder low, and the impact barely made her stumble as the guard went airborne, crashing into the little pillar that was supposed to beep if you were stealing merchandise. April had no idea what those sensors were made of, but they didn't hold up well on impact.

The football-style block seemed to catch everyone else by surprise as April darted out into the mall, all of them slowing down long enough to see that their coworker was all right. April knew those few seconds could mean a lifetime for her. The store security people were essentially out of the race now, leaving her to beat only the three uniformed guys from the mall. April charged toward them, making this ultimately a battle of strength and will. The uniforms were all men, so they had her beat on the former, but when she pulled the little .25 from her jacket pocket and held it up where everyone could see, their will dissolved, and their strength became irrelevant.

"Jesus, she's got a gun!" one of the guards shouted, and all three of them slid to an abrupt stop.

Off to April's right, a lady screamed, igniting a panic like a match ignites straw. Some shoppers dropped to the ground while others took off the other way, and still more just stood, frozen with fear. April had never seen such a response. The security guards seemed most frightened of all, dropping to the hard tile and shouting frantically into their radios.

Whatever she was going to do, this was the time to do it. Never breaking her stride, April sprinted through the mall park, easily dodging the loosely rooted trees and oversize synthetic rocks. Her Keds dug deeply into the mulch as she struggled to find her footing. Reaching the waist-high handrails that separated the public from an intensely chlorinated babbling brook, she scooted under the closest side, landing knee-deep in the frigid water, and scrambled on her hands and knees under the railing on the other side. She plowed through the arrangement of pansies and marigolds, past a small cluster of dogwoods, and finally came out on the other side of the park.

The people on this side seemed much calmer than the ones on the other, as if they were oblivious to the commotion around them. A quick look left and another to the right. Nothing between her and the doors leading to the long hallway to the emergency exit.

She crashed through the double doors, only vaguely aware of the dweebie-looking store clerk—had to be from an electronics department somewhere—that she sent ricocheting off the wall and onto the floor.

Behind her, she could hear the electronics dweeb picking himself up off the floor as the army of security guards crashed through the same doors. April heard the impact against the poor guy's body, and as he said, "Oof," someone else said, "Oh, shit. Sorry."

She didn't know why that struck her as amusing, but this trip to the mall had been so surreal that everything had a bit of a twist to it now.

She turned her body sideways at the emergency door to hit the crash bar with her hip. It flew open as if it were made of cardboard, and as advertised, the tiny speaker on the lock bleated an ugly screech of an alarm.

Finally out in the daylight again, April headed for the parking lot, still wishing that she had some semblance of a plan. Where could she hide? How could she get away? She briefly considered firing a shot back at her pursuers, just to get them to hold back, but dismissed the idea as stupid. With her luck, her random bullet would score a fatal hit on somebody.

Running was an option for only so long. Her legs had grown as heavy as her belly, made heavier still by the two pounds of water soaked into the fabric of her pants, and her wind was giving out. To surrender meant losing Justin, though, and she wasn't about to do that. Not without a hell of a fight.

But what kind of fight would it be? The way she figured it, in fifteen seconds, thirty at the most, they'd be on her, and with that many against one, God only knew what might happen.

So, she fired a shot. Into the ground at her feet. In the vastness of the open parking lot, it sounded like nothing—tinier than a firecracker—certainly not enough to put fear in the hearts of her pursuers. So, she fired again. This time, she saw the sunbaked pavement dimple at the spot where the bullet drilled in.

And the pursuing footsteps stopped. She still didn't dare turn around to look, but she'd have heard them if they were still coming. This was good. This was her chance.

Her legs had grown rubbery by the time she reached the end of the long row of cars. Directly in front was a road that crossed her path at a right angle, and beyond that, more parking lot. How on earth—

She never even saw the guy coming. From off to her left—could it possibly have been over the top of a parked car?—she saw a flash of blue shirt, and then she was airborne. She didn't fall, though. Rather, she felt a beefy arm around her waist, and the sheer momentum of the tackle drove her sideways into the back panel of an enormous sports utility vehicle. A wiper arm gouged her flesh, and as her ear rammed into the back window, she heard a crunch and was instantly bathed in a shower of tiny glass beads. Blue and yellow lights flashed behind her eyes as she tumbled to the pavement amidst all the broken glass, but it seemed as if she never made it to the ground. It was just one long fall without an impact. Somehow, though, she found herself on the ground, covered with glass, and surrounded by people who were all shouting at her to do something. When she tried to stand, the glass beads bit deeper, and she saw blood on her hands. Blood? Where did that come from?

Finally, she was able to raise her head high enough to see a face or two. She recognized the flashes of blue uniform, and curiously, she noted that the boy closest to her—that's what he was, too, a teenager; nowhere near old enough to call himself a man—had pretty eyes that nearly matched the color of his shirt. Handsome, too, with teeth that sparkled when he smiled, just like in those toothpaste commercials.

Only, this wasn't a smile, was it? No, this was a sneer, and the sneering boy had a stick in his hand. As April saw the stick coming around toward her head, she tried to say something to make him stop, but there really wasn't any time.

18

BOBBY TURNED OFF the radio and closed his eyes. He sat still in the Explorer for a long time before pushing the button to activate the garage door. This magnificent house—the one they'd extended themselves so far to afford, in hopes of filling its five thousand square feet with a tribe of screaming, laughing children—seemed to mock him now. As daylight entered his side of the garage, he could see the planks that he'd stacked against the far wall with the intention of one day building shelves, and he gasped at the realization that none of the grandiose home projects he'd planned would ever be started, let alone completed.

As the door rumbled upward, he wondered just how long he had. He thought about the letters he should write to his parents and his childhood friends, but checked himself. Everything he did between now and whenever was just so much more evidence to be used against him. He was playing for keeps in a game where every move counted.

His empty spot gaped at him, and his mind conjured a giant bony finger—Death's bony finger—beckoning him to take his foot off the brake and just glide on into the spot from which he'd never be permitted to leave.

Kidnapping.

Murder.

Both capital crimes and he was guilty on both counts. Jesus, what was he going to do?

He knew the solution, of course. All he had to do was muster the courage. There were two solutions, actually, but he knew he could never take his own life.

But he could run away. He could lift his foot from that brake and whip the wheel hard to the right, and he could be doing eighty miles an hour to anyplace else in the universe in less than ten seconds. It was that simple.

He'd miss Susan, of course. Miss her terribly. But she'd have the baby she'd always wanted, and she wouldn't have the sword of his eventual capture hanging over her head. She could get on with her life.

But what could she reasonably expect from her life? How could she ever justify or explain the sudden appearance of this child? A three-year-old child at that. She couldn't possibly explain it. Truly, they were painted into this corner together.

They could move away, he supposed; just disappear from everyone they knew and then raise the child as if they'd always had him, but what would be the point of that? Bobby's whole desire for children was rooted in his need for family, his need to project and absorb even more love than he already felt for his parents and his wife and his siblings. To have a child merely to disappear made no sense. No sense at all.

But to stay meant facing the music. If not today, then certainly another day soon, and when the music played, their future together would evaporate anyway.

What about a midnight drop-off on the steps of a church or a hospital? Given that he could even talk Susan into doing such a thing, would that make his situation better or worse? And what about the boy? How many times could an innocent child be abandoned before the damage became permanent?

These thoughts made his mind lock up, paralyzed by more emotion and information than he could process in a lifetime. He knew there was an answer—there always was in these things—and he knew that if he did things correctly, he could make everyone understand that the story he had to tell was true. The truth sets you free, right? That's what the Good Book said. Or so he'd been told. The Good Book had never quite made it to the top of his recreational reading pile.

Whole minutes passed as he sat in the driveway contemplating his escape from reality. So much of this didn't add up for him. For example, why would a cop be out there in the woods at such a ridiculous hour? And if there was a mysterious partner named Samuel, why didn't he step forward to help?

Why was the little boy so terrified of a police officer who presumably was there to help him out?

Answer: Good deeds weren't on the police officer's agenda. God knew there were enough examples of cops stepping over the line to join the bad guys. And why hadn't any of the radio news reports mentioned that the dead man was a cop? They talked about solid leads and an ongoing manhunt, but never a word about such an important detail.

Bobby understood that perhaps the police would withhold certain aspects of an investigation, but could they possibly keep a detail like that quiet? And why would they want to? It seemed to Bobby that the public would be all that much more willing to assist in the manhunt if they knew that they were hunting a cop killer.

There hadn't been a word about a missing child, either. What about that? Maybe, because it had all happened in West Virginia, that portion of the story was considered of local interest only, and therefore hadn't made the cut for the Washington broadcasts, but surely even the dimmest bulb in the journalistic lamp would speculate on some possible connection between the two stories.

On the other hand, maybe Bobby was simply grasping for straws here and didn't have a clue what the hell he was talking about. Maybe the police and the FBI knew everything they needed to know, and they were merely amassing the forces they needed to swoop down on sleepy little Clinton with a SWAT team the size of the 101st Airborne.

Fact was, Bobby didn't know a thing, and the more he thought about it, the faster his heart raced.

Finally, his foot released the brake and he glided into his parking space, just as if this were any other day. As he opened his door and stepped out into the chilly garage, he realized that he was all alone; Susan's aging Chrysler Concorde wasn't in its slot. The butterflies that had never stopped their frantic beat in his stomach grew three times in size. Where the hell could she have gone? He left the plastic Kmart bag on the concrete floor and hurried toward the door.

His key found the lock, and he rushed into the kitchen, closing the door behind him. "Hello!" he called, but silence swelled all around him. "Susan?"

No answer.

"Susan? Where are you?"

Instantly paranoid, he noticed that the note he'd left on the kitchen counter was missing, and he gently touched the spot. Off to his right, he threw a casual glance toward the sprawling, underfurnished, two-story family room, where the grand stone fireplace stretched a good twenty-five feet all the way up the far wall. No sign of anyone; not even the daily paper, which always lay in neatly stacked sections on the ottoman.

"Susan?" Maybe if he yelled it loudly enough, he'd be able to shake the feeling of dread. He found himself walking on tiptoes as he passed through the bare dining room and on into the faux-marble foyer. Out here, his voice echoed when he called her name. He climbed the sweeping staircase.

What were we thinking when we got white carpeting? Funny what invades your mind when you're scared shitless.

"Susan?"

He moved faster now, and he headed first for the nursery, where once again he found no sign of people.

Oh shit, oh shit, oh shit . . . The only other logical place was the master bedroom. The door was closed, and as he approached, he called out one more time, "Susan!"

Boxes lay strewn about the bed, some opened, most not, and he recognized little bits of festive wrapping paper from the day of the baby shower his staff had thrown for Steven back in December.

What the hell . . . ?

And then he got it. She was digging for baby clothes. But why? That's why he'd sneaked out to Kmart. She had to know that, because she'd obviously read his note. And what good would it do to try to stuff the kid into clothes designed for newborns?

Daniel Portis.

The name popped uninvited into his mind, and in that second, everything became clearer. Daniel was a junior sales rep who dealt only with small-business accounts and had no concept of how large a baby might be. He'd given as a gift an overalls outfit that looked more like a first-grade ensemble than something for a baby. Bobby remembered how hard a time everyone gave the young man for being so out of touch, and how well he took it. "Say what you like," Daniel had countered at the time, "but they'll have forgotten all about your silly-ass presents when the kid is just beginning to appreciate mine."

Obviously, Susan had remembered that as well, and she'd come in here hunting down the outfit for the baby. But why? Where could they possibly want to go?

The hospital. Suppose something had gone terribly wrong, and either she or the baby was hurt. How could he find out if that's what had happened?

Samuel.

That name kept shooting to the forefront of his consciousness. The mysterious Samuel, who refused to help his friend. Maybe he'd finally figured out who they were, and he'd come to get his revenge. Maybe he'd come and taken them.

No, that was ridiculous. "Stop it, Bobby," he told himself. He spoke aloud, as if audible wishes were somehow more binding. "Just stop it. There has to be a logical explanation for it all."

People don't just disappear.

He scoured the bedroom for a note, for some indication where she might have disappeared to, but all he found was unending neatness, marred only by the mess on the bed. He searched the nursery next, and finally the entire downstairs. Not a trace.

So, what was he supposed to do now?

This was a silly, stupid thing to do, and Susan knew it.

She should have stayed cloistered in the house, with the shades pulled, but she just couldn't stand it anymore. Bobby had run off, hadn't he? He *never* did any shopping—*always* bitched when she wanted him to go, even when the trip to the mall was to replenish his wardrobe. Why, then, did he decide to go today? It was obvious, wasn't it? He needed to get out of the house. She couldn't blame him for that, and she certainly harbored no ill feelings because of it, but she had to have a life, too, didn't she? If she spent one more minute cooped up in that house, she'd surely go crazy. There hadn't been any cheer in that place in weeks, and even with the new addition to their family, the depressing pall still lined every room like so much black wallpaper.

Besides, Steven needed a change of scenery, too. Now that he was rested and fed, there was no containing him anymore. He bolted non-stop around the house, exploring every corner, turning every knob, and opening every drawer. Watching his antics reminded her of the Tasmanian Devil from the old Bugs Bunny cartoons. She'd never seen a child so intent on exploring his surroundings. And his touch was anything but light. Jamming the buttons on the hundred-disc CD changer in the family room, he might as well have been using a hammer as his fingers, and as she tried to keep up, her mind conjured a vision of abject destruction. It was just Susan, Steven, and the ever-present Tiger. The poor creature's ear would likely never recover from the crushing grip it had endured all morning.

So, here she was, in Montgomery County, Maryland, unloading her new son out of the car, and wondering what exactly she was going to say if she ran into someone she knew. Thanks to a huge haul in shower gifts, combined with Steven's relatively small size, she'd been able to dress him and to provide him with a car seat. (And just who were the brilliant engineers who designed a piece of safety equipment that required four hands to operate?) As she wrestled the stroller out of the trunk, she kept a vise grip on the boy's hand to keep him from bolting out into the parking lot and playing the chase-me game through acres of shopping mall.

Steven whined and squirmed against the restraint, pulling with all he had to get away from her. For someone who couldn't yet weigh thirty pounds, he pulled with the force of a tractor, making it impossible for Susan to keep her balance. Finally, she'd had enough, and she turned on him angrily.

"Steven, now stop it!" she commanded, but he wouldn't listen. He let his legs fold under him and he dangled from one arm, his knees barely suspended over the pavement. Susan jerked him once to his feet and gave him a quick shake. She couldn't possibly have hurt him, but judging from the look of shock on his face, she'd finally gotten his attention.

"You will hold my hand while we're in the street, do you understand?"

He just stared, though she could see in his eyes that he considered pulling against her again.

"I said, do you understand me?"

Finally, he nodded, pulling Tiger in a little closer.

She rewarded him with a smile. "Good. Then you just hang on a minute and I'll get your stroller."

This time, the boy stayed still, and a few seconds later, she had the stroller out of the trunk. She nearly cheered when the whole thing came together with the push of a single button.

"I'm guessing he's two," said a voice from close behind.

Susan jumped and whirled to see somebody's grandmother crossing the parking lot behind her. The lady was smiling, but the warmth in the smile cooled when she saw the look in Susan's face.

"Your little boy," the woman explained. "I haven't had a two-year-old in my house for nearly forty years, but you learn to spot them at a distance."

Susan felt hot as she forced her shoulders to relax. "Oh, he's a handful, all right."

The grandmother smiled and kept walking.

That was precisely the kind of encounter that made this trip to the mall so foolish. That woman could have been her next-door neighbor, for God's sake, or someone they knew from Bobby's work—people who knew about the real Steven and would undoubtedly ask questions she was ill-prepared to answer.

At that moment, she realized what Bobby had wanted to talk to her about. They needed to leave Clinton, needed to leave Virginia altogether, and maybe even the East Coast. They had to go someplace where no one would ask questions for which there were no reasonable answers. They had to buy time to let things untangle a bit; time to let people forget about the body in the woods, and for Bobby and her to get to know this little boy who was now such a part of their family.

Suddenly, it was all so clear. This was what God had ordained when He set this little boy loose in the woods for them to find. His will be done.

There'd be problems, she was sure. Some bitter memories from the boy's past that he'd have to grapple with, and maybe even some acting out as he got older. She'd seen a piece on television once how neglected children from the old Soviet Union had difficulties with their emotions, long after they'd been thoroughly assimilated into wonderful, loving American families. There was just no predicting the results of early-childhood emotional trauma.

But that was a mother's job, wasn't it? To protect her baby from all things that might harm him, whether the threats be physical or emotional. She and Bobby were fortunate to have the means to provide for Steven in a way that many other children would never see. They could afford the best doctors, whether here in the United States or somewhere abroad. And God knew they had a big enough and deep enough reservoir of love from which to nurture the boy to his full potential.

Steven's days of mistreatment were over. No more filth for him; only the best clothes and toys. The world would be his for the asking, and she would personally guarantee the delivery. Just look at how well he responded to her gentle discipline out there in the parking lot. If she weren't a natural at parenting—and if all if this weren't as preordained as it obviously was—then he would never have responded as well as that.

Inside the mall now, Susan strolled tall and proud. Oddly enough, this was one of the moments that she had most looked forward to back in the days before Steven was born. Just as she was sure that Bobby had fantasized about vicarious victories on the baseball diamonds and soccer fields, she used to dream of the all-day trips to the mall. They'd buy some clothes and eat some junk food and maybe even play on one of those little McDonald's playgrounds for a while. This would be their bonding time, when they could just stroll and talk and watch the people as they walked by. In her fantasy, her little boy would tell her about his fears and his loves. There'd be none of those communication problems you hear about in other families. Not in the Martin household, no indeed. Susan and Bobby would provide an environment where the children could talk about anything without fear of disapproval. And part of that environment came from places like this, where mother and son could be friends among strangers.

She knew it was unreasonable to push so hard, but she worried about the boy's refusal to talk. If he wanted something, he would point and whine and squeal, but he wouldn't form words. She wondered if that didn't have something to do with the filth and the lack of care for the boy. He probably suffered from some developmental challenge that his former mother had never thought to have checked.

But he sure said the word *Tiger* clearly enough. That one rang like a bell in his sweet little angel voice.

How could anyone ever hurt such a beautiful child as this?

Their first stop was the children's department of Saks Fifth Avenue. She'd long ago surveyed all the stores in the area and decided that her baby would have only the best, and the best of the best was right here in Saks. In just over thirty minutes, she'd bought him four new pairs of pants, six shirts, a pair of nightie-nights, and a stack of underwear. For the most part, he behaved like a champ, diverting himself by pulling on the dangling price tags and squealing with laughter when something would pop off the rack and fall down on his head.

Susan didn't even bother trying things on. He was way too squirmy for that. Besides, why should she risk it? She'd never forget the words of wisdom she'd received from her mother, back before . . . well, before the bad times: *Never try to make a happy baby happier.*

Finally, it was time to check out. Susan carried the mound of clothes in one arm as she wrestled the stroller with the other.

"Isn't this one a cutie?" the salesclerk bubbled, coming around the register to tickle Steven with a playful poke to his tummy, and getting the giggle she'd been mining for. "Good heavens," she said as she stood up again. "He looks just like you, doesn't he?"

Susan beamed.

19

CARLOS ORTEGA HADN'T driven himself in years. He could afford any car in the world, but chose a Jeep Cherokee. Decked out with every trinket the manufacturer offered plus a few more, the Cherokee gave him all the comfort and status he wanted, without the baggage that accompanied glitzy limousines and flashy sports cars. He wasn't a pimp, and he had no desire to make people think otherwise.

Peña drove. That was it; no big entourage of bodyguards and hangers-on. He left that shit for the Italians in New York. Carlos believed that strength was a perceived commodity, rooted in fear and respect. People who traveled from place to place surrounded by paranoid thugs projected weakness, a fear that they could not handle themselves without reinforcements. By keeping an image that was close to the population he served, Carlos demonstrated that he was first a friend, and then a businessman. Those who needed to know differently were fully informed, in terms that were universally understood. If anyone wanted to take a shot at him, they'd first have to get past Peña. To date, only two people had tried, and neither of them had lived through the experience.

Carlos didn't think about his own death much anymore; not since he'd settled on his franchise theory of operation and educated all his suppliers on the benefits of mutual dependency. In the Milford neighborhood, everybody knew Carlos, and most admitted that life was a hell of a lot better for them now than it had been when a different gang controlled every corner. Even the cops knew, and they showed little interest in interfering with the flow of commerce. As long as things stayed peaceful, everyone was happy.

Which brought him to the reason why his black cherry Cherokee was navigating the litter-strewn street en route to his surprise meeting with Logan: he was here to keep the peace.

As Peña whipped the Cherokee into a narrow space between two junkers in front of Logan's brownstone, Carlos noted the three young men who lounged at the foot of the stairs. The tallest of the three saw the vehicle first, and from there the word spread in less than a second. The tall one dashed up the concrete steps and disappeared inside, while the other two closed ranks down below.

"Oh, they look tough." Peña laughed.

"Take it easy on them," Carlos warned. "They're young."

"And impressionable."

When Peña said *impressionable,* Carlos knew he was thinking *dentable.* "I don't want any scenes out here in the street." Carlos slid out of the passenger seat and waited by the front bumper till Peña joined him, then together they headed for the front door.

A kid Carlos had never seen before—all of maybe eighteen years old and sporting a head of orange hair—stepped forward to block their path. "Can I help you?" the kid challenged.

"I don't think so," Carlos said, and he elbowed past.

"Hey!" Recovering his balance, the kid reached under his jacket, but then froze as Peña clamped a claw around his windpipe.

"That's Carlos Ortega, asswipe," he said, and the recognition in the kid's bulging eyes was instantaneous. "Now stay the fuck out of the way." Peña released the kid, but didn't wait for an answer before joining his boss climbing the steps.

Carlos tried the knob, then rang the bell. The door opened ten seconds later, revealing the kid he'd seen run inside. Up close like this, Carlos recognized him as Ricky Timmons, Logan's poor imitation of Peña. The kid looked as if he was about to say something when Peña stiff-armed the door and sent him backpedaling into the foyer.

"Where's Logan?" Peña growled.

A moment passed—an instant, really—where Timmons considered turning this confrontation into something that would have ended his life. He kept his gaze locked with Peña's for a moment more, but it was all for show, with no resolve to do anything stupid.

"I'm in here," Logan's voice called from behind a closed door to their left.

Carlos pulled open the pocket doors and entered a cheaply furnished living room. He waited while Peña followed and closed the doors behind them. The walls screamed for paint almost as loudly as the furniture screamed for slipcovers. Carlos knew a thing or two about Logan's upbringing and knew that to him, this was Buckingham Palace.

Logan sat with his feet propped up on his auction-reject desk, making a show of cutting a telephone conversation short. Despite his warning from Ricky Timmons, he feigned surprise as he stood to greet his visitors. A big man with too many freckles and a nose that labeled him a boozer, he had a single eyebrow that traversed a Neanderthal ridge over his eyes. Look up *Irish thug* in the dictionary and they have a picture of Logan.

"Hey, Carlos. What brings you here?"

Small talk wasn't on Carlos's agenda. "What's this shit I hear about you kidnapping some baby?"

Logan went right to the lie. He pretended to look confused, then realized that Carlos wasn't buying. "I had some business concerns I needed taken care of. Since when do you tell me how to do my business?"

The Irishman had a good five inches on him in height, yet Carlos noticed that the bigger man backpedaled as Carlos leaned closer. "It's not *your* business, Patrick. How many times do I have to pound that into your thick mick head? This isn't your business. This is *my* business, and I just happen to let you take a piece of it."

Logan rolled his eyes. "For God's sake, Carlos—"

"Shut up. I'll say it again so I know you hear it. This is *my* fucking business. You think of yourself as a franchisee, okay? That means you've got corporate rules and regulations to live by. Am I going too fast for you?"

Logan's face turned red. "Who the hell—"

"Shut up!" Carlos yelled it this time, and Logan jumped. "Just shut the fuck up and listen. And sit down."

Logan sat.

"I'm hear to make a speech, and you're here to listen. I don't even want to know why you nabbed this kid. I don't care. It was a stupid fucking thing to do."

The Irishman slammed his hands on the desk and shot to his feet. "Stupid! You come into my office and you have the balls—"

"Sit down!" This time, when Carlos yelled, the whole building seemed to move.

For a long moment, Logan tried defiance, but as Carlos narrowed his gaze and his eyes bore straight through Logan's body, the big man shrank. And he sat down.

"Stupid," Carlos said, locking onto Logan's eyes. "That's what I said, and I'll say it again. It was a stupid fucking thing to do. You got a beef with somebody, make it good. That's your business, and so long as you keep the blood off my streets, I don't care."

"Then why the hell are you here? That kid's old man owed me eighteen hundred bucks."

"His *father*, Patrick! His *father* owed you money. Not his mother, who visited me after you shit all over her, and not the kid himself, but his *father*. What exactly have you done to this father?"

"I took his fucking kid so he'll find a way to get me my money."

Carlos lashed out in a blur and slapped Logan across the face. Furious, the Irishman bolted to his feet and Carlos slapped him again. "Sit down." This time he said it so softly that Logan might not even have heard him. For a long moment, the two men just stared at each other.

"I could kill you," Logan seethed.

"Then you'd better do it on the first shot," Carlos snarled back. If it were anyone else in the world, this would look like Mutt against Jeff; it would have been comical. As it was, Logan backed down yet again.

"Here's what you're going to do," Carlos went on. "You're going to get that kid back and you're going to polish him up and deliver him to his mother without so much as a hair out of place. And you're going to do it by sundown."

Again, Logan looked at him as if he were crazy. "What about my money?"

"Forget about the fucking money. Or break that asshole's legs or dump him in the river, I don't care. But get that kid back."

"I can't do it by tonight."

"Why not?"

"Because he's not here, that's why."

"Then where the hell is he?"

"What, you think I'd lift a kid by myself? I contracted it out."

"To whom?"

"To some guy I know from in the hills."

"And how much did that cost you?"

Logan shrugged. "Another thousand."

Carlos couldn't believe what he was hearing. He turned to Peña for verification and got a shrug. "Let me get this straight. A guy owes you a couple thousand dollars, but you don't want to hurt him because you want to get your money back. This makes sense to me. But then you call some other asshole friend of yours to kidnap the boy, and that costs you *another* thousand. What the hell were you thinking?"

Logan dared a smile; a humorless twitch, really, involving only one side of his mouth. "Call it 'interest and expenses.'"

Carlos wanted to splatter that smirk straight into the peeling paint job. "So, how much does this Simpson guy owe you?"

The Irishman looked to the ceiling and closed his eyes as he ran some cryptic equation through his mind. "His old lady already made a deposit, so today, he could get by with eighteen hundred. Tomorrow, it'll look more like two thousand."

Carlos saw where this was going, but he wanted to hear it directly from Logan. "So, what happens when he finally tells you that he can't pay?"

Another shrug. "Well, then he's had a really, really bad day." Logan laughed hard at that one and didn't seem bothered that he was the only one amused.

Without a word, Carlos moved around to the end of the ugly desk, and then behind it, where he could get within striking distance. Logan tried to hold his ground, but ultimately rolled his chair backward, until he ran into Peña, whom he'd never even seen move into place.

Carlos rested his hands on the arms of the big man's chair and leaned in until less than a foot separated their noses. He intentionally assumed an open, vulnerable pose, as if to demonstrate that he feared nothing from this beer-swilling son of a bitch.

"And what about the boy?" Carlos hissed. "What happens to him if his father can't pay?"

For the first time, Logan's face began to show signs of real concern; as if he finally understood that he was in peril. He held his hands out to ward off the smaller man's advance and stammered, "Well, hell, Carlos, I—I n-never expected him to."

"What happens to the boy?"

Logan looked over his shoulder to see what might be coming at him from behind. "He, uh, well, you know. He—" The Irishman couldn't bring himself to say the actual words. "Come on, Carlos, for Christ's sake, it's only a kid."

Carlos held Logan's eyes for a long time and then, without shifting his gaze, nodded once.

Logan seemed to know what was coming, but when he tried to stand, Carlos pushed him back down. Before he could try again, Peña looped a thin nylon cord around Logan's neck and drew it tight, yanking the Irishman backward onto the floor. Logan flailed like a fish, fighting for breath, and as his eyes filled with terror, his fingers clawed at the garrote.

"Listen to me, Patrick," Carlos said, his voice much, much softer than before. "It's very important that you pay attention. Are you paying attention?"

Logan nodded as best he could as his face turned purple.

Carlos glanced once at Peña, and the cord loosened just enough to allow blood to flow and air to wheeze through Logan's bruised windpipe.

"You're an idiot, Logan," Carlos said evenly. "A stupid, worthless fucking idiot. Don't you understand why we've been able to achieve such quick success? It's because people fear me, and because they know that I'm good for the community. Me, I'm the United Nations and the Teamsters all rolled into one. We have rules for how we conduct business, and anyone who doesn't follow the rules gets taken care of. You know this, right? Tell me that you know this."

Logan gasped for air and nodded spasmodically. Yes, he understood.

"That's good. It's good you understand. You also understand that the cops leave us alone because we don't give them any trouble. We want to fuck somebody up, we take them someplace else. We don't shit in our own nest. You know this, too, am I right?"

Another gasp, another nod.

"Good. When word gets out, then, that one of the people who works for me is a fucking kidnapper, and that he targets two-year-old children, do you think that the police will continue to look the other way? Do you think that the people in the neighborhoods will continue to be our friends once they realize that you're willing to kill their children over a few dollars? Is that what you think?"

This time, the gasp meant no.

"I agree. That's why you're going to contact your buddy who has this child, and you're going to tell him to bring the baby home. Do you think you can do that?"

Peña held the tension a little longer this time, just to make the point. Carlos didn't wait for the answer.

"As far as the money is concerned, I don't give a shit what you do about that. But the kid comes home. Tonight."

Logan shook his head vigorously, and Carlos nodded for Peña to slacken his hold. Logan gasped, "I can't. Not tonight. He's too far away. Tomorrow. I can have him home tomorrow."

Carlos's eyes narrowed. "Where is he?"

"Someplace out in the mountains."

"In the *mountains!* What mountains?"

"W-West Virginia. I d-didn't want, you know, for the body to be found." Then, Logan added quickly, "If it came to that."

Carlos slapped him again, this time splitting the Irishman's lip. "You sick fuck," Carlos growled. But the slap didn't do it for him, and he followed it up with a punch that shattered the big man's nose. Blood and snot poured down the lower half of Logan's face, and Carlos took the ends of the garrote away from Peña and cinched them tight with his own hands. "You've got eighteen hours, Logan. Eighteen hours. By ten o'clock tomorrow morning, that baby had better be home with his mama, or I swear to God you'll wish that I had killed you here today."

For a long moment, Carlos considered killing him anyway, just for the hell of it. God knew it'd be easy enough, but the rules of business applied to the boss just as they did to everyone else. You don't shit in your own nest. Besides, the *real* problem was getting the kid back. With Logan dead, there'd be no way to fix that one.

"Eighteen hours, Logan," Carlos breathed, "and not a mark on him. Right now, that little boy is all that's keeping you alive."

Carlos and Peña turned and saw Ricky Timmons standing in the doorway, his jaw gaping.

"Hope you're taking notes there, kid," Peña said with a laugh.

Ricky didn't say anything. He just waited till the visitors were gone, then rushed over to help his boss as he gasped for air.

20

THE MORE BOBBY thought about it, the hotter his anger glowed. His nerves were shot; he just flat out didn't think he could take much more of this. In a moment of grim resolve, he realized that unless he took some kind of action right this minute, this terror he was living—this gnawing, low-grade nausea that wouldn't go away—would be the rule for the rest of his life. This was as good as it was going to get. Every knock on the door would be a potential cop, every look of recognition at the grocery store an accusation.

It was absurd. How could one five-minute episode in a thirty-four-year-old life cause so many problems? Jesus, it was just so far out of control. Nothing in nineteen years of schooling, or in his captainship of the debate team, or in the succeeding years of excellence in the business world, had prepared him for a moment like this. Presented with a circumstance totally out of left field, you react instinctively. You live or you die. And precisely by living—by *winning*, for God's sake—he had brought countless complications to his life.

He should turn himself in, evidence be damned. He was innocent—certainly, in his heart, if not by the letter of the law. Certainly, the police and the judge and jury would see that. And once proclaimed innocent, he'd get his life back, right? But what kind of life would it be? He'd lose his job, that was for sure. Benton and Arbrosi would never tolerate the hint of scandal—or felonies—from one of their senior account managers, and neither would any of their competitors. Like it or not, an arrest for murder would forever be the lead sentence in Bobby's biography, and no one would ever read as far as the phrase "not guilty." With his job would go the house, under the shame of foreclosure. The press would have a field day with it all, thrilling in the collapse of yet another successful baby boomer. It was the kind of story that *Dateline* and *60 Minutes* loved to do. Even if found innocent, he'd be lucky to find a sales job at a CompUSA, let alone at another prestigious software firm.

And that was the *good* scenario. God only knew what could happen with a few unlucky turns. Death row, he supposed, was the very worst. Or maybe life without parole. He'd never given any of it much thought before, but right at this moment, he couldn't decide which of those two options was truly the worst.

Bobby sat heavily on the blue tapestry sofa in the family room and eased his head back onto the cushions as he tried to figure out his next step. It had long been a counterproductive trait of his to retreat from difficult life decisions; to bury himself in work or merely to go take a walk or play a computer game instead of facing tough issues straight on. Experience had proven that most crises, if left alone, resolved themselves. But this one was different. This problem only got worse with each passing second.

His emotional pendulum had swung, and for the time being, turning himself in was out of the question. There had to be another way. There *had* to be.

Their first problem was the baby. Specifically, where to deposit him. With luck, a set of parents out there were frantic with worry over the loss of their little boy, and recovering him would make everything all right again. Unless, of course, the kid's father was a cop who just happened to be lying dead in the middle of the West Virginia woods. Either way, they needed to get this kid back to where he belonged.

Bobby liked the idea of dropping him off in a church. The more he stewed on it, the more reasonable it sounded. He'd have to time it just right, of course, waiting until nightfall and then just letting the boy loose inside the church until someone found him. Yeah, that could work just fine, couldn't it?

Until the kid decides to wander off somewhere.

An image of the sweet-faced little boy stepping out into traffic flashed into Bobby's head and made him shiver. What would be the legal liability then?

Jesus, Bobby, what are you thinking? What the hell difference did it make what the legal liability was? How could he even think in those terms?

Wherever they decided, it had to be someplace where they could keep an eye on him until a successful handoff could be made.

What about in a department store? A crowded one, where someone was bound to notice a lost boy wandering through the aisles. Another good possibility, except for the security cameras they had everywhere. Bobby could just see it now: The evening news showing grainy videotape of someone who looked just like Bobby entering the store with a little boy in tow, then leaving without one. He could hear the news anchor's commentary as he called on viewers to help identify this mysterious person who could be so irresponsible with his child.

Every time his brain churned up an alternative, he quickly shot it down again, either because it was too risky for the child or because it was too risky for Bobby. How the hell could anyone possibly lose a child? he wondered. If you couldn't find a way to do it on purpose, how could so many people have it happen accidentally?

The telephone rang, and the sound of it went through Bobby like a shot. He jerked up from the sofa, dashed to the kitchen, and lifted the receiver in the middle of the fourth ring.

"Hello?"

"Hi, Bobby, it's me," Susan said cheerfully. "I just realized that I'd forgotten to leave a note, and I wanted you to know that Steven and I are okay, and that we'll be out for the better part of the afternoon."

A chill raked Bobby's back, like fingernails from an invisible hand. "Steven?" He tried to say it lightly, but hearing the name in the present tense made his stomach flip.

She gave a naughty little giggle. "That's what I decided to call him. I've always liked the name Steven."

He leaned against the edge of the counter and switched the

phone to the other ear as he struggled to control his breathing. "I like the name, too. That's why we were going to name the baby that."

"And now I have." Bobby could see her beaming smile as she spoke. "God, he's so beautiful."

Beautiful. Right. They'd discussed this. "Look, honey, where are you? We need to talk about some things."

"I'm at the mall. I thought we said we'd talk about them later."

"The mall!" he shouted. "Are you crazy? What if somebody sees you?"

Susan laughed. "I'm at Buckingham. I wouldn't go anywhere we might know anyone. Give me credit for some brains, will you?"

"But *why,* Susan? Why would you do that?"

"You should see how Steven interacts with people, Bobby. He's such a charmer. I just love being with him."

Bobby's heart pounded a timpani beat against his breastbone. This was bad. He didn't understand exactly what was going on, but this was really, really bad. "Just stay where you are, okay, Sue? I'll get in the car and come and join you."

"Oh, no, that's okay. We're having a terrific time. Besides, I'm not sure how long I'm going to be here."

"No. No, honey, I can be there in what, forty-five minutes? It'll be fun."

"Bobby, you need to rest. You must be exhausted."

"No, really, I'm fine. Just give me a little while—"

"No, Bobby." This time, her tone was unequivocal, harsh. "We don't need you here. This is our special outing, okay?"

Okay? Hell, no, it's not okay! Thoughts raced at a million miles an hour, tracing a tight circle around his brain. He couldn't think of what to do next. He needed her home. He needed the boy home. Now. "Honey, listen—"

"Time to go. Steven's getting antsy in his stroller. I love you, Bobby."

Those words came all in a rush, almost uninterpretable, and before he could take a breath to argue, he heard the line go dead.

"Shit!" He yelled it loudly enough to echo through the house that he suddenly hated more than he'd ever hated anything in his life—the place that weighted his life like an anchor. He slammed the receiver into its cradle on the wall, then picked it up again and smashed it into into the granite countertop, launching a shower of plastic shrapnel across their shiny kitchen floor.

Detective Tom Stipton rubbed his temples. Sooner or later the teasing would stop. He was sure of it. Problem was, with only twelve years to go before retirement, it probably wouldn't happen while he was still young enough to enjoy the break.

It had been five whole hours now since he'd found out that he'd been shot to death in West Virginia, and all things considered, he felt pretty good about it. He had to smile as he thought about the telephone call from the state police. As luck would have it, Tom was at his desk when the shift commander, Captain Mason, fielded the call and transferred it to his desk.

"Hey, Tom, there's a West Virginia state trooper on line three that wants to talk to you about somebody you know." From the leaden tone in the captain's voice, Tom knew that something was terribly wrong.

"What's the problem?"

"Just take the call. But steel yourself. I'm afraid it's not good news."

Tom punched the blinking button and cleared his throat. "Yeah. Hello?"

The voice on the other end was downright grim. "This is Lieutenant LaRue with the West Virginia State Police. I'm investigating the murder of one of your police officers. A detective."

"Jesus," Tom gasped. "One of ours? Who?"

The voice faltered. "A Detective Stipton."

At that moment, Tom's face apparently displayed just the expression people had been waiting for, and the squad room erupted in laughter; guffaws and knee slaps all around.

When he could hear himself talk again, he explained how his badge had been stolen from his locker at his health club and that was the end of it, beyond the lingering bitterness over the week's pay the incident had cost him, in addition to the five-pound chunk they took out of his ass. The jury was still out on the long-term damage the incident would inflict on his career, but the fact that the property issued to him was now involved in a murder couldn't help. He could hear the wheels spinning inside the heads of the Internal Affairs dicks: Was Stipton involved in a plot to get his badge "accidentally" stolen so that criminals somewhere would have an easier time committing a crime?

As part of his administrative punishment, he'd already been removed from the homicide division and placed on the petty crimes unit—the repository for fuckups and those who were so close to retirement that the department didn't want them in harm's way anymore.

He liked to think of it as the humiliation that kept on giving.

Tom glanced across the squad room and saw his next case arriving. She appeared tall for a woman—five-ten—and she looked like shit in her bloodstained secondhand clothes. An enormous bandage all but obscured her left eye. The effect of it all was particularly startling given her obviously pregnant belly. Her head hung low as the uniformed officers on either side led her to an interrogation room, where they removed her handcuffs and ushered her to a chair.

Tom met the officers as they were on their way out. "Is this our armed robber?"

Sergeant Sammy Feitner was the oldest of the two officers, and at six-eight, the tallest in the whole department. "This is her. Hasn't said a word to us since we picked her up."

"Looks more like a victim than a perp. That bandage on her head your doing?"

Feitner scowled. "Not my style, Tom. One of the security guards got a little carried away. A kid named Brandon. Turns out he's the high school home-run king for this district."

Tom winced at the thought of having one's head smacked out of the park. "Ouch. She been to the hospital?"

The big sergeant shook his head. "Refused treatment."

"Is she okay?"

"As far as I can tell, yeah. But you know, it's been a while since I was in medical school."

Ah, station-house sarcasm. How could Tom live without it? "How about her sheet? Did you pull it?"

Feitner pulled a computer printout from his back pocket. "Not much there. A possession arrest a few years ago, but she walked on it."

Scanning the sheet, the first thing Tom noticed was her address in The Pines. That in itself was nearly as good as a conviction.

"Here are the statements from the store security folks," the second officer said, handing over another set of papers, along with a Macy's shopping bag. "And here's a copy of the video from the security cameras."

Tom signed the chain-of-custody slip and accepted the gifts. "And she's said nothing?"

"Not even a sigh."

"No request for a lawyer?"

Feitner shook his head.

"Well, thank you, gentlemen, for a job well done." Tom said it with exaggerated officiousness that brought a smile from the others.

"You been workin' too much, Tom," Feitner said laughing. "It's starting to get to you."

Oh, if only he knew.

April didn't bother to look up as Tom pulled the door open and walked to the table, helping himself to the chair opposite hers.

"Ms. Simpson, I'm Detective Stipton with the Pittsburgh Police Department. Can I get you anything? A soda? Cup of coffee?"

April didn't move.

Tom nodded. He had infinite patience at times like these. Truth be told, given the case they had against her, keeping silent wasn't a bad strategy. "Okay, well, I'm sure that the arresting officers already read you your rights, but let me do it again, just to make sure all the T's are crossed."

He withdrew his wallet from his back pocket and pulled out a laminated card with the Miranda warnings printed out word for word. This was such an important moment for bloodsucking defense attorneys that he forced himself to read what any fan of *N.Y.P.D. Blue* could have recited from memory. As the words spilled out, he noted how they seemed to hammer his prisoner farther into her chair, each syllable making her shoulders sag a little more. When he finished, her chin was touching her chest. He paused long enough to tuck the card away, then leaned his arms heavily on the table.

"Hey, April," he said softly. "Could you look at me, please?"

She hesitated, then led with her eyes as her head rocked up to full height. Beneath the bruises and the swelling, she was a beautiful woman.

"That's a nasty knock you got on your head there. Are you sure you don't want to see a doctor?"

Clearly, movement hurt as she shook her head, and her fingers gently stroked the lump of gauze that had been taped over the wound. Tom noticed the manicure.

"Can you tell me how that happened?" You always opened with questions you already knew the answers to. "Was it one of our people who did it?"

"Does that matter?" At its face, the question might have been combative, but its delivery seemed genuine.

"Well, I think it does," Tom answered with a shrug. "I don't like the notion of my officers out there beating on civilians."

She considered not answering, but in the end shook her head again, ever so gently. "I don't think so, no. I think it was one of the rent-a-cops at the mall."

Tom pulled a reporter's notebook from his inside jacket pocket and made a note. "Would you like to consider filing charges?" This was the get-to-know-each-other phase of their relationship, and it never hurt for a suspect to enjoy the illusion that you were on her side.

April scowled, then smiled, as if she suddenly understood a punch line. "Maybe I will. I'll have to think about it."

Tom made another note, perfectly masking his disappointment. Had she said no, that would have been a good argument in favor of her own guilt. "Okay, fair enough. Now, what about a lawyer, do you want to have one here while we talk?"

"I've got nothing to say to you."

Tom nodded as if to say he appreciated her point of view. "Well, the fact is, Ms. Simpson—do you mind if I call you April?"

She shrugged with one shoulder. "Call me Abe Lincoln if you like. I don't care."

"Okay, I'll call you April. Fact is, I need you to answer for the record whether or not you want to have a lawyer present here while we talk."

April inhaled deeply and closed her eyes against what seemed to be a jolt of pain. "I don't care."

"Is that a yes or a no?"

"I guess it's a no, so long as you realize that I don't intend to say anything."

Another note. "Okay, fine. Now, let's watch some television together." A television and VCR sat on a rolling cart in the corner, and Tom pulled it closer to the table, positioning it at the end, so neither of them had to turn around backward to watch it. The screen made a crackling sound as it popped to life, and Tom verified that the tape of the crime was a copy—not the original, which would stay in the evidence locker—before sliding it into the player. The image danced for a couple of seconds, and then they were watching in color from a high angle as April walked into the credit office and over to the writing carrel, where she took a piece of paper from the stack and wrote something down.

Tom stopped the tape, then fished through the manila envelope for a few seconds, finally coming up with a Ziploc bag in which someone had placed the three-by-five Customer Comment card. "Just so you know," Tom said, "the person we see there is writing the following note: 'Give me all the money in your cash drawer. Do not panic, and do not set off any alarms. I have a gun.'" He read it verbatim through the clear plastic, in as neutral a tone as he could manufacture.

He started the tape again, and they both watched as the woman turned directly toward the camera and walked first to the line on the left, and then over to the newly opened window on the right. The tape provided no sound, but the woman who looked like April was clearly agitated, and as she slid her note across the ledge, the picture started to zoom in, just enough to get a clear image of her features, but not so close as to lose track of the action. Tom paused the tape, rewound it, and then showed that portion again.

"This is interesting, April. You see, the people in the security office clearly thought that something was out of the ordinary here, and they decided to take a little closer look. The clarity of the picture is amazing, don't you think?"

He started the tape again, and as it ran, they saw more commotion in the credit office, and they watched as the woman who looked like April dashed out of the office. The tape jumped at this point to another angle as the woman ran through the men's department, knocking over displays. Two more edits tracked her throughout the store, all the way to where she tackled a lady at the door and then charged out into the mall. Then the tape turned to electronic snow and Tom pushed the stop button.

"Pretty interesting stuff, don't you think? Would you like to watch it again?"

April said nothing, choosing instead to study a cigarette burn on the table's Formica surface.

Tom shrugged and retrieved the tape before pushing the cart back into its corner. When he returned to his chair, he snugged himself in tight to the table and leaned heavily on his forearms. "See anything interesting in that tape, April?"

She flushed from the neck up, but refused to raise her eyes. "I noticed that she didn't take any of the money," she said softly.

Tom nodded. "I noticed that, too, just as I noticed that she never produced the gun that she talked about in the note. I might even find that encouraging if it weren't for this." Reaching into the manila envelope again, he withdrew another bag, this one containing the little .25-caliber pistol. He laid it on the table and said nothing for a good thirty seconds. April glanced at the gun, then returned her eyes to the spot on the table.

"April, I've got to tell you that none of this looks very good for you, okay?"

She pulled back from the table and looked away. "Look, I already told you—"

"I don't want you to say a word," Tom interrupted. "I know that you don't want to make a statement, and I respect that. But I want you at least to hear what I have to say to you."

She said nothing, but worked her jaw angrily.

"We can make a case here for armed robbery and the use of a firearm in the commission of a felony. That's twenty, thirty years right there. If we pushed a little, we could probably get you for attempted murder, too."

April's head snapped around, her eyes showing terror.

"Those shots you fired in the parking lot. In a strict interpretation of the law, that meets the definition of attempted murder. None of that is my decision, you understand. That's what we pay the prosecutor for. I just wanted you to understand that you're in some pretty deep trouble here."

April made no attempt to acknowledge him. She just looked that much more miserable.

Tom rose from his chair and walked to the water fountain near the door, where he pulled a Dixie cup from the dispenser and filled it. He set it on the table in front of his prisoner. "Let me put all of my cards on the table here, April. I need you to sign a statement that says you did what we both already know you did. This isn't a case of misinterpreted intentions or mistaken identities. I've got two fistfuls of eyewitnesses who can place you at the scene of this robbery, and I've got a full color video of you pulling it off. This is as slam-dunk a case as I've ever encountered."

April brought her gaze around to meet his. "What if—"

Tom held up his hand for silence. "I don't want you saying anything yet, okay? Now, I can't make any promises to you—again, I'm not the one who files the charges around here—but if you make this easier on all of us by signing a statement, then I'll do whatever I can to convince the prosecutor to take it easy on you."

April stewed for a long time before saying anything. Tom watched with growing curiosity as her expression shifted from one of panic, back to sadness again, and finally, of resolution. "Assuming I were to confess to doing this—which I'm not. I'm not confessing."

"I understand."

"But suppose I did. Would it make a difference if I had a really good reason for doing it? Would it matter that in the end—hypothetically, now—would it matter in the end that I changed my mind, and that the only reason I fired those shots—if I fired them at all—would have been to get the people to back off long enough for me to get away? Would any of that matter?"

Tom smiled gently. They were coming close to an agreement. He could smell it. "I suppose it could. But I say to you one more time that I'm not the guy who makes that call."

April considered it all carefully.

"You know," Tom pushed, ever so gently, "I figured when I saw you that there was more to this case than it seems. I mean, look at you. You're a good-looking woman—with a baby in the oven, no less—and with the exception of that one drug thing a long time ago, you've lived your life within the law. I asked myself when I first saw you: Why would this woman choose this day to ruin her life?" He leaned closer to her and lowered his voice almost to a whisper. "What did happen today, April? What was it that drove you to rob that store?"

She was so close; so, so close. She opened her mouth and took a breath as if to begin, but then shut down again. Finally, she looked away. "It's not easy deciding to confess to something you didn't do," she said at last. "I'm going to have to think about it."

Tom sighed. The moment had passed; there'd be no confession today. He forced a smile that looked more like a wince. "Okay, April, suit yourself. Take some time. And while you think, I'll just go ahead and have you booked on the robbery, firearms, and attempted-murder counts."

"But I'll be able to change my mind later, if I decide to, you know, confess to that crime I didn't commit?" The edge of panic had returned to her voice.

Tom didn't answer. This was psychological warfare, after all, and he didn't want to just walk away from his advantage. Instead, he made a noncommittal face and gave a little shrug, as if to say, "We'll see."

As the door closed behind him, he peeked once through the wire-reinforced window. He felt a twinge of guilt when he saw her start to cry.

21

WHO DOES THAT fucking greaseball spick think he is, anyway?" raged Patrick Logan, slamming another hole—his fourth—into the drywall. The whole house shook with every blow. "He comes into *my* house and treats me like some piece of shit in front of *my* people! Who the *fuck* does he think he is?"

Ricky Timmons had seen his boss on plenty of rants over the years, but this one was off the scale. He didn't know what to do. Should he just sit and listen? Should he agree? Should he try to calm Logan down? The only option that he could not choose—the only one that he would not be permitted to choose—was the only one he really wanted, and that was to get the hell out of there. On his best days, Patrick Logan defied interpretation or predictability. When he was this out of control, he was downright scary.

Already, Logan's office was a wreck. The holes punched in the walls were only the beginning. He'd cleared his desk with a single sweep of his arm, his chair lay across the room by the door, where it had landed after a spiraling flight through the air, and the $1,200 television set that had once commanded the corner by the front window had been reduced to a worthless pile of fractured plastic and shattered glass.

"Goddammit, Ricky, I asked you a question!" Logan hollered. "Who the fuck does he think he is?"

Ricky jumped. It had never occurred to him that he was supposed to answer. "Shit, Patrick, I don't know. I guess he thinks he's Carlos. I guess he thinks he's the boss."

"The boss! The fucking boss!" Logan raised his face and his arms to the ceiling, as if to plead for guidance. "He has the balls to think that he's the fucking boss of me? Of *me?* Patrick Logan doesn't have no fucking boss!"

Ricky said nothing, fearful of where this might go. In Pittsburgh, Carlos Ortega was *everybody's* boss.

Suddenly, the raging storm seemed to subside, to evaporate. In its wake, Ricky saw an unsettling calm that was almost more frightening than the fury. The wild flailing of arms and flinging of furniture settled into a pensive stroll around the office as Logan considered thoughts that obviously pleased him.

"I think it's time things changed, don't you, Ricky? I think it's time for someone else to start giving the orders."

Ricky gasped and closed his eyes against the inevitable. This was where he'd feared Patrick was headed.

"What's the matter?" Logan prodded. "You don't want to be king of the hill?"

Ricky opened his eyes to behold a little boy in a big Irishman's body. Logan's eyes were huge with expectation and ambition, and he wore a gaping, stupid grin.

"This is our chance, Ricky boy. This is our chance to take it all."

"This is our chance for war," Ricky replied flatly. "This is our chance to get killed and lose everything."

The smile disappeared. "Are you *afraid* of Carlos, Ricky? Are you afraid of that worthless spick?"

Was it possible that Logan didn't get it? *Everybody* was afraid of Carlos, because Carlos had surrounded himself with a fucking army of loyal people. Hell, even the users on the street would stand up for the son of a bitch. But that's not what Ricky said to Logan.

"I think there's a time and a place for everything, Pat. Yours will come, but right now isn't it. Right now, you're pissed off because he came in here and dissed the shit out of you, and you have all the reason in the world to hate the son of a bitch's guts. But you've got the whole city to think about. All those other Patrick Logans who like things just the way they are. They're fat, they're happy, and everybody's not capping everybody else, the way things were a few years ago. They're the ones you've got to worry about. What makes you think they want to work for you now?"

The look of boyish anticipation morphed into one of bewilderment. "What makes you think I give a shit what those pussies want? If we take out Ortega, they'll have to fall in line, because if they don't, I'll fucking put their asses in the ground, too." Logan spun around on that, turning his back on Ricky, signaling that he'd said the last words he intended to on this subject.

But Ricky wouldn't let him off the hook. "Think about this, will you? Just think it through for a few minutes before you decide to do something that you don't want to do. Think about those Patrick Logans I was talking about. Every one of them hates Ortega just as much as you do, and yeah, it's because they're afraid of him. And they're afraid of the warfare. You think that every one of them hasn't had this very conversation in their office? Every fucking one of them? Of course they have."

"And they're too dickless to do anything about it."

That was way too simple, but Ricky shrugged it off. "Okay, they're too dickless. And not only are they afraid, but they're afraid of their fear. They *feel* dickless. Now if we move in and take out Ortega, those dicks are gonna grow back, and when they do, they're not gonna just roll over for you. Are you prepared—I mean *really* prepared—to fight for it all, block by block? Do you really want to do that?"

Logan turned back to face his lieutenant, his eyes hot. "What I want," he said carefully, his voice quivering with rage, "is for that son of a bitch to be dead. I want him hurt. I want him to beg like a woman for his life, and I want him to know that you never fuck with Patrick Logan and get away with it. I want the whole fucking world to know that."

"That doesn't answer—"

"Fuck the others, Ricky!" Logan boomed. "Fuck 'em all! I don't give a shit if they come and work for me, or if they go and work for the fucking CIA, okay? I've got my business here, and it's about goddamned time for me to start running it the way I want to run it."

Ricky saw what Logan couldn't—or maybe what Logan did see and just didn't give a shit about: that this was all about revenge, and revenge was a piss-poor way to run any business. "They'll come at you, you know. All of them. And I don't just mean Ortega's commandos. I mean that every swinging dick that has an interest in business on the street is going to see you as their prime target. And every one of them will assume that they have the full support of the others. Why do you want to do that to yourself?"

Logan shook his head emphatically. "No, they won't. Every one of them will think they owe me the fucking world for getting that leech off their backs. Like you said, there's not a street boss out there who hasn't had this very conversation. They all want him dead."

"But not bad enough to kill him."

Logan paused. For just a second, Ricky thought that maybe his argument had broken through, but then the big Irishman righted the chair near the door, pulled it in close to the sofa where Ricky sat, and then lowered himself easily into the seat. He crossed his legs. "Killing's not about hate, Ricky. And it's not about anger. It's about guts. Carlos Ortega is alive today because no one's ever had the guts to do what needs to be done."

Ricky's shoulders drooped, as if deflated.

"Well, I have the guts," Logan went on. "And I think you have the guts, too, because you know that if we don't act first, Ortega is going to come at us."

Ricky's head snapped up, his face a giant question mark.

"That kid," Logan said. "The fucking thief's kid."

"You're not giving him back?"

"Hell, yes, I'm giving him back. I'll have the bones in one bag and the guts in the other."

"Jesus, Pat, you heard what Ortega said about—"

"Would you shut the fuck up about Ortega, for Christ's sake? Ortega's dead, okay? He doesn't matter anymore. Come tonight, you'll be quoting a fucking ghost."

"But about the Simpson bitch—"

"She's dead, too. And her husband, too. The whole fucking family. I'm tired of this shit." Logan stood abruptly and again turned his back.

This time, though, from the set of his boss's head and shoulders, Ricky knew that the final decision had been made.

"That's a lot of bodies, Patrick. The cops are gonna go ape shit. They're gonna clamp down on us like a fuckin' anaconda."

Logan shrugged it off. "Just for a while. Then it'll be back to business as usual. They won't care about a dead spick after the papers stop running the story. A month, maybe. Two months, max. After that, it'll be like nothing ever happened."

Ricky sighed. In Logan's mind, this was all a done deal. The rest was all details. "So, how are you gonna do it?"

"You know what, Ricky?" Logan continued as if he'd never been interrupted. "If we do this right, the cops never have to know a thing. We keep this just between you and me, we take a few precautions, and nobody knows a thing."

"The cops are still gonna come after us."

"Well, shit, Ricky, they're gonna come after everybody. Not just us. They're gonna come after Bauer and Jackson and Hernandez, too. Christ, there'll be a fucking witch-hunt. So what? Nobody'll see a thing. At least, not that they'll report to the cops. They'll know better. Or we'll teach them."

This kind of bravado made Ricky nervous as hell. Logan always assumed that everything would go his way—hell, nine times out of ten he was right—but the stakes here were huge.

"You're afraid of gettin' caught, aren't you?" Logan asked, reaching right into Ricky's head and grabbing a fistful of his thoughts. "Is that what's got you looking so peaked?"

Ricky shrugged, suddenly embarrassed. "That's part of it. Plus, I'm not so hot on doing the kid. That's not my thing."

Logan chuckled and shook his head, as if this were the most ridiculous thing he'd ever heard. "First of all, you don't have to do the kid. I got other people to take care of him, okay? That leaves you to take out the Simpsons, and me to do Ortega. We can be done and home by nine o'clock."

Ricky let out a breath he didn't even know he'd been holding. It wasn't as if he hadn't killed before; but every other time, he'd had a chance to plan and to make sure all the loose ends were tied. Most of those poor, dumb assholes on the street cap somebody and they're in jail twenty minutes later. The public liked to think of that as great police work when, in fact, it was just the stupidity of the shooters. In neighborhoods like the ones where they did business, cops didn't exactly lose sleep if a murder went unsolved, any more than the police department shelled out any real money for investigations. That stuff was all for the rich neighborhoods and the television cameras. Out here, if you took a few reasonable precautions, you could get away with just about anything. But this business of killing children was not his bag.

"Okay," Ricky said, musing. "Okay, so I only have to worry about that fuckhead and his wife. You're gonna have a hell of a lot tougher job than me, Pat."

Logan smiled. "And here I thought you were going to be mad for me hogging all the fun."

"We'll need alibis."

Logan laughed. "Fuck alibis. We were together, playing cards over at Champ's. Hell, Champ'd testify that he flew the space shuttle with us if I told him to. This isn't a problem. And, hey, about getting caught? You're lookin' at life just for what you do every day. The worst they can do to you here is death. What's the big deal?"

Ricky's eyes hardened. "When did I ever say I was afraid of going to jail? I just don't want people on the street talking about how fucking stupid we were when we pulled off the highest-profile hit this city has ever seen." *And I got better things to do right now than get executed,* he didn't say.

"When we're done, everybody's gonna be suspecting everybody else," Logan grinned. "You see, Ricky, I don't want to be another Ortega. I don't want to run everybody's business. I don't want to be no fucking father figure to anybody. All I want is to do business the way I want to do it. That's all. That and make sure that I hurt that son of a bitch bad before I kill him. Fucker's gonna know he tried to strong-arm the wrong guy."

Ricky nodded. His boss's arguments had merit. With Ortega out of the way, profits would be higher, and they wouldn't have to jump through all the ridiculous hoops that Carlos put in the way of everything. They'd sell what they wanted to whomever they wanted and not have to worry about pissing off the franchisor. That's what Carlos like to call himself—The Franchisor. What a dick.

"Okay," Ricky said finally. "I think we can do this. Just do me one favor, okay?"

Logan's face remained passive.

"Just let me make all the preparations. You don't touch the guns, you don't touch the bullets, you don't say nothing to anybody else. I'll take care of all that stuff."

Logan shrugged. "I wouldn't have it any other way, Ricky."

Tim Burrows watched as Henry Parker supervised the cataloging of the evidence they'd collected that day, silently wondering how such a mountain of a man could move with such easy grace. The evidence bags—either plastic or paper, depending on the contents—were logged onto a master sheet, which in turn was carefully verified by a second technician, and then placed into various bins, for transport either to the Charleston field office, or back to headquarters in Washington.

Watching the way that Parker interacted with his people strummed a chord of jealousy in Tim. Parker's technicians listened to every word he said, then put themselves through extraordinary efforts to comply with his wishes. Even wizened dickheads like Coates held the gentle giant in a kind of awe. The odor of smoke in the air made everyone move a little more quickly, though. About an hour ago, they'd received word of a forest fire at the far end of the park, along with assurances that they had nothing to worry about there on the Powhite. Instantly, all vestiges of the National Park Service had evaporated from Tim's crime scene, scampering off to do their real jobs, but now that the rangers were finally out of his hair Tim found himself wishing he had more current information on the course of the fire. Judging from sirens alone, things were far from being under control.

"Hey, Agent Burrows!" someone yelled from behind.

Tim pivoted to see Homer LaRue on his way up the hill, waving a thin file folder from his right hand. Now *there* was a guy whose typecasting was dead-nuts right on—the hillbilly hick with a large-caliber sidearm. Tim strolled down the path to meet the trooper halfway. "How close are we to being burned up?" He asked the question as off-handedly as he could.

Homer made a face."Closest spark is still three miles from here. Relax. Take a look at this. We found out who the stiff is," Homer announced. "I mean, *was.*"

Tim opened the folder Homer gave him and read for himself what LaRue told him anyway.

"It took the computer a little while to spit out the identification from the prints we took, because it looks like the guy tried to carve 'em off a few times."

Tim nodded as he paged through the report.

"Anyway, his name popped out as Jacob Stanns, from up in Wetzel County, near the Pennsylvania border. He was in and out of trouble a lot as a kid, and on into his twenties. Had a thing for weed and for boosting other people's wheels. He was arrested about fifteen years ago on a charge of murdering his father, but the state's attorney let him walk for lack of evidence."

Now, Tim's eyes came up to stay. Nothing like the mention of a previous murder to get his attention. "How did he die? The father, I mean."

Homer shrugged. "Best as I can tell, they found his body in the rubble of a burned-up chicken coop. The coroner found evidence that his head had been bashed in, but nobody could say for sure whether it was done by the son or by a fall of some sort."

Tim thought it over. The details were interesting, but he wasn't sure if any of this progressed the investigation very far. "So, is this"—he referred back to the cover sheet—"Jacob Stanns married?"

Homer shook his head. "Don't think so. The file says he lives with his brother Samuel out on the family farm. Samuel, apparently, is a few cards short of a full deck. That's one of the reasons they went easy on that murder charge. Seems if Jacob went to jail, there'd be no one to take care of the brother."

"Is he a little kid?"

"He was then, I suppose. Now he's about thirty."

"And no other trouble from Jacob since the murder thing?"

"Not a peep that made it into the file."

Tim stewed on that. Why would someone on the straight and narrow go to the pain and the trouble of carving off his fingerprints? Christ, think what that must feel like!

"What do we know about the brother, other than the fact that he's a little slow?"

Homer shook his head. "Nothing, really. We know he doesn't have a record, though we do know that a social worker went out to their house a million years ago to check up on a report that the parents were hurting the kids. Hell, that was probably in the eighties sometime. Maybe even the seventies, I don't remember. Anyway, it was before people started taking domestic shit so seriously. The file didn't say what became of that, but obviously not a whole lot, right?"

Homer related some more about the results of Jacob Stanns's autopsy, getting into the details of impact angles and time of death, but none of that was anything that Tim hadn't either suspected or figured out for himself. He found his mind wandering back to the footprints in the woods; that separate set, where someone just stood and watched. What if that other set of prints belonged to the brother? What if, for some reason, he had just stood out there in the woods while his brother was shot to death? What would that mean?

Well, for one thing, it would mean that they needed to talk with this—he consulted the papers yet again—this Samuel Stanns. Frankly, this was looking less and less like any scenarios they had constructed before. The rape was certainly out, as was the scenario where the decedent was an innocent victim. Tim didn't even like Russell Coates's pet theory of the foiled kidnapping. It's a huge deal to have someone try to nab you, and an even huger deal to shoot a man. Why, then, didn't the camping couple report it? Why didn't they go screaming to the nearest park ranger and tell him all about it? Why didn't they run for the safety of the ranger station, where they might at least be protected from further attack?

"Agent Burrows, are you even listening to me?"

Tim snapped back to the present and smiled sheepishly at the big trooper. "I'm sorry, Lieutenant, I guess I blinked out on you there for a minute. I was just thinking things through."

LaRue frowned and sighed. "You know, I don't *have* to share any of this stuff with you out here. I could make you go through all the bureaucracy to get the reports through channels."

"I'm sorry," Tim said, as genuinely as he knew how. "I didn't mean to shut you out. I was just thinking about the footprints in the woods, and wondering if maybe they belonged to this brother."

Homer recoiled from the thought. "What the hell kind of man would just stand there while his brother was getting shot to death?"

"I don't know. Be interesting to find out, wouldn't it?"

Homer returned his gaze to his papers. "Well, we traced the 911 call that led us up here in the beginning. Turns out it was made from a pay phone at a convenience store outside of Winchester, Virginia. My troopers tracked down the night clerk who was working the desk, and he said he remembers only one guy who wasn't a regular coming in after midnight. Said he bought gas and diapers."

Tim's head cocked. "Diapers? As in for a baby?"

"As in Pampers. Said the guy was really surprised at how much they cost."

"Tell me he paid by credit card."

Homer shook his head. "No such luck. Cash. But apparently he didn't have a whole lot of it. He had to change the amount of his gas purchase after he found out about the price of the diapers. And no security cameras either, so we don't have any pictures."

Tim's assessment of Homer LaRue was improving with every passing minute. "The Pampers bring to mind those little footprints, don't they?"

"I was thinking the same thing," Homer noted. "Not exactly ironclad, but we're getting there."

Tim and Homer both knew that every camper who ever entered Catoctin National Forest probably stopped at that convenience store to buy something. Hell, the store counted on that business, else why would they have opened it there? It was a long leap from being in the store to accusing someone of murder. Still, it was worth a chat.

"Just so you know," Homer went on carefully, as if preparing Tim for bad news, "I asked the clerk if he saw what the customer was driving, or what he did before entering or after leaving the store, and he said no."

"So we've got no witness linking the shopper to the phone."

"Right. And just the clerk's best guess as to time."

Tim sighed and lifted his fatigue cap to scratch his scalp. The time had come to do something daring. "Tell you what, Lieutenant. What do you say you and I take a trip out to Wetzel County to pay a visit to Samuel Stanns? Let's see if he can shed any light on what happened up here."

Homer looked confused. "Why don't I just have a trooper bring him in?"

Tim pretended to consider that for a moment before shaking his head. It wouldn't do to tell this hillbilly that he didn't want to share the credit for a good hunch with a bunch of locals. Instead, he just said, "I'd kind of like to see their place for myself."

22

NEVER TOUCH THE *little phone.*

It was the thought that jolted Samuel out of his nap. With the lawn finally done, and with all the excitement and tragedy of the night before, he finally just couldn't keep his eyes open any longer. He'd almost fallen asleep on the tractor, in fact. Lord only knows what might have happened then.

The cell phone chirped again.

Never touch the little phone.

What was he supposed to do now? That was Jacob's phone—the one that The Boss always called on; the one that Samuel was never, *ever* to touch, except to plug it into its charger, which he had done just as he was supposed to when he first got home. The whole drive back from the park last night, that's all he'd thought about—making sure that the phone got back into its charger. It was kind of a test; if he could remember to do that, then he could remember anything.

Except, he almost forgot to undo the alarm. The fucking alarm. The most important thing of all. *Never leave the house without setting the alarm, and never* ever *forget to turn it off.* That would have been big, big trouble.

The phone chirped again.

What would he say to whoever was on the other end? What would they say to him? He wasn't supposed to answer, dammit! See? This was exactly the kind of thing that Samuel worried about most, now that Jacob was dead.

The phone chirped.

He had no choice, did he? He had to answer it. Rising from his spot on the sofa, Samuel walked slowly over to the charger near the television set and poised his hand over the phone, waiting. Maybe it wouldn't ring again, and he wouldn't have to worry about these things.

It rang.

Haltingly, Samuel reached out a hand and lifted the phone from its charger. It felt somehow heavier when it was ringing. He pulled open the bottom part, just as he'd seen Jacob do a thousand times in the past, and he brought it to his ear.

"Hello?" *Dammit, that's not how you answer the phone!* Jacob always said, "Yeah?" And when he did, it always sounded so tough.

The voice on the other end was nasty and abrupt. "Burn the package."

Samuel scowled. "What?"

The voice stopped, as if he were suddenly suspicious of something. "Who is this?"

"This is Samuel. Is this The Boss?"

The line went dead. Not so much as a "good-bye." Just silence. Samuel closed the phone and laid it back on its charger. Two seconds later, it chirped again, startling him. This time when he answered, he made an effort to get it right. "Yeah?"

"Is this Moonlighter?"

Moonlighter! Samuel had heard Jacob use that name before, but he had never explained what it meant. Why would anyone want to call themselves something they weren't? "Um, no, th-this is his brother."

Again, the voice seemed confused. "His *brother?*"

"Yes, you see—"

The line died again, and Samuel began to wonder if someone was playing a prank on him. He'd heard about children who would call people and say things and then hang up. Or maybe he'd seen it in a movie or something. Anyway, people did that sometimes. As he closed the phone yet again, he was sure that was what was happening here.

It chirped again.

This time, the right tone came easily. "What!"

"I want to talk to Moonlighter."

"Why do you keep hanging up?"

"Why do you keep answering the goddamn phone?"

"Because you keep calling. Jacob's not—I mean, *Moonlighter*'s not here right now."

"Well, where the hell is he? He's *always* supposed to be there."

"Who is this?"

The voice paused, and for a second Samuel thought the man was getting ready to hang up again. Now, that would really piss Samuel off. But the man didn't hang up. Instead, he took a deep breath. "Burn the package."

Samuel hated feeling like this, as if he'd walked into the middle of a conversation and he had no idea what anyone was talking about. Only, no one else was talking here; just he and whoever was on the other side of the phone. "Is this The Boss?"

Another pause. Then, finally, "Yes, this is the boss. When will Moonlighter be back?"

Samuel gasped. He was going to have to tell, wasn't he? He was going to have to tell The Boss something. This was the man who always made Jacob so difficult to be around after they talked together. You never ever fuck with The Boss. Jacob had said that a thousand times. You never fuck with The Boss.

"Are you there, or what?" The Boss demanded.

"Huh? Yeah, yeah, I'm here. Jacob—I mean Moonlighter—won't ever be back," Samuel said, surprised by the strength in his voice. This was, after all, the first time he'd said it to anyone out loud. "Moonlighter is dead."

Another pause. "Well, what about the package?"

"*What* package? You keep talking about a package, and I don't know what you're talking about."

The man on the other end of the phone sighed. "You're the stupid brother, aren't you?"

"I'm not stupid!" Samuel shouted. "I'm not always smart, but I'm not stupid!"

The voice laughed. "Yeah, okay, whatever you say. You were with him last night, weren't you?"

Samuel nodded, but not with much enthusiasm. Now he understood why Jacob didn't like this guy. "I was there."

"You don't remember picking up something last night? Something about three years old?"

"You mean the little boy?" Why the hell didn't this guy just say what he had on his mind?

"Hey, shut up, you dwid. This isn't a secure line."

Samuel said nothing. He didn't have to talk to anyone who spoke to him that way. Maybe he should be the one to hang up this time. Maybe that would teach the guy to watch what he said.

"Well, were you there for the pickup, or weren't you?"

"Yeah, I was there." Samuel made sure that he put all of his anger in his voice, so the guy would know he'd pissed him off.

"And you know where Moonlighter put him?"

Samuel felt himself blushing as he shifted feet. This was the embarrassing part. "Well, I know where he tried to put him," he mumbled. *You don't fuck with The Boss.*

"What do you mean, 'tried?'"

Samuel stuffed his hands in his pockets, the phone cradled into his shoulder. How was he going to explain this? How was he going to explain how he'd fallen asleep and how the little boy just got away? He didn't want to explain any of that. He wanted to hang up. But that would be fucking . . . well, you know.

"He sort of got away," Samuel said, trying to make it sound like something less than the huge deal that he knew it was.

"What the hell do you mean, he got away!"

See? The Boss thought it was a big deal, too. He thought it was a *really* big deal or he wouldn't have shouted like that.

Samuel's mind raced, trying to come up with something he could say that would make The Boss less angry. "I—I mean, we had him, and then, well, he got away. He ran through the woods. We tried to catch him, and that's when Jacob—I mean, Moonlighter—got into the fight with those people and then got killed. That's why he won't be home again. Did I tell you that? Jacob got killed last night."

"So, you don't know where the package is?"

While Samuel was talking, his hands found a piece of paper all crumpled up in his pocket. He wondered what it was—Samuel liked papers, and he liked writing, because he wasn't good at that stuff himself—and when he pulled it out, he almost didn't read it. What a mistake that would have been!

"Answer me, you stupid shit!"

Suddenly, the names this guy was calling him didn't matter anymore. Suddenly, Samuel had an answer that he knew would make it all sound better. And The Boss wouldn't be all pissed off at him anymore. On that little sheet of paper—the one he remembered picking up as he was going to kiss Jacob good-night—he saw a name and address. The little slip of paper said Robert and Susan Martin, and Samuel remembered the nosy nellies calling each other that. Well, she called him Bobby, which is almost the same as Robert, but he definitely called her Susan. And the slip of paper had their address on it.

"I know where he is," Samuel said triumphantly.

"Yeah? Where?" The Boss sounded as if he didn't believe him, but before Samuel could answer, The Boss quickly corrected himself: "No, wait. I don't want you to say it here. Not on this line."

"But I can get him." Samuel thought The Boss would be at least a little happy about that.

Silence from the other end while The Boss thought about things. "Tell you what," he said finally. "I want you to get the package—you know what I mean by 'the package?'"

"You mean the little boy."

The boss growled. "Okay, right. Well, I want you to go get him and meet me tonight at midnight at the place where you lost him. Do you think you can find that place? You're not too stupid for that?"

"I'm not stupid!" Samuel shouted. "I drove all the way home from there all by myself. I can find it."

"Good." The Boss's voice did sound a little lighter. "Then you meet me there with the package—with the boy—at midnight tonight."

Something in the tone of the voice made Samuel feel funny. "You're not going to hurt him, are you?"

Another silence. "No. No, I don't want to hurt anyone."

Samuel listened, wondering whether he should trust the voice. "Because I don't want to hurt him. We never wanted to do that. It was all a game. Jacob told me."

The voice laughed. "Jacob told you that, did he? Okay, well, we certainly don't want to turn Jacob into a liar, do we? No, we're not going to hurt anyone. You just be there at midnight, okay? It's time to bring him home."

"I'll be there," Samuel said, worrying that it might be risky to make promises like that without first looking at a map to see how far he had to drive. He hoped that he could get where he needed to go and be back in the park by midnight, but he wasn't completely sure, and he didn't want to fuck with The Boss. On the other hand, he didn't want to talk with him anymore either, and he figured that by saying yes, he'd be off the phone that much sooner.

"I'll be there," Samuel repeated, but the line was dead again.

Samuel liked maps. He was good with them, just as he was good with some numbers, such as lock combinations and telephone numbers. He could remember them without even trying, and maps were just plain fun to read. It wasn't even like reading, really, not in the way you had to put words together in your head to make a story.

The atlas was right where it was supposed to be, on the shelf in the living room, and he found Virginia by running the alphabet song through his head until he got to the *V*'s. Sure enough, there was Clinton, Virginia, just outside of Washington, D.C. It looked like maybe a four-hour drive. He checked his watch. If he moved quickly, he could be there and then back to West Virginia in no time at all. He'd make the midnight deadline easy as pie.

But then what? Suppose the nosy nellies—the Martins—didn't go back to Clinton, Virginia? Suppose they—

What? What else could they have done? He remembered how scared they were out there in the woods, and he knew that people who were that scared do only one thing—they go home. He'd find them there, and then what?

You get revenge.

"Jacob?"

Get revenge. Isn't that what Jacob would have done for Samuel?

He'd already thought about that. He'd get revenge on the nosy nellies who'd shot his brother.

And he and Jacob could get back to the game with the boy. The game that Samuel never fully understood. Usually, when they went out to do a job, it was a snot-pounding and then maybe a shooting, but it was always with adults. They only snot-pounded bad guys. Jacob would never hurt a little boy. He'd never hurt anybody that Samuel liked.

It bothered him that the kid—Samuel was pretty sure his name was Justin—didn't really want to play their game. And what a harsh game it was! Jacob called it hide-and-seek deluxe, but no matter what they called it, that hole looked pretty scary. Even scarier than the gunnysack, and that had to have been pretty scary, too.

Once Jacob pulled the Simpson guy over and showed him the badge, Samuel's job had been to say nothing while they approached the car. Jacob had insisted that they watch rerun after rerun of *Cops* to make sure they had the walk down just right. Then, once the punching started, Samuel was to throw the burlap sack over the kid's head and tie him up real tight.

"Just relax, little boy," he'd said as the kid wriggled and squirmed and screamed. "It's only for fun. We're not really gonna hurt you or nothing. We'll be really, really nice if you'll just shut the fuck up." But it was as if the kid didn't understand English or something. The first time Samuel knocked the bag against the ground, the kid just got louder. Same thing the second time. By the third knock, though, he'd settled down to a quiet little whimper, and he stayed that way.

It was a long drive—every bit of two hours—and Jacob was in one of his quiet moods. As the roads deteriorated and they bounced around the interior of the cab, Samuel noticed the clinking of the baby-food jars as they rattled against each other in the back. "Why did you buy such tiny jars of food?" he asked, if only to break the silence. "There's not much in them."

"That's baby food, you idiot. Nobody buys big jars of baby food. A little kid would explode if you tried to stuff a whole jar of apple sauce down his gullet. Jesus."

Samuel tried to picture that in his mind, and he didn't like what he saw. "So, is that food all for little Justin?"

"Every bit of it."

"Wow, he must really be hungry."

This time, Jacob laughed, and Samuel remembered how refreshing a sound it was. A good laugh always made Jacob more pleasant to be around. "He's not going to eat it all at once, dum—" Jacob cut himself off before he said the word, and Samuel really appreciated that. "He's going to be out here for a while."

"In the woods? By himself?"

"He's got his house," Jacob said, referring to the hole they'd dug, "so he'll be safe from animals down there, and the food will keep him from starving."

Samuel winced at the thought and rubbed the back of his neck. "I don't know, Jacob. That doesn't sound like much of a game to me. Sounds more scary than fun."

Jacob got quiet for a while and then said, "Well, you know, Samuel, there are different kinds of fun. Sometimes you have to think that something's fun just because it's more fun than doing something else that's really *not* fun. Does that make sense?"

Actually, it didn't, but Samuel said yes anyway because he was too tired to hear it explained.

Finally, they arrived at the spot they'd so carefully prepared. It was quite a hike from the road to the little clearing, through thickets and briers. Samuel carried the sack with the kid inside, but it wasn't very heavy, and even though the kid moved around a lot, he kept his mouth shut, which was just fine. The woods were spooky enough in the middle of the night without adding the sounds of a screaming kid to it all. Samuel carried the jars of food, too, all stuffed into a backpack that weighed a ton. Jacob carried the water and the flashlight.

"Here we are," Jacob announced, setting the water jug down on the ground. He shined the flashlight on the rectangle they'd cut out of the ground. Samuel moved closer and peered into the hole. It looked deeper at night than it had during the day. "This just doesn't look very fun," he mused aloud.

"Remember what I said, Samuel. Trust me, this is a lot more fun than some of the other games we could have played."

"It looks like the boxes you built for Mama and Daddy. The coffins."

Jacob's patience was thinning. "It's not a coffin, Samuel. It's much, much bigger than that. For a kid this size, there'll be plenty of room for him to crawl around and get his food and stuff."

"Jeez, Jacob, I don't know . . . "

Jacob moved quickly around to the other side of the hole. "Besides, look here. You see? I built a lid for the box that has a big air vent in it."

"But you're gonna put dirt on top."

Even in the dark, Samuel could see Jacob roll his eyes. "I'm not going to put dirt on the vent, for Christ's sake. I'll put the dirt *around* the vent, so the kid will be able to breathe. It's nothing like a coffin, Samuel. Nothing at all like a coffin, so just get that thought out of your mind."

He heard what Jacob was saying, and he knew that his brother wouldn't lie about stuff, but it sure seemed like a coffin to him.

Jacob changed the subject. "I want you to take care of the kid for me, okay, Samuel? I want you to let him out of the sack and put him in the hole and maybe even get down there with him for a little while and show him where you put his food and all. He won't have much light to see with, so he'll need to know how to feel his way around."

"Where are you going?"

"It's dark out here. I need to get some firewood so we can see what we're doing."

Samuel didn't like the sound of that; no, sir, not one bit. "You're not going to go far, are you?"

Jacob gave him one of those looks. "There's nothing out here that can hurt you, Samuel. There's nothing to be afraid of."

"But you're still not going far?"

Jacob laughed. "No, I won't be going far."

"How long will you be gone?"

"Just a few minutes, okay? Relax."

Yeah, right. Relax. Easy for Jacob to say. He understood things. He *knew* when there were things to be afraid of, and when there weren't. For Samuel, it was always a guessing game, and right now, he was guessing that maybe his brother didn't know what he was talking about. Before Samuel could say any of these things, though, Jacob was gone, leaving him out here in the dark woods all by himself. Just him, the kid, and a flashlight.

Well, at least he left the flashlight. That was better than darkness.

Moving cautiously, Samuel approached the burlap sack and nudged it a little with his toe. "Hey, kid," he said in one of his stage whispers. "Hey, Justin, are you still there?"

The boy didn't say anything, but the bag moved. Samuel thought Justin must be nodding.

"Okay, kid, I'm going to untie the bag now, okay? I'm going to show you where you'll be playing. But you've got to promise not to make all that noise like you did before, okay? Noise makes me real nervous, and when I'm nervous, I, well, I just get nervous."

Part of him wondered how much the boy could understand of what he was saying. The kid was pretty little. And it couldn't be much fun to be inside that bag. He figured that Justin would probably like it if he let him out.

So, that's what he did. No matter how he moved, Samuel had trouble staying out of his own shadow, making untying the knot more complicated than it should have been, but once he got it, he pulled open the bag, and there was the boy. Red streaks stained his face from where he'd been crying, and his eyes seemed to take up the whole top half of his face.

"You look scared, Justin." Samuel reached out to pet the boy's head, but the toddler recoiled, making Samuel jump, too. "Oh, you don't have to be afraid of me. We're just going to let you play out in the woods for a while, that's all."

The boy stared. His lip trembled some, but he never made a sound. It would have been better almost if he had. Some sound to indicate that he at least heard what Samuel was saying.

"Are you cold? Is that why you're twitching like that?"

Dressed as Justin was in those heavy pajamas with feet—the kind that only children got to wear, even though grown-ups got cold, too—it was hard to tell how he must feel.

"Okay, Justin, Jacob says I need to show you your new playhouse, so why don't you come with me?"

The boy's eyes got bigger still, and he scooted back a little more.

Samuel stood and held out his hand. "Come on, Justin, I'll show you."

Justin's lip trembled even more, and finally tears started to flow. He started to cry, making that loud, little-boy crying sound that just filled the woods.

"Hush, Justin!" Samuel hissed. "Shut up! You want everyone to hear us?"

But the boy kept on wailing. The tears tumbled out of his eyes and down his cheeks, where they combined with snot and drool to form a wet, slippery mess on his chin.

"I said shut up!" Samuel took a quick step forward, and the boy shot to his feet, trying to run away. But Samuel was faster, catching the kid around his middle, and picking him up effortlessly. Justin squirmed and kicked and did all those little-kid things that Samuel had seen spoiled-rotten kids do in the stores, but he only tightened his grip around the boy's tummy.

"Here you go, kid. Here, see your new playhouse." Samuel tried to lower him gently into the hole, but he was moving around so much that Samuel's grip slipped, and Justin ended up falling down the sides of the excavation and down onto the wooden planks, landing with a hard thump.

And then the screaming started for real, pouring out of the hole as if someone had cranked a volume control all the way up.

"Shh," Samuel said again and again. "Shh, you've got to shut up." He knew that Jacob would worry about other people hearing the kid, but Samuel was much more concerned about Jacob himself. If he heard how much noise the kid was making, then he'd start in with all that talk about "I give you one stupid little job to do, and when I turn my back, you fuck it all up." Samuel didn't need to hear any more of that.

So, he jumped down into the hole with Justin and gathered the boy into his tightest bear hug, trying his best to avoid the flinging knees, elbows, and head. "Please stop, Justin," he begged. "Stop making all that noise. Just look around, will you? This could be fun. We'll give you food and all kinds of stuff, but first you've got to shut up. I don't want to have to drop you again."

The boy did get quiet, and then—

And then Samuel couldn't remember any more. The next image he could see in his brain was Jacob standing over the hole yelling things at him. "You stupid fucking idiot! I give you one simple job to do, and you fuck it all up!"

Samuel remembered that he'd had to stifle his pride that he'd predicted his brother's words exactly. He'd hit the nail on the head. Right on the money. Word for word.

And then the chase started and Jacob got killed.

Now, Samuel was alone forever; no one to tell him what to do or how to do it. No one to help him with hard decisions. A sense of gloom seemed to grow out of the ground and surround him in a sticky black shroud, and as he tried to shrug it away, it only wrapped tighter around him.

Revenge was the way to break the bonds. He knew this, even without Jacob telling him. Once he paid those nosy nellies a visit, he'd feel better. And when he returned the boy, The Boss would be happy.

Maybe then everything would be all right again.

23

RUSSELL CURSED UNDER his breath as he slid the heater control on the dash to off. Again. Never in his life had he been in a rental car where everything worked properly. Today, the gremlins resided in the heater, which cycled between only two settings: sweat and freeze. It's the little things, sometimes, that make life most miserable. The good news was, he was almost there.

Somehow, in the crush of Washington's suburban sprawl, time had eluded Clinton, Virginia. Neat, trim clapboard houses, each with its obligatory three-foot fence (white pickets, of course, or black wrought iron), led the way to a downtown commercial district consisting of three restaurants, a self-consciously rustic general store, a Baptist church, and more trinket and specialty shops than Russell could count.

This was the shopping hub of the surrounding horse country, where people paid big bucks to live in a color-coordinated, Disneyfied vision of small-town America. The residents here couldn't quite afford to live among the old-money foxhunters in Leesburg or Middleburg, but this place teemed nonetheless with all the trappings of nouveau wealth.

Beyond the confines of this little downtown district, Russell piloted his rental Chrysler through the winding roads of mansionland, where huge homes dominated the rolling landscape, but where nobody seemed to be home. Only the horses roamed about on the vast stretches of pasture that somebody's forebears had carved out of the steep forests. The owners—Russell imagined they called themselves "masters"—

were still toiling away at their downtown jobs, preparing for the daily gladiator battle that northern Virginians euphemistically called a commute. This far out, Russell figured they spent a solid hour, hour and a half each way, and he could just imagine their foul humor as they snatched custody of their kids back from the private day-care centers of choice, on their way home to collapse in the splendor of their unfurnished palaces. He didn't get it. Certainly, this was a gorgeous place to live, but what was the point if the living was shitty?

Welcome to the new millennium, Russell thought. Since his latest divorce, his own tastes ran more toward the two-bedroom condominium, where $3,000 furnished the whole thing, and all he had to worry about in the way of maintenance was vacuuming once a week and locking the door on his way out. This was especially fortunate given his uniquely poor luck before judges and his ex-wives' attorneys.

Surrounded by this much opulence, it was easy to be glib and dismissive, but as he drove past acres of wealth, he found himself slipping right back into the funk that his trip to the Caribbean had been supposed to deliver him from. The last marriage was the one that was supposed to have worked. Looking back on it now, he tried to figure out just exactly what had gone wrong with it— beyond that Vicki had been fucking one of her English students. He marveled at people who somehow managed to stay married to a single partner for an entire lifetime, and he wondered what it was about his particular chemistry that made things fall apart after only a couple dozen months.

His therapist had told him that perhaps it wasn't his fault at all—that perhaps it was his wives' fault—but the therapist was such an edgy little twit in his own right that Russell couldn't help but discount every word he said. In fact, by the end of their second session, Russell had determined that a role reversal was in order there, and he decided that life was too short to seek emotional guidance from someone who looked perpetually on the edge of tears. His decision to fire the therapist had propelled Russell into that small minority of three-time losers in love who choose to tackle the world on their own. Chasing bad guys while heavily armed helped some, but that still left moments such as these, stuffed into a tiny rental car with nothing to do but feel sorry for himself. And envy the shit out of the people who could afford to live in mansions.

The three-by-five registration cards that Sarah had given him were evidence now, so before leaving the park, he'd transferred all the information into his little notebook. He was more than a little aware of how terrible a hazard he was creating as he negotiated the hairpin turns of the ridiculously narrow road with one hand while trying to decipher his own handwriting.

Russell sensed that this case was about to close. He felt in his gut that this Martin couple were the people who could answer all of his questions, in all likelihood on the heels of having their rights read to them. He was still missing motive, but opportunity was there, and he'd just learned via cell phone that they drove a late-model Ford Explorer—the very type of vehicle that often used Firestone Wilderness AT tires—and which just happened to have been pulled over by a park ranger in the wee hours this morning. Unfortunately, the ranger made no note of the license plate, so Russell was short of ironclad proof, but sometimes, if enough independent factors line up just right, it's time to relabel coincidence as evidence.

But Russell wasn't ready for that yet.

Russell Coates had a gift. His disgruntled contemporaries in the Bureau called it blind luck, while his bosses—the ones who got to share his limelight—called it outstanding professional commitment, but the reality was that Russell had a knack for seeing things for what they really were. He'd figure this thing out, and when he did, the evidence would appear. It always did.

He nearly missed the house he was looking for—number 7844—and he hit the brakes hard to keep from blowing past it. From the road, there was no house really; just a mailbox next to a long driveway that curved up a steep incline and disappeared behind the trees. Russell wondered what a psychologist would say about the different psyches of people who preferred to have their wealth on display where everyone could see it, as opposed to those who, as here, preferred their privacy.

Pausing in the middle of the road while he verified yet again that he had the right address, Russell pulled the wheel hard to the left and started the long climb up the hill to visit the Martins.

• • •

Bobby was a wreck.

Where the hell were his keys? Christ, he had had them just a couple of minutes ago. They had to be . . . Oh, there they were, right in his pocket.

"Okay, Bobby, just calm down, take a deep breath. Everything's going to be fine."

But it wouldn't be fine. Nothing would ever be fine again.

He tried to remember what Barbara Dettrick had told him; that he had good reason to be optimistic. Even if they caught up with him, he had a perfectly good explanation for what had happened, and an even better one for not coming forward right away. He did report the body, didn't he? That had to be worth something.

With his keys clutched in his fist, he quick-walked through the kitchen, pausing to arm the alarm system before opening the door and walking outside.

He'd almost made it to the door of his Explorer when he saw a Chrysler climbing up his driveway. The man behind the wheel bore a look on his face that ruled him out as a salesman, or a welcoming new neighbor. Ten bucks would get you twenty that this guy was a cop.

24

SOME PEOPLE ARE natural criminals. Russell had spent hours with suspects who had committed horrendous crimes, but to talk with them, you'd think that they were deacons of their local church. They were positively aghast—sometimes downright insulted—that he could suspect them of doing something illegal. Even when faced with incontrovertible evidence of what they had done, these criminals would never bat an eye. Russell believed with all his heart that supreme criminals are supreme liars.

Robert Martin of Clinton, Virginia, was not one of them. This guy looked like the proverbial kid in the cookie jar. As Russell piloted his Chrysler up the sweeping driveway, he caught his prey in the garage, clearly in a hurry to go somewhere. In an Explorer, no less. As he saw Russell's car approaching, the guy nearly jumped out of his skin. Color drained so quickly and so thoroughly from his face that Russell wondered if his suspect was going to faint dead away.

You can tell a lot about someone by the way he reacts to an unpleasant surprise, and the longer you watch him, the more information he gives. Some of it—such as Russell's observation that the guy had turned pale and that his gait had faltered a bit—was actually usable in court. But mostly, Russell liked to absorb the way people responded to different stimuli, then plug those observations into his internal people-meter. Thus, he took his sweet time getting out of his car. He watched for a full minute after pulling to a stop in the driveway, as his suspect watched him back.

Russell noted that the guy didn't come forward to meet him. Nor did he run away. He just stood there, watching. Russell wondered what that meant, just as he wondered what the bruises on his face meant. In his current frame of mind, just about anything the guy did would have told Russell that he was guilty, revealing the chief weakness inherent to hunches: they tended to bear out whatever preconceptions the huncher brought with him to the situation. Appeals-court dockets sagged under the weight of cases where overzealous police officers had trampled on suspects' rights in blind pursuit of hunches that fell short of court-tested probable cause.

The time to be most cautious, then, was when the hunches ran hottest. This thought weighed heavily as Russell finally climbed out of his car and strolled over to Bobby.

"Hi there," Russell said in his most cheerful voice. "Beautiful house."

Bobby dropped a beat as he either winced or smiled. Russell couldn't tell. "Thanks."

"Are you Robert Martin?" Russell had closed the distance to an uncomfortable three feet of separation, effectively trapping his suspect against the Explorer's tailgate.

Bobby circled around his visitor and stepped back outside onto the driveway. "Yeah, I'm Bobby Martin. What can I do for you?"

Russell made a point of keeping his back turned for a moment as he scanned the inside of the garage, keeping Bobby's reflected image in the tailgate window. As Russell turned, he reached into the pocket of his suit coat and produced a leather wallet with his credentials. "I'm Russell Coates with the FBI." For the first time in his career, someone actually reached for the creds and pulled them closer to get a better view. In the process, Russell realized, he'd also been drawn back out of the garage. Was Martin doing that on purpose?

"So you are," Bobby said. "Why are you here?"

The initial fear seemed to be gone now, replaced by a wariness that told Russell that his visit did not come as a total surprise. "I'm investigating a murder." Sometimes, it's best just to lead with the harshest words and knock the suspect off-balance.

"Oh, that," Bobby said, nodding. "Terrible thing. I guess I've halfway been expecting you to call."

Russell raised an eyebrow. This interview wasn't yet a minute old, and it was already moving in an unexpected direction. "And why would that be?"

"You're talking about the killing up in the park, right?"

"You know about that?"

"Well, my wife and I were camping up there last night, so when I heard about it on the news I figured that sooner or later somebody would want to talk to us. I can save you some trouble, though. I don't have anything to offer."

Russell thought about that. Or at least he pretended to. "Why don't you tell me what you do know."

Bobby shrugged. "I know I was there last night, and then I heard that there'd been a killing. This time of year, when there are so few campers, I just figured that sooner or later you'd have to come around and talk to all of us."

"To all of you?"

"I mean to all of the campers who were there last night."

Russell pulled his notepad from the pocket opposite the one that held his creds. "How about you? Who were you there with?"

"My wife."

"No one else?"

"It's just the two of us."

Russell tried to be subtle as he eyed the box of Pampers on the floor, but Bobby caught his gaze.

"The diapers."

Russell responded with an interested shrug.

"We lost a baby a few weeks ago," Bobby explained, looking down. "We, uh . . ."

He didn't bother to finish the sentence, and Russell decided not to push. This Martin guy was either a hell of an actor or he'd tapped into a genuine source of pain. Either way, it never made sense to prod tender spots until a solid groundwork was laid. "What's your wife's name?" Russell asked. A softball, nonintrusive question always helped to bring people back on track.

"Susan."

Russell wrote it down. "So, you saw and heard nothing?"

"I saw a lot of dark and a lot of cold," Bobby said with a chuckle.

Something pinged in Russell's head. The suspect's words were just a little too glib—a little too nonspecific.

"Did you see or hear anything related to the murders?" Russell's words conveyed his fraying temper.

"Like what?"

The guy was good. If they followed this tack, Russell would in effect put himself in the situation of proposing scenarios that Martin could easily—and truthfully—deny. It was, in fact, a role reversal. Russell was supposed to be the one putting his suspect on the spot, not the other way around.

"Tell you what," Russell said, flipping his notebook closed and stuffing it back in his pocket. "It's kind of cold out here. What do you say we go inside and talk? It won't take very long."

The panicked look flashed again behind Bobby's eyes as he shook his head. "I'd rather not."

"Why not?"

"I need a reason for you not to come into my home?" Bobby said it as if he'd never heard of something so appalling.

"Do you always entertain guests out on the driveway?"

"You're not a guest," Bobby said simply enough. "You're an FBI agent, and I can tell just from your demeanor that you suspect that I had something to do with this mess in the park."

"And frankly, your behavior here isn't doing much to make me think otherwise."

Bobby shrugged. "All the more reason not to talk to you anymore." He turned to walk back into the house.

Russell almost laughed at the absurdity of the situation. "You know, we don't *have* to do this the easy way."

Bobby stopped and turned. "Meaning what?"

"Meaning that I can take you into custody as a material witness and question you all night long."

Knowing a bluff when he saw it, but nonetheless recognizing the wafer-thin ice on which he stood, Bobby strolled back toward Agent Coates, taking his time as he formulated his response. "Is that what you intend to do?"

Russell braced as the other man approached, as if preparing himself for a fight. "I may."

Bobby wanted to tell him to go ahead, to call his bluff, but he worried about seeming overly aggressive. The last thing he needed was to inadvertently give Coates the probable cause he was looking for.

"I don't think so," Bobby said. "Else you would have come here with an army of agents and a lot of big guns. Instead, it's just you on a fishing trip."

Russell allowed himself a smile. "And a suspect who's doing everything he can to make himself look guilty as hell."

Bobby's head bounced noncommittally on his shoulders, as if to acknowledge the point. "I think you need to call the ball here, Agent Coates. Either you've got your probable cause, and you're going to haul me in, or I'm going on inside to watch television."

Russell cocked an eyebrow. "What about your trip?"

Bobby didn't know what he was talking about.

Russell nodded toward the Explorer. "When I was driving up, you were headed out to your vehicle. I assumed you were about to take a trip somewhere."

Bobby looked as if he was thinking of a retort, but he ended up letting it go. "Have a nice day, Agent Coates."

Russell watched as Bobby strolled self-consciously back toward the house and pushed the button for the garage door. The tiny electric motor sounded overworked as the overhead door started its downward trek. "Nice truck," Russell yelled over the noise, bending at the waist to keep eye contact below the descending door. "I see you've got the same tires as the prints we found at Powhite Trail." He enjoyed watching the words land on their target.

"I'll see you in a little while," Russell called, but by then the door was all the way down.

Bobby made it only as far as the mudroom before he grabbed the wall and slid down onto the floor. To keep from passing out, he sat Indian-style, with his forehead dangling just inches above his crossed ankles. He opened his mouth wide and gulped huge lungfuls of air, keeping his eyes clenched tight until the spots stopped dancing.

What had he done? Sweet Jesus, God Almighty, what had he done? It was all over now. It had to be. The tires were the key to it all. He'd seen the fucking tires, and soon there'd be the army of cops with their search warrants. In what—two hours?—everything would come crashing down. It couldn't possibly take any longer than that. In two hours there'd be the shame of the mug shots and the television camera crews. There'd be the announcements from all of his neighbors and coworkers about how surprised they were that a guy as nice as Bobby Martin could turn out to be a murderer and a kidnapper.

That quickly, they'd all turn against him. He'd seen it happen on the news countless times and always with the same result. Somehow or other, the networks would get a picture of him being led out of some courthouse somewhere with his wrists and ankles shackled and his head bowed low. Everyone in the world would see that and know unquestioningly that he was guilty. The FBI handled this case, after all, and the FBI always gets it right.

Why hadn't he just come clean?

Of all the countless thousands of questions that swooped and swirled in his mind, that was the one that took center stage, like a giant condor flying among sparrows. Why hadn't he just sat Agent Coates down and spilled his guts? Told the whole story? At least then the truth would have been on the record. Now, no matter what he said to anyone, whether under oath or just in passing, it would be judged as just another lie told by a frightened criminal who'd already established his propensity for lying.

But you didn't lie, he told himself. He'd been very careful about that. Everything he'd said had walked the feather edge, but he'd never crossed it. There was something to be proud of there, no?

Pride. Now there was a concept that didn't mean a lot anymore. Pride seemed like a luxury now; something that he'd be lucky ever to attain in a dream, let alone in the real world. Right at this moment, he'd pay a fortune just for some guaranteed dignity.

Raising his head and looking around the room, he tried to think of something to do; something that might possibly bring him a step closer to a solution for all of this. He could still run; just hop on a plane while there was still time and jet off to wherever. That was ridiculous and he knew it. Others had tried, and they were always caught.

Again, the vision of his retirement party jumped into his head. People crashing the doors and throwing his guests to the floor.

No, that wouldn't do at all.

Climbing back to his feet, Bobby wandered back into the kitchen and helped himself to a tall glass of orange juice. What he really wanted was a good stiff drink, but that was a bad idea. If ever there was a time for him to be fully awake and alert, this was it. He had some serious, serious thinking to do.

He hadn't realized how dry his mouth had become until the cold, acidic juice cut its way through. It felt great, even if it sat a little uneasily on his stomach.

"You know what you need to do," he told the room. "You've got no choice here."

He chugged the rest of the juice, then made a face as his gut decided whether it was going to send it back. In the end, it all stayed down.

And then it was time to make his phone call.

Judging from the sound of the receptionist's voice, Barbara Dettrick had alerted her to be ready for his call. The lawyer picked it up on the first ring.

"Bobby?"

"The FBI just left," Bobby said, and for the first time he wondered if he was going to be able to keep his composure. "I think he knows."

"What did he say to you?"

"I could see it in his eyes. I could hear it in the way he asked his questions. He knows it's me."

"It doesn't matter what he knows, Bobby," she said sharply, trying to get him back on point. "And it doesn't matter what he thinks. All that matters is what he can prove. Now tell me what you talked about."

"It was just like I was afraid of. He knew that we'd been in the park last night, and he wanted some information from me."

"Dammit, Bobby, quit being so vague, will you? Tell me what he asked, and tell me what you told him."

Bobby recounted the conversation as best he could from the increasingly fuzzy recollections. He told her he admitted to being in the park last night, and that he thought he'd done a stunning job of never straying from the truth.

"Don't be so proud of yourself, Bobby," Barbara admonished. "This guy isn't some hayseed deputy. He's the FBI, and he knows when he's being evaded. Did he ever ask to come inside?"

"I told him no. I said I could tell that I'm a suspect in his mind, and that I didn't see where I could do myself any good by inviting him inside. Kind of like inviting a vampire in, you know? Once they cross the threshold, they never have to leave."

Barbara laughed, and the sound was refreshing. "That was good. Very good, in fact. What about that permit thing you were so worried about? Did he ever mention anything about that?"

Damned interesting point. "No, he didn't. What do you think that means?"

"Well, I hope it means he never found the damned thing, or that maybe it blew off the mountain and into the river. The way I see it, the lost permit is only important if they found it within a reasonable distance of the crime scene. Frankly, with that kind of evidence, you'd be under arrest now. How about a search warrant? Did your FBI buddy mention anything about coming back with one of those?"

"Not in so many words, no. But he did say that the tires on my truck were of the same make as the ones found at the crime scene."

"I thought you parked down the hill from the crime scene."

"I did. About a mile, I guess."

Barbara nearly cheered. "A mile! He's bluffing. A mile might as well be a light-year. Besides, if I recall right, your tires don't look very new."

"They're the originals. Got nearly sixty thousand miles on them."

"Well, shit, Bobby. That means that every Explorer on the street is using the same tires. I don't think we've got a lot of exposure there. Sounds like you did a good job."

"So, what happens next?"

"That depends. At this point, the next move belongs to the other side. We just sit and wait."

Bobby fell silent. There had to be something more than that. Just waiting for the other shoe to drop would drive him over the edge. "I want to turn myself in." There, it was out on the table. "Let's explain it all and see where it turns out."

The silence on the other end unnerved him.

"Barbara?"

"I'm here. I think that's a mistake."

"What do you mean, you think it's a mistake? It's what you wanted me to do earlier this afternoon."

"That was earlier. Since then I've had a chance to talk with some of my colleagues, and I've changed my mind. I think you ought to hang tight for a while."

Well, shit. "Why, for God's sake?" The anger in his voice startled him.

"Truthfully? Because the feds have a death penalty now, and they're always looking for a place to test it. Until I know more about what they know, then I think we should just keep our mouths shut."

"Why don't you ask, then?"

"Well, that's what I want to do, but it'll take a little while. I want to tell them that their little visit caused you some concern, and that I want to know everything they have."

"Will they tell you?"

"Probably not. Not until they've officially named you as a suspect. Right now, they won't want to tip their hand, and that makes sense. I think you should wait and keep your mouth shut."

Bobby made a growling sound. "But, Jesus, Barbara, I don't know if I can take it."

"You can take it," she soothed. "You have to take it. For a while, anyway. Just remember, a lifetime is a long time to regret a hasty decision. I can't emphasize that point to you enough."

She was right. He knew she was right, but he also knew that he was telling the God's honest truth about being ready to crack under the stress. "How long will this stretch on?"

"Don't ask questions you don't want the answers to, Bobby. Now, let's talk about this stray human being you have on your hands."

The abruptness of the change of subject startled him. "I've made no progress there. Susan took him out shopping while I was meeting with you."

"*Shopping?* As in out of the house where people might see her? Is she out of her mind?"

Bobby closed his eyes and took a deep breath. "Right at this second? Yeah, I think she is. And I'll be goddamned if I know what to do about it."

25

RICKY TIMMONS DID his best to sit still as he listened to the change of plans. He waited till Logan was done, and then another fifteen seconds before he spoke. When he did, he carefully measured his words, knowing that he could never win an argument with his boss by shouting. Once voices were raised, logic went out the window, and everything became an issue of pride.

"I don't think we can do it all, Patrick. Even if we could get to West Virginia by midnight, the chances of getting away clean are way too small."

Logan waved him off. "We don't have any choice. I already told you that. This Samuel asshole is a fucking nutcase, and with his brother dead, we've got to plug the holes. There's no other way."

And this was exactly the reason why poorly planned hits got you into trouble. Things just never went perfectly. Never. And you had to plan for that. This vendetta against Carlos Ortega boiled so hot in Logan's gut that he couldn't think past it anymore. It was making the boss think that he was infallible.

"Then let's take Ortega out with a rifle," Ricky suggested. "We'll hit him from a hundred yards away and skate off into the sunset."

Logan shook his head. "No. The son of a bitch has to know who hit him."

"But everybody else at the whole school will see you, too. You don't think that'll be a problem?"

Logan smiled. "Not with the disguise my right-hand man is going to put together for me."

Ricky laughed. "What am I supposed to do? Give you some Groucho nose and glasses? Jesus, Patrick, this is big shit here. You need to start taking it seriously."

"I take it *very* seriously!" Logan boomed. "You're being an old woman! What the hell's gotten into you?"

Ricky bristled. If anyone else in the world had called him an old woman, they'd already have been dead.

Logan seemed to sense his lieutenant's anger, and he toned it down. He leaned back into his seat and motioned for Ricky to do the same. "Relax, Ricky. I just wanted you to know exactly how much faith I have in your abilities, okay? You're nobody's old woman, and I apologize for calling you that, okay?"

Ricky didn't say anything, trying to measure sincerity. Finally he nodded. Yeah, it was okay.

"Good. And I want you to know that if there was another way to do this, I'd do it. But there's not. Ortega drew his line in the sand, and I'm walking all over it. If we don't take him out tonight, then it'll be us in body bags tomorrow. This thing in the woods, well, what the hell? Sometimes things go wrong. Maybe this is the fuckup you've been worried about. Maybe this is the one thing that always goes wrong, and from here on out, it's smooth sailing."

Ricky had to smile. Only Logan could take comfort in twisted logic like that. Still, that kind of confidence couldn't help but rub off. Maybe he had a good point. One thing was sure: right or wrong, making other people dead beat the hell out of being dead yourself.

Ricky took a deep breath and nodded his surrender. "Okay, Patrick, we'll do it all tonight. But I want your promise on something first, okay?"

Logan cocked his head.

"I want you to promise me that we'll do the hits my way. I'll get you in close enough that Ortega will know who's popping him, but beyond that, you do it my way, okay?"

Logan looked as if he wanted to argue, but he nodded nonetheless. "Your way."

"Because this is what I do. This kind of thing is my specialty."

"Ricky, quit selling. I already said I'd do it."

Ricky searched for signs that the boss was lying, but ended up liking what he saw. "All right, then." Ricky reached into the zippered backpack that had been lounging at his feet and pulled out a Ziploc bag with a Glock nine-millimeter inside. Holding the bag by a top corner, he dangled it in front of Logan.

"Here's your weapon. It's clean. It'll trace back to some doper in Spokane."

Logan reached for the bag, but Ricky pulled it back out of reach. "Listen to me now. There's not a fingerprint on this thing. I loaded it with gloves on, and you need to handle it with gloves. Don't take it out of the bag until you're at the school. That way, you won't get fibers on it that'll trace back here."

"What about a silencer?"

Ricky shook his head. "No way. You're going to be shooting in a crowd, so you want the noise. You want the panic. And don't worry about the brass. Just let it fly."

Logan nodded. Clearly, he was imagining the scene in his head.

"Now your biggest problem is gonna be Peña, okay? You gotta take him out first, and you gotta do that one fast. I'd prefer that you take them both fast, but I know you'll want to play with Ortega, so I won't even bother to tell you. But Peña's a fucking animal, okay, Pat? An animal. You don't take him out first, he'll shoot every fucking person in that room till he gets you, understand?"

"I understand. What kind of ammunition did you load me with?"

"Devastators. Seventeen of them. You hit an arm, it's coming off. Anywhere above the belly button and between the shoulders, the guy dies with hamburger for guts."

Now there was an image Logan could wrap his mind around. "How are you gonna take the Martin bitch and her hubby?"

Ricky smiled knowingly and slung his arm over the back of his chair. Hoping to make a point, he answered, "With as little drama as possible."

"I need to talk to you about Bobby and Susan Martin," Russell said, tucking his credentials away. Heather Gannon seemed oblivious to the two-year-old who hung from the sleeve of her Eddie Bauer sweatshirt. The kid wore a diaper and a T-shirt and its name was Terry. For the life of him, Russell couldn't tell if it was a boy or a girl.

"What have they done?"

"We don't know that they've done anything, ma'am," Russell replied as cheerfully as he could. Fact was, no one had yet invented a way to casually inquire about someone's neighbors without raising eyebrows. "I just wanted to ask some questions, if that's okay."

Heather looked on the cusp when little Terry decided the issue for her, pulling her off-balance into the foyer. "Come on in," she called over her shoulder.

Russell stepped into Tara. A grand stairway rose steeply from the center of the entryway to join a railed balcony that ran along all four walls overhead. On the ground floor, where Russell would have expected wallpaper and a few paintings, the Gannons had opted for a ten-foot-high mural that spanned the entire perimeter of the entry hall, featuring red-jacketed men on horseback scaring the living shit out of a fox that, to Russell's eye, was nowhere to be found.

"How nice," he said. A much better icebreaker than "This is tackiest waste of money I've ever seen."

"Thank you," said Heather, prying her child off her arm. "It was done by Antoine Phillipe." She pronounced the artist's name with a kind of awe that he was clearly invited to share, but the effort was wasted. Call him a cynic, but Russell's mind conjured up the image of a pony-tailed, out-of-work artist named Tony Phillips who needed some folding money and had devised a way to score big.

"You're welcome to study some of the detail if you'd like."

Russell smiled politely but didn't respond. As he pushed the door closed behind him, he instinctively opened his jacket. Carrying a gun made no sense if you didn't have quick access to it, and he wasn't yet ready to rule this woman out as delusional. "Is there a place where we can sit down?"

Little Terry was crying now, sitting on the stone floor and kicking his feet.

"What do you *want?*" Heather barked at the child, and the crying became a wail. Heather raised her head to the ceiling and yelled, "Margarita!" When Margarita—whoever the hell she was—didn't respond in five seconds, Heather called the name again, only this time much louder.

Russell heard a long string of Spanish words spilling over the railing above and behind, and he looked up to see a round, little woman of about fifty hurrying to get to the stairs. She wore the uniform of a maid, and the expression of someone who feared losing it.

"For God's sake, Margarita, where have you been? He's been just crazy this afternoon!"

Margarita answered in heavily accented English that Russell could understand only slightly better than the Spanish. He distinctly heard the word *bathroom,* though, and he found himself feeling sorry for the woman, who apparently needed permission to take a dump. She bowed and apologized and then hurried off with little Terry in tow.

Finally alone, Heather straightened and brushed herself off. "There," she said with a puff of air that made it sound as if she'd just won an arm-wrestling match. "He can be quite a handful."

"Must be nice to have a stunt mother on standby," Russell said with a smile.

Heather hesitated a moment before deciding to take the comment in good humor. "Margarita's a godsend. Shall we go and sit in the parlor?"

Another first, Russell thought. To his knowledge, he'd never been in a parlor before. Lots of living rooms and family rooms and even the occasional library, but never a parlor. He followed his hostess through an archway off the foyer, in effect turning his back on Tara and entering the Cheyenne Social Club. He wondered where one shops to find so much red velvet and gold tassels.

"Please help yourself to a seat."

Heather perched on the edge of a garish chaise lounge while a deceptively innocent-looking chair consumed Russell whole.

Heather smiled as her visitor struggled to rescue his butt. "I should have warned you. But don't you just love antiques?"

Artists and yard sales see you coming for miles, he didn't say. "So, how long have you known the Martins?"

Heather stewed on that one for a few seconds and appeared to be close to answering when her features darkened. "I don't know how I feel about answering questions like this without knowing what it's all about. I mean, suppose I get them in trouble?"

Russell took out his notebook. "Do they regularly engage in activities that would get them in trouble?" He loved asking questions like that, and Heather's reaction made it all the more worthwhile.

"Oh, heavens, I don't know," she blustered, pulling on her sweatshirt as if suddenly struck with a hot flash. "I don't think so. I mean, well, I don't really know, come to think of it. Certainly I haven't witnessed any, but you never really know about people, do you?"

Russell smiled patiently and wrote doodles in his book that he hoped might look like illegible handwriting. "No, I guess you don't." He scowled thoughtfully as he doodled a little more. Finally he looked up. "You were saying?"

As planned, Heather seemed utterly confused. "Was I saying something?"

"About the Martins."

"Oh, yes, of course." She paused. "Where were we?"

"You were about to tell me how long you've known them." Nothing like drawing a few squiggles in a notebook to get hesitant neighbors to squeal on their friends.

"Well, they've lived next door for maybe six, seven months, I guess. But I can't say that I've ever really known them." She added that last part quickly, as if to separate herself from whatever bad things they might have done.

"How would you characterize them as neighbors?"

She shrugged. "Nice enough, I suppose. They keep to themselves a lot, but then so do we all around here. These five-acre lots sort of keep people at arm's length."

"Do they seem to get along well together? Mr. and Mrs. Martin, I mean."

"I suppose. Like I said, we don't spend much time with them."

Russell jotted a note. "When was the last time you spoke with either of them?"

Heather thought for a moment, then snapped her fingers. "Oh, of course, that's easy. That would have been at the reception after the miscarriage."

Russell looked confused. "Miscarriage?" When Bobby had told the story, he'd made it sound as if a child had actually died.

"Yeah, a few weeks ago, I guess. I think it was pretty late-term, too. They took it very hard."

This detail interested him. At what point does a miscarriage become a stillbirth? He couldn't put his finger on why this could matter, but his instincts told him that it was significant. He wrote a note—a real one this time—and boldly underlined it, so he wouldn't forget. "You say they took it hard. How do you mean?"

"Well, they seemed to be in mourning, you know? I heard from some of the other neighbors that they'd been trying and trying to have a baby, and then to lose one so late. Well, I guess they just took it hard."

"You said this happened a few weeks ago. Could you be more specific? Four weeks? Eight weeks?"

Heather thought for a moment. "I guess it was maybe six weeks ago, two months max. It really was very sad. Bobby in particular seemed torn apart over it. Susan got real quiet—probably quieter than she should have been—but Bobby was just a mess."

"'Just a mess' doesn't mean anything to me. Could you be more specific?"

Heather grunted in a way that showed growing exasperation. "He was, you know, a *mess*. You could see it in his walk, in the way he'd wave back when I said hi. He just seemed to be a very, very sad man."

Russell nodded sympathetically. Your heart has to go out to anyone who's suffered that kind of loss. He thought of the box of Pampers in the garage and remembered how long his own mother had hung on to his father's clothes after he'd passed away. Like Bobby Martin, she'd been able to get the box as far as the garage, but for years was unable to actually let go of them. Up in the bedroom, she'd bought a wooden valet stand just to hold his dad's favorite sweater vest and hat.

At least for the Martins, the diapers would still have a valid use, he thought, once they got around to having another child.

Footprints.

Russell had delved so far into sentimentality that he'd nearly forgotten a piece of the puzzle. The only set of footprints common to the grave site, the murder scene, and the road belonged to a child. If the Martins had no children, then where did those prints come from?

"Have you seen anything of the Martins in the past few days? Say, within the last week?"

"You mean to speak to?"

Russell shrugged. "To speak to, to wave to, to casually observe."

"I think they went away this weekend. On Friday I saw them loading camping gear into the car." Heather shivered at the thought of it. "You've really got to love the outdoors to camp in this weather. It's cold out there."

Russell allowed himself a chuckle. "Not the frontier type, eh?"

She recoiled from the thought. "Me? Keep your tents. I'm room service and cable TV all the way."

Okay, Russell thought, she swam in money, had no taste, and never worried about where to put her mother-of-the-year awards, but at least she was honest about herself. In his book, that counted for quite a lot.

Frankly, he'd been hoping that this interview would be more productive. As it was, all he'd really got out of it was that the people he suspected of murder were in fact really nice folks. Why was that always the case? He was just about to ask the sweeping is-there-anything-else-I-should-know question and move on when his cell phone rang.

Russell took a whole two rings to find the damn thing in his jacket pocket. Between his wallet, gun, handcuffs, credentials, and cell phone, he swore he carried an extra ten pounds of crap around with him every day. Offering an apologetic smile to his hostess, he opened his StarTAC and brought it up to his ear.

"Coates."

"Hi, Russell, this is Tim," said the familiar voice from the other end. "I thought I'd catch you up on a few details. We got a positive ID on the stiff. His name was Jacob Stanns, and he lives out here in West Virginia with his brother, Samuel. I'm heading out there to chat him up and see what we can find."

Russell wrote the victim's name into his book. "Okay, good. Anything else?"

"Not much, really. But I did get the 911 call traced to a little all-night convenience store outside of Winchester, Virginia. Some state troopers talked to the kid who was working last night, and while they didn't have any pictures to show, the description the kid gave of the customer came awfully close to the description on the Martin guy's driver's license. It might be time to reach out and touch him."

Russell glanced awkwardly at Heather, who acknowledged him, but made no effort to leave him alone. "I can't really talk about that now," he said as pointedly as he knew how, and wrestled himself out of the man-eating chair. As he made his way out to the foyer, Heather followed. "What did they buy at the store?"

He could hear pages rustling as Tim searched his notes for that detail. "Well, I know he got gas, but other than that, not much. Oh, here we go. The clerk said he bought a candy bar and a box of diapers."

26

LIKE THE LITTLE lady that she was, Christa Ortega waited patiently in her seat while Tío Jesús walked around to open the car door for her. She had the position of honor in the Cherokee tonight—the back right-hand corner where her father usually sat. Carlos could barely contain his pride as he watched her take Peña's hand and then rise like an angel out of her seat. For her part, Christa handled the attention like a queen. Once she was out on the sidewalk, Carlos's wife, Consuela, followed, sliding across the seat and likewise accepting Peña's hand. Carlos himself stepped out last, from the front seat, and walked his ladies down the long sidewalk toward the school, one draped on either arm. Peña followed closely behind, Christa's cello dangling from his left hand.

He kept his right hand free.

"Carlos, this is so silly," Consuelo said, laughing. "You'd think that we were arriving at the Oscars."

"This is better than the Oscars," Carlos said, nudging Christa. "This is my daughter's big chance to show everyone how talented she is."

"Dad-dy." Christa blushed. "I don't even have a real solo part."

"Real enough." Carlos beamed. As a father, it was his job to gush over his daughter's talent, just as it was her job to be embarrassed by it. Every little girl needed to know that she was special. Even more importantly, she needed to know that her daddy would do anything in the world for her.

The Ortegas were not the first family to arrive at the auditorium, but they were far from the last, as they slipped into the crush of parents and siblings who represented 90 percent of the audience for this middle-school orchestra concert.

Carlos craned his neck to see over the heads of the people in front but couldn't determine the source of the bottleneck. Christa stepped off to the side to take a peek of her own, then rejoined the family, frowning.

"It's Sister Inez," she said quietly. "I don't think she likes me."

"That's silly," said her mother. "I'm sure she likes all her students." Then, much more quietly, Consuela whispered to Carlos, "It's her father that she can't stand."

He smiled. What could he say? Consuela was right, and it had been that way ever since he was a little boy here at St. Ignatius School—St. Iggy's to the locals. Never one to abide by the rules, little Carlos Ortega had been a terror, and no amount of beatings from home could change that. When he'd be planted in Sister Inez's office and she'd rant at him, he'd feel truly apologetic. It wasn't that he *tried* to get into trouble. It's just that he could never get over the surprise that the rules actually applied to him.

Perhaps to make amends—or perhaps to rub their noses in it—Carlos had since donated over $200,000 to the school. In fact, the entire music department would not exist were it not for his contributions. So, Sister Inez had little choice but to be cordial these days. But that didn't mean she had to be friendly.

He waited patiently for his turn in the receiving line, and when he found himself face-to-face with his old nemesis, he smiled politely and shook her hand. "Good evening, Sister."

She barely made eye contact before she bent down to greet Christa. "Play well, young lady."

To which Christa replied, "Good evening, Sister."

Sister Inez reserved her most withering look for Peña, who sort of grunted as he looked her over as if to spot a weapon she might be carrying.

Carlos and Consuela parted company with their daughter at the door to the music room. Christa accepted the cello from Peña and headed on in to the practice room to tune up and get ready.

"She's nearly as beautiful as her mother," said a voice from behind.

The Ortegas turned to see Father Eugene, smile beaming. "Father!" Carlos rejoiced. "So wonderful of you to come! I don't know that she could ever hope to be *that* beautiful, but it will be close." That last part earned him a shot in the ribs from his wife.

If Sister Inez had come close to driving young Carlos to paganism, then Father Eugene bore the single-handed responsibility for keeping him near the Church. Ever kind, and always willing to listen, this quickly aging priest was a particular favorite among the kids whom Carlos used to hang around with and also taught a kick-ass history lesson. Father Eugene hated everything about what Carlos did for a living, but still managed to treat him as one of his flock. Father Eugene had been there for every significant event in Carlos's life, from his marriage to Consuela to the christening of his daughter to the funerals of both his parents.

After embracing first Carlos and then Consuela, Father Eugene even offered a warm handshake to Peña, who returned it with a smile.

"I presume you're here early for a front-row seat," the priest said as he ushered the others toward the auditorium.

Carlos smiled and produced a camera from his jacket pocket. "Of course. Would you care to join us?"

Father Eugene smiled. "I would love to."

As it turned out, the third row was the best they could manage. As always, Carlos noted the sideward glances from the other parents as they took their seats, and as always, he returned the glances with a smile and a nod. He wondered how much of the radiated discomfort came not from offended citizens, but from customers who were afraid of being outed in front of their families.

Let he who is without sin cast the first stone. Carlos always liked that parable.

The orchestra at St. Iggy's was big. Between the Strings Ensemble and the much larger and more accomplished Concert Orchestra, over a hundred kids would play tonight. Given two parents per kid, more or less, along with the faculty and staff who had decided to stick around to listen, there had to be upwards of two hundred people in the auditorium, which was designed for two seventy-five. Unless you wanted to split hairs, this house was full.

At seven sharp, the houselights dimmed and the stage lights blossomed. The combined footsteps of the children filing onto the stage sounded like distant thunder, to which was soon added the metallic clanking of music stands and the scraping of chairs as the kids all took their places.

When all the seats onstage were filled, Carlos's heart rate doubled. "Where's Christa?" he whispered.

Peña saw the look on his boss's face and stood. The set of his eyes and his jaw told everyone that he was prepared to fight.

Consuela pulled on Peña's suit coat. "Sit down!" she hissed. "These are the beginners. Christa won't be out until later."

If Peña felt embarrassed, he didn't show it. He merely smiled to his neighbors and lowered himself back into his seat. Leaning forward, he whispered to Carlos, "You want me to go back and check on her?"

Carlos thought about it briefly, then shook his head. "No, she's fine," he whispered. "I'll never hear the end of it if I embarrass her. She'll be fine."

Behind them, a man dressed all in black stepped into the rear of the auditorium. Filling the doorway as he did, he drew looks from people in the quick-exit seats, but they thought nothing of this man wearing a clerical collar and a gentle smile. Truthfully, the bushy mustache made him seem rather unlikely as a priest, but not so much that anyone would inquire.

The man could see clearly enough in the wash of the stage lights to find a seat about halfway down, in the center section, three seats from the nearest end. When he arrived abreast of the row, he stooped down till his mouth was inches away from the occupant in the aisle seat.

"Excuse me," he whispered, "but would you mind scooting over so I don't have to climb over you?"

Clearly the man did mind, but what could he say to a priest? He nudged his wife in the arm and they each scooted over one seat.

The priest smiled and nodded his satisfaction. "Thank you so very much. I have a bad back, don't you know."

The former seat owner grudgingly nodded and turned his attention back to the stage.

No one would ever think to ask the priest why he never took off his gloves.

William Simpson was furious. Where the hell had that bitch run off to?

He wasn't April's fucking secretary, and he was tired of fielding all of her phone calls. How the hell were they supposed to make ends meet if she didn't show up to her jobs? Jesus, where was her head?

Well, he knew the answer to that one, didn't he? Her head was stuck a foot up her ass worrying about that damn kid. Oh, sweet little fucking Justin. Who needed that little shit around here in the first place? Today had been the first day of peace and quiet in years. It just never stopped. I want, I want, I want. That's all he ever heard. I want a cookie, a juice, a fucking toy. Swear to God, the kid was worse than having a dog. At least a dog'll shit outside. Not dear little Justin. That kid could crap a whole pound on one push.

Did April cut him any slack for that at all? Fuck no. Well, fuck her. And her kid. Let them both go to hell the hard way.

Just so long as she kept her fucking yap shut. If she went to the cops with this, Logan would no-shit for real kill them all, no questions asked. Surely she believed this. Christ, could he have explained it any more clearly?

So, where the hell was she? He could just imagine her wandering through the city, looking in trash cans and alleys, searching for her precious baby. Boo-fucking-hoo. Maybe now she'd feel a little pain for her own miserable self and start treating her husband with a little respect. It was about time for her to start earning her keep. To hell with this burgers and maid shit. With her looks, she could haul in serious bucks off the street.

And he could be her pimp. She'd by God show him some respect then or he'd beat the living shit out of her.

He needed a drink. To hell with all of this shit. Let them both fucking die. Grabbing his keys and jacket off the sagging little table in the hall, William headed out.

This playground was a problem. He had never liked walking through such a wide expanse of open space with no place to duck and run to when the gang-bangers got out of hand. It wasn't so bad during the day, but once it got dusky like this, he began to feel uneasy.

Out of nowhere, an invisible horse kicked him in the gut. The impact knocked him backward a good three feet and landed him in a twisted pile of arms and legs, with his butt in the air and his weight pressed against his shoulder and his face. The half somersault had flopped his legs all the way over his head, leaving his feet in a tangle on the cold, wet grass. When he tried to straighten himself out, though, the legs wouldn't work. Gasping for air, he willed them to move, but they wouldn't; they just lay there, as if they belonged to someone else. Panic flashed behind his eyes as he grabbed at the useless appendages and tried to uncoil them by hand. His fingers registered the rough texture of the denim pants, under which he could feel flesh, but the flesh couldn't feel him back.

What the hell . . . ?

As he struggled for a handhold on his pants leg, the horse kicked him again, and he shrieked in horror as his right hip exploded in a gnarled mess of bone and tissue. The impact seemed even greater than before, spinning him on the ground like a break-dancer and landing him flat on his back.

"Oh, shit! Oh, fuck, I'm shot!" That had to be it. It *had* to be. But where was the pain? Where was the fucking pain? Feeling nothing terrified him more than any agony he'd ever endured. What the hell was happening?

His breathing wasn't right. He felt an odd pressure in his chest. Not a pain, really, but every bit as oppressive as if someone heavy were sitting on him. The harder he tried to inhale, the heavier the weight became. And the chest-sitter slurped when he breathed. He made a horrid, snoring sound as he struggled for air, and William couldn't understand it.

That's when he saw the blood. With his jacket zipped, it had taken a while for it to ooze out where he could see it, but now it was everywhere. And there was the hole, no bigger around than a pencil. If it hadn't been for a protruding tuft of down filling, he might have missed it completely.

"Aw, fuck, help me!" he cried, and a third bullet screamed in, this one passing maybe an inch from his ear and drilling itself into the grass behind him. William tried to roll over onto his belly to crawl away, but his dead legs were like anchors, keeping him rooted flat on his back.

He tried to scream out for help again, but the weight in his chest had filled his throat, rendering his vocal cords as useless as his legs. Maybe he could just scoot out of there on his back, he thought, but when he tried to lift his arms, the beast on his chest grew to the size of a building.

Godammit, the fuckers won, he thought. As he lay there, staring up at the black sky, he wondered where all the stars had gone.

A block away, in the third floor of a condemned rattrap that had done stints as a hotel and a homeless shelter, Ricky Timmons settled his aim and took his time, savoring what had to be one of the easiest hits of his life. Thanks to his chat with a kid named Fuzzy—the very one who would be found in the river in a day or two, dead of an overdose—Ricky had found out that William Simpson lived by a routine you could set your watch by.

That made all of this just a matter of waiting.

It bothered Ricky that no one had seen the woman. April, that was her name. No one had seen April. He'd asked two people in passing, and both of them had said no. He'd paid Fuzzy fifty bucks to ask in more detail, but he'd come up empty as well. This was troubling to Ricky. The woman was a loose end, and sooner rather than later it would need to be tied.

As he'd set up his sniper's nest, he'd considered holding off on William until he could nail them both, but logic told him that whacking the husband now would at least serve to make the lady think twice before opening her mouth. She was a pretty ballsy broad, though. It wasn't beyond the realm that this would cause her to panic and take everything public.

When William stepped out of his apartment into the open, however, the target decided the issue himself. Some opportunities are so juicy that you can't turn away. Ricky watched through the rifle scope as William walked straight toward him. The target looked a little nervous, but no more so than anyone else walking out into this neighborhood at night. The few working streetlights provided just enough illumination so that Ricky didn't need the nightscope.

He'd thought about ending it quickly with a head shot, but with the silencer in place, he could afford to play around a little. Logan always wanted his enemies to know they'd crossed the wrong guy, and without a few moments of panic—the kind of panic that comes from seeing your own guts spilling onto the sidewalk—the lesson could be wasted.

It was always hazardous going for the spine if you didn't want an outright kill; even more difficult when shooting head-on as he was here. The heart, the liver, and the lungs all bled like sons of bitches, and if you weren't careful, the target would bleed out before he had a chance to realize what was happening.

So, that first shot was something to be proud of. Three inches above the belly button and out through the backbone. Perfect. Instant paralysis. The leg shot, on the other hand, was so artless that he almost felt ashamed for firing it. Sure did make the target fly, though. Ricky laughed at the spectacle and allowed his concentration to sag, and now he couldn't believe he'd completely whiffed with the last shot.

Now it was about pride. The guy was propably dead already, even if he was still breathing, but Ricky was not in the business of taking chances. There's dead and there's damned dead. Ricky never liked compromise.

Kneeling just far enough away from the window to remain invisible, he assumed a classic kneeling pose and locked his elbows in. He took his breath, let half of it out, and held it. Settling his crosshairs on the target, he slipped his finger through the trigger guard and squeezed, gently and slowly.

The silenced weapon hissed, his shoulder easily absorbing the recoil. Even from this far away—even at night—he could see the brains fly.

27

BY THE TIME he saw Susan's headlights sweeping up the driveway, Bobby's anger had blossomed to rage. Here he was, trying to keep his sanity, even as the friggin' FBI was closing in on his ass, and Susan was out *shopping*. And not by herself, thank you very much, but with a child who, by any other definition in the world but hers, had been kidnapped.

Not misplaced, not misdirected, not lost, but *kidnapped!* Jesus.

He'd never before endured the kind of fear he'd lived with over the past twenty-four hours. The specter of getting caught far outweighed the physical fear he'd felt in the woods last night when he was fighting for his life. That kind of fear you just reacted to; there was no thinking to be done; no weighing of options. When someone threatened to kill you, you just did what you did, and it wasn't until after the fight that you even knew who won.

This new terror brought with it too many options; too many decisions with consequences that he couldn't even begin to calculate. He realized now that his visit to Barbara Dettrick's office, and the phone calls that had followed, weren't really about finding a way to avoid prosecution. They were really about seeking permission to turn himself in. He'd wanted somebody to tell him that all was lost; that he had no choice but to do the right thing.

But that's not what she'd told him at all. And when he turned to his best friend—his life partner, with whom he was supposed to grow old—

she wasn't there. She was off in some make-believe world where she could claim a lost child as her own, as if he were a lost puppy.

Jesus, she was calling him *Steven.* How sick was that? How could she blaspheme their son's memory like that? Was she so unbalanced over his loss, or was this just a way to escape the pain that their life had become? And who the hell was she to leave him all alone to deal with such unspeakable terror?

Now that he saw the headlights, though, the jumbled emotions all drained away, leaving behind only a miserable sense of dread. He stood framed in the living room window, the space behind him darkened so he couldn't be seen. Ever since Agent Coates had left him in the garage, he couldn't shake the feeling that he was being watched. What was the word from the cops show? Oh, yeah. Surveilled. He couldn't shake the feeling that he was being surveilled.

Susan's Chrysler stopped short of the garage, and as the overhead door climbed its track, a dim rectangle of light crawled across the driveway to meet her. Instead of pulling inside, though, she climbed out while still on the driveway and walked around to the backseat on the passenger side. For a second, Bobby wondered what she was doing, but then he saw the little boy's head bobbing in the glare of the dome light, and he remembered that Susan probably didn't have enough room on that side of the garage to wrestle him out.

The way she moved, and the way she smiled as she lifted him out of the car, you'd think she hadn't a care in the world. It seemed like a million years since he'd last seen that expression on her face, and seeing it now only deepened his anger. What gave her the right to feel anything but miserable? Their next stop was the trunk, from which Susan lifted half a dozen shopping bags before closing the lid again. She handed one of the bags to the boy at her side, and he hugged it to his chest, beaming. A stuffed tiger dangled from his left fist.

Bobby continued to watch just long enough to make sure that they were coming in through the garage before he headed back toward the kitchen to meet them. He and Susan arrived at the door at the same time, each startling the other.

"Oh!" Susan exclaimed. "Bobby, you scared me."

"Sorry," he said, but he didn't mean it. "Nice to have you back."

"Steven and I had such a wonderful time! You wouldn't believe how many mothers are at the mall this time of day. We just shopped and shopped and shopped. Steven was a perfect little angel." She gushed on breathlessly, the whole way ushering the boy across the kitchen into the family room, where he zealously tore into a package, which, as it turned out, contained another stuffed animal, this one a foot-tall Pooh bear. He beamed as Susan sat down next to him on the floor to play.

Bobby tried a half dozen times to interrupt, but she was on a roll that wouldn't be stopped. Finally, as she paused to remove her coat, he said quickly, "The FBI came by this afternoon." He hoped to rattle her, but his words apparently missed their mark.

"Oh, really?" She didn't even look up. "What did they want?"

Bobby's eyebrows launched up to his hairline. "Excuse me? They wanted to talk about a certain dead body they found up in the woods last night, remarkably close to the place where we pitched our tent."

Susan had the tiger now, and the stuffed animal flew through the air to tickle the boy's tummy, competing with Pooh for attention. Giggles bubbled up from the toddler's toes.

"Susan, are you even listening to me?"

"I'm right here, Bobby. Of course I'm listening to you."

"Think you could look at me, too?"

She lifted her face and threw a smile over her shoulder, batting her eyes in exaggerated flirtation. "How's this?"

The anger in Bobby's gut froze to a block of fear. "Honey, are you drunk?"

She laughed. "You know me better than that. I don't get drunk, I get sleepy. Besides, I'd never drink with Steven in the car." She switched to pouty baby talk as she added, "I was driving precious cargo today, wasn't I, my little Steven?"

Bobby moaned. "Honey, they're getting close to us. We need to do something."

"I am doing something. I'm playing with my son. You ought to come down here and join us."

"Your son? Susan, stop it! Goddammit, just stop it!"

She looked horrified. "What? What's wrong with you today?"

"I just told you. The FBI—"

"I know. I heard you the first time. The FBI came by here today." Suddenly, Susan's voice took on a condescending tone that Bobby wasn't used to. She sounded as if she were lecturing a child in school. "What you keep forgetting, Bobby, is that God sent this child. He's not going to let anybody take us away from him. Not the FBI or anyone else. So just relax."

A headache erupted behind Bobby's eyes. "You're not hearing me, Susan. You may be listening, but you're not hearing the words. They know. They already know. It's just a matter of time—"

Again without looking: "If they were all that close, we'd be in jail now, wouldn't we? Or at least we'd be on our way *downtown for questioning.*" She leaned on that final phrase, lowering her voice as if to mock a television announcer.

Bobby's jaw dropped. "I don't believe this. Are you telling me that you don't think—"

"That's exactly it," Susan said abruptly, cutting him off. "Stop right there, because you hit the nail on the head. I don't think. Not about this. I don't waste my time thinking about it, because I know that it will all work out somehow. Where you have fear, I have faith. It's that simple." She turned away from him again. "And I don't think this is something that we should be discussing in front of Steven."

"He's not Steven!" Bobby roared, making them both jump. "Steven is dead, Susan! He was never born, don't you understand?"

The boy started to cry and Susan gathered him into her arms. She shot a look to Bobby that came as close to pure hatred as he'd ever seen. She looked possessed. She looked insane.

"Shut up, Bobby."

"I won't shut up! Jesus, Susan, do you see what you're doing? Do you see what you've become? Our son *never* lived! He never *will* live. And this one here"—Bobby gestured to the terrified boy in her arms—"he's *not* Steven. We don't know who the hell he is, but the one thing we do know is that he's not our son!"

Susan rose abruptly to her feet. "I'm not going to sit here and listen to this."

"Yes, you are!" Bobby boomed. She tried to push past him and he grabbed her arm. "That's exactly what you're going to do! These are capital crimes, Susan! These are the crimes that people get sent to the electric chair for. You can't just climb into some fantasy world and pretend that it will all go away."

Susan yanked hard to get her arm free, then smacked Bobby's face. "You keep your hands off of me."

"Jesus, Susan."

"And you keep your hands off of my son, do you hear? He's mine. He's my Steven. I don't give a shit what you do. Leave if you want. Go turn yourself in. But nobody's taking my little boy away from me again."

She shoved past him toward the center hall, knocking Bobby off-balance. He couldn't believe she'd struck him like that. They'd never even had a serious argument before, let alone exchanged blows. This whole thing was even further out of control than he'd feared.

Susan's footsteps fell like hammers on the marble of the foyer and like bass drumbeats on the stairs. Bobby ran to catch up, clearing the foyer in a few strides, and nearly tearing the railing off its mounts as he slid the turn to head up after her. Susan sensed his approach and quickened her pace, heading for the bedroom, where he knew she would lock him out. Bobby wouldn't have that.

His trot became a run as Susan hit the top step, and as he closed the distance, he zeroed in on the look of terror in the little boy's face as he watched, facing backward over Susan's shoulder.

God, what must the kid think of me?

With a two-step lead, Susan scooted through the open door and tried to push it shut with her free hand, but Bobby was already there. The door banged his shoulder, then rebounded open. Susan caught it again with her hand and tried to slam it shut, but by then, Bobby was already inside.

"Get out!" she screamed. "Get out and leave us alone!"

"Us!" Bobby yelled back. The boy was screaming now, too, and pushing his hands against his ears. "Which *us,* Susan? Which *us* am I supposed to leave alone? Until this morning, *we* were us. Now you're telling me I'm not a part of my own family anymore?"

"Not if you're going to take my baby away, you're not!"

They'd been down this road already, and Bobby knew it was a loser. He let the moment pass. He let Susan's words just hang there, hoping that she would hear them for herself. Hear how bizarre a situation she'd created.

"Look," he said softly, trying to make peace, "I'm sorry I yelled, okay? I'm sorry I got mad at you. It's just that things are so wrong now."

"Don't take Steven from me."

Bobby looked at Susan hard. He looked at the commitment in her eyes, and he realized with perfect clarity that until he conceded that one point, until he swore to her that he would not take the little boy—that he would not take *Steven* away—nothing he said would be heard. Until that ground was covered—*unless* that ground was covered—he'd find himself wading through this nightmare alone.

Bobby Martin never was any good at being alone.

"Okay," he said at last. "Okay, I won't take Steven away from you."

"Give me your word."

"I just did."

"*Say* it."

Part of him wanted to laugh. What was next, a pinky swear? But she was dead serious. He nodded. "Okay," he whispered. "I swear I won't take Steven away."

"Ever."

He hesitated. He could lie. He could tell her anything that she wanted to hear just to get past this crisis, but if he did that, what would they have left? If he betrayed her in the hour when she needed him most, the trust would all be gone. And without trust, there was no such thing as marriage. He loved her too much to lie to her.

"I can't say that, Susan."

"Then we have nothing to talk about." She turned away and headed for the bathroom.

"Goddammit, Susan, will you please wait and listen to me?" If there was anger in his voice, he didn't mean for it to be there. He was just tired. And confused. And scared to death.

Susan turned.

"I promised I wouldn't give him away, okay? Not tonight, anyway. That I can swear. Not tonight. But I can't vouch for *ever.* I mean, think about it. You have your faith that it will all turn out, but I just don't have that. I've already talked with the FBI today. I heard what he had to say, and I'm telling you that they're getting close enough to smell what we did. Sooner or later, they're going to come back. Don't make me swear now to what might happen then, okay? That's just not fair. I can't do that."

Susan's eyes narrowed as she considered his words; weighed them. After a long moment, she finally nodded. "Fair enough," she whispered. "But for tonight, we're a family, right?"

Bobby took a deep, deep breath. Certainly, this was no time to argue the finer points of what defined a family. This was a time simply to nod and smile. "Okay. Tonight, we're a family."

One look at the jailer's face told April that something was terribly wrong.

She sat among a dozen other women, any one of whom could have broken her in half at a whim. April had no idea what they'd been charged with, but most of them seemed to know each other, and as a group they'd made it perfectly clear that she was not welcome in their little club.

The place stank of sweat and urine, and the filthy concrete walls reflected and magnified the room's conversations into a swirling, meaningless din. She had nothing to prove to these women, and no desire to learn from them. She sat where they told her to sit; moved elsewhere when instructed to do so. She just didn't care.

All she could think of was Justin. When would Carlos make good on his promise to bring him home? And once home, where would he stay? Certainly not with her. Not for a long time. Twenty to life was what they told her.

But these were concerns for later. First, she had to get Justin to a safe place. When that was taken care of, everything else would rise above the distant third-place slots they occupied in her mind.

All the prisoners turned as the jailer approached with her keys, but the cop looked only at April, quickly looking away as April met her gaze.

"April Simpson, front and center," the guard called, as if she didn't know which prisoner was which.

April stood, knowing instinctively that something terrible had happened. "I'm April Simpson. What's wrong?"

"You need to come with me." Another guard stood at a distance behind the first as she pulled the door open, a radio in one hand and a nightstick in the other, ready to move in fast if the prisoners decided to rush.

April stepped through the door, and the guard slammed it shut behind her. "Is there something wrong?" April asked again.

"All I know is Detective Stipton asked to speak with you again. Now, I need to cuff you, so please turn around and put your hands behind your back."

April did as she was told, facing the wall of bars, but seeing none of the faces behind them. "Just tell me if something is wrong."

With the cuffs locked in place, and her prisoner's hands secured behind her back, the guard grasped April's elbow, firmly but not harshly. "The detective will tell you everything you need to know upstairs."

This was about Justin. She could feel it. Something terrible had happened to him. Maybe they'd found his body somewhere. What else could it be? These jail officers were hard as granite, yet their expressions showed something balanced between dread and compassion. What else could it possibly be?

Detective Stipton was waiting for her when she arrived in the interview room, his back turned to the door, staring out at the parking lot through the steel-grated window. When he turned, his face looked even more grave than the guard's. Stipton communicated something with his eyes to the officer, who in turn unlocked April's handcuffs and then slipped out the door, closing it behind her.

"Can I get you some coffee, April? A soda?"

"What's wrong?"

Stipton inhaled deeply through his nose and gestured to the seat he'd occupied during their last session together. "Please have a seat."

The politeness rang warning bells throughout April's body. *Oh, God. Oh God oh God oh God . . .*

She sat. So did Stipton, directly across from her.

"April, I wish there were an easy way to tell you this, but there just isn't."

She felt her guts tense as tears rushed to her eyes. *Poor Justin. Oh, please, God, take good care of my boy . . .*

"I'm afraid your husband's been shot. He's dead."

April scowled as her brain struggled with the words. *Did he say my husband? William?* For some reason, the words didn't compute for a moment, but down deep in her gut, she felt as if her heart had started beating again.

"Apparently, he was walking out of your apartment and someone was waiting for him. They shot him three times and he died on the spot. I'm terribly, terribly sorry for your loss."

April had to work hard to suppress her smile. She wanted to shout, *Is that all?* On a different day, under different circumstances, this might have been terrible news—and judging from the look on Detective Stipton's face, it *should* have been terrible news—but for the moment, all she wanted to do was let out a war whoop of joy.

Justin was still okay!

28

ST. IGGY'S AUDITORIUM erupted in applause. As one, the audience rose to their feet, cheering with the kind of enthusiasm that only a group of proud parents can generate. After directing the orchestra to bow as a whole, Mrs. Vonder then presented their star soloist with a flourish of her open palm.

Christa Ortega stepped forward and the thunder swelled even louder. Just as she'd practiced a hundred times in the mirror, she acknowledged her public first with a nod to the left, then to her right, and then a demure curtsy for all.

As she glided back to join the rest of her friends, she paused just a moment more to blow a kiss to her father.

Carlos could barely see through his tears. He didn't know that he'd ever been so proud. He felt Consuela's arm slip around his waist and draped his own over her shoulder. This was a night they'd remember for a long, long time.

"She's beautiful," Father Eugene said, leaning in close enough to be heard. "Just beautiful."

Carlos acknowledged the compliment with a nod and a smile, knowing full well that it would be a moment before his voice would work.

The Canon was the final piece of the concert, and as the applause finally withered to a rumble of countless conversations, the musicians remained standing, awaiting their turn to file out as their parents gathered coats and purses in preparation to leave.

The children's route of retreat would take them out the backstage door and down a side hallway that would lead them to the music room. Having worked closely with the architect, Carlos knew the way as well as anyone and didn't hesitate to climb the short stairway leading up from the audience to stage right, and from there to join the parade of children on their way to pick up their coats and music cases. Some parents followed, but most did not, preferring to wait in the lobby of the auditorium for their cellists and violinists to join them.

The mood of the children raised Carlos's spirits to their highest point in days. They knew that they'd done a terrific job, and they could not contain their enthusiasm. Was there anything better in the world than the sound of happy children? Carlos didn't think so. He walked hand in hand with Consuela, just listening, trying his best not to let his presence as an adult dampen any spirits. As always, Peña remained just a step or two behind, continually scanning the crowd. Even he sensed that this was a happy time, and he did his best to keep his lips bent into a smile that just didn't seem to fit him well.

Total bedlam reigned in the music room, as half the kids made an earnest effort to recover their belongings and the other half ran around out of control, playing tag, or violin keep-away. Above the din, Mrs. Vonder tried to keep some semblance of control.

"Children!" she yelled. "Children, your parents are waiting for you, so please don't waste time. You had a wonderful concert; you should all be very proud. Now please hurry along and collect your belongings . . . "

For the contingent who were not already busy doing those very things, she might as well have been reading from the phone book.

"I bet I could get their attention," Peña whispered to his boss, who couldn't help but chuckle.

The laughter disappeared, however, when Carlos caught the glare from Consuela. The silent reprimand registered instantly with Peña, too, and he took a step backward.

"Relax, Consuela," Carlos whispered. "He meant no harm."

"You know how I feel about such things." She resented even the slightest mention of violence, even in its most oblique form.

"Just don't be angry."

A flash of black off to the left briefly caught Carlos's eye, and he turned to see a priest entering the music room. Carlos noted casually that it might well be the largest priest he'd ever seen, but when Christa asked for help with her cello case, he never gave the priest a second thought.

You'd have thought that it was Carnegie Fucking Hall the way everyone jumped to their feet. They actually *cheered!* Like you'd expect to hear at a football game. And it went on and on and on.

Logan joined them, of course, if only to blend in, but he felt foolish for doing it. It was a kids' strings concert for God's sake, and all they played was elevator music. It was all he could do to keep his eyes open. Was it possible that what seemed so endless could have been only ninety minutes?

He thought he'd spotted Ortega early on, recognizing his helmet of jet-black hair, but he couldn't be sure until the ovation started and everyone stood. Were it not for Peña's unmistakable silhouette and glistening pate, he might still not have known beyond doubt, but that pit bull's presence always and forever meant that Ortega was within arm's reach. Logan didn't recognize the woman who stood between them, but he could only assume that she was Ortega's wife. Funny how he'd never thought of the asshole's being married. Not that he should be surprised. After all, they were here at a school, weren't they? It only made sense that where there was a father and a daughter, there'd naturally be a mother. He'd just never thought about it before.

Logan followed his target's gaze up to the stage and picked out which child belonged to him. The fucking star of the show, of course. Logan kept applauding with the rest as the conceited little bitch took her bows, and when she blew her father a kiss—as if she were some fucking movie star—it was all he could do to keep from throwing up.

The houselights came up as the children filed out, and Logan suddenly felt terribly self-conscious of his gloved hands. He shoved them into the pockets of his black overcoat and stepped out into the aisle, fighting against the flow of the exiting crowd to make his way closer to the front, near the stage. He wanted to get it over with here, while they were all still in the auditorium and his targets had no place to go, but as he half-stepped and excuse-me'd through the crowd, Ortega disappeared.

Where the hell could he be?

Logan's head whipped to the left, taking in every face in the crowd that jammed the opposite aisle, but none of them was Ortega.

There! Up by the stage. Wasn't that Peña disappearing behind the heavy velvet curtain? Of course it was. Who else could it be?

The thought flashed through Logan's head that his target might get away, but then he noticed the kids filing out in the same direction, and he put it all together. This was okay, he told himself. He still had plenty of time. Ricky Timmons's speeches echoed in his brain. *Take your time,* he told himself. *He's got no place to go.*

The crowd had thinned to practically nothing down near the stage as the audience bottlenecked at the rear exits. Logan walked purposefully across the front row and up the four steps to the stage. From there, he joined the tail end of the musician parade as it made its way down the long beige and white hallway.

He could see Ortega, but was still too far away. Besides, until he dropped Peña, Ortega remained number two on his target list.

Logan found himself smiling as he passed a few straggling violinists to close the distance. Up ahead, he noted the red exit sign and nearly laughed out loud. Easy hit and easy escape. What more could he have asked for?

He wondered about the kids, though. When they panicked, what would they do? Would they cram the exits, just as they crammed the entrance now? He hoped not. He only had but so many bullets.

A woman Logan recognized as the director shouted something as he entered the room, and the sharpness of her tone startled him. His hand tensed on the weapon in his pocket, but in an instant, he realized that she was yelling not at him, but at the kids.

Ortega stood across the room with his wife and his human bulldog, watching his bitch kid putting her stuff away. As Logan entered the room, Ortega actually turned and looked right at him, but then looked away, back to his little girl. Peña looked, too, but he wasn't so easily distracted. The bulldog's brow knitted as Logan held his gaze just a second too long.

Logan's mind screamed, *Now!*

His hand found the pistol grip, but as he moved to pull it from his coat, he found that he'd grabbed the plastic bag as well. He looked down long enough to yank the pistol clear of the bag, and by the time he brought the weapon up to fire, Peña was already moving.

"Get down!"

Peña barked the words with explosive force as he rammed his beefy hand like a piston between his boss's shoulder blades, sending him stumbling forward.

All Carlos knew was that he'd been punched hard, and as he tried to catch his balance, his foot caught the leading edge of a riser. He dove face-first into a group of children, who yelled and tried to get their hands up to protect themselves. A cello gave way under his weight, its strings thrumming a painfully dissonant chord that was nearly lost in the sound of splintering wood.

Instinctively, he knew this was a hit, and he desperately tried to decipher the swirl of activity. He watched in horror as Peña charged forward, his hand disappearing under his coat and emerging with a gun. Who the hell was he going to shoot?

"Tío Jesús!" Christa yelled from Carlos's left. "Look out!"

Carlos grabbed his daughter's wrist and pulled her down to the ground with him. "Stay down!"

From somewhere out in the gathered crowd, he heard Consuela shout, "Oh, my God, no!" But Carlos still didn't get it.

A gunshot fractured the air, sounding more like a grenade in the acoustically enhanced practice room, and the crowd panicked. Carlos just heard screaming. No words or meaningful instructions to get down or to run, just screaming. Shrieking. It was the sound of raw terror.

A second shot seemed somehow even louder than the first, and out of the corner of his eye, Carlos saw Peña's gait wobble.

Oh, shit, this is it! He gathered his daughter closer to him and rolled on top of her, shielding her body with his own, even as he craned his neck to see what happened next.

A third shot launched a horrific fountain of brains through the top of Peña's head and sent a two-inch disk of bald scalp spinning into the air as his body just dropped where he stood.

Carlos's head rushed to make sense of this. Why was Peña exchanging gunfire with a priest?

Not that it mattered. He knew that this would be the night when he died, and the best he could hope for was to save his family. His instincts, honed by years on the street, told him that he needed to rush this prick. He needed to charge him at full speed, shove that pistol of his down his gullet, and blast his heart from the inside. But in the instant that he needed to make that decision, he felt Christa move beneath him, and he hesitated. If he got up, he'd leave her exposed.

He waited.

Logan didn't. As a swarm of students panicked and ran, the tall man with the fake mustache and the imitation priest suit closed the distance to his target in five strides, leading with his giant Glock. As Carlos moved to defend himself, Logan fired.

The bullet disintegrated his target's knee, nearly severing the limb at its joint. Carlos felt as if his whole body had been slammed with a hammer, forcing the air from his lungs in a croupy bark.

Consuela screamed. "Carlos! Oh, God!" She darted forward to help, but froze in place as Logan wrapped his fist in Christa's hair and dragged her to her feet.

"Daddy!"

Carlos tried to form words, but the best he could produce was a growl.

Logan held the girl in front of him, his left hand gripping her throat, his thumb and first two fingers turning white as they squeezed the pressure points below her ears.

"Take a step, lady," he hissed to Consuela, "and I'll shoot you first and then your little bitch daughter." Christa's face contorted grotesquely as he forced the muzzle into her cheek and the skin gathered up before it. "Do you understand me?"

Consuela nodded, her eyes huge.

"Say it!"

"I—I understand. Please don't hurt her."

Logan wasn't listening anymore. He turned to face Carlos again, whose hands were clamped above his knee in a futile effort to stanch the flow of blood.

Christa's terrified eyes pleaded and her lips formed the words *Daddy, help* but the sound came out only as a terrible gurgle.

"You son of a bitch!" Carlos growled.

The room exploded as his other knee erupted into a flowery display of blood and tendons. Carlos yelled as the searing pain shot all the way to his neck, but when he saw the look on his daughter's face, he swallowed the noise and locked his jaw tight. If she had to watch her father die, she could watch him die with dignity.

"You know who I am now, don't you, Ortega?" Logan asked, returning the hot muzzle to the little girl's face. The faint odor of burning flesh energized him. "Say my name, though, and I'll blow her fucking head off. Just nod. You know who I am."

Carlos hadn't until just that moment, but once he put the priest's size together with his voice, Carlos recognized Patrick Logan. He nodded.

"Good," Logan said. "It's important that you know that. Because I want you to beg me not to kill you."

"Fuck you."

Logan savagely smacked the bridge of Christa's nose with the Glock's barrel, launching a fountain of blood that cascaded over the girl's lips and chin and down across Logan's hand.

"Stop that!" Consuela yelled, and he fired a shot into the ceiling over her head.

"I told you to shut up, bitch." Logan turned back to face Ortega. "Beg me not to kill you."

Carlos didn't see his own blood anymore; didn't even feel his own pain. He just saw what this animal was doing to his daughter, and suddenly he cared about nothing else. "Please don't hurt her," he moaned.

This time, he didn't even hear the gunshot. A bullet slammed through his right shoulder, spinning him in place on the blood-soaked carpet. This one was bad. Carlos could tell from the way his breath didn't want to come that this bullet had hit more than just a joint. He fought to keep consciousness from slipping away.

"Look at me, goddammit!" Logan yelled.

With his arm and legs ruined, Carlos couldn't find the leverage to push himself up.

"Beg for *your* life, asshole. Not hers. By the count of three, or I swear to God I'll blow her head off. One . . ."

"I'm trying, goddammit," Carlos yelled. But there was no volume to it. His words made a whistling sound as they passed through his throat.

"Two . . ."

Logan would do it. Carlos knew he'd do it. Not a doubt in his mind. Grunting against unspeakable agony, he used his good left arm to push off the carpet, forcing the momentum to flop him the rest of the way. The mechanism to make his right arm follow no longer existed, however, and he howled as ligaments became entwined with severed bone.

"Beg me, asshole," Logan said again, pressing the gun even harder into the side of Christa's face. "Let me hear you whine a little."

Carlos looked into his daughter's desperate features and saw nothing but fear. He found himself weeping as he choked out the words, "Please don't kill me."

"Fuck you." Logan laughed.

Carlos refused to look away as the muzzle took aim at his face.

He saw a flash.

29

AFTER TWO HOURS with Homer at the wheel, Tim Burrows couldn't wait to put his feet on the ground again. A farm boy at heart, Lieutenant Homer LaRue rejected the notion of speed limits and seemed to believe that every tire rut and pothole was a target to be rammed at not less than thirty-five miles per hour. The more nervous Tim became, the more Homer seemed to enjoy it.

This was often the case with backwater police departments, Tim thought. After a few hours of feigned cooperation, their pride got the better of them and they succumbed to this petty my-dick's-longer-than-yours bullshit. On days when he was in good humor, Tim found it annoying. After a day like today, he just wanted to shoot the son of a bitch.

The Stanns place turned out to be about three miles past nowhere, way the hell out in the wilds of West Virginia, where the architecture seemed to predate the Civil War, and even the farm machinery looked like something out of the Depression. But for the mailbox at the end of the driveway, they'd have missed the house entirely. Even at that, they had to extrapolate that "St n s" really meant "Stanns."

Even in the sparseness of late winter, the woods still owned the driveway. Unpaved and still muddy from rains that had fallen days ago, the impossibly narrow road bore tire ruts deep enough to prompt even Homer to slow his approach to a crawl, lest he separate his cruiser from its undercarriage. Branches and dangling vines slapped and screeched along the windows on both sides of the vehicle.

"How spooky is this?" Homer mused aloud.

The road went on like this for a good two hundred yards, up hills and through gulleys. At one point they even had to ford a stream.

"How sure are you that there's a house at the end of this?" Tim asked.

Homer shrugged. "You saw the same sign I did. We keep going as long as the road does, though. Ain't no turnin' around in here."

Interesting point. Tim rarely approached a building anymore without giving at least passing consideration to the tactical challenges of staging a raid. Even when he visited friends' houses for dinner or a football game, his mind casually calculated fields of fire and routes of approach. Such were the casualties of effective training, such as the weeks following his surveillance-avoidance and evasion training when he'd found himself watching the rearview mirror as much as the windshield.

Given a savvy, intelligent bad guy, a driveway such as this would be a nightmare in a hostage-rescue situation. The terrorist would merely have to wait until all of the law enforcement assets were committed to the road, then attack with impunity. If Tim were the bad guy, he'd probably choose claymores placed at ten- or fifteen-yard intervals, rigged to detonate together once the lead element tripped a trigger at the three-quarter mark on the approach. In less than a second, the entire team would be shredded by tens of thousands of high-velocity BBs.

Ordinarily, such strategic musings didn't bother him, but tonight, as the tree limbs and bushes loomed white under the assault of Homer's high beams, only to disappear like so many ghosts, the thoughts unnerved him. What exactly did they know about this Samuel Stanns? That he was "slow." And what the hell did that mean?

They *did* know that his older brother got himself killed while impersonating a police officer, and that said brother was the chief suspect in the murder of his own father.

Beyond that, they knew nothing, and it occurred to him now that this was precisely the kind of knowledge vacuum that could get you in trouble. With incomplete intelligence data, bad guys and the cops were on equal ground, and that was always a problem. Law enforcement wasn't about equality—it was about force and superiority. To win, you had to guarantee yourself the upper hand at all times, in every element from intelligence to firepower. That way, you always negotiated from a position of strength. And if negotiations broke down, you could still blast the hell out of them. The cop knew it, and so did the bad guy, keeping the rules of engagement clear for all parties involved.

"You're looking pretty stressed there, Agent Burrows," Homer said, taking his eyes away from the road for longer than he should. "You got something you're not telling me?"

Tim glanced across the seat and said nothing for a long moment as he weighed his driver's motives. It wouldn't do to admit even an ounce of fear to a yokel like this. Why give the guy bragging rights when he went back to his buddies at the state police barracks?

"No, I've told you everything I know."

"Kinda makes you wish we had backup, doesn't it?"

Tim snorted, forcing a chuckle. "I'm not sure how the West Virginia State Police handles things, Lietenant LaRue, but at the FBI we don't bring an army to ask a few questions." *Whose is bigger now, asshole?*

Homer laughed. "I gotta tell you, Special Agent Timothy Burrows, I've met a lot of people in my time on this planet, some of them not all that pleasant to be around. But being a prick comes easier to you than any five people I've ever met." Homer turned his eyes back to the road.

Tim glared at LaRue, who never gave the satisfaction of a return glance. "Thanks for sharing that, Lieutenant. I'll be sure to pass your sentiments on to your commander."

Homer's smile grew even bigger. "I appreciate that. Just make sure you spell my name right on the report, okay? Because I assure you I've got yours down."

The cruiser climbed another hill, and suddenly the trees disappeared. They found themselves at the edge of a wide-open field, and in the light of the crescent moon, they saw the dark outline of a one-story farmhouse at the crest of a long, gradual slope. Hundreds of feet off to the left of the house—it was hard to judge distances in this light—stood the classic silhouette of a barn.

Homer stopped the vehicle just long enough to get his bearings and then, without a word, started driving again.

The place looked empty as they pulled to a stop out front, thirty feet from the front porch. No lights burned anywhere. Homer kept his high beams trained on the front steps so they could see where they walked, and he pulled his long-handled Maglite from its clamp on the edge of the front seat, right next to his twelve-gauge shot gun—or riot gun as they still called it.

"Ready?" Homer asked.

Tim answered by opening his door and stepping out into the cold air. A single breath brought the heavy odor of freshly cut grass, and Tim drew his weapon. Someone was home, all right. They just wanted it to look as if they weren't. Off to his left, across the wide expanse of the cruiser's hood, he saw a spark of reflected headlight off the barrel of Homer's monstrous revolver.

"Three fifty-seven?" Tim asked, referring to the caliber of the trooper's cannon.

Homer shook his head. "Forty-four. If I shoot somebody, I want 'em to stay shot."

Tim pulled his six-inch mini-Maglite from its loop in his nylon utility belt and twisted it on with his mouth. If this were a full-scale assault, he'd have clamped it under the barrel of his automatic, but as it was, he wanted to be able to point a light in somebody's face without threatening to blow his head off. Nerves aside, they weren't even sure this guy they were visiting had done anything wrong. It was an important point to remember. On the other hand, he could have been the shooter, for all they knew.

Homer and Tim approached the porch steps shoulder to shoulder, both of them in a half-crouch, their weapons tucked out of sight behind their thighs.

"We don't look too paranoid, do we?" Homer whispered.

"There's a difference between paranoia and caution, Lieutenant."

Homer sighed and shook his head. "How about you lighten up and take about a pound of pull off the trigger?"

Tim Burrows had no desire to lighten the moment. He had no desire to do anything but concentrate on the job that lay ahead. If any single mistake killed the most cops at crime scenes, it was a lapse in concentration.

Homer paused at the base of the steps, so Tim decided to go first. He'd only made it to the second riser when LaRue interrupted his concentration a second time.

"Yo, Burrows," Homer said, stooping down on his haunches. "Take a look at this."

Tim didn't move, but instead grumbled, "What is it?"

"Come and see for yourself, you prick. It's what we country boys call evidence." Homer exaggerated his accent for maximum effect.

Keeping his eyes focused on the front door, Tim retraced his steps, then looked down just long enough to see what had so captured LaRue's attention. It was a footprint, embedded in the soft, muddy grass at the base of the steps.

"Look familiar?" Homer taunted.

Sure enough, the print looked identical to the one they'd found in the woods, where someone had stood and watched a murder. Just that quickly, Tim Burrows knew that he'd found the critical link to the case. Samuel Stanns was either a killer or a material witness. Either way, this was a big moment. He could already see the look on Russell Coates's face when he found out.

Tim started back up the stairs, this time with his weapon out front, leading the way.

"What are you doing?" Homer whispered.

"I'm going to make an arrest."

"The hell you are! Remember wondering a few minutes ago about backup? Well, we need it now."

"No, we don't." Tim's mind conjured images of a dozen potbellied deputies pouring down that driveway and swarming all over the place, getting in the way and clamoring for credit at a time when the career spotlight was rightfully his. "It's not your call. This is a federal operation, on which you are merely assisting. So, are you going to assist or not?"

"What is wrong with you, Burrows? Quit being such a tight ass. Let me call for assistance, and we'll wait here and keep an eye on things. It's not like the guy can run off without us seeing him."

"No, but he can dig in and build himself a hell of a defensive position. Turn this into another Ruby Ridge. You want that?"

"I'd prefer it to getting capped by some guy who knows the inside of his house a hell of a lot better than I do."

"Jesus, LaRue, there might not even be anybody in there."

"Then there's no harm in waiting, is there?" Homer turned and walked back toward his cruiser. "I'm calling."

"I'm going in." Tim climbed to the porch.

Pausing at the open car door, Homer called to Burrows in a harsh stage whisper, "Would you hold on just a second?" No, he wouldn't. Just one call for help. Five seconds on the radio. Why was that such a big deal to this asshole? These were great questions for the reports that would follow this incident—and, oh, you betcha, there'd be some kick-ass reports when Homer was done. For right now, though, Burrows was by God going ahead with his plan, and Homer couldn't abandon him.

"Goddamn fucking know-it-all feds," he grumbled as he brought the .44 to arm's length and hurried up the stairs after him.

With Burrows already standing on the knob side of the door, Homer took the hinge side, both of them standing with their backs pressed against the front wall. Tim shot a glance to LaRue, who said, "This is your game, buddy. I'm just here to take notes."

Shifting his weapon from his right hand to his left, Tim balled his free hand into a fist and hammered on the wooden door. After about fifteen seconds, when no one answered, he did it again, this time calling out at the top of his voice, "Samuel Stanns, this is the FBI. Open the door."

Another ten seconds passed.

"I'm breaking the door," Tim announced at a whisper.

Homer scowled. "You got a warrant I don't see?"

Tim glared at LaRue as if the trooper were an idiot. "I don't need a warrant when I've got a footprint. That's what we call probable cause."

"So you're just gonna crash on in there—" Homer saw the glare and shut up. "Suit yourself."

Tim took a step back and balanced himself for a mighty kick. "Cover me."

"Why don't you try the knob?"

"What?"

"The doorknob. Why don't you try the doorknob? Maybe it's not even locked."

Tim tried his best to look annoyed, but mostly looked embarrassed for not having thought of that himself. He stepped in closer and put his hand on the knob. Sure enough, it turned. He saw Homer's big grin but refused to acknowledge it.

"Now, cover me, will you?"

Homer's .44 was up and ready. "You going in fast or slow?"

"Watch me." Tim settled himself, took a deep breath, then in one smooth motion, shoved the door open and swung his weapon down to confront whoever might be lying in wait for him.

From the corner of Homer's eye, the muzzle flash looked like a camera strobe in the darkened foyer, and the noise of the blast was deafening. He watched, horrified, as Special Agent Tim Burrows of the FBI bent at the waist, pirouetted once in place, then stumbled backward down the porch steps, leaving both his pistol and his flashlight on the wooden decking, amidst blood spatters and a heavy crimson gob of tissue.

Homer yelled at the sound of the shot and launched himself away from the wall. A lifelong hunter, Homer knew a shotgun when he heard it, and this was a big one. That thin wood siding wouldn't even slow down a double-aught pellet. Scrambling for the porch rail, he fired blindly over his shoulder, deafening himself with the heavy concussions of his own weapon. He didn't care about hitting anything; he just wanted the gunman to duck long enough for him to find decent cover.

In his mind, Homer saw himself vaulting the rail and landing feet-first in the little garden out front, but he'd seen too many years and too many pounds to pull it off. It felt like forever as he slung his right leg over the top of the rail, then sort of rolled himself over the rest of the way on his belly. As his left leg cleared, he dropped like a sack, landing heavily on his right side. Five feet away, Tim Burrows lay sprawled on his back at the foot of the stairs, the left side of his camouflaged BDUs soaked black and shiny in the beam of Homer's Maglite.

The agent's mouth opened and closed, and his lips worked as if trying to say something, but all Homer could hear was the high-pitched screech of his bruised eardrums as his fingers wrestled a speed loader out of the leather pouch in his belt. His hands suddenly felt too big for his arms, and they felt disconnected from his brain. The simple reloading procedure that he'd practiced thousands of times on the shooting range felt foreign to him, and he found himself trying to reload the six-shot cylinder without emptying it first.

He cursed, unable to hear his own voice, as he slapped the eject rod and dumped the spent casings into the dirt. Reloaded now, he threw two more quick shots toward the front door and scrambled on his hands and knees to where Burrows lay, still trying to move, but apparently unable to make his muscles work in unison.

"I got you, Burrows," Homer said, finally able to hear again. "You've been hit, buddy. You've been hit. And we're out in the fucking open here." Homer grabbed a fistful of the agent's shirt collar and pulled. Burrows wailed, in obvious agony, but Homer didn't have time for any of that. "I know it hurts," he said as soothingly as he could, "but we've got to get you under cover."

The ground was more gravel that grass, and the sharp stones dug at Homer's hands and knees, drawing blood from both as he dragged Tim around to the back of his cruiser, into the shadow of the trunk. "Okay, buddy," Homer said hoarsely, "we got you under cover now. You're safe now. You're safe." He dared a peek over the trunk lid, and when nobody took a shot at him, he ducked down again. "You just wait here, okay? I've got to get some help."

Grabbing Homer's sleeve, Tim grunted, "No."

Homer fought the instinctive urge to pull away and instead leaned down closer. "I'm not leaving you, pal, okay? I'm just going up to the front to call this in. That's it. And to get us some more firepower. Then I'll be right back. I'll never be more than ten yards away."

The look he saw in Burrows's face was unlike anything he'd ever seen. Desperate pain combined with desperate fear. Tim's mouth worked some more, but to no effect.

Homer gently pried the agent's fist from the fabric of his jacket, then held it in his hand for a moment. "I gotta get you a chopper, kid. I need to get you flown out of here."

With that, Homer laid Tim's hand back on his chest and duck-walked down the passenger side of the cruiser toward the front, keeping the vehicle between himself and the shooter the whole time. He pulled open the door and was instantly awash in the cast of the dome light. On a night as dark as this, he might as well have been onstage. Three swings of his heavy steel Maglite took care of the problem. If it had taken more than five, he would have shot it out.

Relieved to be back in the blackness, he found the microphone on the dash and pulled it free. "Four seven seven to control!" he shouted at a whisper, trying his best to sound collected on the air. "Signal thirteen, shots fired, officer down!"

He heard some distant static, then the familiar voice in the speakers. "All units hold your traffic," the dispatcher commanded to other units that Homer couldn't hear. "Unit declaring signal thirteen, repeat."

"Four seven seven," Homer repeated, this time much more slowly and distinctly, and he gave the rural route address and approximate map grid number. "Shots have been fired, and I've got one adult male badly wounded. Control, do you copy?"

"Ten-four, four seven seven. We've got help on the way. Life Flight will be airborne in two minutes, and ground units are being dispatched as we speak."

"ETA?"

"As fast as they can get there, four seven seven. Stand by and I'll advise."

Homer sighed. "Negative, control. I need to pull back to a more secure location. I will not be at my vehicle, and the portable's useless up here." One of the great frustrations of the new UHF radios the state police had purchased five years ago.

The dispatcher paused before transmitting, "Good luck, four seven seven."

He could use some luck. He could also use some manpower. Goddammit. He let the microphone drop to the floor mat while he reached across the center console to pull his keys from the ignition and fished in the dark for the one that would unlock the shotgun. He found it on the second try, and as the short-barreled twelve-gauge fell into his hands, he pulled the portable radio from its charger as well.

Since the initial exchange, the gunman hadn't fired a single shot, and Homer didn't know what to make of it. It was possible, he supposed, that those rounds he'd fired into the open door had actually hit something, but that would make the guy the unluckiest son of a bitch ever to pick up a gun. The only other reasonable alternatives were variations on the theme of the bad guy moving for a better angle from which to finish what he'd started.

Homer returned to his wounded partner. "Yo, Burrows, you still with me?" Homer worked hard to keep a light, nothing-to-worry-about lilt in his tone.

"Where the hell have you been?" the agent grunted. "I feel like my guts are on fire."

"I had to make a phone call. I got the cavalry started."

"How long?"

Homer dropped a beat before answering. "About five minutes," he lied. "About five minutes and we're set." Even in the darkness, he could see the frightening smear of blood. This guy was leaking out fast. "Tell you what," he went on, fishing his keys back out of his pocket. "I've got a first-aid kit here in the trunk. Let's see if I can patch you up a little while we wait."

"The light," Tim wheezed. "You'll get a light when you open the lid."

Homer sighed. Actually, he'd already thought of that and couldn't figure a way around it. "Well, if you hear more shooting, you just stay low. And if I fall down next to you, just remember that there's a first-aid kit in the trunk." If he wasn't mistaken, Burrows might actually have cut a smile.

Opening the lid, snatching the kit, and slamming it closed again took all of five seconds, and luckily for both of them, their man hadn't taken advantage of his opportunity.

The first-aid kits provided to state troopers were designed primarily for auto accidents on the interstates and were therefore long on dressings and Cling-Pak, but that was about it. Heavy-duty Band-Aids. Something's better than nothing, right?

The silver bandage scissors gleamed at him as he lifted the lid on the onetime tackle box and pulled open the retractable shelves. He grabbed the scissors, then repositioned himself so he could get in closer to his patient.

"Okay, Special Agent Timothy Burrows, I'm going to make you a little naked here, okay? I need to see where you're bleeding."

"Check the big fucking hole in my side," Tim moaned.

Homer smiled. Wittiness was a good sign. He slipped the blunt end of the angled scissors into the space between two buttons and cut away the blood-saturated cotton to expose a drenched T-shirt, which he likewise cut away.

Everything felt slippery and sticky as he peeled the material away to reveal a torso smeared crimson. At first, he couldn't see the source of the blood; it seemed to be everywhere.

The instant he saw the wound, he wished that he'd minded his own business.

30

APRIL WANTED TO feel sad about William, felt that she *should* feel sad about him. The man who'd been there for her when she really needed him was dead, never again to utter another word or to breathe another breath. She thought back to the times when he'd been tender, the times when they'd really made love to each other, hoping that somehow those memories would trigger something more than the hatred that burned front and center in her heart. As much as she tried to conjure the image of a warm, loving man—and, yes, there'd been times when he'd been exactly that—all she could see was the useless drunk he'd become. The man who'd let her baby be used as collateral.

He *deserved* to be killed all right, but it should have happened last night, when Logan's men came searching for their money. If he'd been even half a man, he'd have laid down his life right there in the filthy streets outside Wilson's tavern, rather than let them take away a little boy whose only offense was to have been born to someone as incompetent as she.

So, now William was dead, just as Carlos had warned, and she accepted that as a fair trade.

So, Carlos had been true to his word. He'd gone to Logan and he'd had his little talk with him. There were lines never to be crossed, and Logan had finally seen the light. Soon, Justin would be home.

But what about her? What was April going to do about this armed-robbery charge? Such a stupid thing to do! If she'd just waited, everything would have been fine. She'd be at home, waiting for her son to return, rather than in a police station waiting for some court-appointed lawyer to come in and screw everything up.

Screw everything up. There was a thought that made her laugh. She was perfectly capable of screwing up her own life, thank you very much. She certainly needed no help from outsiders.

At least Justin would be safe. No matter what else happened, at least he would have a future. Who knew? Maybe while she was rotting away in prison, the system would find a set of foster parents who would *really* take care of him; provide him with a real house with a real yard, and neighbors who wouldn't recruit him as a drug runner. It could happen.

What kind of people might they be? How could people take a baby into their house for just a few days or a few weeks at a time, only to give him up again? Wouldn't that tear their hearts out? And once torn a few times, would those hearts grow a kind of emotional scar tissue that would prevent them from ever truly loving the children in their care?

It turned her stomach to think of someone caring for her Justin merely for the paycheck.

Well, she should have thought of that before she went and tried to hold up a store. A store with security cameras every ten feet, for God's sakes. What had she been thinking?

Nothing, that's what. She hadn't been thinking a thing. She'd been in a blind panic, and she'd been stupid.

Maybe the judge and the jury would take it easy on her, when she explained how she'd been in fear of her child's life, and that she'd had no choice—

In a flash of realization, a brand-new wave of panic overwhelmed her. She gasped as she realized that she'd *never* be able to tell the real story of what had happened. That would mean implicating Logan and Carlos, and if she did that, they'd kill her for sure. The baby, too, probably. And God help her if the jury *didn't* believe her. She'd be trapped in a cage, surrounded by countless felons who'd be thrilled to kill her in return for an extra pack of cigarettes.

She was trapped, with no choice but to take the whole fall. It had been her choice, after all. No one had forced her to be this stupid, and now that she'd done it, once little Justin was safe and sound, she'd do what she had to do.

For Justin.

She could do anything for her son.

They'd left her alone in the interview room, presumably to allow her to deal with her grief without the glares of the women in the holding cell, but as she sat there in silence, trying to force her mind to grapple with the problems that lay ahead, she couldn't shake the feeling that she was being watched. The big mirror on the wall did that to you. She could almost hear them asking each other why she wasn't more emotional over the death of her husband. How could she make them understand that there comes a point when you've felt so many emotions for so long that they don't register one at a time anymore? They just combine to form a kind of general misery that settles on your life like a blanket.

It had been a good half hour since she'd seen anyone, and Detective Stipton had been clear that he would be returning shortly to ask her a few more questions. As if there'd ever been a cop in the history of police forces who *ever* limited himself to just a few questions.

When the door opened, she wasn't surprised to see him standing there, but the expression on his face unnerved her. Cops were supposed to be rocks, but this one looked as if he'd just been rolled down a hill. If she wasn't mistaken, she'd have thought he looked close to tears.

"April, I'm sorry, but we're going to have to continue this conversation tomorrow. I'm going to send an officer in to take you back to the lockup."

"Is everything okay?" Clearly, it was not.

Stipton looked at April for a moment, considered not saying anything, but then said, "There's been a shooting at St. Ignatius School. There's at least two dead. During a student orchestra concert." He spoke as if he needed to share the news with someone, *anyone.*

As the door closed, April shook her head pitifully. What was the world coming to? Every day, it seemed, you opened the paper or listened to the news and heard about another shooting in the schools. And St. Iggy's, no less—known throughout the universe as one of the finest private schools in the country. Who would have thought—

"Oh, my God!" she exclaimed. In a rush, she remembered the sound of cello music wafting from Carlos Ortega's library while she waited in the hallway to be announced. She remembered the beautiful little girl with her long black hair who glared at her as she exited through the pocket doors as if April were a piece of gum stuck to the bottom of her shoe. With the greatest clarity of all, she remembered the sweatshirt the little girl wore. It was white, with a green-and-black plaid design around the cuffs and the collar.

And over the left breast, where there might have been a logo for Hilfiger or Izod or any one of a thousand designer names that April could never afford to own, was an elaborate school crest, under which were the embroidered words ST. IGNATIUS SCHOOL.

The panic rushed toward her like an out-of-control freight train. She brought her hands to her head, inhaling spasmodically, and her eyes grew huge as she understood exactly what had happened.

That's when she started to scream.

The rain came from nowhere. Steady but not hard. Drenching.

Burrows was slipping away and Homer could do nothing to stop it. The hole in Tim's gut was huge, about the size of Homer's fist, and from what he could tell by feel alone, it was through-and-through, both wounds to the right of midline, and both below the rib cage. In between the two holes, it had to look like hamburger in there.

The agent hadn't said another word since giving Homer a hard time. That was what, ten minutes ago? Fifteen, maybe? And the flow of blood had slowed to a trickle around the pressure bandages Homer had tied in place. Or at least that he *thought* he'd tied in place. It's tough work in the dark when your patient won't sit up for you. Whether the trickle meant that he'd controlled the bleeding, or that Burrows had simply bled out, was hard to tell.

"C'mon," Homer growled impatiently, searching the dark clouds for some sign of an approaching chopper. "C'mon, guys, or there won't be nothin' to save."

Beyond the incessant hammering of his own heart, though, combined with Burrows's raspy breath, the night brought nothing but the sound of the rain. Even the shooter remained still. Why would he do that? Why would he shoot a man at the door and then not even attempt to finish the job?

What was that?

He listened carefully, and the sound disappeared. He thought at first that maybe it was the approaching beat of helicopter rotors, but now wondered if maybe it were just more of his own pounding pulse.

No, there it was again! That was definitely a helicopter. But was it *the* helicopter? Was it Life Flight?

Homer scanned the sky for some visual sign, but when the sky returned only blackness for his effort, he picked up his portable radio. If the medevac helicopter were approaching, it should be trying to raise him on the radio. Why wasn't he doing that?

Because you've got to turn the goddamn thing on, you idiot.

Jesus, he'd never been so unraveled. He twisted the knob on the top of the radio, next to the antenna, and was instantly greeted by the sound of an electronic voice.

". . . four seven seven, this is Life Flight one, do you copy?"

Homer's hands shook as he brought the radio to his lips and keyed the mike. "West Virginia State Police unit four seven seven to Life Flight one. I copy and I can hear your rotors approaching."

"Nice to hear from you, West Virginia four seven seven. We've been trying to reach you. How is your patient?"

Homer glanced at the man lying next to him and pressed two fingers into the notch alongside his windpipe. "I've got a pulse, but he's been hit pretty bad. Lost a lot of blood."

"I copy that, four seven seven. You're going to need to set out four flares in a rectangular pattern to give us an LZ. It's nice to know we're in the neighborhood, but from up here, everything looks the same. Do you have a visual on us yet?"

"That's a negative, Life Flight one. No visual."

"Okay, four seven seven. We'll keep an eye out for each other. By the way, your scene is secure, is it not?"

Homer hesitated. "Uh, negative, Life Flight. But we've had no further shooting."

"Be advised, four seven seven, our procedures require a secured scene before landing."

Homer's heart sank. He'd been afraid of that. And as much as he wanted to rail against them, he understood their position. They were medics, after all, not soldiers or cops. That meant that they were defenseless.

It didn't make sense even to ask someone to take such a risk. There was a guy in there with a gun, for God's sake. A guy who was more than willing—hell, maybe even anxious—to add another trophy to his case. And a helicopter was one hell of a trophy.

Homer hated the thoughts that were knocking on the door of his brain. Why on God's green earth should he even think about taking on this nutcase by himself? Why shouldn't he just do what they should have done from the very beginning—wait for backup to arrive and then go in with superior strength and firepower and blast this guy right out of his socks? That would be justice, after all. That would be showing this scumbag what it meant to shoot at a cop.

But a federal officer lay beside him dying.

God, how he wished there was a better way. Yet the more time he wasted out here trying to decide what to do, the longer Stanns had to dig himself in, and the more blood would drain from Burrows's body.

Worst of all, if he waited, he'd be a coward. No one would call him that—hell, he'd probably already qualified tonight for a damn medal of commendation—but every day that he woke up, he'd realize it for himself, and he wasn't sure how well he'd be able to live with such a thing.

"Goddamn you, Burrows."

He checked to make sure he had all six chambers loaded. Next, he checked the magazine on the shotgun. Full to capacity. He shucked a double-aught round into the breech and was suddenly out of time-killers.

Well, this was it. He keyed the mike on his portable. "State police four seven seven to Life Flight one. Be advised, I'll be securing the scene right now. Stay close."

The medevac responded with something, but Homer wasn't all that interested. This being the night he was going to die in the line of duty, he frankly didn't care what a pilot in a clean uniform had to say.

There were two ways to make an assault such as this one: you could go in fast and noisy or you could go in slow and stealthy. Frankly, Homer didn't think his nerves could handle stealthy right now. Instead, he chose the frontal assault. Straight up the stairs, into the front door, and maybe the bad guy would either freak or he'd take pity on someone stupid enough to pull such a crazy stunt. Either way, it was time to go.

Homer rose to his haunches, steadied himself with a huge breath, and after checking to make sure that he could handle the Maglite and the forward grip of the shotgun in the same hand, he leapt forward like a linebacker. A loud, guttural, animal yell rose from his throat as he dashed straight up the stairs, across the porch, and on into the foyer, the shotgun ready at his shoulder, the brilliant beam of his flashlight illuminating the whole path.

He saw the gun before he saw the gunman and fired. The riot gun bucked hard, and before the roar of the blast died in his ears, he chambered another round and fired again, dropping down to his right knee to provide a smaller target.

Gun smoke choked the air, looking like so much fog in the beam of the Maglite. He'd expected return fire, and when he got none, he felt simultaneously elated and frightened. Where was this guy?

Homer allowed himself the luxury of lowering the riot gun to his hip as he searched through the wreckage he'd wrought. He saw no body on the floor, and no signs of blood, either new or old.

Yet the shotgun that had wounded Burrows was still there; or rather, bits and pieces of it were—mostly just the barrel. The stock and the grip had been mauled by Homer's assault. The shredded weapon appeared to be floating on its own in the air, a gun with no one to fire it.

He took a step closer, and as he did, he got his first glimpse of the heavy fishing line on the floor, and then of an elaborate arrangement of pulleys mounted near the door, and another near the stairs.

The stairs where someone had lashed a shotgun to the post.

"Well, I'll be goddamned." Homer found himself laughing in spite of the adrenaline that coursed through his veins. It had been a trap. A fucking booby trap, and Special Agent Timothy Burrows of the FBI had charged right into it.

31

THE SCREAM THAT rose from Interview Three seemed to shake the entire station house. Tom Stipton had nearly made it to the hallway when it stopped him dead at the threshold. In a business where screams were a part of everyday life, this one was different. This one had an edge of horror to it that raised the hair on his back and his neck.

He drew his weapon without thinking and charged back toward the door he'd just closed; one of a half dozen detectives with a half dozen drawn weapons. Tom arrived first and threw the door open, his arm uncertain where to point the gun.

"What is it?" he shouted. "What's wrong?"

April's eyes were like saucers, her features twisted and contorted by panic. Instinctively, Tom whirled around to see if someone was standing on the dark side of the door behind him.

"They're going to kill him!" April sobbed. "They're going to kill my baby!"

Tom looked to the other detectives to see if they knew what she was talking about, only to find them staring back at him. Right until this very moment, he hadn't even known she had a baby. Pretty damned shoddy police work, come to think of it.

"Who, April?" Tom asked, holstering his weapon. He heard a rustle of fabric and leather as others behind him followed his lead. "Who's going to kill your baby?"

"Patrick Logan," she said quickly, and then the look of panic deepened, as if she'd frightened herself with her words.

She looked desperately at Detective Stipton, and then, all at once, something changed behind her eyes as she gave herself up to the inevitable. Just like that, she seemed more relaxed, even as she stayed on the verge of tears. "The shooting at the school. That was Carlos Ortega, wasn't it?"

Again, Tom looked to the others, wondering who had leaked the information. "How did you know that?"

April opened her mouth to speak, but then checked herself. "Can we talk alone for a moment, Detective Stipton? I'd rather not have to watch everybody staring at me."

Tom didn't have to say anything. The others all filed out, and as they did, one of them told Stipton to take his time, that they would handle things over at the school.

With the room empty save for the two of them, Tom took his old seat, crossed his legs, and laced his fingers around his knee. If April was ready to tell a story, he was ready to listen.

Samuel waited in the truck for a long time before walking into the little restaurant for directions. He'd stopped at the 7-Eleven to look at their maps, but there were just too many little roads around here, and the way the words sort of wrapped around each other on the page, he couldn't figure out where he was supposed to go.

You're such a fucking dummy.

"I'm not a dummy," he declared. "And why don't you just keep your mouth shut?"

He wasn't sure why Jacob had decided to come driving with him, but when he'd first heard the voice, he nearly drove the truck into a tree. He couldn't see him, but he could sure hear his voice, so close that he swore he could feel Jacob's hot breath on his ear.

He hated asking for directions. Not just because he scared people sometimes, but because when they started to tell him, the words oftentimes came too fast. Turn left here, go for a mile, go right and then left and then right and then right again before you get to a stop sign . . .

God Almighty, sometimes they'd go on and on forever. But he'd always pretend that he got it all on the first try. Otherwise, they'd think he was a dummy.

The place he picked looked as if it probably cost a lot of money to eat there, with the people hanging around dressed in suits and ties, dresses for the ladies. They'd probably look at him funny when he came in there in his blue jeans and his flannel shirt and denim jacket, but that was okay. He was used to people looking at him funny. Sometimes, he kind of enjoyed catching them looking, just to see the expression on their faces before they quickly looked away.

The restaurant was called Hats Off, and it sat at the very end of a short block, the last building before the railroad tracks. He parked his truck near the tracks and walked back across the gravel parking lot, up the three steps to the porch, which actually turned out to be more of an elevated sidewalk, and on into the brightly lit anteroom, where a thin little lady stood at a podium and tried to smile at him.

"Can I help you, sir?"

Samuel heard the conversation stop as people noticed him standing there, but he paid no notice. Things like that didn't bother him so much anymore. She'd said the right thing and tried her best not to look at him badly, and sometimes that was the best you could hope for.

"Yes, ma'am," he said, scraping the filthy John Deere cap off of his dirty hair. "I was wondering if you could point me toward an address." He pulled the rumpled camping permit out of his pocket and read the street number to her.

The lady looked genuinely relieved to know exactly where that place was. "Okay," she said, and Samuel found himself bracing for an onslaught of turns and directions. "You drive straight across the railroad tracks there, and around the curve and at your very first opportunity, hang a left. That will put you on Clinton Road. Then you just go straight for a mile, maybe a mile and a half, and you'll find this address. If you get to Bradlick Road, you've gone too far."

Samuel closed his eyes as he listened, trying to visualize what she was saying, and when he opened them again, he thought he had it.

"Thank you very much." He turned for the door. His hand was on the knob when he caught a glimpse of a mother forcing her five-year-old's head around so as not to stare. "That's okay, ma'am," Samuel said in his friendliest tone. "He can look at me if he wants to."

The woman looked horribly uncomfortable while the little boy smiled triumphantly.

"This is what will happen to you if you don't study in school, little boy. So take a good look."

Samuel's words did nothing to ease the tension. If anything, the mother drew the boy in closer, and the little one's smile looked very much as if he were about to cry. Samuel stood there for a long moment, watching the boy's features cloud, and wishing that he could say something that would make the boy feel better. But Samuel knew that he didn't own those words, so in the end, he just walked out and back across the parking lot.

He hated it when children made those faces. Samuel loved kids, wished that he could have one of his own to play with and stuff.

Little Justin had cried, too. All children cried when they were around him, and Samuel was tired of that. Why did they do that? People either laughed, looked scared, or cried. Why couldn't they just say nice things—like "hello, sir" or "Have a nice day, sir"—the way they used to talk to Jacob? Why did everyone have to make him feel like a freak all the time?

It was a good thing the lady at the podium told him about Bradlick Road's being too far, because it seemed as if he got there in no time. Without her saying that, he might have missed the address completely and then just driven on till morning. He turned around in the apron of a closed driving range and headed back in the other direction, driving slowly now, and examining the house numbers that were posted on trees or posts or rocks, all along the road.

Lots and lots of driveways, but precious few houses that he could see.

There! That was the number right there! He saw it on a post next to the mailbox. He had to back up a little, but he made the turn easily.

Drive in slow now, Jacob told him.

"I will. You just hush up. I know what I'm doing."

Turn your lights off.

Okay, so that was one he'd forgotten about. Jacob had taken him on a lot of the jobs he used to do and shared in detail every little thing. Only before—well, you know, *before*—Jacob would be the one to go inside, while Samuel waited in the car with the engine running, the doors unlocked.

Samuel's job was mainly just to keep an eye out. If somebody approached a place where they were working, Samuel was to call Jacob's little phone, let it ring twice, and then hang up. They'd never say anything, but Jacob would know that there was trouble. Samuel was also supposed to keep close watch on the door. If Jacob came running out quickly—and he never did, but *if* he did—then Samuel was supposed to stomp on the gas the instant his brother's butt hit the seat.

Sometimes, Jacob would come back bloody, and when that happened, Samuel would know that things hadn't gone well, and that he should probably keep his mouth shut. Most times, though, Jacob came back clean—clean as a whistle—and those times, Jacob's mood was always high. Way up in the clouds, he liked to say.

For a few seconds after he turned off the headlights, Samuel couldn't see anything, but as his eyes adjusted to the darkness, he finally saw a serpentine black ribbon climbing steeply into the less black woods.

One thing you could say about the engine in their truck was that it ran smooth and quiet. *Like a top.* Jacob always insisted that everything be kept in tip-top working order for just such times as these.

Surprise is important, Samuel, never forget that. Sometimes it's most important of all. A squeaking fan belt can get you killed if you're not careful.

Samuel never fully understood how a squeaky belt could kill, but when Jacob said something with such forcefulness, it was always best just to listen to what he had to say.

Add to the quiet engine this smooth driveway, and it was like driving on a cloud.

Bright carriage lights on either side of the front door, combined with the light of a lamppost, made the night seem like day up near the house, so Samuel decided to park in the shadow of the trees, where no one would see the truck if they happened to look out the window.

Surprise means everything.

The truck's door latch clicked as he pulled the handle, and the hinge moaned a bit as he opened it, but Samuel didn't think they were loud enough to cause a problem. He swung his legs around and lowered himself to the ground oh so softly.

Don't forget the gun, Jacob told him.

"I'm not forgetting anything," Samuel whispered sharply. "I just haven't gotten to that yet." He was lying, of course, but he wasn't in the mood for a lecture right now about how all the little things mattered. Of course they mattered, but what did Jacob expect from him on his first time doing this stuff alone?

The Ruger automatic lay in the glove compartment where it always stayed, requiring Samuel to climb back into the truck and lie across the front seat to grab it. Back on his feet again, he stuffed the weapon into the waistband of his jeans.

Don't blow your balls off.

That one didn't even require a response. But he did check the safety, just to be sure.

One of Jacob's most important rules was to always enter from the rear of a house. People didn't pay as much attention to the back sides of their houses as they did to the front. If they had lots of lights on, they were almost always concentrated on the street side of the property, probably to make petty burglars think twice about picking that house instead of the darkened one next door. If he and Jacob had been petty burglars, that would probably have worked, but their business required a certain person from a certain place at a certain time. Lights or no lights.

He made an effort to stay in the shadows as he worked his way around the left side of the enormous brick home, and he was almost halfway there when he drew up short. How sure was he that this was the right house? Was he absolutely positive? It wouldn't do to help himself to the wrong house with the wrong people inside. He pulled the camping permit out of his pocket one more time and tilted it till he could see the writing in the dim, distant shine of the lamppost.

You already checked it, Samuel.

"But I need to be sure."

You are *sure.*

Jacob was right, of course. Again. Samuel had taken a lot of care down there at the end of the driveway to make sure that he had the right address. Sometimes, you just have to trust yourself to be right.

"I need to find the phone line first," he whispered, getting a jump on his brother. Sometimes, phone lines came in on poles, and other times, they came up from the ground. Out here, he didn't see any overhead lines at all, so he shined his flashlight along the foundation, looking for the telltale wire to the gray box.

Samuel giggled with glee when he found it within seconds. Sometimes just dumb luck goes in your favor. He'd learned to recognize them quickly, but just to be sure, he glided through the darkness over to that spot on the wall, and he clicked on his light again. Sure enough, there was the raised picture of a telephone with a bell in the middle of it. He used a Swiss Army knife to turn the screw that kept the little plastic cover closed, and as the four-inch door swung open, there were the phone connections: two wires with little plastic clips on the end, just like the one he'd seen inside his own house. The second wire could mean a second telephone, but probably meant they had an alarm system with an automatic dialer. For all the good it would do them tonight. Noiselessly, he slipped the blade under the wires and cut them cleanly away from the plugs.

He remembered the one job he'd done with Jacob a long time ago when they'd just unplugged the phone line long enough for Jacob to go inside and do the job, and then they'd plugged it back in before leaving. Jacob had said something about keeping them guessing, but Samuel wasn't sure whom he was talking about, and he didn't pursue it.

He smiled. "Things are going just fine now, huh?"

You're doing great, Samuel. You're doing just great.

Now it was time to find a way inside.

Russell Coates had finally gotten around to checking in with the Fairfield County police, a courtesy that should have been his first order of business, but in fact was an easily delayed pain in the ass to do. Sometimes, local police organizations were just plain difficult to work with, and after his long drive in from West Virginia he wanted to get some work done before he played politician. Besides, if he waited long enough, the big brass and big egos would be on their way home before he had to deal with them.

As it turned out, he needn't have been concerned. He'd heard about Fairfield County for a long time—it being one of the largest and most progressive suburban departments in the country—and from what he could tell from his dealings so far, their reputation was well earned. After exchanging pleasantries with the duty shift commander, Captain Himler, they'd made him feel right at home, granting him free access to all the files he needed and all the coffee he could drink. They even gave him a desk and a phone, courtesy of a detective who wouldn't know of his sacrifice until he started his shift in the morning.

"Why don't you just reach out and touch this guy if you're so sure he did it?" Himler asked after being filled in on what Russell had found so far. "I mean, you've got the tires and you can put him at the park and at the convenience store where the shooting was called in. What more do you need?"

Russell thought for a moment before answering. "I guess I'm just not comfortable with it yet. It's like I've got all the pieces, but none of the glue to hold them all together. One stiff breeze and I'm out of business."

Himler considered that and shrugged. "Well, it's your case. But if it were mine, the guy would've been in interrogation for two hours now."

Russell shook his head. "Not this guy. He's smart and he's rich. He'd lawyer up before you even thought of the first question. I guess I want to give him another couple of days to hang himself on something, and then if I can't come up with anything, I'll pull him in based on what I've got."

"Just let me know what I can do to help," Himler said before getting back to the stack of papers on his desk.

That had been ninety minutes ago, and since then, Russell had been on the phone with the Washington field office, getting them caught up on the same details. Everybody in the world was ready to go, it seemed, as soon as Russell pulled the rip cord. Until then, it was all a matter of plowing through—

His cell phone chirped, interrupting his thoughts. Russell snapped it open in the middle of the third ring. "Coates."

"This is Chuck Wheatley." Russell recognized the voice the instant he heard the name. "I've got news for you, some of it tough."

Russell didn't like the tone he heard. Wheatley was ordinarily the life of the party at the office. "Hit me."

"We just got word that Tim Burrows has been shot."

Russell's heart stammered, and he gasped reflexively. "Oh, shit, is he all right?"

"We don't know yet. Seems he was checking out a lead on your murder case and he opened a door that was rigged with a shotgun. Nailed him in the belly. He's in surgery now, and the doctors won't commit to anything."

"Jesus."

"He's still alive, but he's lost a lot of blood."

"I should be there." Russell checked his watch. "Shit, I'll never get a flight at this hour. I'll catch the first one out in the morning. Keep me informed, okay, Chuck? When he gets out of surgery, you give me a call. Even if they don't have a prognosis yet, I want to know."

"You got it. And there's one other thing."

Russell waited a beat until Chuck got to it.

"You said you were looking for any reports of kidnappings, and when we talked, we didn't have anything on the boards. We just received an all-points from Pittsburgh, though, about a little boy—a two-year-old named Justin Fitzgerald—who was yanked from his stepfather's car last night and is apparently being held as leverage against some drug shit on the street. The details are kinda hard to figure out from what's on the wire, but apparently since then, the stepfather's been whacked by a sniper, the mother's been arrested robbing a department store, and the whole deal is somehow tied in with the murder of a drug lord inside a private school."

It came too fast, leaving Russell awash in details. "Jesus, and all that happened tonight?"

"All within the last few hours, yeah. Think it has anything to do with your park killing?"

Russell shrugged. "Hell, I don't know. The kidnapping I was looking for was an adult. I don't know how a little kid could fit—"

The footprints. The Pampers.

That door in his mind opened and shut again, teasing him with the solution he needed. "Thanks, Chuck. Remember to call me about Tim."

Russell slapped the phone closed and leaned forward with his elbows on the desk. The answer was there. Right *there,* so close that he could touch it. He pressed his temples hard, trying to squeeze the answer out.

What did he know? He knew that a child was kidnapped from someplace in Pennsylvania, and either coincidentally or otherwise, a lot of people shot up a lot of places as a result. He knew that one Jacob Stanns was shot dead while either being buried alive or burying someone else alive.

But the murder was so far away from the burial site.

Yeah, how about that?

Could this be the key? This Justin Fitzgerald? Could this be the boy for whom Robert Martin shelled out more money than he expected for a box of diapers, at the same convenience store where someone happened to call in a 911 report of a murder?

Russell still didn't have his arms completely around it, but he sure as hell knew enough to bring this Martin guy in for questioning. Rising from his desk, he headed across the squad room toward Himler's office.

It was time to see about some reinforcements.

32

EXHAUSTION CRUSHED BOBBY'S body like a blanket welded from steel. Mentally and physically, there was nothing left. He'd spent it all in the past twenty-four hours, and now, as they lay together in the bed, the three of them—Bobby, Susan, and . . . Steven—his body demanded that he sleep, but his mind wouldn't let it happen, cycling through rushes of intense fear and then anger, and finally, sadness.

This was their truce. They would spend the night as a family together, either with the adults sleeping on the floor of the nursery or Steven sleeping in the bed with them, and then in the morning, they'd start anew, firing volleys at one another at full volume.

But there it would end, simply because Bobby couldn't take it anymore. His first act in the morning would be a telephone call to Agent Coates. He'd come by the house, he'd find whatever he found, and Bobby would be led away in handcuffs.

What was that?

Something startled him, making his whole body convulse in the bed, and jolting his heart. He realized now that he'd dozed off, if only because he was so conscious of being wide-awake. He must have heard a noise; why else would he have jumped so?

He sat there for a long time, bolt upright in the bed, his legs lost under the blanket and bedspread, the flesh of his bare chest pimpling into gooseflesh. He listened to the night, but it didn't move. He heard only the syncopated rhythms of Susan and Steven breathing. Even in the darkness, he could make out their forms in the bed, Susan flat on her stomach, with her head buried under her pillow, only a two-inch stripe of flannel nightgown showing above the line of the covers.

Next to her, Steven lay sideways, likewise on his stomach, but with his knees tucked under and his bottom sticking straight up into the air, as if he'd collapsed while praying. Not that the kid didn't have a lot to pray for. Didn't they all?

Steven was a snorer, a world-class one at that. Bobby had to smile as he listened to the boy saw at his sleep like somebody's grandfather. Bobby remembered from the baby books that such aggressive snoring was a sign of future tonsil and adenoid problems, and he fleetingly wondered who was going to take care of those for the little guy.

The longer he listened, the safer the night seemed. Perhaps it had just been the snoring that woke him up, a hitch in the breathing that registered somewhere deep in his psyche as danger. That was probably it.

Moving as gently as he could, so as not wake the others, he settled back into the bed, into his pillows. He wished he could burrow in as Susan did, blocking out all traces of sound and light, but if he slept on his stomach, his back wouldn't be right for days. A cruel reminder that his fortieth birthday lay not so far down the road. Instead, he lay on his back and brought the covers up to his chin—his "coffin position" as Susan liked to call it.

He closed his eyes and tried to think about something pleasant, images that would let him sleep peacefully through the night.

It wasn't snoring, his subconscious told him. *It was more like a crash.*

That was silly. If there'd been a crash, then the security alarm would have gone off, and God knew there'd be no sleeping through that. Just to reassure himself, he turned his head to the left and strained to see the backlit annunciator panel on the wall just beyond Susan's nightstand. His heart skipped again as he saw a green light glowing where there should have been red. In all the excitement and acrimony of Susan's arrival home, he'd forgotten to set the damn thing.

Cursing under his breath, he quietly pulled back the covers and swung his feet around to correct his omission. He froze in place, though, even before his feet touched the floor. This time, there was no mistaking the sound he heard, and with a sudden head rush of recognition, it was all he could do to keep from fainting.

Somewhere downstairs, a door opened and then closed.

Climbing in through the basement window had been Jacob's idea. *Houses this big always have alarms,* he'd told Samuel, *but a lot of times, they don't hook anything up to the basement.*

Samuel had thought about arguing but in the end deferred to his big brother just as he always did. Samuel had landed right in the middle of a stack of boxes, sending all kinds of shit tumbling onto the concrete floor. God, what a noise that made!

The gun! Jacob told him. *Be ready with the gun.* Samuel quickly picked himself up off the floor, struggling to keep his balance among the junk, and held the pistol straight out at arm's length, his flashlight in the other hand, waiting to blast whoever might come tearing down the steps to get him.

He waited there for a good minute, not moving even a muscle, listening. When nothing happened, he decided it was safe to move on.

Samuel's hands shook. Even as a little boy, he refused to play hide-and-seek, because he hated the way he jumped every time he discovered someone. And then they'd laugh at him. They always laughed at him. He got used to it after a while, but still.

Walking around inside other people's houses was way worse than hide-and-seek.

Keep going, you pussy.

"I'm going," he whispered. "I just want to make sure that nobody heard me."

You've got a gun, asshole. Why the hell should you care?

Letting the flashlight beam lead the way, he made his way quickly and quietly across the basement over to the wooden stairs that led to the main level. As he walked, he tried not to let himself be distracted by all the boxes and tools and exercise equipment that lay strewn everywhere. He tried not to think about how much fun it would be just to spend a day down here looking at stuff and trying to figure out how it worked. He had a job to do, and he was going to do it.

The Boss said he had to, and you don't fuck with The Boss. Never.

The risers creaked under his weight, and there were a lot of them. Normally, a staircase had thirteen steps—unlucky thirteen. Jacob had taught him that so he wouldn't trip and fall if he was walking around the house at night. Thirteen steps was *standard.* That was the word Jacob used. Standard. But standard didn't mean always, because this house had fifteen steps up from the basement. Not thirteen. Fifteen.

He nearly turned around at the top of the climb just to count them out one more time to be sure, but he knew that Jacob would yell if he did. As it was, Samuel spent too much time thinking about shit that didn't matter.

If this place had an alarm, it would probably be hooked to the door at the top of the stairs. People did that sometimes, just to save money. Not that it mattered with the phone lines cut, but he really hated the sound of those attic sirens. He opened the door quickly, just to get it over with, and laughed a little when everything remained quiet.

He lost concentration, though, as he stepped out into the huge kitchen—it looked bigger than his whole house!—and let the door close too quickly behind him. It didn't slam, exactly, but it made a lot more noise than he wanted.

His mouth gaped as he did a slow-motion pirouette there in the breakfast nook, trying his best to take in the hugeness of this place. How was he going to find Justin in a place this big?

People sleep upstairs.

That was true, wasn't it? Chalk up another one for old Jacob. And from the looks of this place, people were certainly asleep. They sure weren't downstairs watching television. But where was upstairs? He followed his light beam around to the right and on into the short hallway that led to the foyer, and there he found it. In the mottled artificial light, the curved stairway seemed to be floating in the air, twisting around to join a bridge-looking thing that likewise seemed to float.

"Wow," he whispered. This was the fanciest house he'd ever seen.

He pointed the automatic up over his head now as he started up the treads, keeping his aim focused at the very top step, where anyone who wanted to stop him would have to appear.

Get the boy. Just get the boy, don't worry about anybody else. Do whatever you have to do.

"I will, okay? Just let me think. Just let me think . . ."

Captain Himler was nodding his head even before Russell had finished with his explanation, and he made a quick phone call the instant he was done. He chatted, nodded, then hung up the telephone. "I can get you six patrol officers if you can wait a couple of minutes."

Russell checked his watch without even seeing the time. "Sure. A couple of minutes can't hurt, and I'd like to have the manpower, just in case."

The footsteps were in the foyer now.

Bobby couldn't believe it. This couldn't be happening. He wanted it to be a dream. He wanted it to be his imagination, but the noise was too rhythmic, too regular, to be anything else but an intruder.

He jostled his wife sharply. "Susan! Wake up!"

Ordinarily, she was slow to rouse, but something in his tone brought her instantly awake. "What?"

"Shh. I think there's somebody in the house."

"*What?*"

"Quiet. I hear someone walking around downstairs."

"Who is it?" she asked groggily. Then she got it. "There's someone in our *house?*"

Bobby snatched the telephone off the nightstand to call the police, but it was like listening to an earmuff. "Oh, shit, it's dead. *Shit!*"

Why hadn't he kept the gun? Why hadn't he *bought* a gun back when he was single and no one would bitch to him about having it? What the hell was he supposed to do now?

"We've got to get out of the house," he said.

"Why? Let's just lock the door and let them have whatever they want."

"What if they want *us,* Susan? Suppose this is the cop's buddies coming back for revenge?"

Susan didn't hesitate an instant. Gathering Steven into her arms, she tried to strip the blanket off the bed to keep him warm, but it snagged where it had been tucked under the mattress at the footboard.

"Leave that," Bobby said. "We don't have time." His mind raced to find a solution, but came up only with disasters. If they tried to go out the front windows, they'd fall two stories; out the back, it'd be three. How stupid was that? Why hadn't they thought about that before? Suppose the place was on fire?

The back porch! That was it! They needed to cross the bridge over the foyer, and if they made it to the nursery, they could climb out the back window onto the porch roof, and from there, it was only ten or twelve feet to the ground. They could survive that.

But they had to get there first.

"Come on," he said, leading the way to the bedroom door. "Quickly."

"What are you doing, Bobby? They're out there! I hear them on the steps."

"It's our only chance." Bobby had no intention of turning this into a long discussion. They were dealing with seconds here, if they even had that. It'd be a dead heat as it was getting across the hallway in time to dash into the nursery and lock the door. From there, he didn't know what would happen. It couldn't take long to kick in one of these doors, but it was the only chance they had. That, or fight it out on the stairs. Fat chance.

Susan didn't want to go, but she didn't argue, either. Maybe she was just too drowsy.

Praying silently to whoever might listen, he pulled the door open and stepped out into the hall.

Samuel had just been wondering which room to start in when he heard all the noise. People were talking, moving around quickly. The noise was coming from the set of double doors directly across from the top of the stairs.

He quickened his pace, the gun outstretched.

Remember, no one matters but the kid.

He didn't bother to answer. Too much going on. This had to work. The Boss was waiting, and he was running late. He had to—

Just as he reached for the brass handle, the door flew open.

There in front of him, not five feet away, was the man he remembered from the woods last night, standing in a pair of drawers and nothing else. The man yelled as he saw Samuel, and Samuel yelled back.

For a long moment, they all just seemed to stand there, staring at each other.

Shoot them!

The gun! That's right, he had a gun! Without even really thinking about it, he brought the weapon up. He hesitated, though, when he saw the woman standing right behind the man, holding the little boy he was here to retrieve. It was him! He wasn't going to let The Boss down after all!

He allowed himself a little smile as he pulled the trigger.

Bobby jumped a foot. Susan screamed, and then so did the boy, finally startled out of his sleep.

"Bobby!"

Jesus, he had a fucking gun!

Bobby saw the stranger's arm move, and somehow he knew what was going to happen next. They were all dead.

But his body wasn't so ready to write him off. He launched himself at the burglar, hitting him square in the chest. It was like tackling a wall. For just an instant, he wondered if the explosion that rocked his body was the sound of his bones shattering.

For all his size and strength, the intruder seemed as surprised as Bobby, and off-balance, too. The impact drove him backward toward the railing, and the marble foyer below. The wood of the railing cracked on impact, but it held. Bobby had the momentum, though, and that gave him the upper hand at least until the gunman regained his balance and composure.

Gathering the fabric of the man's jacket into his fists, he hauled him away from the railing and then tried to heave him back toward the same spot on the rail. But the surprise had evaporated by now, and the intruder was having none of it.

"Susan, run!" Bobby yelled, just before a punch to the side of his head left him feeling rattled. He refused to let go. "Go, Susan, go!"

The intruder roared, "I'm not a pussy, goddammit!" And then he hit Bobby with everything he had.

Yes, you are! You're a fucking pussy! You missed, for God's sake! You missed! How the fuck did you miss?

Samuel felt the half-naked guy's grip loosen on the first punch, and on the second, he went reeling across the hallway, letting Samuel regain his balance and move away from that long drop. He brought the pistol up to shoot, but then he saw the woman and the little boy darting down the hallway.

All that mattered was the boy.

Shoot!

"I can't! I'll hit Justin!"

Instead, he charged after them. People were always surprised by his speed. For a big guy, he could move like lightning. He didn't know where they were running to, or why they'd try to get to another room on the same floor, but then again he didn't much care. They never had a chance.

He took the woman off her feet simply by snagging her hair in his fist.

Susan thought for sure he'd ripped her scalp clean away from her skull. She was moving fast, as fast as she knew how, when suddenly her head stopped as her feet kept going. She felt herself going down and hugged Steven in close. They hit hard, and the boy leapt to his feet, screaming.

He turned and started for the stairs.

"I got you!" the intruder yelled, and he made a scooping motion with his arm. He got Steven around the middle, but the boy squirmed like a grounded fish, arms and legs flying, back arching severely. Samuel couldn't hang on. The boy fell to the floor, rolled to his feet, and scrambled for the steps.

He'd nearly made it when Samuel went for an ankle. Again, he missed, but he managed to knock the boy's feet out from under him.

"Leave him alone!" Susan shrieked, and she launched herself at the gunman, snaring his head with her arms, and digging her nails deeply into the flesh of his face.

• • •

"What the fungh—" Samuel yelled as the nails slashed his cheeks. He hadn't expected this kind of fight. Jacob was right again. He should have just shot them when he first saw them.

But now, this bitch was on his back, where he couldn't get a shot, and little Justin was going to get away.

Get the kid, goddammit!

"I'm fucking trying!"

But the bitch wouldn't let go. In fact, it seemed that the more he struggled, the tighter her hold became.

Through a haze of tears, Samuel saw the boy nearly at the stairs and he lashed out with his foot.

He was kicking the boy down the steps for God's sake! Bobby couldn't get his vision to clear completely, but he sure as hell saw Steven teetering at the top step, just as he could hear the screaming from his wife, and the cries of pain from the little boy.

A fall from here would kill him; that's all there was to it.

Bobby scrambled drunkenly across the carpet and snagged the little one's nightie-night—a brand-new one, with *Tigger* embroidered on the blue blanket material—the very instant he began to topple. For a horrifying instant, Bobby thought that maybe he'd grabbed too hard and actually pushed him over, but both his grip and the material held, and he was able to pull him in close to his body—in close to safety.

But the boy was hysterical. He kicked, he screamed. All he wanted in the world was to be somewhere else, and Bobby realized with crippling sadness that this was the second such night for this child. That was two of two. What the hell could he have done to deserve this?

"Oh, my God! Bobby!" Susan's shrieks reached a new level, one of sheer panic.

Bobby whirled to see the enormous stranger standing upright again, his massive forearm tucked tightly under Susan's chin, his pistol at her head.

"I will!" he shouted as if someone else were there on the bridge with them. Then, to Bobby: "I only want Justin. I don't want you and I don't want her. I have to take Justin back."

The icy hand returned to Bobby's insides as he realized that he could no longer win this. "Please put the gun down."

"Give Justin back to me, and I will."

Bobby wondered if the man was drunk. His words seemed thick. Not slurred really, just labored. Drugs maybe? "Who's Justin?" Bobby asked, a play for more time. Time to think.

"You know who he is. Give him to me and I won't hurt her." He pressed the muzzle in harder to emphasize his point.

"Oh, Jesus, don't do that!" Bobby begged.

Susan's eyes burned red and wet. She was terrified. "Let him kill me," she sobbed. "Just let him kill me. I can't lose my baby. Not again."

Bobby's breaths came in quick, short gulps. He looked from his wife to her captor, wondering what to do.

"I'll do it. I'll count to four, and then I'll kill her and I'll kill you, and I'll still get Justin. Let him go."

"No, Bobby! Please."

"One . . . "

"I'll do it!" Bobby shouted the words and hurried forward with the boy. "Here, take him. Let her go."

"Bobby, no!"

He ignored her, concentrating his gaze at the intruder's eyes. "Please don't hurt my wife. This boy is not ours, and we're sorry we got involved in this at all. You have to realize that."

"Bobby!"

"She doesn't understand," Bobby went on quickly, hoping that the big man wouldn't be distracted by Susan's hysterics. "She's not feeling well, okay? She's confused. Here, the boy is yours."

Steven went nuts, squirming and kicking. It was all Bobby could do to hang on to him.

"But you'd better take him now. I don't know how long I can hold on to him."

"Bobby, I'll kill you!" Susan shrieked. "You can't give up our baby! You can't!"

"Do it now, goddammit!" Bobby yelled. "Do it now and get out of here."

For a long moment, the intruder just looked confused, unsure what to do. Then, as if a veil had lifted, he nodded. In one quick motion, he let go of Susan and scooped Steven out of Bobby's arms.

Susan attacked. She charged at the intruder, screaming nonsensical words, her eyes filled with murder.

Samuel started around with the pistol, but Bobby tackled his wife, wrestling her to the ground and doing his best to pin her there.

"Go!" Bobby shouted. "I've got her! Just go!"

Samuel tried to hold his aim, but the squirming boy was giving him fits. "I heard you!" he shouted angrily, and at first Bobby thought he was talking to him. Then he realized that this man who'd broken into his house was embroiled in a shouting match with someone who wasn't even there.

"The boy's the most important!" the intruder ranted on. "You said so yourself. He's the most important, and I've got him and I'm gonna go back. That's all I need to do. I'm gonna take him back."

He shouted on like that the whole way down the stairs, and on out the front door, his voice ultimately drowned out by Steven's high-pitched squeals—or Justin's, or whoever the hell he was.

Bobby would never have guessed that his wife could be so strong. Hanging on through her struggles was like riding a bucking bronc in a rodeo. She squirmed and twisted and screamed, trying to break a hand or a leg free. She tried to bite him.

"Susan, stop! Goddammit, stop!"

"My baby! You let my baby go! You gave him away!"

"He's not our baby!"

"He's *my* baby! God sent him to *me!*"

"He was going to kill you, Susan! He was going to kill you and then take him anyway!"

"Let me go!"

"No! Not until you settle down."

"Let me *go!*" She got a wrist free, and it all went south from there. She pummeled him, pounding his face and his ears, the blows landing with stunning force. When she got a leg free, she jammed a knee into his crotch, and Bobby felt the fight drain out of him in a wave of agony. He let go and rolled himself into a protective ball.

Susan didn't hesitate an instant. She jumped to her feet and tore down the stairs, taking them two, three, four at a time.

She dashed through the foyer and the opened front door, shrieking to the night, "Steven! Bring him back, you bastard! Bring back my baby!"

33

RUSSELL COATES OPTED to ride in the lead cruiser, with none other than Captain Himler himself at the wheel, leading a procession of four vehicles through the downtown center of Clinton. Out here in the sticks, reception on his cellular phone was fragile at best, and he had to keep a finger pushed into his other ear to hear the latest report from Agent Wheatley on Tim Burrows's condition.

Himler waited until his passenger hung up to ask, "How's he doing?"

Russell shook his head. "They don't know yet. Apparently it's a pretty bad belly wound, and he's still in surgery. Beyond that, my guy didn't know much."

Himler shook his head. "Damned shame. And you think these folks we're after had something to do with it?"

"That's what my instincts tell me, yes. I think the Martins are up to their eyeballs in something they shouldn't be involved with, and I think they've probably kidnapped themselves a child. Beyond that, there's not much I can say for sure."

Neither of them spoke as they bounced over two sets of railroad tracks, then Himler broke the silence. "Mind if I ask a question?"

"Word it that way and the answer is probably yes."

Himler chuckled. "Still happy with your decision to wait?"

Russell considered the question for a moment. "Haven't you ever had a gut feeling that a case just hasn't evolved far enough yet? You know you're close, but if you pull the string too early, it'll just unravel?"

Himler nodded. "All the time. I wasn't criticizing. Just asking."

"Well, there'll be plenty of criticism to go around. With Agent Burrows getting himself shot, I can guarantee that every single decision I've made today will be second-guessed and overturned."

Himler turned his head in the darkness to face Russell. "Sounds like burnout to me, Coates."

Russell chuckled. "Maybe the first symptoms. Another couple years and I'll have my twenty in. From there, I think it might be time to move on. It'll be up here on the left in about a quarter mile." Russell wasn't in the mood for career counseling.

A few minutes later, the invasion of the Martin house was complete. In total, six police vehicles scattered through the front and side yards, their light bars shimmering. As officers moved to assigned locations throughout the property, the air crackled with the sharp staccato sounds of constant radio traffic.

"It's your scene, Agent Coates," Himler deferred as they approached the front door. "You may do the honors."

Russell nodded, then stepped up and rang the bell. Through the leaded glass that lined the doorjamb, they could hear the sound of Big Ben.

"Is that the doorbell?" Himler laughed. "Sounds like Buckingham Palace."

Ten seconds passed and Russell switched to the knocker. On a quiet night like this, people were likely to report the knocks as distant gunfire.

"Robert Martin!" Coates yelled. "This is the FBI. I have a warrant to take you into custody. Open the door!"

This time, he didn't even wait for a reply. If the suspects hadn't answered by now, to hell with them. He'd shown due diligence in front of a half dozen witnesses. Now he could break down the fucking door.

The two patrol officers stepped forward with a battering ram, and after one practice swing, they sent the decorative cherry-stained door exploding open in a hailstorm of wood fragments and broken glass. They heard a similar crash elsewhere in the house as more officers carried out the same operation downstairs, at the back door.

Two minutes later, the primary search was completed, and the house was declared empty.

"Looks like your people bolted," Himler said to Russell.

Russell pulled his notepad from an inside pocket and flipped through it till he got the right page. "Do me a favor, will you, Captain?"

Himler took a step closer.

"Put out an APB for this Explorer?"

"How far, do you think?"

Russell mused for a moment. "Well, certainly the D.C. metro area, and why don't you throw in West Virginia, Pennsylvania, Delaware, and Ohio just for grins."

"Those will take some time, you know."

"Fair enough. I'll be interested to see just how big a head start they've gotten." Even as Himler passed the assignment on to a junior officer, Russell held little hope that the all-points bulletin would bear any fruit tonight. It was hard enough spotting the color of a car at night; reading the license number could be a bitch. And that's if they didn't do something to disguise it.

So, I spooked them, Russell thought. *Where would I run if I were them?* He wondered if they'd even thought that far ahead. Was this part of the larger plan all along, or were they merely reacting to Russell's getting too close?

A patrol officer yelled from above, "Captain Himler, I think you might want to take a look at this."

Every eye in the house turned to face the gray-shirted cop on the bridge over the foyer.

"We got signs of a fight up here. And a bullet hole in the doorjamb."

Samuel hit the sack with his flashlight and it stopped squirming. "Quit making me do that!" he scolded. "Just be quiet and enjoy the ride. This is a game, okay? I don't want to hurt you. I don't want to hurt anybody, so just settle down." After a pause, he added, "You dummy," just to hear what it sounded like coming from him instead of toward him.

He didn't like it.

"I'm sorry I called you that. Nobody should call anybody that." The sack said nothing. Just as well. It never talked anyway; it just screamed.

Why did they call the boy Steven? he wondered. If his real name was Justin, why would they go and call him Steven? It didn't make any sense.

Just like a lot of things that didn't make any sense.

Like, why did Jacob have to die like that? Why couldn't he have won the fight and gone on to do all of this stuff with The Boss? Samuel hated this stuff. Every time he thought about The Boss, his heart would hammer so hard in his chest! He just didn't know that he was up to the task of doing business with the only man in the world that his big brother had been frightened of.

You should have killed them.

"Who? The people back at the house?"

Who else, you pussy?

"I didn't have to. I didn't want to. I already had the boy, why should I have killed them? That man was actually *helping* me there at the end. It wouldn't have been nice to shoot him after that."

Did you touch anything?

Samuel gasped hard enough and loudly enough to trigger a cough. He had! He'd touched lots of stuff, hadn't he? Quickly, he raised his hands in front of his face, one at a time in the darkness of the cab, so as not to lose control, just to make sure he hadn't left any parts of himself behind.

Well, did you?

He hated that tone in Jacob's voice: that taunting, know-it-all tone. Maybe he didn't wish that Jacob had lived after all.

Well?

"You were there, Mr. Smarty! You were there! You already know I did!"

Remember the electric chair, Samuel? Remember how I told you about that?

"Well, why didn't you say anything? You were there!"

Jacob didn't bother to answer. More and more, he was getting like that. His daddy had been a lot like that, too, right after he died. He always talked to Samuel, ragging on him day and night about stuff, calling him names, telling him terrible things in his sleep about Jacob. Things that Samuel didn't want to hear.

Jacob wasn't like his daddy said. He wasn't a bad boy. Mama had died of the cancer. They knew she was going to die, so it was just a matter of time anyway. The way she cried out in the middle of the night, and the way she didn't recognize them when they came in the room, that was all part of the cancer. That's what Jacob had told him, and Samuel knew that Jacob never lied. Jacob was the one person in the world who was always on his side; the one person in the world who would always stick up for him, no matter what else was going on. No matter who else was making fun of him.

It was okay for Jacob to call him names, but if anybody else even tried, then Katy bar the door, boy. Jacob would be all over them like . . . like stink on shit. That's right, like stink on shit. That's how Jacob liked to put it.

And those pills that he gave to Mama? They were just her medicine. Daddy got that part all wrong. He said that Jacob *wanted* her to die. Said that he was *tired* of her yelling out all the time, and tired of having to clean her bottom as if she were a baby. Who the hell did Daddy think he was, saying shit like that about Jacob? He was a good brother. The best brother a boy could ever have.

But Daddy never saw it that way. Hell, he didn't like any of his kids.

The sound of the switch slicing through the air startled Samuel, making him jump in his seat and look around the inside of the truck cab. He swore that he could almost feel the searing pain. Smell the chicken shit.

Why was he thinking about that day so much? He hadn't thought about that in so long. Why was it all coming back now? And with such clarity? It almost felt as if he were traveling with ghosts in the truck.

Screams.

He jumped again. Where did those come from? God, they were so loud. Where the hell did they come from? Were they even real?

Samuel tried to force himself to concentrate on the winding road that stretched out in front of his truck, but inside his head, he kept seeing that great column of smoke rising from way off in the backyard. Jesus, that was so long ago, but he could still see it with perfect clarity and detail.

The sun burned bright and hot, and Samuel's butt and back still ached from the switching. He couldn't move his arms or his legs without tearing a scab, but he still had work to do. The tractor needed an oil change, and after that, the hay wasn't going to stack itself, you know. Out there at their farm, either you pulled your weight or you didn't, that's all there was to it. A few taps with a switch was no reason for a man to shirk his work.

At first, he'd thought he heard the sound of a cat caught somewhere it didn't belong. But the more he listened, the more he realized that no cat could ever raise a howl like that. It was a much bigger sound—much bigger animal. Human maybe? Jacob!

Samuel dropped what he was doing and tore out of the barn, out into the yard, only to see that it was empty. The screams got louder still, and from way off to the right—near where the chicken coops were—he saw a giant column of smoke rising into the air; black, greasy smoke, like you'd expect to see out of those old steam trains he'd seen on television.

"Jacob!" he yelled, and took off in the direction of the smoke and the screams, running as fast as he'd ever run, not even worrying about the torn scabs and the purple bruises. There'd be plenty of time to worry about those. Right now, Jacob needed his help.

The closer he got, the quieter the screams became, until the human sounds were gone entirely, and all he could hear was the horrible cackles and shricks of the chickens. What could possibly be happening? he asked himself, even though he probably already knew. These were sounds of birds being roasted alive.

"Jacob!"

Up close, the thick smoke clung to the ground, rolling around along the grass before lifting off into the sky. The heavy, bitter smell of the gray fog made him feel sick to his stomach. As he rounded the final little mound of earth that separated him from the chicken coop, he stopped dead, in midstride.

Orange flames shot out from everywhere, the entire building completely consumed by fire. Horrified, Samuel watched as half a dozen chickens jumped free from the little windows, their feathers on fire, and scrambled in circles on the ground, making sounds that he'd never even imagined such a bird could make.

"Jacob!"

"Shut up, Samuel, I'm right here."

The voice came from his right, and Samuel whirled to see his big brother sitting on the chopping block, his face locked into an expression Samuel had never seen before or since. Deep wrinkles furrowed Jacob's forehead, right above the spot where his eyebrows nearly touched each other. The way his jaw muscles worked, he looked as though he'd trapped something in his mouth and was trying to keep it from escaping. A five-gallon gas can lay on its side at his feet.

"What happened?" Samuel noticed the blisters on his brother's hands and forearms. "Jacob, you're burned."

"No shit, Sherlock." There also were tiny blisters on his face, where the wispy sideburns he'd been trying to grow had been singed off.

"I heard screaming."

"That was Daddy," Jacob said, just as easily as if Samuel had asked who'd been on the phone. "He had a little accident."

Samuel choked down a wad of panic as he whipped his head around toward the blast furnace that had once been the chicken coop. "Is he going to be all right?"

Jacob laughed, but looked as if he might cry. "Fuck no, he's not all right. He's dead." Jacob stood and pushed past Samuel, on his way back to the house. "Damn shame about the chickens, though."

Back in the days right after he died, his daddy had visited Samuel a lot, trying to tell him that Jacob had set the fire on purpose; that he'd murdered him, just as he'd murdered their mama. He'd say that it was all because of Samuel, too. If he'd been a better son—if he hadn't been such a pansy-assed dummy every fucking day of his life—then his daddy wouldn't have had to be so rough on him.

"Them switchings was for your own good," his daddy used to say. "They was to make you a better boy. If you'd been good to start, then I never would've laid a hand on you."

According to Daddy, Jacob set him on fire because of that last switching. What a stupid thought! Jacob'd never do something like that. Not to somebody Samuel loved. It had happened just like Jacob had told the police when they came by: Daddy had been using the gasoline to get rid of yellow jackets when the idiot drunk had lit a cigarette. The whole place had just gone up so fast.

Samuel remembered how Jacob had offered up his scarred hands and face as proof of his efforts to save their daddy. Jacob had even started to cry when he talked about it. Jacob never cried, for heaven's sake. For him to do that, he had to feel really bad about what had happened. And why would he feel bad if he'd done it on purpose?

Over time, Daddy had stopped visiting Samuel at night, and as the boy grew into a man, and he and Jacob had started their little business with The Boss and others like him, Samuel hadn't thought much about any of this stuff.

On the days when Samuel allowed himself to be brutally honest about everything, he knew very well what their business was all about. Samuel was not as stupid or as dense as people thought he was—or even as he sometimes pretended to be. He knew that these nighttime outings, with all the secrecy and the occasional blood, were sometimes about killing the bad people. Not always, but sometimes. Other times it was just about snot-poundings, but as long as they were picking only on bad people, and not good ones, then Samuel didn't really have much of a problem with that. Especially since he never had to do any of the real work. He just stayed outside and watched things.

He wondered, though, about this stuff with Justin. Jacob said it was a game, and as long as Jacob said it, then it must be true. Take that to the bank. But Samuel didn't much like this notion of stuffing a little boy in a sack and then putting him in that room underground. He didn't like that at all. Part of him wondered just how asleep he really was when the boy got away the first time.

Now that he thought back on it, he could almost remember watching the boy struggle his way out of the hole and take off into the woods. He could almost remember thinking how nice it would be if the boy got away this time.

Of course, that was before Jacob had come up and seen that he was missing. That was before he got so mad and called Samuel all those names and told him to stand still in the woods while he got himself shot.

Those were all really bad memories, and that same part of him that remembered them also wondered why he was going back out to the same woods all over again.

By all indications, it had been a hell of a fight. The railing over the foyer was barely holding itself together anymore, and the bullet hole in the doorframe spoke volumes to Russell. The bags of new children's clothes and toys intrigued him as well. He could understand the furniture in what was obviously the nursery, and the little shrine on the wall explained most of what he needed to know. But what about the stuff that was still in the bags? The ones with the receipts dated today?

"I'm entertaining any theories you might have," Himler said, his arms folded across his chest. Given the location of the violence—in Fairfield County, on his watch—he'd rightfully taken over jurisdiction of whatever crime might have been committed here.

Russell shook his head. "Wish I had one for you."

"So, do you think the Martins were the shooters or the shootees?"

Damned interesting question. Russell still couldn't make the link between what clearly was a foiled kidnapping and all of the bloodshed that had followed. He supposed that the Martins might have surprised an intruder and fired off a shot, but it seemed equally likely that the intruder surprised them with intent to murder. Of course in the second case, that begged the question, why and how did he flub it up so miserably?

"I don't know what to tell you," Russell said as honestly as he knew how. "For all I know, the Martins were murdered in here tonight, albeit very neatly. Your guys still haven't found any blood, right?"

"There's a tiny little smear on the carpet over there, but the technician says it looks more like the result of a boo-boo than a bullet."

Russell pinched the bridge of his nose, hoping to ward off the headache that had started to bloom. "What I need is a way to snap my fingers and be back in Pittsburgh. Whatever's going down here, that seems to be the common denominator."

"What'll it take, four, five hours to drive?"

"Something like that. But I'm dead on my feet. I probably need to crash someplace for a couple of hours before I head out."

"I can get you a ride," Himler offered.

Russell waved the offer away. "I can't put one of your officers through a drive like that just so I can sleep in the car."

Himler shook his head. "I wasn't talking about a car. I was talking about a helicopter."

34

WE'LL GET HIM back, Susan. I swear it."

She refused to speak to him. Instead, she stared out the window at the passing darkness, her silence broken only by occasional tears and snuffles.

"Dammit, Susan, don't do this. He was going to kill you!"

"And now he's going to kill Steven," she shot back, her first words in over an hour. "That's what you wanted all along, I suppose."

"Susan!"

"It is."

"Oh, yeah, that's why I've done this whole thing your way. That's because I wanted the boy to die."

"His name is *Steven.*"

"No, it's not. But that's not the point."

"You're right. That's not the point. The point is that you've been trying to get rid of him all day long."

"Because he's not ours. Jesus, how many times do I have to say that? He's not ours."

"God—"

"Yes, God sent him to us. I hear you. I've heard you the thousand times you said it. And maybe He did. Who am I to say otherwise? That doesn't mitigate the fact that you can't just take possession of another human being."

"Well, you *killed* a human being."

Her comment landed like a slap.

But she wasn't done. "There's your big problem. It's not Steven, and it's not me. It's how are you going to get away with killing a police officer? You can't deal with one without the other, you said it yourself. We're good people. Why else would God have created such a dilemma for us if He didn't intend for us to keep the baby?"

"He wasn't a police officer," Bobby said, instantly and deftly changing the subject.

"What?"

"The guy in the woods. He wasn't a police officer."

"How do you know?"

He paused for a moment to collect his thoughts. How exactly was he to explain this? "Well, I guess I don't *know*. But I know. It's because there's been no mention of it. Not anywhere. Not in the news, not when the FBI guy came to the door this afternoon. If he were really a cop, then we'd have heard something about it by now."

"Then who was he?"

Bobby shrugged. "I don't know that either. But remember when he and I were struggling out there in the woods? Remember he kept calling out for Samuel?"

Intrigued, she half-shrugged. "I remember."

"Well, I think that Samuel just came and took Steven away."

Susan's scowl began to show fear. "But why?"

"I suppose to finish off whatever it was that his buddy had started. Whatever we interrupted."

"But he had a badge."

Bobby's mind skipped a bit as he kept up with the shift backward in the conversation. "The dead guy, you mean?"

"Right."

"Okay, so what? Anybody can have a badge. Go down to the army surplus store, and you can have one, too. It's not like I checked his credentials or anything."

"So what does that mean?"

Again, Bobby paused before answering. "If I'm right, it means that the guy I killed didn't think I was a kidnapper, but rather was a kidnapper himself. He wasn't shooting to protect the boy; he was shooting to get him back."

"So it *was* self-defense."

Bobby nodded. "If I'm right, I think so, yes."

And that meant that Bobby's instinct about calling the police from the very first had been the correct one; and that but for his cowardice, maybe little Steven would not be in danger all over again.

"So, is that why you think they're heading back to the woods?" Susan asked. "To finish off whatever they were going to do?"

Bobby nodded. "Yes. I certainly think they're out to finish whatever they started, and did you hear what Samuel said to Steven in the hallway? He said they were 'going back.' To me, that means back to where all of this started. I can't begin to guess why, but the good news is, it's not to kill him."

"What makes you so sure?"

"Killing is easy. He could have done that in the house. He could have done that out in the driveway. But he didn't. Whatever he's got planned, it has to take place 'back there.' I'm just hoping that it turns out to be the woods."

They drove in silence for a long time before Susan said, "Do you think we should call the police now?"

Bobby had to laugh. Where was that question ten hours ago? "No, not anymore. I don't think we have the time for it now. If we call it in, they're going to want us to sit down and talk through it all. That takes time, and this guy's got too much momentum to give him any more time than he's already got."

As they drove on through the narrowing roads and deepening woods, Susan found herself watching Bobby drive, just as she'd done last night from the backseat. When he'd sense her gaze and turn, she'd look away, as if staring straight ahead.

Her eyes shifted back to her husband; back to that hard expression that she'd never seen before they lost Steven the first time and now seemed never to leave. She watched the way his jaw muscles flexed, and how his lips seemed almost white from the pressure as he pursed them so tightly.

As if someone had lifted a veil, she realized for the first time what he must have gone through these past hours—God, through these past weeks. That expression on his face said it all. He'd worked so hard to be the rock that suddenly she wasn't sure that she'd ever given him the room to grieve on his own. He'd been so busy serving as her emotional scaffold that he'd never taken the time to deal with his own feelings.

Suddenly, Susan saw things with a remarkable clarity—a view of the world that was every bit as different as the view she'd seen after finally being fitted with her first pair of glasses. What once seemed fuzzy and confusing now seemed perfectly sharp and utterly self-explanatory. This man who sat opposite her—this man who'd been her best friend since her freshman year in high school, and who had forever endured her efforts to change his style of dress and the jokes he told—was not her enemy after all.

Why did this come as such a shock to her? How could she have ever thought otherwise? With this newly cleared vision, she understood that she was alive now because he'd been selfless enough to throw himself in front of a madman's gun. That scene back on the bridge in the house wasn't about giving up Steven. It was about saving her.

It was about loving her more than he loved himself. And now, here he was, every bit as terrified as she, driving through thc night to rescue a little boy he'd never even come to know.

"You know," she said, finally breaking the silence, "I really do love you."

"I love you, too." He said it mechanically as he tossed a forced smile her way.

"And it occurs to me that I've been something of a shit today."

"Have you?" he asked, a genuine smile finally cracking that look of stress and gloom. "I hadn't noticed."

As it turned out, discovering the body in the woods, and all the attendant nonsense surrounding it, was the best part of Sarah Rodgers's day. Ten minutes after Agent Coates drove out of Catoctin National Forest, she received a report of a brush fire on the far southern end of the 73,000-acre facility, and by the time they were able to muster the necessary fire-fighting forces, the blaze had charred over twenty acres of old-growth hardwood. But for the arrival of a cold front around six-thirty, and the rains that came with it, things might have been a whole lot worse. As it was, the fire was contained, and the local fire chief assured her that there'd be no problem with flare-ups tonight.

As the chief put it so succinctly, "Ain't no fire yet been made that can burn wet wood."

Thank God for small favors.

But even that wasn't the low point of the day. According to the National Weather Service, they could expect the temperatures to continue to drop through the night to an unseasonable twenty-five degrees, with the rain to transition to snow that would accumulate up to six inches by morning.

All of this would mean stranded campers, short staffs, and a workday for Sarah that would stretch to every bit of sixty-five hours. Even now, as she piloted her green Chevy pickup into one of five narrow parking slots in front of the Area Five ranger station, she noted the big heavy flakes that tumbled through the beams of her headlights.

Gardner Blackwell looked up from the pile of papers on his desk as Sarah walked through the door. "Coffee's on the burner," he said, offering a big buck-toothed smile. "Just made a fresh pot."

Sarah's addiction to caffeine was the stuff of legend. "You're a lifesaver, Gard. So, what's your bet? The weather says up to six inches from this one."

Gardner shook his head. "Nah, I say four at the most. It's been too warm for too long."

"Just to be ornery, then, I'll say eight." Sarah poured a half inch of coffee into the bottom of a heavy white mug, swirled it around, then tossed the rinse into the wastebasket. "Nobody up here's got communicable diseases, do they?" She refilled the cup and helped herself to a thinly padded, gray metal chair in front of Gardner's desk.

"That's my cup," he replied, eyeing her less-than-complete washing regimen. "I was about to ask you. By the way, you look like crap."

Sarah laughed. "It's too late to try and sweet-talk me now." A moment passed while she watched him sift through park passes. "Got any murderers in there tonight?"

"Only three that I know of," he replied without dropping a beat. "But I sent them all down to Area One. Thought the Tourist Center could use a little excitement."

"Kinda weird, though, isn't it?" Sarah mused aloud. "I mean, chances are we've handled paperwork that was filled out by a killer."

Gardner cocked his head as he regarded her. "How weirdly morbid. I think it's time for you to take a nap."

"That time passed unnoticed about twelve hours ago."

They shared a laugh before Gardner changed the subject. "Oh, before I forget, we've got to get some new chain strung at the entrance road at the top of Challenger Trail. It's busted again. I just noticed it on my last rounds."

Sarah closed her eyes as she tried to remember precisely where Challenger was.

"Connects to Powhite," he reminded her. "Leads to Route 630."

Of course. Now she remembered. She never ceased to be amazed by the extent some people would go to save a few bucks on a permit. "Put it in tomorrow's briefing for everybody to be hard-asses on permits for the next few days. No excuses. If they can't cough up a permit, hit 'em with a ticket." As outdoor lovers themselves, rangers too often let such transgressions go unchallenged, their hearts going out to people who just want to commune. Sarah couldn't help but wonder if last night's murderer hadn't been just such a scofflaw.

As an afterthought, she added, "Have you looked around up there? Seen any signs of who might have broken the chain?"

Gardner shrugged. "I just assumed it was kids. Why, you think it had something to do with the murder?"

"I think I should include it in my next chat with my FBI contacts."

"Speaking of which," Gardner teased, "a little bird told me you were charming the hell out of a fed."

Sarah blushed and leaned over to rest her head on the front of the desk. "And someone doesn't have enough to do. What have you heard from the patrols about the condition of the roads?"

Gardner rose from his chair and carried her empty cup back to the coffeepot. "So far, none of them have mentioned anything, so I guess things are still in good shape. I'll be sure to ask when they check in on the hour." He didn't bother asking her if she wanted a refill. "Come on now, heads up. There's plenty of work to do. You are our leader, after all."

But she'd already fallen asleep.

35

IT HADN'T OCCURRED to Samuel until he cleared the pass at the top of the mountain that he'd forgotten to put the bolt cutters back into the truck. If someone had replaced the chain across that road, he'd have to think of something pretty quickly. As he pulled off Route 630, he nearly cheered when he spotted the barricade right where they'd left it, lying in the dirt.

He tried turning off the headlights the way his brother had done the night before, but he turned them back on after barely missing a tree in the darkness. Fifty yards later, he realized that even the headlights weren't enough to see properly, so he just parked the truck and turned off the ignition.

The night was so much darker out here in the woods. So dark that Samuel couldn't find the flashlight on the seat without first opening the door for the dome light. Walking around to the passenger side, he pulled open that door and lifted the sack from the floorboard down onto the wet ground. When did it get so cold? he wondered.

The boy didn't move while he untied the cord that knotted the mouth of the bag, and for a brief moment, Samuel worried that maybe Justin was hurt. As the fabric fell away, though, he saw that the little boy was just fine. He lay on his side, with his eyes open, his thumb stuck into his mouth.

Samuel squatted down as low as he could without getting his pants wet in the sopping mulch. "Hey, little boy," he said cheerily. "We're almost there, okay? We're almost done. Now, are you going to be a good boy this time?"

Justin said nothing. He didn't even make eye contact. He merely lay there on his side, staring straight ahead.

"I need you to stand up now, okay, Justin? Can you do that for Uncle Samuel? Can you just stand up for a minute?"

But still the boy did not move.

Anger churned in Samuel's stomach. "Dammit, boy, get up!" He raised the heavy flashlight over his head, ready to hit him with it, but little Justin didn't even cringe. He didn't seem to care anymore.

The anger went away. Maybe Justin was just too tired to play right now. Maybe that was it. Maybe he was just plain too tuckered out to do what Samuel told him to do.

"Want me to carry you instead?" The boy didn't respond, but Samuel knew that his answer would have been yes. That was it, he was just too tired.

Justin fought some as Samuel worked his hands under his armpits to get a handhold, but it was nothing like the fights he'd put up in the past. And once Samuel got him up so his little butt was resting on Samuel's forearm and the mussed mop of hair was resting on his shoulders, the boy seemed to relax again. His thumb never left his mouth.

Justin smelled just like babies always do, kind of sweaty and pissy, but tonight, there was a new smell—one that Samuel hadn't sniffed in a long, long time. His brain flashed more pictures he hadn't seen in years. Jacob and Samuel were little boys, and they were playing with their mama. She had a huge smile on her face, and everyone was having fun. In these pictures, no one was angry, and no one was afraid. It must have been because Daddy wasn't home. He must have been on the road.

Things were always so much better when Daddy was on the road.

Baby powder. That was the new smell. Baby powder. And it smelled delightful, filling Samuel's sinuses with the kinds of memories that never seemed to come anymore. Each night, when he closed his eyes, all he saw recently were the jobs he'd done with Jacob. He saw the way the people lay so still when Jacob was done. He remembered too much blood. And if he thought real hard, he could remember the screaming.

Not many of the jobs screamed—Jacob was too good for that, but even he made mistakes sometimes. But when they did, it was a terrible, terrible thing to hear. Those were the times when Samuel would take one of his trips.

Those people were all bad, he thought, and The Boss said that they had to be taken care of. That's all Samuel needed to hear. When The Boss wanted something, he got it; that's all there was to it. And Jacob said it was all okay.

The screaming.

The sound built in Samuel's mind even as he worked feverishly to shut off the flow of thoughts.

What kind of game makes you bury a little boy?

That was a new voice in Samuel's brain. That was his *own* voice. He didn't think many thoughts in that voice anymore, and hearing it now startled him.

There's nothing fun in that. That's no kind of game.

Samuel found himself hugging Justin closer to his chest as he worked his way through the thick woods on the way toward their special spot. The boy's breathing seemed to be coming faster than it should, and his little body trembled in his arms. "Are you cold?"

That was a stupid question, wasn't it? Of course the boy was cold! It was snowing out, for God's sake!

Without slowing his pace much, Samuel unzipped his coat and wrapped one of the flaps around Justin's pajama-clad body. He hugged him tighter still and vigorously rubbed the outside of the coat where the lump curled himself into an even smaller boy.

"Just a little bit further. Just a little bit further and we'll be with The Boss. Then everything will be just fine."

The Boss is going to hurt him.

There was Samuel's own voice again. Why was it saying things like that?

"No, he won't," Samuel insisted aloud. "He's not going to hurt anybody. He told me so. Jacob told me so, too. Isn't that right, Jacob?"

He waited for an answer, but when none came, Samuel just shook off the bad feelings that climbed his spine. Jacob wouldn't ever do anything to hurt this boy. Samuel liked the boy, and Jacob would never hurt anybody Samuel liked. Jacob had said so himself countless times. That voice in his head didn't know what it was talking about, pure and simple. It was just crazy. As crazy as Samuel. Maybe even crazier.

Games should be fun, you dummy!

Of course they should be fun, but as Jacob said, sometimes they just have to be more fun than the alternative.

And what is the alternative?

"Stop it!" As Samuel shouted at the voices, Justin jumped in his arms and began to cry.

The sudden shriek of the telephone nearly launched Sarah out of her chair. Out here in the area offices, the annual budget didn't allow for the beeps or the electronic warble of modern phones. Out here, they were still stuck with good old-fashioned ringing phones. In the fog of her grogginess, Sarah could have sworn it actually rang *inside* her head.

Gardner was still laughing as he brought the handset up to his ear. "Area Five. . . . Oh, yeah, she's here, but it may take me a minute to get her fingernails out of the ceiling."

Sarah stuck out her tongue at him and reached for the phone. "This is Sarah Rodgers."

"Your fingernails are in the ceiling?"

"Never mind. Who is this?"

"Jerry Bartlett down at entrance four. Thought you'd like to know that your favorite Explorer is back in the park."

Sarah's brow knotted as she tried to decode what he was trying to tell her. "I'm not sure . . ." Then she got it. She jumped to her feet, instantly wide-awake. "Oh, my God, you mean the one from last night? The one you pulled over?"

"Yeah, I just finished collecting the entry permits, and I happened to notice the license number matched the one we were told to look out for. Once through the gate, I don't know where they headed, but I thought you'd want to know right away."

Jesus, she couldn't believe it. Criminals really do return to the scene of the crime! "Okay, listen to me, Jerry. I need you to make a phone call for me, and then I want you to meet me at the bottom of Powhite Trail, okay?"

"What, you think—"

"Exactly." Then she read a number to him off of a business card from her pocket. "Call that number, tell whoever answers exactly what you told me, and then get your ass up to Powhite."

Dropping the phone into its cradle, she turned to Gardner. "Get your coat. And grab a shotgun. I think this evening is about to get really exciting."

The Bell Jet Ranger was all over the sky. Approaching the Blue Ridge, the fine, chilly weather of northern Virginia had quickly turned to shit. What had once been clear, starry skies now looked like thick, gray ink as the heavy clouds reflected the chopper's blinking strobes.

Russell sat in the back this time, watching over the shoulders of the two pilots for some signs of panic on their part, all the while trying to decide which direction his supper would ultimately travel. "You're sure it's safe to be up here, right?" he asked over the intercom. It felt slightly unfair to him that the pilots both wore helmets while all he got was a pair of green plastic headphones with a boom mike.

The uniformed cop on the right—the command pilot—half-turned as he keyed his intercom. "Agent Coates, you need to relax. I promise that neither one of us has a death wish, okay? If conditions go below minimum, we'll turn around. It's a little rougher than usual, but you're perfectly safe."

Russell loved the way pilots practiced the art of understatement. And the edge of annoyance was not lost on him. They were flying through this crap as a favor to him. If they were in fact unnerved by the weather, his whining wasn't making it any better.

According to his latest information, Tim Burrows was out of surgery, and the doctors had sent out word to the vigil in the waiting room that things had gone well, and that there was every reason to be optimistic. His flawless physical conditioning made it all the better. Russell said a little prayer of thanks.

As a gust of wind rolled the helicopter sharply to the right, Russell shot out a hand to grab the Jesus bar. Suddenly, he felt as if he were field-testing Dramamine.

"Agent Coates," the pilot's voice cracked in his earphones.

"Still here."

"Okay, I've got a call for you here. I'm gonna patch it through to your headset. Just talk like you would on the intercom. Remember to push the talk button."

If there was one task in the world at which Russell was an expert, it was talking on radios. He heard a brief burst of static, followed yet again by the pilot's voice: "Go ahead, Charleston Center."

"Am I speaking to Special Agent Russell Coates?" The new voice sounded scratchy and mechanical.

"That's affirmative. Who is this?"

"This is the air traffic control center in Charleston, sir, with an urgent message from your office."

Oh, God, Russell thought. *Tim didn't make it.*

"I'm reading here, sir, so I hope it makes sense. Park Ranger Sarah Rodgers reports that the Martins' Explorer has been spotted in Catoctin National Forest."

Russell's eyebrows nearly left his forehead.

"Do you copy, sir?"

"Affirmative, I copy. And it does indeed make sense. Thank you very much."

"Thank you, Charleston Center," the pilot added. In another hiss of static, Russell's headset was disconnected from the main radio.

Now, this was a damned interesting development. Why would they go back? Why would an attack in their home bring them back to the woods? You'd think it would be the very last place they'd go; which meant, of course, that it was the very place that Russell needed to be.

"Okay, guys," he said into his intercom. "We need to change the plans a bit . . ."

The accumulating snow masked many of the landmarks that Bobby remembered from last night. It was colder, too, and while his down jacket kept his body warm, he found himself wishing he'd brought a hat.

"Suppose this isn't where they went?" Susan asked as they walked up the Powhite Trail, her hands tucked into her armpits for warmth.

"This is it," Bobby replied, hoping that saying it firmly enough would make it true.

"But suppose it isn't?"

"If this isn't it, then we're all screwed."

"You're sure we're still on the Powhite?"

"I don't know how we couldn't be. Sure looks a lot different in the snow. It's beautiful."

Susan didn't bother to answer. Nothing was beautiful anymore.

Bobby's logic for being here was as simple as it got: last night, Steven had come running to them from upstream, which meant that wherever his ordeal had started was centered somewhere uphill from where they'd camped. His plan was merely to go there and wait. And watch. And listen. It was that simple. Now that he was here, though, it seemed *too* simple, too driven by coincidence. These woods were big, even on a clear day. On a snowy night, they felt even bigger. The more he thought about it, the more stupid and hopeless it all seemed. But what was the alternative? Nothing, that's what.

Suppose they're not even here? Suppose they went to an airport, or to South fucking Carolina?

These thoughts tortured him as he continued his climb up the steep incline. If he was wrong, they really were out of cards. If they didn't find what they were looking for up here, then he supposed it would be time to make that phone call to the FBI.

As for Steven, it would be time to pray. Hard.

36

IT NEVER OCCURRED to Samuel to wonder about the other car. He saw it sitting there among the trees, and he assumed it belonged to The Boss, but he kept on walking toward the special place in the woods—the place where they would play their game. The snow fell and fell and fell, making the woods look like a Christmas special on television.

Justin didn't seem to like it, though. As the temperature dropped, and the snowflakes accumulated on the outside of Samuel's jacket, the little boy curled tighter and burrowed deeper. He still hadn't said a damn thing.

Samuel's doubts about this game grew steadily deeper. For the life of him, he couldn't see the fun in it. If it were anyone but The Boss that he was going down the mountain to meet, then he might have considered breaking the appointment—a very, very bad thing to do. Jacob never missed an appointment and always yelled at Samuel if he did something to slow him down. If you missed appointments or let people down, they might never work with you again.

But maybe Samuel didn't want to continue working Jacob's job. Maybe he didn't want to get into the snot-pounding business. He wasn't nearly as good at it as his brother was, and he certainly didn't enjoy it as much. Yessir, maybe this would be the very last time that Samuel ever dealt with The Boss. Maybe he might just mention that to him, too.

So, why keep going at all, then? If he was never going to work for The Boss again, why not turn around and take Justin home, away from the game that had never sounded very fun in the first place? What did he care if The Boss got pissed off?

The only man Jacob was ever afraid of.

Well, okay, was that an argument in favor of meeting him or walking away? If he was so damn terrifying, why even meet up with him? Why not just leave now?

Because he knows where you live, you dummy.

"Don't call me that!" The snowy insulation made his voice sound three times as loud as he intended it to be. "You just keep your big fat mouth shut, Jacob!"

At the sound of the shouting, Justin jumped under his jacket and started to cry again.

Instantly, Samuel felt terrible. "Oh, it's not you, little boy. You didn't do nothing wrong. I was just talking to Jacob." He bounced the curled child gently as he spoke.

It was Samuel's turn to jump when a voice boomed from the shadows, "Who in the fuck are you talking to?"

He whirled around, leading with his flashlight. "Who is that?" he yelled. As an afterthought, he remembered his Ruger and shifted the boy and the flashlight to his left hand while he dug the pistol out of his pocket with his right.

"Whoa, there, Sammy," said a new voice, this one coming from farther over to his left. "You just be careful with that gun."

Samuel shifted the beam accordingly and caught a glimpse of a young man standing in a clump of trees, holding his own pistol. He thought he recognized the voice. "You're the one I talked to on the telephone. You're The Boss."

"No, *I'm* the boss," said the first voice. A big man with red hair stepped forward. Samuel responded with two steps back. "I understand you have a package for me."

Give him the boy, Jacob told Samuel.

Samuel shook his head. He didn't like the looks of this. Didn't like the looks these men had in their eyes.

"What do you mean, no?" challenged the big man.

Samuel was confused. "Huh?"

"Do you have the package or not?"

People might call him names, but Samuel was smart enough to know that when the man said "package," he really meant Justin. The man on the phone had meant the same thing. Come to think of it, how nice is it to call a nice little boy a package? Samuel took two more steps backward.

"Not thinking of leaving us, are you, Sammy?" asked the man with the gun.

Actually, that's exactly what he was thinking.

In fifteen years as a park ranger, Sarah had never once pointed her firearm at another human being. In fact, until recently, weapons weren't even part of the ranger's ensemble. As she understood the story, about a decade ago, a generation of psychotic hunters started taking out their anger against rangers who dared to enforce the game limits, at which point Congress approved the use of sidearms by uniformed park rangers.

From the very first day of the new regulation, Sarah had seen her obligatory pistol as more of an ornament than a weapon—no more threatening than her Smokey the Bear hat or her badge. Just between her and the tooth fairy, if it ever came down to a confrontation between her little .38 snub nose and some redneck's high-powered hunting rifle, she had every intention of just staying out of the guy's way.

Gardner seemed impressed that she'd known exactly where to find the Explorer parked. "I figured there was only one place for them to be," she explained. Still, it felt good to absorb that kind of admiration from a subordinate.

As they climbed the Powhite, following the steadily filling footprints on the trail, she found herself wishing that she hadn't been quite so aggressive. These people were murderers, after all, and she felt psychologically unprepared for a midnight shoot-out. Gardner's twelve-gauge helped, but even a hail of buckshot wouldn't do much to stop a well-aimed bullet from piercing her unarmored body.

"Well, I'm pretty much scared shitless," Gardner said as lightly as he could. The proud owner of a degree in forestry, he made no bones about his distaste for the law enforcement aspects of his job. "You sure we can't just wait for the sheriff's deputies to take care of this?"

As much as she wanted to say yes, she found herself shaking her head no. "In good weather, it takes them twenty minutes to get up here. Tonight, it'll be twice that. Maybe three times. And that's if they're not all tied up working wrecks on the highway."

"Suppose there's like a whole militia group up here or something?"

Sarah shot him a look that he couldn't see in the dark. "It's not like we're going in there with guns blazing, Gard. Maybe we just go as close as we can and stay out of sight. Hell, I don't know what we're going to do, but if it helps, I'm not feeling particularly suicidal or heroic this evening."

"Makes me feel all aglow and comfy."

Torn stubs of crime-scene tape still clung to the trees all around them. Without those clues, Bobby wasn't sure that he could even have found the old campsite. Even after only a day, it all seemed so different. In the distance, they could still hear the rush of the river, but with the snow muffling everything, even that sounded different.

As they walked into the tiny clearing, Bobby hesitantly illuminated the area at the base of the tree where the body had lain. He felt a sense of genuine relief when he saw that it was gone.

"Steven!"

Susan's cry made him jump a foot. He whirled to see what she saw. "Where? Where is he?"

"Steven! I know you're out there, honey, come to your mommy!"

He understood now that she didn't actually see anything. She was hoping. And drawing a hell of a lot of attention to herself if their attacker was out there. He'd have admonished her to be quiet, but realized the fruitlessness of it. If everybody stayed quiet, no one would find anything.

"Give us the boy," said Ricky Timmons, his voice as menacing as anything Samuel had ever heard.

This wasn't a game.

Maybe Samuel had known that all along, and he'd just been trying not to see it, but everything was clear as day right now. This was no game. No one was interested in Justin having any fun out here; it wasn't even about having more fun than the alternative, or whatever it was that Jacob had tried to tell him last night. These men wanted to hurt the boy. Samuel took another step backward.

"Y—you stay away," he stammered.

"Give us the boy," Ricky insisted again.

Samuel backed up faster now. "No! No, you just go away!" *Fuck the Boss,* he thought. They wanted to hurt this little boy he liked so much.

"Oh, for God's sake," grumbled the tall, redheaded man. "Just end this shit."

Samuel saw Ricky's gun hand arc up, and he raised his own. Ricky fired first, his body disappearing behind an enormous muzzle flash that seemed to rock the whole forest. Samuel turned sideways to the gunman, his body protecting the screaming child who was only now struggling to free himself, and pulled the trigger on his own weapon.

The Ruger split the night as well, kicking hard against the heel of his hand as Samuel pulled again and again and again. In the strobes of the muzzle flashes, Samuel thought for sure he saw the other man fall.

He thought it, but couldn't be positive because now he was running, plunging through the woods downhill, his momentum moving him faster and faster down the slope. From behind, he heard still more gunshots, but he never even glanced around to see. There was no time for that. He had to get little Justin back to safety. He had to get him back home.

You stupid fool, the car's behind you!

"So are they!" he tried to yell, but he was breathing too hard to make any real noise.

The flashlight splashed through the woods in mottled patches, casting weird shadows that camouflaged the real hazards of branches and tree limbs. He ducked and dived past branches and over rocks, moving faster than he'd ever run in his whole life.

And the boy was cooperating now. He stayed perfectly still, allowing himself to be hugged tightly to Samuel's chest.

The very same chest that glistened black and wet in the night.

Susan screamed at the cacophony of gunshots. They sounded so close, but as they echoed and deflected through the forest, they could have been coming from anywhere. Instinctively, she and Bobby drew closer together, shoulder to shoulder, and scanned the trees for some sign of movement, or even another sound.

"I think it was from up there," Bobby said, pointing straight up the trail.

Susan pointed more to the left. "No. From there."

Bobby didn't want to argue. They split the difference and left the trail, heading up the hill and toward the river. Susan wanted to run, but Bobby held her back. "If we make too much noise, we'll never hear anything."

"But Steven!" she breathed. "He's hurt. I know he's hurt. I *feel* it."

"I hope not," Bobby whispered. "But if he is, we'll never be able to help if we can't find him."

Down the trail, Sarah and Gardner recognized the sounds for what they were and quickened their pace, breaking into the closest thing to a run that the steep slope would allow.

"Sounds close," she gasped. "Keep your eyes wide open."

"I'll keep them open for the deputies is what I'll keep them open for."

"Oh, God, little boy, are you hurt?"

Even as Samuel stumbled through the forest, he brought the little boy out from under his jacket and held him out in front to get a better look. The lower half of his nightie-nights were soaked in blood, the heavy fabric sticking to his stout little legs.

"Oh, no. Oh, no, you're hurt, aren't you?"

But Justin didn't seem to be. Now that he was out from under the coat and exposed to the snow and the cold, he started wriggling all over again.

It's not him, you idiot. It's you.

Samuel gasped at the thought of it, and as he did, a terrible pain stabbed him, deep in his guts. The intensity of it made him yell out, an animal-like howl that rose from his throat without his even thinking of it.

"You lied to me, Jacob. You *lied* to me!" Samuel choked the words out of his throat as he continued his downhill stumble, propelled by his momentum. "You promised me it was a game. You *promised!*"

Just as he'd promised that Mama and Daddy had died accidentally, even though Jacob had been the only one close enough to see anything.

Just as he'd promised never to hurt anything that Samuel ever loved.

"Oh, Jacob, you *promised . . .*"

It was as if someone had pumped concrete into Samuel's legs. Suddenly, each of them weighed a hundred pounds and was getting heavier by the second. Sheer force of will kept them moving, one after the other down the hill, and it took all the concentration he could muster to keep from falling face-first into the branches and leaves and bushes.

If he fell, he'd hurt the boy. *Can't do that . . . can't do that.*

His stomach hurt *so* bad. There was blood in the back of his throat now, making him want to cough, while at the same time making him afraid to cough—afraid of what might come up if he did.

And still he plunged through the woods. He wasn't making half the speed that he was before, but it was taking three times the effort.

Tears streamed down his face as he realized just how stupid he'd really been. How stupid he'd been for as long as people had been calling him names.

"That sounds like a person," Susan said hurriedly as the two of them jolted to a halt.

Bobby agreed. That's exactly what it sounded like. And they both knew exactly the direction from which it came.

Finally, it was time to run.

37

RUSSELL HANDED THE pilot the sheet of paper on which he'd jotted down the radio frequencies from that morning. "Dial these into your radio," he said over his intercom. "I want to see what I can find out from them."

For the first time, the pilots seemed unnerved by the weather. They didn't say anything, of course, but Russell could see it in their faces. He wondered if maybe they should have opted for some Dramamine as well.

When the frequency was set, Russell heard the familiar pop in his headset, and then the pilot's announcement that the radio was his. Mimicking what he'd heard the others say, he opened with, "Fairfield County Helicopter Eagle One to Catoctin National Park ranger units, how do you copy?"

For a long moment, the radio was silent, prompting the pilot to recheck the numbers he'd dialed in. Russell was ready to key the mike a second time when a tinny, breathless voice crackled in his earphones. "Go ahead, Fairfield Eagle One."

Russell instantly recognized the voice. "Ranger Rodgers, I presume," he said, smiling.

"They're here!" she shouted. "They're here at the murder scene from this morning and shots have been fired."

This got everyone's attention. Without prompting, the copilot started digging for the map that would show the layout of Catoctin National Forest.

"Is anyone hit?" Russell asked.

"I don't know. The shots were not directed at us, but they were close by."

"Do you have backup on the way?"

"That's affirmative, but they're still a long ways out."

"Shit." Russell meant for that to be silent, but it went out on the air anyway. "Okay, Sarah, stand by." This time, he keyed the intercom button. "Hold that map up so I can see it."

The copilot shifted the map and the gooseneck light while Russell leaned in closer. It took him a good ten seconds to get himself oriented, and then he pointed to the spot where he'd spent the morning investigating. "That's where she is. Now, where are we?"

The copilot pointed to a spot east and south of Sarah's location. "That's about seven minutes' flight time from here. But I'm not sure about the flight conditions—"

Russell keyed the radio mike before the copilot could finish. "Sarah, this is Coates. We'll be there in six minutes."

Each step felt as if somebody were running a hot knife through Samuel's guts. His head had begun to feel funny, and while he knew that only pussies cried, he couldn't help himself.

And somebody was following him.

He couldn't bear to turn around and look, but he just *knew* that someone was following him. Trying to hurt him. Trying to hurt Justin.

"Can't let that happen," he panted. "Can't. Got to protect your friends. Got to protect friends and hurt your enemies. Before they can hurt you."

So why did Jacob hurt Mama and Daddy? Why did he hurt them so badly? Why did he set Daddy on fire?

Oh, God, the screams!

The inside of his head whirled as his brain replayed the pictures of the smoke, the sounds of those horrible screams, and the look on Jacob's face. The *happy* look.

Oh, sweet Jesus, he did it for me!

It was so clear now. He saw the pictures of the chicken shit, and of his own blood mingling with it. He heard the whistling of the switch, and somehow, even beyond the agony of the searing pain in his belly, he remembered how that switch had dug furrows into his flesh.

He remembered the look on Jacob's face the first time he saw it. He remembered the look of sheer fury. And how Jacob swore to get even with the son of a bitch who'd done it.

"I'll be okay, Jacob. Really I will, you don't have to do that."

"I'm gonna kill the son of a bitch. I swear to God I'm gonna kill him . . ."

Samuel's steps had slowed to a virtual stagger, though in his mind he was still running as fast as he could. He heard the sound of people.

Were they coming up behind him? Were they coming to hurt little Justin?

He couldn't let that happen.

He'd die first.

Bobby heard the big man approaching at the exact same instant he saw him. Recognition came instantly. This was the man from the hallway. This was the man who'd threatened to kill him and his family.

"Steven!" Before Bobby could move to stop her, Susan bolted forward to retrieve the boy, who reacted to the sound of her voice as if he'd been shot with electricity. He wrenched himself free of his captor's hands and dropped to his hands and knees in the mulch.

"Oh, God, my baby!"

Bobby hadn't ever seen that much blood on one person. Even the man in the woods hadn't bled that much.

The big man struggled to get a hand on the boy, but he never had a chance. He stood there for a long moment, listing off to the side and trying to gather the strength to lift the pistol that just barely dangled from his right hand.

"No!" Bobby shouted, and lunged at him, just as he'd lunged the night before, only this time, his opponent fell easily.

The man howled in agony as he impacted the earth, and blood frothed up from his lips. "Help him," he gasped. "Help the little boy."

Bobby wrenched the pistol from the big man's hand and brought to bear on his face, only to find the slide locked back, the magazine empty. He threw the weapon into the woods. Curiously, Bobby noticed that the man was crying. Not the way that someone cries when he's hurt, where tears come from the sheer agony of it; this man sobbed the way a child cries when he's ashamed. He tried to cover his face, to hide himself from the humiliation, but it was as if his hands were just too heavy to move.

"I'm so sorry," he sobbed.

Bobby didn't know what to do. He found himself torn between wanting to stay and wanting to run. Could he leave another man to die alone in the woods? He leaned in closer. "You're hurt. Is your name Samuel?"

Samuel's lip trembled as he nodded, but he still refused eye contact. "I'm so, so sorry . . ."

Bobby knelt up straight and looked back over his shoulder to see Susan locked in an embrace with Steven. Well, whatever came of all this, at least they were finally safe.

Three inches from his head, a two-inch gash exploded from the side of a tree at the very instant that the woods shook from another gunshot.

Susan screamed and tried to shelter the baby while Bobby scrambled toward them. Two more shots passed within inches.

"Who is that?" Susan screamed.

Bobby ran full tilt, bent at the waist to grab a fistful of his wife's coat and drag her deeper into the woods, away from where he thought the shots were originating. "Run!" he hissed. "Run! Run! Run!"

Susan had difficulty finding her balance as Bobby pushed and dragged her through the woods, the tree branches pummeling her as she tried to shelter Steven from them. "Let me carry him," he said, reaching out to grab the boy, but Susan turned away.

"I've got him."

"Fine. Then move!"

The worst part of all was not knowing where the shooter was. In the darkness of the night, they could be running in circles and never know it. That could mean death for sure. If not at the hands of the man with the gun, then at the hands of Mother Nature as they got lost in the unrelenting expanse of the forest.

The river beckoned him. The sound stood out above all others, a great and constant rush of noise—and as long as he knew where that river was, then he'd at least know basic north from basic south. As they plunged through the woods, he found himself drawn toward the water; not directly, but at an oblique angle that took him ever closer.

If this were a different time of year, the rushing waters might even provide them with a convenient means of escape; but here, in the frigid cold and the snow, the river was a death sentence in itself.

Please, God, just get us out of this alive. I'll take what's ever coming to me, but just let us escape from this alive.

Another gunshot split the night. Bobby didn't know where this bullet went, but he knew that they weren't running nearly fast enough.

Sarah instinctively ducked at the sound of the last shot. It was that close, up ahead and over to her left. "There!" she barked, pointing. "It's coming from over there."

Startled that she'd heard no answer, she turned to face Gardner, but he was no longer next to her. "Gard? Where are you?" Then louder: "Where are you?"

Terrified that he'd been hit, she whipped her head around, and then her body, the strong beam of her flashlight illuminating hundreds of falling snowflakes, which themselves cast a confusing array of shadows on the forest.

Then she saw him. He stood over in the trees, a little to the right of the path, trying his best to stay out of sight. He wasn't hit; he was just scared shitless. "Gard!" she called, but he refused to acknowledge her. She supposed it was shame, but the least he could do was pretend to cover her with the shotgun.

"Gardner, come on!"

He shrank farther away.

"Shit." She didn't have time for this. Somebody had to do the right goddamn thing, and at the moment, the torch had been passed to her. "Try not to wet yourself!" she shouted, and she took off again in the direction of the running shoot-out.

Footing was becoming treacherous now, and as she ran through the punishing branches, she found herself reaching out more and more to keep from falling. It was all way too noisy, she knew, but she hoped that the increasing noise from the river would help to mask some of that. In fact, now that she thought about it, the forest was an extraordinarily noisy place tonight, thanks to the acoustical tricks of the snow.

She heard another shot and this time saw the muzzle flash that came with it. The gunman still looked to be far away, but she knew that had to be an illusion. Even though the foliage was skimpy, the bare branches allowed only a limited line of sight, and she figured she was no more than fifty yards away from him.

She killed her flashlight and drew her .38, cursing Gardner one more time for being such a wuss. With luck, maybe he'd at least be able to screw up enough courage to point the way for the sheriff's deputies when they arrived.

The woods ended abruptly at the rocks, and from there, the Martins had no place to go. Susan took one step out onto them and her feet went right out from under her. Airborne acrobatics kept her from landing on Steven.

"My God, Bobby, we're trapped." Susan had to nearly shout to be heard over the roar of the water.

He hadn't counted on the ice. Where the raging torrents splashed up onto the current-smoothed rock faces, they froze solid and invisible, making it impossibly treacherous. They couldn't stay here. It was that simple. To stay was to die.

This time he didn't even ask for the boy; he just took him from her. Steven must have sensed the urgency, because he didn't fight. He just clutched Bobby for all he was worth. "We've got to move on," Bobby shouted.

"Where?"

"This way!" He eased himself onto his butt and scooted across the slick surface. Ahead and below, he could just make out a complex tangle of rock outcroppings. If they could make it that far, he thought they'd be safe for a while. Maybe even long enough for the gunman to give up for the night. That's all they really needed, after all: just a night. By this time tomorrow, Bobby would be safely in jail or stuffed into a drawer in the coroner's office. He wished there was a third choice, but for the life of him, he couldn't see what it might be.

Clutching Steven to his chest with his left arm, he tried to control the speed of his slide with his right, but to little avail. Once he got on the far side of this first rock, he found it much steeper than he'd expected and he dropped feet first a good yard, straight down, landing up to his shins in a puddle of standing ice water. The chill took his breath away. He had to steady himself against the rocks to keep from falling over into the river itself.

Susan was visible to him only as a black silhouette against the lighter black sky. She inched down the rock as he had, on her backside, only as she approached, she had two hands with which to control her descent, so things went a little better for her. He let her feet rest against his chest, and then her knees.

"It's cold down here," he warned.

"It's cold up here, too," she said, offering a smile.

He'd just grabbed hold of her hand when the gunman fired again. The report was nearly as loud as Susan's yelp of pain.

Sarah had just gotten into position to see what the gunman was aiming at when she heard the shot and saw the woman on the rocks drop out of sight.

"Freeze!" Sarah yelled, bringing her pistol up into the two-handed shooting posture she'd learned so long ago.

But her target didn't freeze. He spun quickly around to face her and fired off two quick shots that spattered her with tree bark.

Sarah retaliated with three shots of her own, but they were wild. She cursed herself as she dove for cover. She should have anticipated that. She remembered the FBI range instructors at Quantico telling her to expect that very thing.

Nobody freezes when you tell them to.

Why could she remember the instructor's voice so clearly now that it was too late?

They panic instead, and you need to be prepared for that. You need to be prepared to squeeze off a shot before they can react. That's the trick here. You stay calm, while they do the stupid stuff.

She couldn't remember if the "stupid stuff" specifically included crawling on your belly through wet mulch, but if it didn't, it should have. She couldn't see a thing beyond the thick tangle of branches and tree trunks, but her target obviously knew where she was. Inches over her head, a bullet split a sapling in two, the whip crack of the passing round causing her ears to ring.

Cursing herself for not staying behind to hide in the trees with Gardner, she decided it was time for a full commitment. She needed to be aggressive. She needed to make the other guy be the one dropping to the ground, if only to give her enough time to dash away. Leaping to a squatting position, she fired off her last two rounds in the general vicinity of the silhouette she saw in the distance. As she'd hoped, he dropped to the ground.

Yes! she cheered silently. She had the break she needed. She took off like a sprinter, heading back in the direction she'd just come from—back in the direction of protective ground cover, away from the wide open killing zone around the river.

She ran for maybe thirty yards, until she found herself comfortably ensconced in a thicket of evergreens. *In the midst of a Christmas tree farm,* she thought. The irony was too much.

Out there, somewhere, she heard movement. She already knew that if she'd hit her target, it would have been an outrageous accident; that he was probably still out there, looking for her; looking to finish the job he'd made such a mess of. She froze as the sound of cracking sticks and rustling leaves came ever closer, their sounds still masked by the roar of the river and the quiet hiss of the snow falling through the trees.

Moving as slowly as she knew how, Sarah thumbed the release on her .38 and flopped the cylinder off to the side. She cringed as she pushed the eject rod, praying that the noise would be slight. She hoped to catch the spent brass in the palm of her hand, but working in the dark, while keeping one eye pasted to the compass point from which her attacker would most likely come, two of the casings rolled out of her grasp, landing with a soft thud on the damp, muddy ground. She paused, listening for some sign that she'd been recognized. Ten seconds later, she breathed again.

God, how she wished she'd listened to the warnings of those instructors! How many times had they warned that more bullets were better than fewer? That automatics were better than revolvers? Even at that, she knew other revolver-toting rangers who at least equipped themselves with speed-loaders. But Sarah had never seen the sense in them. When would a park ranger ever find herself embroiled in a shoot-out?

Instead of dropping in a speed-loader and twisting a knob, then, Sarah found herself slipping spare bullets one at a time out of the loops on her belt, with hands that suddenly were way too big. Located behind her hip as they were—cowboy style—she had to work exclusively by feel, pushing each bullet up with her forefinger, and catching it in her palm.

She'd slipped out the last of them when she first heard the sound of approaching rotor blades. *Thank God,* she thought. Help was finally—

"Sarah, this is Eagle One," crackled her radio. "We need help zeroing in on your position."

She'd never heard anything so loud in her entire life.

38

SUSAN CLUTCHED HER face as she toppled toward Bobby. She fell like a tree, first spinning a quarter turn, then collapsing right at him. He tried to catch her, but with his left arm filled with a panicked Steven, he could work only with his right, and that just wasn't enough. He spun, too, under the force of the impact, and as he tried to recover his balance, his feet tangled.

He yelled as he fell backward, grasping at the air for a handhold, then clutching the boy tightly to his chest.

The frigid water registered as fire against his skin, agonizing needles of cold gouging his flesh as the torrent engulfed him. Suddenly, up and down meant nothing. As the waters swept him downstream, he struggled to find the surface, but it seemed that every time he thought he'd popped through, the waters dragged him down again. With Steven clutched tightly in both arms, he struggled to roll onto his back, even as the little boy fought desperately to break free. He kicked and scratched and bit at Bobby's hands, but Bobby refused to let go.

This is it, Bobby thought. *This is the end.*

Finally, his head came up and he was able to choke his way to a solid breath. He nearly cheered when he heard Steven choking and sputtering for air as well. The boy was still alive, and still strong enough to fight for air. That had to be good for something. It had to be a positive sign.

He sensed more than saw that the current had ripped him away from the riverbank and into the main channel, where the water moved even faster. Rocks pummeled mercilessly as he shot blindly through narrow chutes and over four- and five-foot water falls. He wasn't sure how he managed it, but somehow he'd gotten himself oriented feetfirst and on his back, clutching Steven on his chest the way an otter cradles his food.

He felt as if he were moving sixty miles an hour through the water, and as his butt and back scooted along the bottom, he thought for sure that the heavy impacts had to be breaking bones.

This couldn't go on. The frigid water siphoned his energy away by the pound. He could already feel his feet getting more clumsy as he used them to push away from approaching rocks. If he didn't find a way to shore soon, then he wouldn't find it at all. He and Steven would both drown. As it was, he was coherent enough to realize that he'd probably die of exposure anyway, but that had to be better than drowning.

Just about anything would be better than drowning.

Up ahead—it was nearly impossible to judge distances in the dark—he could just barely make out the silhouette of a deadfall across the water. It stuck out about halfway, extending from the right-hand bank. If the big old tree—it looked like a pine from here—had fallen recently enough, the branches that extended down toward the water would still be green and pliable enough to cushion their impact and slow them down enough for Bobby to grab hold of something.

If it was years old, however, those same branches would be so many spears, waiting to run them through on impact.

His legs were his rudder. By moving them to the left, his torso shifted right, and from there it was a matter of willing his leaden right arm to paddle for him, while his left trembled under the strain of holding on to Steven so tightly. He kicked and paddled, spitting out mouthfuls of water that now tasted like blood, but the current wouldn't relent. It had them in its grasp, and it had no intention of letting go.

He didn't see the last waterfall until he was right on top of it. Two boulders guarded its entrance, skulking just under the surface, and as Bobby's ankle found the spot where the two rocks were joined and jammed to a stop, the rest of his body kept going. As he rose out of the water in a giant somersault, the bones connecting his knee to his ankle twisted against each other and snapped.

Bobby howled in agony as his driving momentum carried him completely over, the rocks finally releasing their grasp on his foot at the last possible moment before it was simply torn from his body.

Not until he splashed back down in the water and his brain was swimming in agony did he realize that Steven was no longer in his arms.

The spare bullets scattered as Sarah moved quickly to slap her hand over the radio speaker. The gunman reacted with frightening speed, firing off a panicked shot. She could tell by the sound, though, that he was more than a few degrees off. He still didn't know where she was exactly, and he shot again. This one was a little closer, and she figured that he was trying to flush her out of her hiding spot. Right now, he couldn't know that she was essentially unarmed, and he therefore had to be more careful.

Sarah waited until she heard the rasp of her radio's squelch before quickly twisting the dial to the off position. Her heart hammered faster than she thought was possible as she patted the dark ground with her hand, searching for the bullets she'd lost. The movement outside her little thicket started up again, suddenly sounding much closer than before, and from a different direction.

Christ! He'd circled all the way around! He knew where she was hiding!

Please, Jesus, just one bullet. Just let me find one bullet. At least she'd have a chance. As it was now, she was merely a target, as harmless as the silhouette targets on the FBI range. And at the moment, she felt twice as vulnerable.

Overhead, the sounds of the approaching chopper grew exponentially as it drew closer. *He knows,* Sarah thought. *Somehow, Russell knows where we are.*

A stick cracked immediately behind her hiding place, and Sarah froze. Jesus, he was right there. He was right outside her hopelessly thin wall of vegetation! From there, he *had* to be able to hear the sound of her heart. The whole eastern seaboard had to be able to hear it!

In all the distraction of the helicopter and the gunman who was close enough for her to feel his breath, her fingers almost passed right over the stubby little cylinder that her mind initially dismissed as a piece from a broken stick.

That was a bullet!

Her mind screamed it so loud that for a moment she thought yet again that she'd announced her position. Her one bullet! She finally had it! She'd pay a million dollars for four more, but one would give her the chance she needed.

She felt the beat of the rotor blades in her chest now as Eagle One closed in on her.

Suddenly, she was surrounded by daylight; bathed in the blinding white light of the million-candlepower searchlight mounted on the helicopter's chin. Shadows circled and danced around her as the beam cut the night, making her feel strangely disoriented. She looked down to keep from falling over, and as she did, she saw among the shadows of the branches and the leaf buds and the snowflakes, a pair of shoes, and they stood not a yard away from her.

A gasp escaped her throat and the feet moved, taking five quick steps backward.

Sarah jumped to her feet and brought her weapon up. At this range, she couldn't miss. The muscles of her forearms tightened, and in the crazy light, she saw the hammer rock back.

"Jesus, Sarah, no! It's me!"

Realization came instantly. "Gardner!"

"I heard—" His eyes changed. And his jaw dropped as he focused on something behind her. He brought his shotgun to his shoulder. "Look out!"

Instinctively, Sarah dove to the right as the night erupted in gunfire. Both men fired and both men fell, the twelve-gauge spinning off into another stand of trees. Just from the way he dropped, Sarah knew that Gardner had been hit.

"Gard! Oh, no, Gard!"

Still on her hands and knees, she scrambled over to where her friend lay, a crimson stain spreading quickly across his chest. "Gard, you're hit. Is it bad? Does it hurt real bad?"

Gardner just lay there. His eyes were open, and he was alive, but his expression seemed empty, confused.

"That's okay," she cooed. "You'll be okay. I'll make sure. You'll see."

A wracking cough seemed to bring him back to alertness, but the pain it caused seemed terrible. "Oh, God, that hurts," he moaned. He hawked up some bloody sputum and struggled to raise his head. Sarah helped him, and he forced a smile.

Then the smile transformed to a look of horror as he focused past her again. His mouth tried to form words, but Sarah didn't need them. Letting his head drop against the soft ground, she spun on one knee, her weapon extended to the full reach of her arm.

Ahead of her, in the whirling shadows of the searchlight, a huge man with flaming red hair struggled to his feet. The whole left side of his down coat looked as if it had been through a shredder, and as he raised himself to his full height, he sagged to the side of his wounds. A pistol dangled from the fingers of his good hand.

"Drop your weapon!" Sarah yelled.

But the man appeared not to hear. He took a step closer.

"Freeze! And drop that weapon. Now!"

Another step.

"Don't make me shoot you!"

Two more steps. Only ten yards separated them now.

"Goddammit, stop!"

The man raised his weapon.

"Shit!" Sarah pulled the trigger. And nothing happened. The snub nose just clicked.

The big man smiled at her, revealing a mouthful of slick red teeth. It looked as if it took an enormous effort for him to bring his big pistol up to a shooting position.

Sarah pulled again, and again the hammer landed on an empty chamber. When she'd loaded her one bullet, she'd obviously not put it in position.

The man's hand moved faster now. So fast in the whirling shadows that Sarah couldn't even see it. She was going to die. Right here in the woods she loved so much, some asshole was going to blow a hole right through her.

Bullshit. This time when the hammer fell, it launched a bullet right through the bridge of her attacker's nose.

Five seconds later, she was back on the radio. She had a life to save.

Pain knotted every muscle in Bobby's body as he jolted against even more rocks.

"Steven!" he cried in to the night, and from somewhere, he heard a choking cry. "Steven!"

The water here was much shallower than it had been in the channel. The boy had a chance, he thought, so long as the current didn't throw him out in the middle again. He had to be here. He *had* to be.

Bobby howled in agony as the currents and boulders battered his useless left leg, but he never heard any of it. He was face-first in the water now, his hands scraping mercilessly along the bottom.

"Steven!"

There! Not five feet away, he caught a flash of baby blue as it shot past him, heading back out toward the center of the channel. It was him! That blue was the new pair of nightie-nights!

Bobby lunged at him, his hands missing the boy by inches. "Shit!" Bobby tumbled sideways in the water, scooting along the rocks, trying to get one last shot at grabbing the boy. The speeds were amazing. His arms weighed two hundred pounds apiece, and he felt his consciousness slipping. With the deadfall zooming in closer by the second, this was his last shot at saving the boy. And himself.

Bobby screamed to the night as he launched himself one final time at the boy, who was now floating on the surface of the water like a bobber, no longer struggling to save himself. Bobby came all the way out of the water, reaching out in desperation, looking like a frantic basketball player struggling to score a slam dunk on his belly.

Extended as he was, there was nothing to protect his face as he crashed back into the water, where more rocks awaited him under the surface.

But he had the boy. He didn't know at first if he'd snagged an arm or a leg, but he by God had a hold on him, and nothing on earth was going to pry him loose this time. He pulled Steven in close and hugged him tightly in both arms.

There was the deadfall! Only yards away now, Bobby spun himself in the water yet again, until he was on his side, protecting Steven from a direct impact with the fallen tree. He hit hard, the tangle of branches snagging him in a hundred places all along his back and butt and legs.

Oh, God, his leg! He shrieked as the bone ends scraped against each other, and his mouth filled with water. Now that they were no longer moving, the current was like a battering ram, pinning them both against the branches, which themselves had begun to sag under the weight of their onslaught.

Hanging on with one hand to the thickest part of the trunk he could find, Bobby hoisted Steven into the air with his other hand, the tiny, limp body making no move to fight him. By heaving himself up a little, he could get the boy high enough out of the water to wedge him into a kind of cradle that nature had formed in the twisted boughs of the grand old pine tree.

"Up you go," he grunted as the boy rolled out of his grasp. "And don't you dare die on me, you little shit." In his heart, though, he knew that it was already too late, whether from the cold or from a lungful of water. He harbored no hope that the boy would see another day.

Any more than he harbored hope that he would see another one himself.

His muscles were dead. Suddenly, nothing worked anymore. It was as if that final heave to raise Steven out of the water had spent his entire reserve of energy, leaving him just plain empty.

Bobby didn't feel anything anymore. The broken leg was numb, the bruised and torn flesh was numb. The best he could do—and it took an amazing effort—was to lift his right arm maybe three inches out of the raging water, just far enough to wedge a medium-size branch into his armpit. He hoped that it would be enough to keep his head out of the water when the oncoming unconsciousness finally overtook him.

As the darkness engulfed him, his thoughts turned to Susan. She was out there somewhere, too. He hoped that her next husband would be able to provide a better life for her than he had.

39

THE LIGHT OF heaven was blinding, just as all the New Age televangelists had claimed on late-night television. Bobby tried to look away, it was so bright, but still it got brighter. And it was cold. Oh, so impossibly cold and windy.

And noisy. Heaven roared with an unspeakably loud growl; a thrumming noise that sounded every bit like a . . .

Helicopter!

" . . . hear me?"

Was someone talking to him?

"Mr. Martin, can you hear me!"

Of course I can hear you, Bobby thought, but his mouth wouldn't work. As he forced his eyes open, he thought for sure that he could see the face of that FBI agent—what was his name? Oh, yes, Coates!—staring straight at him.

"I'm gonna need your help, Mr. Martin!" Coates shouted. "I need you to slip this collar over your head so we can both get the hell out of this water!"

Water! The river! This wasn't heaven at all. He was still in the freezing Catoctin River. He was still in hell.

"B-boy," Bobby managed to say. "B-boy."

"We got him! He's already in the chopper! And if you don't cooperate, sir, I'm getting back in there myself! You understand? In a couple of minutes, we're all dead!"

Bobby nodded. Or at least he thought he did. He managed to let go of the deadfall long enough for Russell to slip the collar over his head, from which point the agent had to manipulate Bobby's arms to bring them the rest of the way through. From there, Bobby just lay back silently while he was manipulated some more: a strap here and there.

And then the darkness returned.

Samuel wouldn't let himself cry.

Now that the helicopters and the lights were gone, he was left there all alone in the dark, among the trees. His belly didn't hurt him so badly anymore. That was good. He was grateful for that.

But he was so, so cold. And thirsty. Maybe if all this snow had been rain, then he would have had something to drink, he thought. Or maybe he could catch enough snowflakes on his tongue to make a difference. He supposed that there were all sorts of solutions, if he were only smart enough to figure out what they were. That was the problem with being a stupid dummy: sometimes, you knew there was something you should be doing, but you just couldn't figure out what it was.

He wished that Jacob was with him now. He'd know what to do. He'd protect him from The Boss and from the other man with the gun. He'd protect him from the nosy nellies who ended up with Justin all over again.

"I'm so sorry, Jacob," he tried to say, but his lips felt as if they had been rubbed raw, and his throat as if it had been packed with sand. No sound came out at all. "Please help me."

And then, there he was, staring right down on him, shining a light in his eyes. Samuel tried to squint and look away, but the muscles in his neck felt disconnected from the rest of his body. All he could do was stare.

But what a sight it was! Jacob was alive again, wearing a heavy green jacket with a fur collar around his neck. It looked warm. But the hat looked stupid—like something Smokey the Bear would wear. Samuel tried to laugh. Jacob always liked it when Samuel laughed at his jokes, but still, nothing worked. He had to laugh on the inside.

Jacob was shouting something at him and then he talked into a radio, but Samuel couldn't make out any of the words. He tried to lean in closer to listen, but it felt as if somebody were pulling him farther and farther away.

"You'll be okay, buddy . . ."

That time he heard it, but the sound came without pictures. He slipped further away, smiling even wider. Jacob said he'd be okay.

And he'd called him his buddy.

Bobby Martin awoke slowly, his steady movement toward consciousness driven by the terrible ache in his leg. He inadvertently flexed a toe, and a bolt of pain launched like a missile all the way up into his groin and beyond. The crystal-like clarity of the pain vaulted him over the wall of wakefulness in his mind and landed him squarely in the middle of reality.

He knew instantly where he was, and why he was here, and a knot of panic seized his insides. Yelling against the pain, he raised himself up to his elbows there on the medevac cot and took a swipe at the man whose back was turned to him, hoping to get his attention.

The man whirled around, startled, revealing the now familiar face of Special Agent Russell Coates.

"My wife!" Bobby yelled over the thunderous vibration of the rotors. "We have to go back for Susan!"

Russell smiled and put his hand on Bobby's shoulder, moving out of the way so he could see the patient on the other side of the narrow aisle. Susan lay under a huge pile of blankets, her eyes closed and her skin bearing a yellowish tinge in the blazing artificial light.

"Is she okay?" Bobby shouted.

"She'll be fine."

"But she was shot!"

"Medic says it looks like a ricochet." Russell pointed to a spot over his ear. "All three of you are hypothermic as hell, and your leg's going to need some mending, but it looks like you'll all be fine."

"What about Steven?" Bobby saw the look of confusion and rephrased the question. "What about the boy?"

Russell nodded toward Susan. "He's breathing fine and sleeping away on the other side of your wife. Everybody will be just fine."

Bobby felt as if he should have more questions, but for the life of him he couldn't think of any. Not until he saw yet another supine form on a cot that was actually *under* Susan's. "Who's that?"

Russell's features dimmed. "That there is Ranger Blackwell with the

Park Service. He was shot." Bobby saw a trace of anger in the agent's eyes before he looked away.

Shot trying to save my sorry ass, Bobby didn't say. He strained to get a look at Blackwell's face, but a stab of pain stopped him. "Is he going to be okay?"

He didn't know how to interpret the look he received in return, but he knew better than to pursue it. Instead, he laid his head back down and tried to relax, wondering whether his nightmare had finally ended, or if it was just beginning.

April knew the instant that she heard the heavy door open at the end of the short cellblock that the approaching footsteps were coming for her. She'd been transferred to a four-person cell and relegated to a top bunk. From her perch, she could tell that none of the other ladies had stirred an inch at the sound of the approaching guard.

April's bare feet landed soundlessly on the concrete floor, and she was waiting at the barred wall when Detective Tom Stipton stepped into view. He looked tired and jumped when he saw her so close to the bars.

"You know something," April said, anxious to hear it, no matter what.

He looked so grim. "Before I go into the details for you, April, I want you to know that Justin's going to be just fine."

"You've found him?" she gasped. Behind her, her cellmates grumbled for silence.

Stipton nodded. "Yes, but—"

"And he's alive?"

"Well, yes, but he's had a tough go of it. Apparently, the plot to kidnap him was interrupted by—"

"Wait," April said, holding up her hand. She smiled and her vision blurred with tears. "Before you get to the rest of it, just tell me that first part again."

The grimness left Stipton's eyes and dimples formed in the corners of his smile. "He's going to be just fine, April."

40

TOM STIPTON PULLED his unmarked vehicle up to the curb and threw the transmission into park. Neither he nor April said anything for a long time as they took in the war zone that was The Pines. "You could do better than this," Tom said.

April offered a half-shrug and a quarter-smile. "I tell myself that my ship will come in someday, but it keeps getting stranded on the reef." She didn't like the feeling of sadness that dominated the car. "But, hey, it's better than the digs I almost had, right? At least here I can come and go as I please."

Tom forced a chuckle. "Well, I think I'd avoid that mall for a while. They're still not real happy about the DA looking the other way on this."

"That reminds me. I need to write him a thank-you note."

Tom cringed. "Um, I'm not sure that's the best idea. He is, after all, an elected official, and this decision is going to be controversial enough without a record of your thanks. Take it from me that he was happy to do it."

"Can I thank you, then?"

Tom smiled. "Sure you can. It's not necessary, though."

April leaned across the seat and gave him an affectionate peck on the cheek. "Thank you, Detective Stipton. And that comes from Justin, too." They both looked to the back, where the boy was sound asleep in a car seat.

"Can I tell you a secret?" Tom asked with a conspiratorial twinkle.

"He's the one I really did it for. He's been through too much to lose his mom just because she was a little crazy one day."

April held Tom's gaze long enough for it to become uncomfortable for both of them, and then they both broke away. "Why does a cop car have a kiddie seat anyway?" she asked as she climbed out of the car.

"We keep them in the trunk all the time," he answered, climbing out himself. "You know, just in case."

April laughed at the absurdity of it. "You mean you keep it back there with the bulletproof vests and the tear gas?"

Tom laughed along with her. "Don't forget the road flares and shotgun." He waited while she lifted out the sleeping boy and rested him on her shoulder. "Want me to walk you to the door?"

This was getting awkward. "You know, I do this all the time. I really don't need a bodyguard."

"But you're not armed anymore."

"Well, don't tell *everybody,* okay?" She laughed. They stood there together for a long moment. "Tell you what. You want to escort me, then you call me for a date and escort me to a nice dinner, okay?"

Tom's smile became bigger. "I might just do that."

"And I might just say yes." She bounced her eyebrows playfully and walked away, enjoying the sensation of his eyes burning into her back.

Turning the lock on her door, April stepped into her dingy little apartment and instantly knew that something had to change. Tom was right: she didn't belong here. She had dreams, and none of them centered around this shit hole. These two bedrooms and roach-infested kitchen were too much of a shrine to what she used to be; a shrine to William and all the misery he'd brought into their lives. She had talent, dammit, and where the talent fell short, she had more drive and desire than any five people she knew. It was about damn time for her to start believing in herself as much and as deeply as her father had believed in her.

It was time for a *huge* change.

The first step was to exorcise the remnants of her worthless husband from this place. Laying Justin gently onto his own bed, she watched him sleep for a moment before heading into her bedroom to begin the great purge. She wanted to feel sad as she gathered up

William's clothes from where they lay on the floor and draped over the footboard of the bed. She'd have settled for something other than hatred. It was wrong to hate the dead, wasn't it?

She walked to the living room to deposit the first armload of clothes, then returned to the bedroom for more. The closet was next; first the stuff from the hangers, and then the shoes and shirts and pants and underwear that littered the closet floor. How had she ever convinced herself that she needed this man?

This was a question to be answered years from now, when she had the luxury of looking back on things objectively. Right now, she felt too much shame.

She finished the final scrapings of the floor on her hands and knees, straining to reach all the way to the back wall for a stray white athletic sock, which, for some reason, appeared to be stuck to the wall. More accurately, she supposed, it appeared to be stuck *into* the wall.

"What is this?" she asked the room. She reached in even farther and had to tug hard to pull it clear from the hole in the wall. But it wasn't just one sock, it was four of them, and the hole had to be the size of a saucer. As the socks tumbled free, a $20 bill tumbled out, too.

April frowned as she slid under the hems of her own dresses, and over her own shoes, to get a better look.

As she moved in close enough to see into the hole, more money came into view. Wincing at the thought of what her fingers might find, she reached in and touched stacks of bills. She pulled out first one, and then two more: twenties, tens, fifties, and hundreds, in no particular order, but there had to be hundreds of dollars here. Thousands, maybe!

Gathering the money in her arms, she hurried out to the living room and piled it onto the coffee table for sorting. Even as she separated the stacks by denomination, she knew that she was looking at more money than she'd ever seen. William must have—

The realization of what had happened nearly made her scream. She fell back against the threadbare sofa, her hand clasped to her mouth. He'd had it all along! The bastard had had the money from the very first minute! None of this had had to happen to Justin. He'd never had to be sucked into William's world of booze and drugs.

Jesus, they were going to bury her baby alive! April's entire body went cold, and grief descended like a great black cloud.

"Oh, God!" she whispered.

When Justin walked into the room, she felt suddenly wrought with shame.

"Mommy?" Justin said hesitantly, his own face clouding with sadness. "Don't cry, Mommy."

April held out her arms, and the little boy ran to her. She gathered him in and kissed his hair and his face. "Oh, baby, I love you so, so much. I'm so sorry." The tears burst from her in a rush.

"Be okay," Justin croaked through tears of his own. "Be okay."

"You bet we will."

April wondered if she'd ever be able to let go of her little boy again. Holding him close like that, after he'd been ripped so far from her, felt like perfection. She held him there on the couch until she lost track of time.

When someone knocked on the door, she nearly didn't answer it. But thc visitor was persistent, and when she finally caved in to ask who it was, Tom's voice greeted her.

"Just a minute!" she called. Moving quickly, she scraped the piles of cash onto the floor, and from there shoved it all under the sofa. That was drug money, she knew, and she didn't yet know what she was going to do with it. Until she did, she didn't need anyone asking tough questions. "This is our little secret, okay, Justin?"

"Secret," the boy echoed, but he clearly didn't know what she was talking about.

When she opened the door, Tom had his back turned, looking out toward the playground. He turned and greeted her with a huge smile. "I'm back." he said. He held a shoe box in his hand.

"So you are," April replied, nervously adjusting her hair. She stepped off to the side. "Would you like to come in?"

Tom shook his head. "Um, well, no, actually. At least not now. I'm still on duty. This came for you in the mail today, addressed care of the police department. Thought you might like to have it."

Curious, she took the box and opened it to reveal an orange stuffed tiger. From behind, Justin recognized it instantly and squealed with glee. He rushed up and grabbed the toy, giving it a big hug. As he pulled it free of the box, a note fluttered to the floor.

"Have you read this?" April asked as she bent to pick it up.

"Well, under the circumstances, we didn't want it to be a bomb or anything."

It was written in blue ink on expensive stationery:

To whom it may concern,

Our lawyer tells us that you wish to remain anonymous, and we therefore are sending this in care of the police department. Meet Tiger. He once belonged to a very special boy who never got a chance to play with him. Now he belongs to your little boy, whose name we're told is Justin. And such a pretty name it is.

We hope one day that you'll feel comfortable enough to drop us a line, just to tell us how he is doing. You probably already know this, but you have a terrific little boy on your hands. It was an honor to call him ours, if only for such a short time.

Very sincerely yours,
Susan and Bobby Martin

41

I THINK THIS is the one," Bobby said.

Susan shook her head. "Nope. If it were, I'd know it. A woman can feel these things."

"I can feel things, too, you know."

They sat on the hardwood floor, just outside the bathroom off the foyer, waiting for the timer to ring.

Susan teased, "Not every shot hits the target, you know."

"But this one did. I'm telling you, this one did."

Susan cocked her head and frowned. "But suppose it didn't? We've been disappointed before, and I don't want—"

Bobby took his wife's hand gently into his own. "If it didn't, then we'll try again. But this one did."

She smiled and shook her head. He was hopeless.

When the timer dinged, they both jumped a little. It was time to go look.

"Think we should give it another couple of minutes?" Bobby asked quickly.

She gave him her scolding look. "I already put on an extra thirty seconds."

They stood, and Susan opened the door. Bobby put his hand on hers and pulled it closed again. "Hey," he said softly. "I love you. No matter what, I love you."

Susan kissed him lightly and hugged him. "I love you, too."

And then they stepped inside together.